GODHEAD

Also by Greg McLeod

King of Dreams

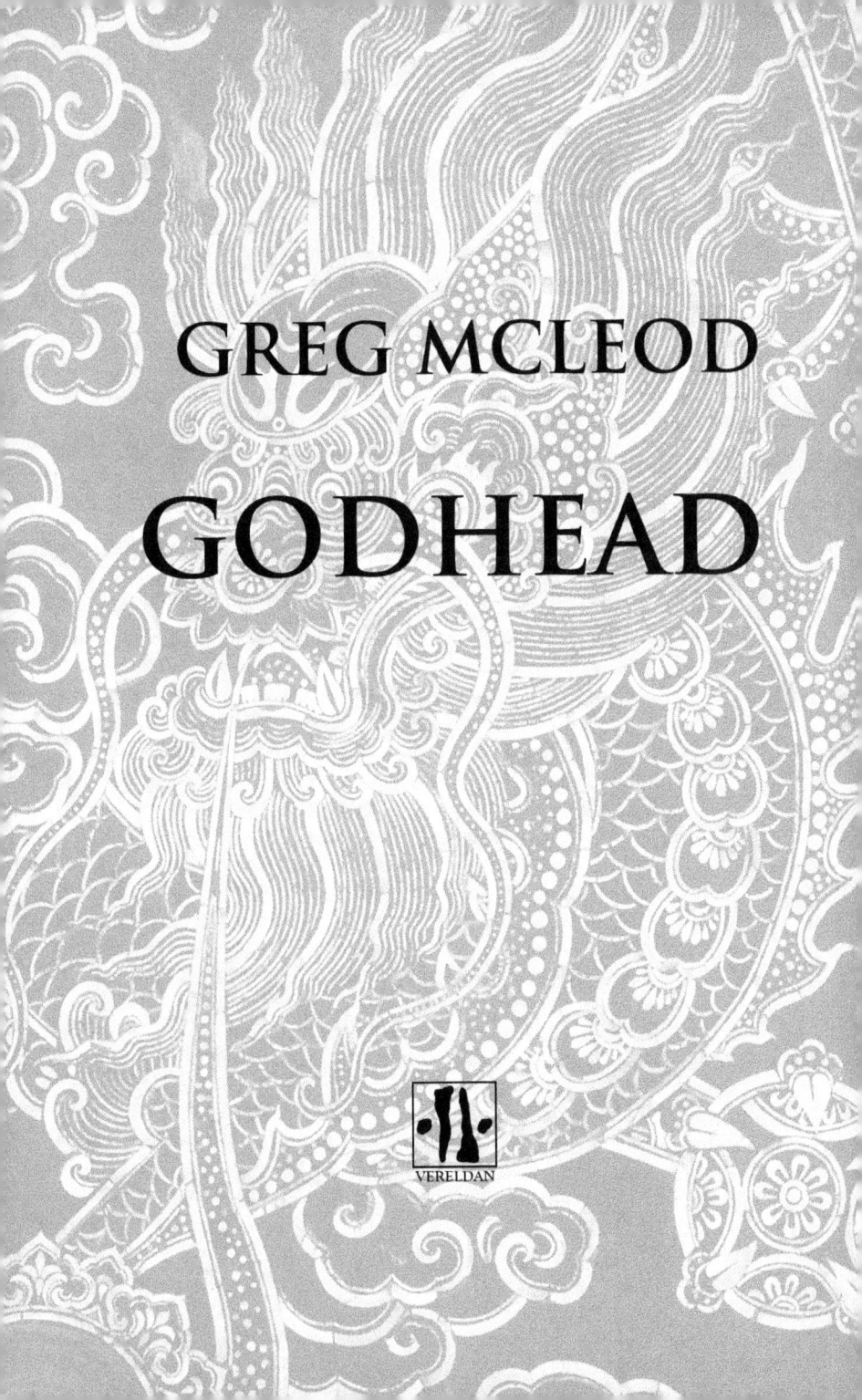

GREG MCLEOD

GODHEAD

VERELDAN

ISBN 978-88-940221-5-5

Caps: Neugotische Initialen by Dieter Steffmann

Dragon image: Wiki Commons

*This one's for all of you out there whose turn it is
to nurture the spark and shepherd it through difficult times.
You're not alone.*

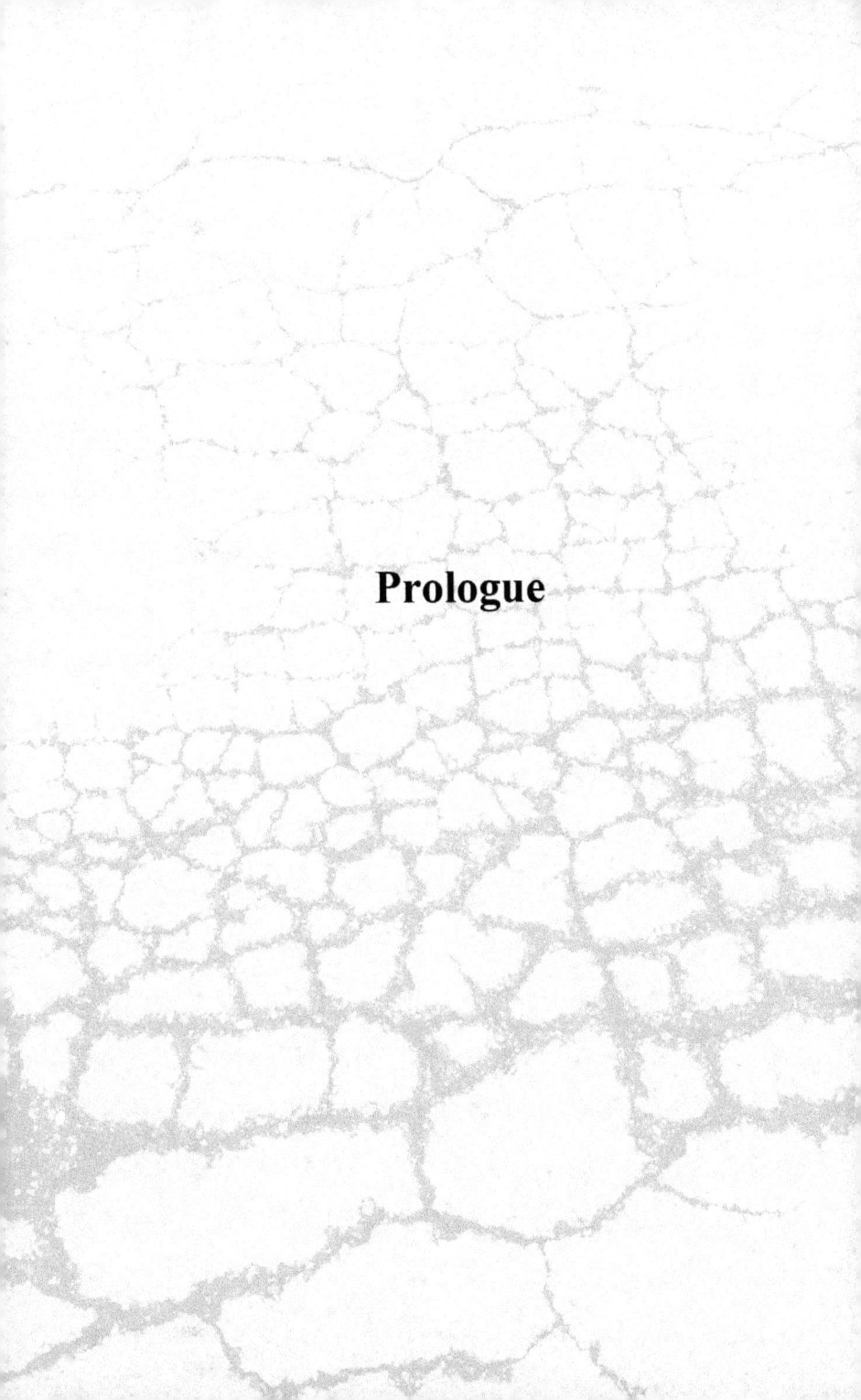

Prologue

Digger's Row

(AD 2001 / 1210, 4th Empire)

Lazily, a lone snowflake drifts out of the diffuse glare that on this day passes for a sky. Descending amidst dark, silent pines, it refuses to alight on branch or limb and instead continues on down to the forest floor. There, two boys are running through the strangely shadowless half-light, completely immersed in the game of the hunt. The tracking is easy enough with an inch of yesterday's snow on the ground and regular though ever more widely spaced traces of blood marking the trail of the wounded deer Billy and Eric have so far failed to catch up with. They should – and do – know better than to shoot deer with a .22, but they are boys, a bit wild, and today they are up to no good.

The deer isn't seriously injured, and eventually there are no more drops of red dotting the snow, but the tracks are still clearly visible. Going slower now, the boys move through a ghostly zone of stunted, dead, and dying trees, and a quick, half-thought explanation for this desolation involving beaver dams and changing water tables flits along the edge of Eric's mind but does nothing to dispel the creepy feeling that is suddenly stirring the small hairs on the back of his neck.

Another hundred yards, and they find themselves on the edge of a large, almost perfectly circular clearing. Here the snow abruptly peters out as if it never touched the hard, dusty ground inside the round of dry brush and dead weeds. The deer seems to have run right

9

up to where the snow ends, and then vanished into thin air. There is no trace of its passing beyond the snowline, which means the boys will have to circle around the whole clearing and see if they can pick up the tracks where they come out again.

If they come out again. From all the evidence they can find at the deer's point of entry into the circle, it might well have slyly backtracked in its own prints, climbed a tree, and could right now be hiding somewhere up there among the pine boughs, laughing at the two-legged, bumbling fools down on the ground.

For a moment the boys stand and rest, leaning forward with their hands on their knees, their breath pluming white in the chill air, and Eric notices the unnatural stillness that has descended on the woods seemingly out of nowhere. Suddenly Billy straightens up and points to the middle of the clearing, about fifty yards from where they stand.

'Hey, check that out. What's a couple of telephone poles doing out here in the middle of Bumfuck?'

Eric squints warily through half-fogged glasses. He really doesn't like this place. 'I don't know, man. Shouldn't we be thinking about heading back? It's getting late, and we've never been out this way before. This is, like, nobody ever comes here. It's spooky, bro.'

'Yeah, okay, okay. Chill, dude. Just lemme have a look.'

'What about the deer?'

'It'll be okay. I think we just winged it. Come on. One quick look, and then we're outta here.'

From up close, the two objects don't look like telephone poles at all. Instead, they are something radically and disquietingly different. Roughly twelve feet tall, they stand about nine feet apart on a patch of earth that is blackened as if by a recent fire. A closer look shows that the soil is covered with a layer of some kind of lamp-black, lichenous or fungal growth. The same stuff has grown up both columns, covering them completely and making it impossible to tell whether they are made of stone or wood or metal – or something else entirely. Either the black stuff is thicker here, growing in a totally weird pattern, or the columns themselves are carved from top to bottom with strange, convoluted designs that send the eye slipping and sliding in impossible directions. Twisting perception and fooling the brain into seeing things that surely can't be there. Tricking the mind into imagining a shimmering in the space between the columns, like hot air over sun-baked blacktop or the slightly fogged and distorted view in the uneven glass of an ancient mirror. Repulsing and at the same time drawing you in with sweetly poisoned promises never intended to be kept except maybe in a place you never, ever want to go.

Just looking at it makes Eric feel nauseous. And scared. Shitting-himself scared. Drop-everything-and-run-for-his life scared.

'Dude, this is mental! It's creeping me out. Let's get the fuck outta here. Hey Billy, c'mon man. You coming?'

'Yeah, I'm coming, I'm coming. Just a sec.' But Billy continues to move forward until he is nearly in line with the two columns. He raises a hand as if to touch the translucent curtain before him.

'Don't do that!' Eric feels the situation is about to go seriously bad. 'Billy, you stupid moron! That shit's dangerous!' Eric couldn't say where this information has just come from, but he knows it's true, no doubt about it.

Billy pulls back his hand, hesitates, and then in one swift movement and following no clear decision of his own sticks the barrel of his .22 into the space between the columns. With a cocky grin he starts to turn towards Eric as if to say, 'See? No big deal'.

But then an altogether different expression overtakes him as the gun somehow begins to change and wriggle in his hand, while simultaneously the black stuff that seems to have grown up around his ankles and caught hold of his feet is pulling him inexorably forward.

Before he can put up much of a struggle, it suddenly picks up speed and literally yanks him over the line and through the curtain, where momentarily a dark shape can be seen moving on the other side. Eric catches a glimpse of something huge and impossible that his mind immediately shuts out and refuses to acknowledge it has ever seen – except later, when the image will surface time and again in terrifyingly vivid dreams and a few years down the line leave him, already not the most stable of persons, hanging from an extension cord tied to a rafter in the attic of his parents' house – and just like that, Billy is gone.

'Billy!' Eric yells, totally losing it. 'Billy get back here, d'you hear me? Oh jeeze, oh fuck, Billy! Billeeeee!'

There is no answer from beyond the curtain, no sign of life whatsoever. Eric is frozen in panic. The urge to help his buddy is undoubtedly there, but then suddenly the ground under his feet is moving like black sand shifting or inky ichor flowing, pulling him towards the shimmering maw, and fear beyond his every imagining backs him away until, sobbing with terror and shame, he drops his gun, turns, and runs.

❖   ❖   ❖

Part I

AD 1984 – 1985 / 1198, 4th Empire

An old man sleeps, an old man dreams.

Yet his is no ordinary dream like you or I would have. It is more than a dream, real as life in the waking world. More real, even. The old man is inside a tree – no, he is the tree.

He is roots and trunk and branches and twigs, he is bark, sapwood, heartwood. He is buds and leaves, coming and going with the seasons, dancing in the wind, whispering in the rain. He bows and rests under snow and ice, and under the warming sun spreads out and grows, above ground and below.

But that is only a part of it, for he is also connected to the tree's living heart, and to those of its neighbors near and far, brothers and sisters, parents and grandparents, aunts, uncles and cousins, children and grandchildren. The old man is all that, and more. He is part and whole of the great network spanning the planet, for through the tree he communes not only with other trees but with every living thing that cares to listen.

His body, half lying, half sitting propped against the tree's enormous trunk, is so deeply lost in sleep it appears to be that of a dead man. He looks gaunt and starved, and what clothes he once wore have long since been reduced to rotting rags, overgrown with moss and sprouting small mushrooms. But he is alive and well, nourished and protected by magic more potent than food and drink, than a roof and sturdy walls, and neither predator nor scavenger can touch him.

And so he dreams, and sometimes slightly stirs, but for now he doesn't wake.

In a very different place lies another old man – or what is left of him. This one doesn't sleep, and he doesn't dream. Instead, his thoughts beat like great, dark wings around and around the walls of his light-less prison, seeking, seeking, always looking for that one tiny flaw that, once found, can be made to grow into a tremor, an avalanche, an earthquake.

Meanwhile, his only escape lies in the past, in memory, and so he drifts back through centuries to times when he Wanted, and he Took. First it was a city, then a kingdom, and finally a whole continent that squirmed beneath the heel of his boot, that flinched and groveled at a word from him and bowed to his every cruel and senseless whim.

And yet, with every appetite he indulged, his hunger only grew. Soon an empire was no longer enough. He wanted a world, but not to simply conquer, to subjugate and rule. No, he wanted to consume it whole, to bleed it and suck it dry and then destroy it in one vast and final conflagration. That was the kind of hunger he felt. That was the kind of being he had become, or perhaps had always been. Better to let him rest undisturbed, if not in peace.

No, never in peace.

❖ ❖ ❖

A journey of a thousand miles begins with a single step.

Lao Tzu

1 Orr

here to begin? Which thread to choose among the countless strands leading to and from, around and through our story? All of them are interwoven, knotted and tangled with the infinitely larger pattern, with the endless, ever unfolding weave that makes up the Great Story, the One Story of which history is but a very small part, a sketchy footnote, a short and dodgy byline written by those most interested in the shading and coloring of the light that falls upon them in the aftermath of whatever it was all about their time around.

Where to begin, if not with that one, tiny thread-end sticking out provokingly from the fold of the grand fabric containing the events that are of interest here? Small as it is, it marks out what looks suspiciously like a high-intensity collision point of the possible and the probable, a temporal distillate of incipience and momentousness, one of those famous instants when things are about to pick up some steam, or at least the fire under the pot is being vigorously stoked. Call it fateful, if you like.

Let's give that thread a gentle tug, and see where it will lead.

❖   ❖   ❖

Orr: there was no city on Vereld to rival it.

Its days of glory were long past, yet it grandly persisted in calling itself 'The Empire'. Over the past few centuries it had lost nearly all its vast territories and provinces that once sprawled over half a continent, and yet the place still managed to live up to the title. Certainly where trade was concerned, it continued to be an empire.

Situated at the tip of a wide peninsula, it boasted the largest man-made harbor in the known world, enclosed by heavily fortified seawalls. In truth, those walls were beginning to show their age, and it had been a long time since Orr had gone to the trouble of keeping them properly manned. Not that there wasn't enough human material available in a city of half a million. But the authorities just couldn't seem to be bothered anymore with the upkeep of costly defenses that in the eyes of many had become largely obsolete ever since Orr had shifted its instruments of conquest from armies to commerce, from weapons to gold.

Better to invest in useful things that kept revenues flowing, in docks and quays, customs sheds and warehouses, ships, wagon trains and caravans, instead of wasting it on defenses against a hypothetical enemy that most believed would never come.

Now, the city's sole guardian on the seaward side was the Therion.

The fifty-foot bronze statue of the first emperor, Antherion I, was counted among the wonders of the world. Boosted by a clever arrangement of large mirrors, the beacon fire burning day and night within the statue's hollow head shone forth from its eyes and open mouth to guide arriving ships safely into harbor – though among sailors and passengers alike, the glowing face rising like a demonic apparition over the nighttime horizon was apt to evoke a frisson of deep, primordial unease along with the relief over a safe arrival.

While the beacon burned without fail, the sea forts on both sides of the harbor channel were deserted. The huge chain meant to be raised and block the entrance in case of an attack from the sea was overgrown with barnacles, fused to the ocean floor by centuries worth of silt and sediments.

In the city, no one was bothered by this state of complete unpreparedness. Practically everyone around the Middle Sea did business with Orr, and it couldn't conceivably be in anyone's interest to bring war and strife to its doorstep. Granted, there were the tribes from the southern desert. Every now and then, their raiding parties would nibble at the fringes of the three-hundred-mile swath of farmland that fed the city and was the last vestige of its once formidable holdings. So far, the tribes had proved no more than a nuisance. And should they ever arrive in force, they would find another of Orr's and the world's wonders squarely in their way: the Great Wall.

No one coming to Orr from the landward side for the first time failed to be awed by this titanic bastion, grand enough to be the work of gods rather than men, its looming shadow still that of an Empire and seeming to reach far into the continent.

If a traveler arriving at the Wall had been able to avoid the bustle at the gate – farmers and craftsmen to market with their produce and wares; carts and wagons backed up in the gate's bottleneck by hard-faced guards and busy customs officers collecting tolls or bribes; nobles coming in to carouse or going out to ride, hunt, or inspect their holdings; the sudden scramble to make way for a palanquin bearing some important imperial official – if our traveler could have bypassed the congestion clogging the passage under the gatehouse by simply rising over the Wall and taking a bird's view of Orr, he would have seen yet more of the city's extremes.

Here, side by side, could be found every condition of human existence, from abject poverty to immense wealth, from unbelievable squalor to perverse opulence, from utter despair to supersaturated tedium.

Though the space enclosed by the Wall was enormous, towards the edges it was crammed to the point of bursting with buildings of every shape and color, set so close together that over some streets there remained only a narrow, crooked strip of daylight between the mass of projecting alcoves and balconies.

In the poorer quarters hugging the wall, many of the smaller alley-ways had been completely built over and thus turned into dark, fetid tunnels inhabited by scavengers and vermin both animal and human. Here, there was hardly a larger structure without one or more smaller ones built piggyback onto its rooftop, and those in turn supported a wild assortment of tilted, tottering shacks and hovels. The whole jumbled mess seemed forever on the verge of collapsing, and in fact the odd, particularly ramshackle structure did sometimes end up as a large pile of rubble on the street – squalid furnishings, miserable inhabitants and all.

Farther into the city, the architecture took on a semblance of normalcy, with inns and taverns, stableyards, small businesses, and a few minor temples interspersed among modest but decent dwellings.

In the third circle lay the major temples, the banks and trading houses, shops selling luxury goods, and the sprawling homes of the affluent and respectable citizenry, walled enclosures with courtyards and gardens growing ever grander and richer the closer they lay to the center. Beyond, the scenery changed dramatically.

In an almost perfect circle around the hub of the city stood the towers of the nobles. Huge, vertical hybrids between forbidding fortresses and resplendent mansions, they rose ten or more stories above the abodes of the unwashed masses, surrounding the core of the city, the heart of the empire, like a ring of giant stone sentinels – or monolithic prison bars. Neither point of view would have been far off the mark.

They were definitely a force to be reckoned with, teeth of granite and tough, fired brick that could bite both ways, inward and out, depending first and foremost on where their owners' interests lay at any given time.

Inside this ring of stone there was a sudden abundance of open space. Embassies and administrative buildings were nearly lost on acres upon acres of verdant, blooming parks and gardens, in the very center of which lay the Imperial City.

Its walled compound housed the Imperial Palace, a structure to rival the Great Wall if not in size, then in sheer imposingness. Where the one was all about war and deterrence, the other allowed for no necessity other than pure pleasure, a symphony for the senses set in stonework so light and airy it seemed to have been coaxed and grown from the very soil of the paradisian gardens surrounding it by some benign, arcadian magic rather than built by human sweat and toil.

And in fact, this point of view also wouldn't have been too far off the mark.

But the thread we've chosen doesn't lead us this far into the city – at least not yet – and so we leave our hypothetical flying traveler to float in the late afternoon sun and gaze in awestruck silence on the imperial splendor spread out beneath him, while we turn back to find a quiet street flanked by the modest private homes of the second circle.

Here, a tall, rangy man looking to be somewhere in his early thirties, wearing a scruffy, prematurely graying beard and a sky-blue blue cloak designating him a practitioner of the healing arts, is just now being led over the doorstep of a small but well-kept home by a rotund, elderly man whose features are set in worry lines old and new.

And here the trail grows warmer.

❖ ❖ ❖

'Please, Doctor, it's just through here, my son's room is.'
Joceyn Frair led Rather down a narrow corridor towards the back of the house. 'You'll have to excuse the clutter.'

Rather saw only spotlessly scrubbed floorboards and a pair of scuffed work boots standing by the last door on the left. He supposed that those constituted the 'clutter'.

'Here we are.' Frair used a foot to shove the offensive footwear a fraction to the left and closer to the wall, neatly aligning them while at the same time knocking softly on the door. 'Doctor's here,' he called out in a low voice.

The woman who opened could have been Frair's twin sister.

'My wife, Felda,' the old man said.

'Thank the gods,' she said. 'He's in a bad way, Doctor. Please, do come in.'

The first thing Rather noticed as he stepped into the room was the smell. Roses. Not at all what you'd expect from a sickroom. He put it down to the old lady having dispersed a few drops of essence of rose, perhaps in an attempt to ameliorate the underlying sick-person smell. Only he couldn't for the life of him detect even the faintest trace of one. Strange. But the more immediate problem was that, apart from a small oil lamp casting a feeble glow in the far corner, the room was dark.

'Can we have some light, please,' Rather said, moving towards a large shape that he took for the bed. 'Open the shutters, maybe. Let in some fresh air.'

'He's over here,' the old woman said, gesturing towards the lamp-light. Rather, his eyes slowly becoming accustomed to the dark, made out a slim, frail figure crouched in the corner, facing the wall and scratching at the plaster.

Oh, boy, he thought to himself. *Looks like we've got us a head case here. Or three.*

'And I'd rather not open the shutters, if you don't mind too much,' Felda was saying. 'He can't stand the daylight. It hurts his eyes and scares him something fierce. And then he cries and cries for hours on end until we have him calmed down again, and I – we – just don't have the heart or the strength for it anymore. Please, can you manage with the light there is? I'll fetch another lamp, if you like.'

'Not to worry, mistress,' Rather said, employing his Hearty Doctor's Voice. 'Light or no, we'll treat the patient and make him better.'

A deep, phlegmy cough from the figure in the corner answered this breezy statement. Somehow, it managed to sound derisive.

'Right,' Rather said, approaching the corner, 'let's have a look at you.'

He set his bag on the floor and knelt beside the patient. The smell of roses was suddenly much stronger.

'Hey, there. How's it going? I'm Rather. What's your name?'

'Jareth,' the mother said. 'His name's Jareth.'

The sick man stopped scratching the wall. Turned his head away from Rather and started rocking back and forth on his haunches in a rhythm Rather knew all too well. A person dear to him had suffered from the same affliction, as he recalled with a short, sharp stab of sadness. Back then, back where Rather came from, there'd been a name for it. But the term would tell these people nothing they didn't already know, seeing as this was their son and they'd lived with his disability pretty much since he'd been born. Besides, it wasn't what they'd called him here for, as another ugly-sounding cough reminded him.

At least now he knew how he needed to deal with the patient. Softly, delicately, carefully.

He began to talk to Jareth in a low, calm voice, trying to project cautious interest and caring while he told him about his own day, everything from waking in the morning with the memory of a strange and funny dream up to how and why he'd come to be here in this room.

It was a one-sided conversation but an exchange all the same. Empathy and help were offered, trust was built, and barriers lowered. Gradually, the rocking slowed. The tension in the narrow shoulders lessened. Jareth was listening.

Finally, he turned his head back to face the wall in front of him, offering Rather his profile – an act of faith and trust for one such as him, Rather knew. He saw the face of a very young man, far too young to be these people's son, unless the old lady through some miracle had conceived him in her fifties. Grandson was more like it. A boy.

There was something ethereal about those pallid features, a sensitivity and deeply vulnerable beauty hidden in the soft lines and shadows of an otherwise plain and ordinary face. And, Rather thought, something like ravaged innocence, or a baffled weariness with the world that seemed to say, 'What am I doing here? There must be some mistake. This is not the planet where I belong.' Rather knew the feeling.

Meanwhile, he'd reached the end of his account.
'I'm here to find out what's making you sick, and to make it go away,' he said. 'That means I'm going to have to touch you, here, and here, and here.' He touched his own chest, back and throat.

The boy's eyes flickered. None of Rather's movements had gone unobserved. But Rather sensed more alarm from the old couple, looking on from behind and doing their best to keep quiet, than he felt in Jareth.

'We'll start with something easy.' Rather touched his own wrist. 'We'll measure your pulse, see how fast and how strong your heart is beating. Can we do that?'

The rocking intensified for a moment. Then it stopped.

A nod, no more than the slightest inclination of the head. With no hurry, Rather reached out and gently took hold of the boy's wrist. His bones were slight as bird's, the skin papery thin, dry and hot to the touch. While Rather felt for a pulse, his eyes followed the boy's other hand as it reached out to touch the wall, holding what looked to be a long carpenter's nail driven through a round length of wood, its end sharpened to a needle point. His writing utensil, or rather scratching tool, made by a loving father's hand, no doubt. An attempt had even been made to shape the wooden grip so it fit the boy's hand.

Rather's gaze was caught by a fragment of the scratchings.
Gradually what he was seeing penetrated into his awareness, and sudden recognition nearly froze him in shock. Sensing Rather's confusion, the boy tensed and made a feeble effort to withdraw his arm from Rather's gentle grasp.

'It's okay,' Rather said, willing them both back to the previous calm, and the boy relaxed somewhat. Rather finally detected a pulse, weak and erratic. Not good. 'Kid,' he said, 'no matter how important what you've been doing here is, you need to be in bed. Now. Doctor's orders. Are you prepared to follow them?'

The boy took a moment to process Rather's request. Then, surprisingly, he took hold of Rather's arm, and they rose together. On shaky legs, the boy made his way over to the bed, never letting go of Rather.

One-love for the medical team, Rather thought.

Once Jareth was settled in, his face turned to the wall, Rather was able to conclude the rest of the examination. 'Okay,' he said. 'I'll bet this all started with a bad cold, am I right?'

Nod. The mother – grandmother? – cleared her throat, but said nothing.

Good woman. Got it in one.

'What happened is, you didn't take proper care of yourself with the cold. So it went into your lungs, making them all sore and inflamed. That's not good, but we'll get you through it. You are going to get better, but you're going to have to take some pretty evil-tasting medicine for a while. You ready for that?'

Nod.

'Good. It's going to take me a while to prepare the medicine. In the meantime, you need to rest. So I'm giving you something that'll help you sleep without waking up every time you have to cough. I'm afraid it tastes even worse than the other stuff, but the sooner you start getting better, the sooner you can go back to your work.'

Abruptly, Rather sensed another presence in the room.

Obviously the boy did too, for, already pale, he turned whiter than the bedsheet. He began to rock intensely, hammering the side of his hand against the wall. Hard enough to do himself harm.

Rather turned and caught a glimpse of a short, nondescript, black-robed man retreating from the open door and muttering, 'Sorry', though he didn't seem sorry at all, just curious.

'Our lodger, Par Severt,' the mother whispered, closing the door. 'He's a priest at the temple of Amut. We need the money, else we wouldn't have taken him in. Jareth doesn't like him.'

And neither do I, Rather thought, though he could think of no earthly reason why he shouldn't. Except that the Black Priests of Amut were generally regarded with uneasiness bordering on suspicion, even fear. But Rather wasn't usually impressed by general views.

Suddenly he needed to be out of there. He gave the boy a mild sleeping draught, asked Felda to apply leg compresses against the

29

fever, and made his farewells, promising to return later in the evening. Once he was outside, his thoughts were immediately drawn back
to what he'd seen on the walls of the boy's room.

Top to bottom and end to end, as far as he had been able to make out,
they'd been covered not with aimless scratchings, not with childish
doodling or clumsy little drawings but with row upon row upon row
of neat, miniscule writing. And one glance had been enough to show
him that not only was the boy – who as a result of both his disability
and his social circumstances should have been entirely, resoundingly
illiterate – not only was he capable of writing; no, these were not just
random scribbles, not some jumbled, meaningless thought-bubbles
escaped from an impaired mind to disfigure pristine, white plaster but
carefully worded, well constructed sentences coherently and concise-
ly expressing clear, rational thought.

So maybe, somehow, someone taught him. Or not.

When his kind latched on to something, they didn't really learn in
any conventional sense. They seemed to just know and understand in
less time than it took a 'normal' person to sit down to his or her first
lesson.

No, there was no doubt about it: the boy was a savant, and language was his thing. But where and how he'd picked it up, living as
he did…

Same argument, Rather told himself. *Just been there.*

And anyhow, the worst of it, the really bad part as far Rather was
concerned, the part that had shaken him down to his roots, was that
the boy wrote in a language he couldn't possibly know, for it was a
foreign language – and not just foreign to Orr. It was foreign to this

whole world.

Rather knew. Although it wasn't his native tongue, he had, in another time and place, learned to read and write and speak it.

As he sat at his workbench preparing a carefully measured mixture of thyme, peppermint, buckthorn, anise and fennel, Rather once again found himself wishing for the kind of medical resources he'd had at his disposal during his previous life. And once again cut himself short, reminding himself that, in the here and now, he had something equally useful and effective, if not more so: he had magic. Though it wasn't, really. Just something that worked a lot better here than elsewhere, provided you had the knack for it.

Where fate had seen fit to rob him of one thing, it had gifted him with another, a rare occurrence he was duly grateful for, considering how fortune seldom bothered to compensate her victims.

A modest amount of Talent was his to command, too little to perform dazzling displays or miraculous deeds with, but enough to enhance his medicines and treatments to a point where professionally he lacked for nothing in comparison to what he'd had before. Besides healing, he was also pretty good at small Glamors, a skill that brought the ageing wives of the nobility and the more affluent citizenry flocking to his practice to have their appearances uplifted and beautified. Nothing dramatic, mind. Just a bit of shine and polish, a nip here, a tuck there. But the overall effect was always very favorable. The ladies returned with unfailing regularity every two months or so — that was about as long as a Glamor held before it began to fade.

Rather wasn't really enthusiastic about this aspect of his work, but it provided him with a steady, handsome income, which in turn al-

31

lowed him to treat his real and predominantly poor patients for free. Or, when their dignity wouldn't allow it, for as close to nothing as he could get away with.

And it amused him no end to imagine what certain of his colleagues back home would have given had they been able count such an instrument of trade among their blessings.

When Rather returned to Jareth's street, he nearly ran into the priest, Par Whatshisname. Instinctively, Rather recoiled.

The man chuckled, as if at some private joke, and Rather wasn't slow to get it. The priest had his hood up, and in the gathering dusk the face beneath it was hidden in impenetrable shadow. So how had Rather recognized him so quickly? And how did the priest know he'd been recognized? And what …

The priest interrupted this train of thought.

'Doctor,' he said. 'Back already? I do hope the patient will recover speedily under your expert ministrations.'

'Oh, he will, he will,' Rather said, still distracted. 'I don't know about speedily, but he's definitely going to be all right. Now, if you'll excuse me, I've got his medicine to deliver.'

'Wouldn't want to keep you, then. I'm sure I'll see you again soon. Enjoy your stay.'

Before Rather could think of a reply the man was gone, swallowed by the descending dark. Impossible even to say in which direction he'd gone.

Rather shook himself. He definitely didn't like Severt. The guy gave him the shivers. In what would have seemed like a perfectly normal exchange to anyone happening to overhear it, the priest had

32

with only a few, seemingly innocent words managed to convey something entirely different, a projection of what felt uncannily like creeping malice and oily threat.

Come off it, Rather told himself, moving on. *You've got a patient waiting.*

Felda awaited him on the stoop, light in hand.

But instead of leading him straight through to the back, she motioned him into another room and closed the door behind them, setting the lamp on the table in the center of the room, kitchen, parlor and dining room in one. Here too, everything was spotless and tidy. The furnishings – table, chairs, a sideboard – were not new but well cared for, simple but well proportioned, and in the small but endearing imperfections and irregularities of their making showed the same hand that had crafted Jareth's writing tool. Or so Rather imagined.

Felda pulled out a chair for him before seating herself.

'Forgive me, Doctor,' she said. She seemed distraught. Close to tears. 'But I'd have a word with you, if I may.'

'Why, certainly,' Rather said. 'What is it? Is Jareth all right?'

'No, he isn't, that's just it.' She sniffled, and he noticed her gnarled hands nearly wringing the life out of her apron. 'He's gotten worse, but it's not from the sickness. It's because of that dreadful priest. I think he went into Jareth's room earlier, when I was out in the garden for a moment. I'm sure of it actually, because there was this smell in the room when I came back, like spoilt meat going to rot. That's him. That's Par Severt. I don't know why he smells like that. Maybe he should change his diet or wash more often, though I shouldn't be saying that about – '

'Felda,' Rather gently interrupted her. 'First things first. Let me go look after Jareth, and then we'll talk. All right?'

'Of course!' Felda said, tears now seriously threatening to spill over. 'What was I thinking? I'm a foolish old woman. Please forgive me.'

'Nothing to forgive,' Rather told her. 'Jareth's sick. You're upset. I'm the Doctor. That's what I'm here for. Everything as it should be.'

Rather was alarmed at the change in the boy.
He was barely conscious, muttering and tossing, burning with fever, and his breathing had become short and labored. The infection had developed into full-blown pneumonia.

He asked Felda for a cup, boiling water, and honey, all of which she promptly supplied. He made an infusion from the mixture he'd prepared, liberally dosing it with honey. Then he held the cup for a few moments while he charged it with every ounce of healing power he could muster.

There were no muttered incantations, no arcane gestures, not with him – just quiet, deep concentration on what he imagined to be the Source of All Things, and willing, willing, willing the liquid in his hands to become something more than just a simple herbal remedy, something miraculously potent and beneficial.

When the brew was cool enough to drink, he got Jareth up into a sitting position, bracing him with one arm and feeding him the tea in small sips. There was no to-do about space and touching this time. The boy was limp as a rag doll in Rather's arm, trusting as a baby. He slipped off again as soon as the cup was empty, this time into some-thing closer to true sleep and, hopefully, restful and healing. Rather remained sitting on the edge of the bed, feeling the boy's pulse. Only now did he notice that the smell of roses, all but absent until a moment ago, was beginning to permeate the room again.

He took it for a good sign.

'The worst should soon be over now,' he told Felda.
'But I'll stay for a while. Maybe for the night, depending.'

'Thank you, Doctor. Gods bless you.'

'Pull up a chair,' Rather offered. 'Sit with me, and we'll talk some more.'

Felda shot an anxious glance at the figure in the bed.

'Don't worry,' Rather said. 'He's well and truly out of it. He won't hear a thing we say.'

She sat perched on the very edge of her chair as if ready to rise and scurry at some severe master's bidding, though he reckoned it was her own inner despot that denied her rest. She was clearly on the brink of collapse.

'Perhaps your husband could spell you later on,' he said. 'It's going to be a long night, and you look exhausted.'

'He's out,' she said. 'He's a night watchman at the foundry.'

'Then I *will* stay the night.' The boy had rolled over towards the wall, and Rather carefully shifted and eased his aching back up against the headboard. 'So,' he said. 'You were telling me about the priest.' He saw her shudder. 'Can't you simply ask him to leave? Find yourself another lodger?'

'I would,' the old woman said, fidgeting. 'Believe me, I would. But I don't dare. He's said things – well, not in so many words. But he has a way of saying things without really saying them, if you know what I mean. In any case, he's made it clear that we'd be sorry if we went back on the lease. And he's capable. He's a Black Priest after all, one of Amut's, and anyone can tell you they're bad news. I still can't fathom why we ever took him in – it just somehow happened. And now we're stuck with him in our house, only he's killing Jareth, though the gods only know why he would want to do such a thing.'

If not for his earlier encounter with the man, Rather would have dismissed Felda's words as the darker fancies of a superstitious and slightly hysterical old crank. He didn't for a moment believe that the priest was trying to kill the boy, but something troubling was going on here, that much was certain.

'So at least make sure he stays away from Jareth,' he said, knowing as he spoke the words that they were utterly inadequate. Just being under the same roof with the man was too much for the boy, would have been intolerable for Rather himself.

Felda stared into her lap, knotting fingers warped and swollen by arthritis. Rather made a mental note to bring her some salve on his next visit.

'Doctor,' she suddenly blurted out hopefully, 'can't you do something to make him go away? You have magic, and – '

'I'm sorry, Felda,' Rather gently interrupted. 'But I don't have that kind of magic. And even if I did, I wouldn't use it in such a way. I'm told that even the battle-mages of old tried to avoid going one-on-one with an enemy if they could. Too easy to get drawn in by the Dark Side if you meet them on their own level and conditions. I've no personal experience with the Amut lot, but from what one hears they are a bit unsavory, to say the least. What I can do, though, is have a quiet word with the man and see if he's amenable to reason.'

Or to a substantial enough bribe, he didn't say. But he'd pay it if he had to, and if it worked put it down to his fabulous powers of persuasion. No need for these people to feel even more indebted to him.

'Thank you, Doctor,' Felda said, but her disappointment was obvious.

Rather decided to change the subject.

'Felda. Forgive me if I seem to be prying. But I'm a doctor, and the more I know about my patients, the better I can treat them. I don't know how else to put this, but Jareth – he seems very young to be your and Jaceyn's son. Are you sure the boy is yours?'

'Oh, he's mine all right,' the old woman said, her tone at once defensive and resigned. 'Though to look at him, you wouldn't think so, and you're forgiven for asking. And he's no boy either, but a man of forty-six years. It's just that he ages differently from other folks. I'm ashamed to admit I thank the gods he's like he is, keeping to the house and all, else how would I explain his looks to people? They'd have accused me of witchcraft years ago and taken him away from me if they'd ever gotten a proper look at him. Yes, Doctor, even if it's hard to believe, Jareth is my son.'

Rather gestured at the walls. 'Do you have any idea what he's been doing here?'

'Yes,' she said, and there was something akin to pride in her voice. 'He's been writing.'

'So you can read?'

'Me?' She seemed shocked at the idea. 'Oh no, not a word. Reading and writing's for the priests, not us simple folk.'

'So how can you be sure Jareth is writing, and not just spoiling the walls?' Rather asked.

Felda went still for a moment. Then she sighed. 'Oh, well. I might as well tell you. As it is, it's been a weight on my mind for all these years, and no one to talk to about it. Besides, you're a doctor, and a good man, and you'll keep it to yourself.'

'That I will,' Rather said solemnly.

'Where to begin?' Felda mused.

'For one thing, though he doesn't know it, Jaceyn isn't Jareth's real father. Forty-seven years ago, I was working as a serving girl at my uncle's tavern. Until one day a stranger walked in and stole my heart. I'd never seen him before, nor had anyone else, so right away he was a bit of a sensation, leastwise for a spring chicken like me who'd never been out of her circle, let alone the city.

'He started coming in regularly. I thought it was because he fancied me. You wouldn't think so to look at me now, but I was a pretty thing back then. And I certainly fancied him. Though he was poorly dressed, he was a very good-looking young man, and well mannered. My uncle reckoned he must be higherborn, perhaps a noble with a taste for common girls, slumming in disguise and trawling the outer circles for easy meat – or he might have done something bad and was hiding from the bailiffs.

'Which was why, smitten ot not, I turned him the cold shoulder in the beginning. But then we got to talking, and when I came right out and asked him if he was highborn he wouldn't say either way. Instead, he told me he wasn't from Orr at all. He said he'd come on a ship from the south, from Enemathea, but that it wasn't his real home either. Where exactly he was from, he never said.'

Something in the old woman's tale had caught Rather's attention, was nagging at him, but he couldn't quite put his finger on it.

'For weeks, he came almost every day,' Felda went on. 'We became friends, and then more than friends. Fool that I was, I began to dream of a future for the two of us. Even my uncle, who'd been keeping a sharp eye on us, began to regard the young man in a different light. And then all my hopes and fancies were dashed.

'The man I'd begun to think of as my suitor must have realized which way my thoughts were headed, because one day, he took me aside and told me that he'd soon be moving on. He said he had places to go and things to do that honor and duty wouldn't allow him to put off any longer. Said he thought he'd finally found a way to get back home – whatever that was supposed to mean – and that he had to go. I was devastated. But I could see it wasn't any easier for him to say farewell than it was for me.

'To this day, I believe he truly loved me, in his fashion. Don't ask me why, but I decided then and there that I couldn't let him leave without having… lain with him at least once.' The old woman blushed, and Rather caught a sudden, quick glimpse of the young girl she'd once been.

'I was inexperienced as could be, he was reluctant to take advantage, but what was between us was stronger. To make a long story short, we had a tumble in the hay and next I knew, Jareth was on the way. He was gone by then, must have left on my free day. When I came in the day after, he'd left a packet for me. Inside was a white rose, and this.'

Leaning forward, Felda reached under the foot-end of the straw-stuffed mattress. She pulled out a bundle, placed it on her lap and reverently opened it to reveal an old and well-worn book. She handed it to Rather.

He was thunderstruck.

He was looking at a German translation of Stendhal's *Le Rouge et le Noir*, published in Munich in 1921. The implications were almost too momentous to consider all at once. With a thrill of excitement, he understood what had escaped him earlier, the parallels with his own story suddenly glaringly obvious. And the man seemed to have found a way...

'I gave it to Jareth as soon as he could hold it,' Felda interrupted his thoughts. 'It was the only thing of his real father's, and I wanted him to have at least that much. From this, he taught himself to read and write. He started writing his own book' – she gestured towards the walls – 'when he was six. I'm an uneducated person, but I saw what he was putting on the walls, and I looked at the marks in this book, and that's how I knew what he was doing.'

Here lay her secret treasure, and there lay her secret pride, Rather could see, looking from the book to the boy, and felt a sudden, great sadness for these people tug at his heart.

'His father,' he asked, 'did you ever see him again?'

'Never. And I didn't cry over him. No time for that. There was a baby coming that needed a father, and I was very lucky to find Jaceyn early enough to pass Jareth off as his, though it breaks my heart to think how I've had him living a lie for all these years. He's been a good and loving parent to Jareth, where a lesser man would've named the boy a changeling or worse and thrown him to the priests or the dogs. But here I am, gabbing away while you must be starving. I'll go and fix you something to eat.'

She rose heavily and took one of the two lamps.

'Thank you,' Rather said. 'Some food would be welcome. And thanks for your trust.'

He didn't add that the information she'd given him was the most invaluable gift he could have possibly received – though it was still too early to know what it was really worth, and where it might lead him.

Felda, already at the door, simply nodded. Opening it, she suddenly stopped dead.

'What is it?' Rather asked.

After a moment, she shook her head. 'Nothing,' she said, and left. But as she closed the door behind her, he thought he caught a faint whiff of something malodorous, like spoiling meat, drifting in from the hallway.

Suddenly feeling restless, he rose, took up the remaining lamp and began to study the wall opposite the bed's footboard. A closer look showed that the plaster was made from ruddy-ochre clay covered with a thin layer of whitewash, which explained why Jareth's writing was so readily legible. He'd simply scratched his marks through the paint, graffiti-like, and the resulting characters stood out in clear contrast to the white surface.

Rather read.

'... und es wird danach eine Zeit der Unruhe kommen, in der die Leute zu murren beginnen und aufbegehren gegen die Ungerechtig-

keit... ' (… and there will then come a time of unrest when the people will begin to grumble and revolt against the injustice…)

He chose another spot at random.

'... *werden sie merken, dass es den Goldenen Mann gar nicht gibt. Zuerst werden sie wütend und enttäuscht sein, aber dann...* ' (… they will realize that the Golden Man doesn't exist. At first they will be angry and disappointed, but then…)

And another.

'*Er wird durch die Hintertür kommen, und Keiner wird ihn bemerken bevor es zu spät ist...* ' (He will come through the back door, and no one will notice him until it's too late…)

Rather picked out several more fragments of text.

He was perplexed. A whole story, written in the future tense? Odd. Maybe the boy hadn't quite grasped all the intricacies of the German language after all. And where did this strange story begin? He looked around the room. Where would he begin? No, where would a six year-old autistic savant begin? Close to home, close to safety. And the place that to Jareth must have felt safest in the room was the bed. Rather studied the wall over the bed. If Jareth had simply begun writing one day without knowing how grand a task he was embarking upon, he would have chosen a spot he could easily reach, over the headboard or halfway up the lateral wall. If, on the other hand, he had started out with a plan… No, strike all that.

Jareth's condition left no room for randomness or improvisation. He had no choice but to execute anything he undertook in a controlled and precisely organized manner. It was the only way he could do anything at all. Rigid, unchanging order and fastidiously repeated ritual were the mainstays of his existence, the only tools at his disposal to help him cope with the world around him. There was only one logical place for him to begin: the corner over the bed.

Rather took a moment to check on the boy, still rolled up close to the wall. The fever was still running high, but he seemed to be breathing a bit more easily. Rather slipped off his boots. Gingerly, so as not to disturb the boy, he stepped up onto the mattress and held up the light.

And there it was, right up in the corner, at the juncture of walls and ceiling: the beginning.

'*Eine Geschichte der Welt,*' Rather read. '*Geschrieben von Jareth Frair. Begonnen am 27. Ernte 1172, beendet am 3. Saat im 1210. Jahr des 4. Reichs.*' (A history of the world. Written by Jareth Frair. Begun on the 27th of Harvest 1172, concluded on the 3rd of Sowing, in the 1210th year of the Fourth Empire.)

A history of the world? Written in the future tense?

Of a sudden Rather was struck by an idea so far-fetched and crazy, he almost laughed out loud. At the same time he began to feel a growing apprehension. He read on.

By the time he was halfway through the second column, he was sure of what he was seeing, and growing more and more excited.

He wasn't all that well acquainted with Vereld's history, and although Jareth had begun every entry with the date of its writing, he rarely gave precise dates pertaining to the actual events he described. Still, Rather was able to pinpoint several important incidents that had taken place roughly two decades ago.

This meant that, if Jareth's initial dating was correct, which accor-

ding to Felda it must be, then the boy had written down these events –
again roughly – twenty years before they had occurred. No wonder
the future tense. Jareth was predicting.

Astounding as the boy's feat of literacy and the mastery of a foreign language was, it still wasn't his main gift.

This was. The boy was a bloody prophet.

Suddenly Rather had the distinct feeling he was being watched.
The shutters gave a small rattle. He heard the faint creak of a floor-
board in the hallway. He tensed, not knowing which way to turn.

Then the door opened and Felda came in, carrying a tray loaded
with bread, cheese, wine, and a steaming bowl of soup.

Over dinner, Rather decided to tell Felda what he'd found.
He felt it wasn't up to him alone to decide what was to be done – or
not done – with his discovery. She didn't appear to be all that surprised by his revelation. If anything, she seemed satisfied to see the
faith she'd almost blindly placed in the genius of her strange son
validated in such a meaningful way, and by no less than a doctor of
medicine and magic.

Otherwise, to Rather's relief she seemed content to let the issue of
what do with this newfound knowledge lie for the moment and take
the time to think things over before reaching a decision. Rather got
the impression that her innate, simple wisdom was already heading
her towards a certain solution, though in this case he wasn't sure if
simple was the really the right way to go.

And sure enough, she said, 'Perhaps we should just whitewash the
whole room and give Jareth four fresh walls to write something new
on.'

Rather deliberated for a moment.

'Um, to tell you the truth, there's a problem with that. I've seen those walls. And I have what's called an eidetic – ah... an unfailing memory. Meaning I can remember everything I see, down to the smallest detail. I couldn't tell you right now and off the bat what's written there, but it's all in here,' he tapped his head, 'whether I want it to be or not. Given time and enough parchment, quills, and ink, I could write it down for you word for word. Just so you know.'

'But you'd ...'

'No, I wouldn't. Not if you don't want me to. But whitewashing alone isn't going to solve the problem. It's not that simple, is what I'm saying.'

Suddenly Jareth sat up in bed.

Eyes wide with fear, he grabbed Rather's sleeve.

'Kid!' Rather said. 'You gave me a fright there. Calm down, everything's fine.'

The boy shook his head. He turned to the wall by his bed and seemed to search for something. Then he pointed to a word.

'Gefahr' (danger), Rather read. Immediately Jareth pointed to another word, and another, 'bad' and 'man'.

'Bad man?' Rather said. 'Who's that? The priest?' Jareth nodded vigorously. 'What about him?' Rather asked.

Jareth chose another word, 'wants'.

'Okay, what does he want?

'Schlüssel' (key), Jareth pointed out.

'He wants the key?' Rather said. 'What key? What does it open? Jareth gently slapped the wall.

'You mean, he wants the key to this?' Rather indicated the walls. 'The key to understanding what you've written?'

Nod.

'Are you the key?'

Jareth shook his head.

'No, it's not you. But you wrote – ah, I see. You can read and write, but you don't speak. And anyone else trying to decipher this would understand jack, except… Shit! Are you saying I'm the key?'

Nod, nod.

'Bloody hell!' Rather said. 'So who is this damned priest?'

The boy found the fitting word on the wall. *'Hexenmeister'* (sorcerer).

Rather groaned. 'But they're just what mothers use to frighten their naughty children with. They don't really exist, do they? Please tell me they don't – '

Jareth was urgently pulling on his sleeve. This time, he looked Rather directly in the eye. To Rather it felt like a small jolt of electricity, catching an unveiled glimpse of the boy's stupendous intelligence like that, completely unprepared. Momentarily he felt crude and stupid, an inferior being looking at some higher form of existence. But the feeling passed quickly, and all that remained was an immense love for this strange, stricken boy. It must have communicated itself to Jareth, who leaned his head against Rather's shoulder for two heartbeats in a gesture so frail and endearing that Rather felt his eyes go moist.

Jareth straightened up with a new urgency. Back to the wall. 'Bad man,' he showed Rather, and 'coming'. He searched for a moment until he found 'rather' and 'run', emphasizing the last word by tapping it several times with his finger. He leaned over and gave Rather a sketchy hug.

Then the boy pushed him away, motioning him to go.

It was too late.

The door burst open with a violent crash, nearly flying off its hinges. A giant of a man wearing a black, sleeveless habit stepped into the room. Pock-marked, shaven-headed, absurdly muscled, he looked like the worst kind of thug. Using one massive arm, he swiped Felda out of the way with shocking brutality. She bounced off the wall like a bundle of rags, leaving a splash of red on the whitewash, and then came to rest on the floor, motionless, eyes staring vacantly into a crack between two boards.

Rather instinctively rose to his feet, putting himself between the man and Jareth, who was desperately trying to flee this world and retreat deep into his place of hiding, rocking wildly and keening like a freshly widowed Iskari woman.

Seemingly without effort, the brute picked Rather up by the scruff, nearly breaking his neck in the process, and held him there, three inches off the ground, feet treading air. Rather was outraged. He tried in vain to strike a blow at the giant, but he was no fighter to begin with, and hopelessly outmatched. All he managed to do was kick the man's shin with the heel of his stockinged foot. It was like hitting a rock, and probably hurt Rather more than it did his adversary, who just gave him a mild shake that set the vertebrae cracking in his neck. He felt helpless as a rabbit about to make the acquaintance of the chopping block.

Another black-robed man stepped through the door, pulling back

47

his hood, and an icicle of fear speared into Rather's gut. The priest. Or sorcerer. Severt, if that was really his name.

For the first time, Rather got a proper look at the man's face.
He looked frighteningly ordinary – apart from the red-lipped, hungry mouth and the twisted cross tattooed on his shaven pate. You could have passed him ten times in a row on the street and never noticed him. Still, he set Rather's flesh creeping.

'Doctor,' Severt said. 'Surprised? I told you I'd see you again shortly, though even I didn't think it would be quite so soon.'

'What the hell?' Rather snarled, more to keep from wetting his small-clothes than to impress anyone.

The big man shut him up by clapping a huge, calloused hand over his mouth.

'That's better,' the priest said, stepping over Felda's prone figure to pick up something from the floor. Rather recognized Jareth's writing tool. 'You shouldn't interrupt, you know. It's bad manners. Now, where was I? Ah, yes. You've been very busy. Admirable. I've spent months in this hovel trying to puzzle out the problem.' He indicated the walls.

'And you breeze in here and solve it in a matter of hours. But then, you're the only one with the proper tools, aren't you? Still, you deserve my sincerest thanks for saving me so much time and bother. And what's more, you've freed me to finally get out of this stinking rattrap.

'Speaking of which, I'm afraid you'll be accompanying me on a rather longish trip. Sorry, old chap, but you simply haven't got a choice in the matter. Actually, our coach is already waiting. Oh, and, by the way, not to worry about old Jaceyn, he's been taken care of. A quiet word to the City Guard, sped along by a handful of silvers, letting them know that after all these years of caring for a lunatic boy and recently finding out from his faithless wife that the kid's not even his, the poor man is at the end of his tether and likely to do something rash.'

Rather thrashed in the giant's grip.

'Bring him along,' Severt told the giant.

'Mmmmh, mmmh,' Rather struggled and rolled his eyes.

'What?' Severt said. 'Let him speak.'

'I'll go with you,' Rather said. 'But leave the boy alone. You don't need him.'

'My, my, a hero,' the priest sneered. 'Alas, as I've already told you, you're coming anyway, so no deal. But thanks all the same for reminding me. I really don't need the boy anymore, now that I have you. Besides, even I can read the dates at the beginning of... all this.' He gestured at the walls. 'Finished on the 3rd of Sowing, 1210, it says. In case you hadn't noticed: that's today.'

Rather could have kicked himself.

Perhaps if he'd paid attention he'd have been more watchful... but of what? Nothing could have led him to anticipate what was happening now. Severt was studying Jareth. The look on his face ratcheted Rather's fear for the boy up several notches.

'Don't you dare,' he gritted. The priest hardly took notice, just waved a hand, and the giant clapped his evil-smelling paw back over Rather's mouth.

With three short steps, Severt was at the bed. Laying an arm

49

around Jareth's shoulders, he pulled the feebly resisting boy towards him. Briefly, the tableau reminded Rather of a kindly uncle holding his favorite nephew in a fond embrace, although it was nothing of the kind.

In a move so quick Rather hardly saw it, Severt stuck the sharp end of the writing tool into the boy's ear, all the way up to the hilt, and gave it a sharp twist. Jareth immediately went limp. The priest let him drop like so much rubbish, then tossed the bloody tool on top of him.

Rather bit the giant's hand as hard as he could, and the man withdrew it with a grunt.

'Damn you to hell, you sorry piece of shit!' Rather yelled. 'I'm going to make – '

'Hold his mouth open,' Severt said. Bitten or no, the giant needed only a thumb and a finger to force Rather's jaws apart, putting an abrupt stop to his rant. The priest pulled a flask from his robe, uncorked it, and poured the oily, evil-smelling and eviler-tasting contents down Rather's throat, nearly choking him.

'Have a nice trip,' he said. 'I'll see you when we get there.'

Next, he said something to the giant that Rather couldn't understand, because suddenly there was a buzzing like ten thousand bees in his ears and the room was swaying and revolving around him like a mad carousel with all the lights going out, one after the other, until everything whirled away into darkness.

Soon, there was nothing but silence, and then not even that.

❖   ❖   ❖

When the giant had carried Rather away, the man who called himself

Par Severt took a lamp and threw it on the floor, shattering the glass. Flames immediately began to spread and lick at the dry wood. The second lamp he flung at the wall over Jareth's bed. Lamp oil sprayed all over the boy's body and the bedding, setting them alight in an instant.

The black priest stood for a moment, savoring the first whiffs of burning meat. Then he turned and left, satisfaction twisting his fleshy lips.

❖ ❖ ❖

I shall now turn to the most secret matter of the Gates. Of these ancient and mysterious passageways, little is known by few. Owing to their great age, which reaches far back beyond all human remembrance, one can but speculate whether one should hold them to be wondrously advanced artifacts, left behind by incredibly powerful mages of a people so long gone from the face of this world as to have been forgotten even by legend, or whether they are some manner of natural phenomenon, come into existence when the Good Elil (praised be His name) breathed life into the eternal void and thus created the All.

Carric Three Suns, The Secret History of Magic

2 Bonesend

t was near last light. The cold, biting winds that had gusted over the stony wilderness of the Bonesend plateau throughout the day had finally died down, leaving behind an eerie silence unbroken by the call of birds or the rushing of water, for up here there was neither.

In the unnatural stillness that seemed to magnify even the smallest sound, Lansing Durpa went about his chores with the quiet deliberateness of a man long used to being aware of his every move and paying attention to the smallest detail. Up here on the high plains, it was the only way to survive.

He gave the stew in the pot hanging over the cook-fire a last stir.

Then he walked to the edge of the small camp and sent out three long, piercing whistles. From farther out on the plateau an answering whistle came, then another, and another. Only when he heard a fourth did Durpa's shoulders relax a fraction. He went to feed the ponies.

Darkness was setting in by the time the other men arrived in camp, weary from a long day's work. First was Ügmen, Durpa's brother-in-law. Next came Jalme and Pasong, Ügmen's sons, and finally Dorting, Durpa's own son, last as usual. Packs were carefully set down, hands and faces washed sparingly with splashes of water from their dwindling supply, every drop of which had come up on the backs of their pack-ponies. One after another the men hunkered down by the welcoming fire, and Durpa handed out bowls of stew and still crisp rounds of nan bread baked on the hot stones of the morning's fire.

The men were Larnaki bone gatherers, and like most Larnaki they were black-haired and olive-skinned, short and slight but wiry and tough. Twice every year between spring melt and the first autumn snows, they undertook the long and arduous journey to this barren, inhospitable place to search for the precious commodity after which Bonesend was named. It could be found only here, relics of a long forgotten battle, bones of man and beast preserved and hardened to extraordinary toughness, stained many different, vivid colors by a unique combination of local minerals and the cold, dry climate. The bones were much sought after by Larnaki artisans, who cut and carved them into figurines and trinkets that fetched exorbitant prices on the continent and beyond, and especially in the Empire far to the west. Lucrative or no, bone-gathering was a dangerous job, and not just because of Bonesend's treacherous terrain.

Less than half a mile from the bone gatherer's camp on Bonesend's northern rim stood Blacktower, allegedly built by sorcerers in ages past and now many centuries abandoned. It was a grim, forbidding structure made from enormous slabs of black, foreign stone, likely brought from far away and put together by magic rather than animal or human labor. The stuff seemed to swallow the light that fell upon it and made the building's details difficult to discern even on a bright day. With the onset of twilight, the tower became ever harder to see, seeming to fade from the world of tangible things as if its substance were being transmuted and sucked into another dark altogether. At night, only a hole in the sky where there should have been stars betrayed its presence.

Dreadful as the tower was, the true terror of the place resided in a pair of slender stone columns and a night-black monolith standing outside the dark maw of the building's entrance. Just looking at these artifacts for too long, even from afar, could fill a man's mind with utter hopelessness and despair and drive him to the brink of suicide. Or beyond, if his will was weak.

The bone gatherers, ordinarily brave and fearless men, took great care to give the tower a wide berth, even though the best troves were to be found there, as if the ancient battle had raged highest around it. They all knew the tales of men who had been foolhardy enough to let greed lure them too close to the tower. Men who returned as empty, mindless husks. Or not at all. It was the standing stones that ate away at their minds or swallowed them whole, whispered rumor among the gatherers held, and Lansing was inclined to believe it.

There were traces of ancient roads leading south and west, but they were soon lost in the jumble of boulders and scree. No one in living memory had ever attempted to cross the lifeless plain that seemed to stretch forever beyond the tower, and no one knew what lay across its vast expanse, though on clear nights like this one, sharp eyes could just make out a dark bank of clouds far, far to the south and east, sometimes lit by flashes of yellow and red as if strange and fearsome storms raged within or great, consuming fires beneath.

But of these things the gatherers spoke only in the safety of home, if at all. When, as now, they were camped on the edge of Bonesend, campfire talk involved only immediate necessities. If the need to defend against the encroaching darkness became too great, they sometimes told stories or talked of trivial and insignificant matters, though never of home and family, for fear of drawing unwanted attention to things held dear.

Tonight there was no conversation during dinner.

But Durpa saw that his son Dorting was excited about something, even if the boy tried hard not to show it. Durpa nodded to himself. Becoming a man, his Dorting was. Finally, Durpa set aside his bowl and took out his pipe.

'You went out far today,' he said to his son.

'Yes, padhu,' Dorting said.

''Did you find any good bones?'

'I did, padhu. And I also found something else. Something special, I think.'

'Show us,' Durpa said.

Rummaging in his pack, Dorting drew out an object wrapped in one of the squares of soft leather used to protect the better bone pieces. He undid the wrapping and carefully placed the object on a flat stone by the fire.

It was a small, delicate bowl made from light blue stone, its outer rim beautifully carved with a row of flying cranes. The birds were rendered in every detail, and Durpa thought that if the light had been better and his eyes still sharper he could have discerned even the small feathers on their necks and breasts.

'It is very beautiful,' Pasong said, leaning closer for a better look.

'And not the smallest chip or crack,' Jalme marveled. 'A wonder.'

'A good find,' Ügmen said.

'A very fine find,' Durpa agreed. 'It ought to bring a good price in Sirida.'

Dorting looked stricken. 'I don't think it should be sold,' he blurted. Then he blushed, obviously embarrassed at his own forwardness.

'Why not?' Durpa asked.

'Take it,' Dorting said. 'Hold it.'

Picking up the bowl, Durpa immediately felt a tingling in his fingertips. It rapidly spread through his hands and lower arms, and with it a sense of deep calm and great strength seemed to flow into him. He felt completely relaxed and at the same time more awake and aware than ever before in his life.

Very softly, the bowl began to hum.

Durpa quickly set it down and rubbed his hands on his trousers. He took a deep breath and slowly let it out again.

'You're right,' he said. 'This is not something that should be sold. Wrap it up again. We will take it to the Radj. He will know what to do with it. And if not he, then Abbot Tönden.'

He caught Ügmen's eye.

'I think we've gathered enough this trip. We should leave tomorrow. What do you say?'

'Yes,' Ügmen agreed. 'Time to go. There's a smell of snow in the air.'

They broke camp before dawn, and at first light the five men and four ponies dipped down over the rim of Bonesend and vanished into the thick layer of cloud that filled the lower valleys like a sea of cool, grey cotton for as far as the eye could see. It would be nearly three weeks before they reached Sirida in Larnakis, and home.

As to the gods, I have no means of knowing either that they exist or do not exist.

Protagoras

3 The Madal Skog

hen the gods divided up the earth among the tribes of man, so the story went, the Skogon came last. By then, the only thing left was the Madal Skog, the badlands north of the plains of Gomilar. It was bleak, unforgiving country, its inhabitants as harsh and unwelcoming as the land they lived on. In the Madal's warren of mesas and canyons they made a meager living planting crops on the steep, terraced slopes of narrow valleys, herding sheep and goats, and mining and smelting ore.

Once every three-month, a band of dark-clad, hard-faced clansmen brought a pack train's worth of iron ingots to Ulan Bok, a caravanserai and trading post in northern Gomilar, where they sold their product and bartered for supplies. Here too they kept themselves apart, foregoing the inns and taverns for a camp outside the walls, communicating with outsiders only in order to sell or buy, and leaving as soon as the last ingot had changed hands.

Truth be told, no one was sorry to see them go, for these dour, taciturn men with their black head-cloths and veils exuded a hardbitten joylessness, a grim, oppressive atmosphere of sour superiority and unspoken reproach that made others for no good reason feel somehow in the wrong, as if found inadequate and judged wanting on some obscure, intangible scale of reckoning.

As every year at the beginning of October, the clans were gathered in Hunter's Valley for the annual ceremonies in honor of Uilmaz the Riven, God Protector and Father of the Skogon. More than a thousand yurts were clustered around the Great Hall built outside Rivensend, a small box canyon that was no more than a gash in the side of the valley.

There, legend said, Uilmaz had fled when he was pursued by six demon-gods sent to kill him by his evil, treacherous brother Eill the White. The demons found him, in the end, and murdered him, cutting up and dividing his body into six pieces, which they scattered all over the badlands. But, Uilmaz being a god, his flesh was immortal, and so it came that from the six parts of his divine body grew the six clans of the Skogon: Stone, Water, Sky, Mud, Snake, and Black Yurt.

So much for the orthodox version. The more occult mysteries fostered by the Mud and Black Yurt clans predicted that, some day, all six parts of the god would be found and reunited, returning him to his former power and glory. It was a matter of bitter dispute between the Muds and Black Yurts on the one side and the rest of the clans on the other, the latter holding that the god had long since risen and the clans themselves were his living members, with Uilmaz existing in and through them, and thus it was impossible to bring back to life a god who had already been resurrected.

This year, for the first time ever, the ceremonies had been interrupted and the council of elders convened in the Great Hall to deal with an unprecedented emergency.

Hands and feet bound with heavy chains, accused of having committed murder not only during God's Festival but in the holiest of holies, in Rivensend itself, Morlic Silt stood before the council of Skogon elders in the hastily converted Great Hall where he was to be questioned and judged.

There was no doubt as to whether he'd done the deed, had killed in cold blood and in the process created a horrific carnage that had threatened to turn even the most hardened stomachs of those who'd had the misfortune to behold what he'd left behind.

The man even admitted to the deed. But alas, the rest of the story was not so simple, much to the chagrin of Jekkim Flint, chief and priest of the Stone clan, who found himself fervently wishing that there was no 'rest of the story', that the whole sorry mess would simply go away, that he might wake up back in his yurt and shrug it all off like a bad dream.

Jekkim's eyes wandered to the thing lying on a low table set to one side, covered with a white cloth. White, at least, and not black, the color of the god. He shuddered. Abomination! Those thrice-damned, pig-headed Mud and Black Yurt people: fools, fools and heretics, the lot of them. And the guilty man himself – surely not your average murderer.

Not that Jekkim had any experience with murderers, the Skogon being what they were: proud and unforgiving, quick to take offense and quicker to retaliate, a people to whom killing was a matter of honor, not of malefaction. Had Morlic committed his crime at any other time and place, the matter would have rested with the victim's family, and revenge would have been swift and merciless. But this was a different kettle of fish altogether. Murder was the least of it.

What this had quickly become and was now really about was the foundation of Skogon faith. It was about the never-ending dispute between the orthodox and the heretics. It was about doctrine, it was about dogma – meaning, it was about politics.

And there was another factor to consider in all of this: Asukan, High Priestess of Uilmaz, accompanied by her sidekicks Halima and Tomay, a trio of black vultures watching the proceedings with hard, glittering eyes, silent for now but ready to pounce whenever it suited them. For all that there were male priests in every clan, these women represented the real power in all matters spiritual, and from this fact they most unfortunately extrapolated the right to have a say in all other clan affairs as well.

Not yet forty, big-boned and strong-featured, good-looking if you appreciated the aesthetics of, say, a keen blade polished to a high gloss, Asukan was young for the job but had already held it for nearly a decade. Purportedly she had magic, was capable of miraculous feats such as turning water into wine or levitating. But no one outside her inner circle of dedicated followers had ever witnessed such a deed, and Jekkim wasn't prepared to concede these hardcore fanatics – fanatics firstly of Asukan, and only secondly of the god – much credibility. Asukan herself neither confirmed nor denied the rumors, only adding to the mystery surrounding her person and fuelling the superstitions about her supposed powers. Sly tactics, in Jekkim's opinion.

Asukan, he knew, was all about power, and she possessed the necessary patience for long-term strategy, the deviousness to hide her true motives and objectives, and the iron will and determination to fulfill any task and reach any goal she set herself. At the end of the day, if she didn't see a greater gain for herself in staying out of it altogether, it would be she who would decide over whatever religious and political dispute arose in the course of Morlic Silt's trial.

Which meant he had to give this his very best shot.

Jekkim was aware that he was supposed to be an unprejudiced and impartial judge, whatever that meant, but he admitted to himself that, right from the start, he'd felt a spontaneous and intense dislike for the man Morlic.

There were reasons enough. Short and skinny, with a too-large head, jug-handle ears, close-set eyes, a weak chin and a prominent, permanently bobbing Adam's apple, his appearance alone did nothing to attract anybody's sympathies. Just hearing the little turd use the honorific for elder, *dras*, every time he answered a question, made Jekkim feel like puking. And the man was a member of the Mud clan.

To make matters even worse he was all false, slimy attentiveness and obsequious nods and bobs, a willing helper at his own condemnation. The fellow almost succeeded in making one feel somehow complicit, as if one were sharing the same side of the argument with him. Disgusting.

With an effort, Jekkim forced his attention back to the proceedings. This was his one chance – barring interference from Asukan – to shut the Muds and Black Yurts up for good and finally put an end to their heretical fantasies. They thought they had their grand revelation lying there on the table, but he'd show them different. The man Morlic was one of theirs. Jekkim was going to rub their noses in that until he drew tears. The moment he'd heard of the murder and the culprit's clan affiliation, he'd sent out a host of agents to gather every shred of intelligence they could find.

In a surprisingly short time they had unearthed some very interesting stuff, and he intended to use every last bit of it.

❖   ❖   ❖

Morlic, on the other hand, in a fit of dangerous hubris most likely provoked by the afterglow of the killing and the undivided attention he was getting, was almost enjoying himself.

The doddering old fools were about as sharp as wooden knives, and easy to play. The three women gave him the creeps, but they seemed to be there only as observers – and anyhow, no woman was going to dare interfere with Morlic Silt. One glance from him, packed with meaning, would be enough to show them all the horrors that lay in store for them if they did, and shut them up smartly. Or so he reckoned.

The real challenge for him was keeping straight the voices in his head and making sure that only one of them spoke out loud, and the right one at that. If the others ever managed to get a word in sideways, he was done for. He found his eyes wandering to the thing on the table.

Pay attention, he told himself. *This is a game you're good at. Better than them.*

Elder Jekkim, a stout, square man with a broad peasant's face and large, calloused hands, cleared his throat and sat up in his low-slung ceremonial chair.

'Do you mind?' he interrupted elder Fasik, who during the past quarter-hour had managed to get himself hopelessly tangled in his own line of questioning and was about to head off on an even less promising tangent.

'Suit yourself,' short, plump Fasik said ungraciously, leaning back in his chair and clasping pudgy hands over an ample waist.

With perhaps two hundred clanspeople packed into every bit of space not taken up by the court, the air in the dark, low-beamed hall was quickly growing stale, and it was stifling hot. Though it was a mild day, the elders had ordered a fire lit in the huge hearth behind them. Some overzealous fool was keeping it going at full blast, and everyone close to it except the cold-blooded old lizards was sweating copiously.

Forget it. Concentrate.

'Let's take a moment,' Jekkim was saying, his pale eyes fastened on Morlic like righteous leeches, 'and go back a few years. It may help us to better understand the present. I seem to recall an incident some years back involving you and that unfortunate shepherd, Hurim I believe his name was. You were apprenticed to him, if I remember correctly, at the age of...'

'Twelve, dras. I was an unruly, rebellious brat back then, and caused my parents much grief and worry. For that I'm truly sorry, and I'd beg their forgiveness if they were still alive and could hear me. It was all my fault, and they were right to send me away.'

You pulled apart living insects and blew air into frogs until they burst when you were six. You set fire to small, furry animals when you were eight. How they burned! How they screamed! You tortured your younger brother and threatened to cut off his thing if he told. You promised your parents you'd kill them in their sleep if they beat

65

you bloody one more time. That promptly got you another beating, but it also got you sent away. Go ahead. Tell them about it. Seeing the shock on their stupid faces would be worth it.

"Kill them! Kill them all! Blood must flow for the great work to be done. Rivers of blood, oceans of blood! Worlds of blood!" That was the thing on the table. Thankfully, it spoke only inside Morlic's head, and nobody else could hear it.

'Ah, your parents,' Jekkim said. 'They died an untimely and tragic death, didn't they? What can you tell us about it?'

'Only what I was told myself, dras, seeing as I wasn't there at the time. Still herding sheep, I was. Most likely a faulty chimney, they said, and the thatch caught fire. They must have died in their sleep, killed by the smoke before they could wake.'

In their sleep, my arse. They died screaming and pounding on the door that wouldn't open because you'd wedged small, flat stones under it and under the shutters, something nobody would notice in the aftermath of a fire that left the house a smoking ruin, burned to the ground. Should have stuck to tradition and slept in a yurt, the dumb fuckers.

'Yes, well, so you say.' Jekkim considered for a moment. 'How long exactly did you stay with shepherd Hurim?'

'With him, six months, dras. Meaning as long as he was alive.'

'The shepherd too died an untimely death, I believe.'

'Yes, dras. My fault again. A mountain lion was following the herd, killing sheep even when it wasn't hungry. Hurim said it was a very bad thing, a beast that killed for sport. One day it attacked us in our camp. We fought it off with fire and spears, but I was wounded in the fight. I can show you the scars, if you like.'

66

Scars you gave yourself with a sharpened stick, in case anyone ever questioned your story. Because there was no lion. The beast was traveling with the herd, not following it. Oh, there were lion tracks all right, but they weren't as fresh as old Hurim believed. You could find them all over the place. Not much of a tracker, was Hurim.

Hated your guts, that's for sure, just like you hated his, but he never dreamed that you could be the one killing his sheep until it was too late. Didn't catch on to what was happening until you slit that gravid ewe open from head to tail and nailed her unborn lamb to the ground beside her with a couple of tent pegs.

You watched him find her, watched him kneel in the blood and gore and touch that lamb like it was his own dead child. Pathetic. And the look on his face when he suddenly realized you were there behind him – because even a dumb fool like Hurim could feel you, could feel your power raising the small hairs on the back of his neck and sending a chill down his spine.

Oh, the terror when he turned and saw you. It was then he finally understood, and fear knotted his innards and turned them to water because he knew then and there that it was over for him, that a twelve year-old boy was going to kill him and there was nothing he could do about it.

"Kill him, kill him," the thing on the table echoed.

All you had to do was hide and wait. Four nights Hurim managed to stay awake, but it wasn't enough to make it back to safety, back among other people. On the fifth night he fell asleep, and that was it. Lights out. End of story.

'Hurim went to fetch water for cleaning my wounds,' Morlic said.

'He must have taken a shortcut to the stream, a steep, dangerous path down a gully in the canyon wall. He slipped and fell. I found him at the bottom, dead as mutton.'

Morlic saw Jekkim straighten – something must have caught his attention.

Careful.

'And how did you get to the stream,' Jekkim asked, 'wounded as you were? Did you fly?'

'No, dras. When I saw Hurim wasn't coming back I dragged myself there the long way round. Took me half the day but saved my life. Though I wish Hurim had come back then and was here now to tell the tale himself.'

'And after Hurim died, you didn't return? You stayed out there alone?'

'I did, dras. I liked the job and the life that came with it, and I owed it to Hurim to take care of his herd. I did come in for shearing and supplies.'

'And this went on for how long?'

'Five years, dras.'

'During those five years, did you ever by chance come by a place called Farbrook?'

Ah! She was your first. You gave her every chance to recognize your power and your inner beauty, but she just turned up her nose and laughed at you. Mocked you. She needed to be taught a lesson. A lesson in blood.

"Blood, yes!" said the thing on the table. "The more, the better."

'Not that I remember, dras,' Morlic said. 'Don't think I've ever heard of the place.'

'Oram's Crag? That ring a bell?'

That one was a screamer, nearly got you caught.

Not quite so dull after all, the old goat. Hot on a trail that would take him nowhere past a suspicion he could never prove. Sosha was another story, but Morlic already knew how to wriggle out of that one.

'Where are you going with this, Jekkim?' elder Samad asked, his breath wheezing and his bald, liver-spotted head wobbling precariously on his stick of a neck. Morlic reckoned he could break it with two fingers, snap it like a dead twig. 'Aren't we supposed to be talking about the death of that girl, ah, ah…?'

'Sosha,' Jekkim said. 'Patience, Samad. We're getting there. Morlic. After you returned – '

There was a sudden commotion behind Morlic.

He turned just in time to see Sosha's youngest brother Nesud standing in the door, arrow nocked, bow drawn, his handsome face twisted in a feral grimace, radiating hate like a brazier full of demons. Before anyone could move, Nesud loosed.

Morlic stood frozen in place. The arrow came whistling faster than the eye could follow, burrowing through the gap between Morlic's left arm and his torso, the razor-sharp broadhead cutting through his shirt, gashing his ribs and the inside of his elbow. Flying on, it lifted the lone remaining strand of elder Samad's wispy hair with the draft of its passing before it shattered in the fireplace.

Before Nesud could nock another arrow he was pinned down by the men closest to the door. 'Murderer! Monster! Abomination!' he shouted, struggling to free himself. 'Let me kill him! Let me kill him

69

now!'

'Get him out of here,' Jekkim ordered. 'See that he calms down. We'll deal with him later.'

'You,' he said, turning back to Morlic, momentarily at a loss for words.

'I say, what was all that about?' elder Samad piped up, disturbed by the ruckus at the door but blissfully unaware that death had just missed him by a hair's breadth. No one bothered to answer him. The three women sat still as stone statues, unperturbed, as if nothing at all had happened.

'I'm sorry,' Morlic said. 'I'm sorry things had to happen the way they did. Maybe you should just let him kill me. Get it over with.'

'Ha!' Jekkim exclaimed. 'You'd like that, wouldn't you? But trust me, it's not going to be that easy. Now. Where was I?'

'The dead girl, Sosha,' Fasik offered.

'No, I have it now,' Jekkim said. 'After your stint as a shepherd, what did you do next?'

'I rejoined my people. The old caretaker at Rivensend had just died, and I was given the job. I've been there ever since. Six years it's been.'

And the beast slept for most of that time. Only twice it woke up and needed to be fed.

'During that time, did you ever visit the winter camping grounds at Coldridge? The village of Scree?'

Damn him, he's like a dog worrying a bone. Easy now.

'Never been to either place, dras. I'm sure I'd remember.'

❖   ❖   ❖

'Now, Jekkim, I think we've had quite enough of this.'

This from Munnir, chief of the Mud clan, who had so far seemed content to follow the proceedings in silence.

Not that he had Jekkim fooled for a minute. Here was the real enemy, finally stepping up to the line. He'd caught on to what Jekkim was doing, and didn't like it one bit.

'It's leading absolutely nowhere, as anyone can see.' Munnir, a wiry, bird-faced man in his late fifties who looked closer to forty and moved with the verve and agility of a man thirty years his junior, looked around for approval and got it, except from Asukan and her two companions, inscrutable as ever.

'Do you think we can move on to the actual crime? In fact, if you don't mind, I'd like to ask some questions of my own.'

It was time to let him have the floor, Jekkim knew. He could only hope that the foundation he'd so carefully laid would hold when the time came for the final showdown. And that Asukan wouldn't spoil it all at the last moment.

'Please,' he said with a dismissive wave of his hand. 'He's all yours.'

Munnir stood, one hand stroking his short, neat beard, the other resting as if by chance on the hilt of the ceremonial rukh stuck in his sash. Never one to miss a gesture, that one. Jekkim suppressed a sigh.

'Well then,' Munnir addressed the defendant. 'Why don't you tell us in your own words what happened the other night. And I'll take the liberty to interrupt you if we need clarification on some point or other. Is that all right with you?'

Damn the man! He was treating Morlic almost as an equal. And Jekkim was suddenly certain that Morlic had been well coached in advance, probably by Munnir himself. He wasn't surprised, though.

He'd foreseen this possibility as well.

❖ ❖ ❖

Morlic took a moment to envision the layout of Rivensend: the narrow, rock-walled entrance to the small box canyon, the grassy oval with the small temple to the left and the custodian's quarters to the right, both built up against the vertical canyon walls. The holy of holies, the stone altar under the deep overhang at the back of the canyon, decked with vases, candles and incense, perpetually strewn with wildflowers and surrounded by hundreds of offerings. And the seal, a marble inlay on the front of the altar depicting a vertical grey line, bisecting a circle of white and flanked by two round, black dots.

'Master Morlic?' Munnir prodded.

'Yes,' Morlic said, all obsequiousness gone from his voice and bearing. 'This is what happened: I was tidying up the altar, and at first I didn't even notice her. When I did, she was just standing there staring at me with the weirdest look on her face, like she wasn't quite there. Like she was listening to something only she could hear. Of a sudden she slipped out of her dress and dropped her shift, just like that. And then the God spoke to me.'

Jekkim snorted.

Look at Jekkim now, storm clouds gathering on his brow like he's just discovered that every single apple in his root cellar is wormy. Fasik on the other hand is licking his lips as if sweets are about to be served, and Tomman the Snake is actually blushing. Too bad you can't tell them the real story.

Had Morlic bothered to look at Asukan, he would have likely risked wetting his smallclothes. Though not a muscle moved in her face, she was radiating the displeasure of someone about to squash a particularly revolting bug under her heel.

How you wanted her, your cousin Ramin's betrothed, ever since you noticed her young breasts beginning to bud. So sweet, so shy, so beautiful!

How she stood there in the gathering dusk, bewildered by the way you were looking at her, letting her see the power and the beauty of the beast. You frightened her, and she would have turned to leave. But the power already had her in its grip, and when you told her to undress she cast around a last, futile look for help that wasn't there and wouldn't come, and then complied, trembling like a cornered deer.

How Fasik would salivate if you described the wonder of her naked body to him! But when you ordered her to lie on the cold stone floor and spread her legs for you she balked and tried to cover herself, so you grabbed her by the hair and threw her against the altar, knocking over and breaking a vase. You fumbled at your trousers, crowding her from behind, but suddenly found yourself gone limp. She remained hunched over and motionless for a moment, then she turned and looked at you, and you saw relief there, and contempt. Worst of all, you saw pity.

That was when the beast awoke in earnest, filling you to bursting with its overwhelming rage, darkening your vision until all you saw and remembered later were disconnected images springing at you out of the haze-edged darkness like crazily jerking phantoms: her eyes like black glass, flat and alien; her white breasts and belly, soft and

73

oh so vulnerable; her face: relieved, then puzzled, then terrified; your hand gripping a shard from the broken vase; her face again, mouth a gaping hole, small, white teeth bared in a soundless scream, inaudible against the roaring in your ears; and then more red, gaping mouths appeared all over her body, made by the shard in your hand, and they multiplied and fused into a bloody waste of tattered skin and mutilated flesh.

"Bloody, yes," the thing on the table said. "But not a waste. Oh no, not a waste at all."

Finally, bathed in the stink of blood, piss, and excrement, you found sweet release. And that was when the God really spoke to you.

'The God spoke to you,' Munnir said with just a touch of reverence in his voice. 'What did it say?'

'It said, "Behold, I have brought this woman here, and I have brought you. For she shall be my sacrifice, and you shall be my reaper. I hunger. I thirst. Too long the Skogon have neglected to see to my needs. Too long they have forgotten their true purpose, which is to free me from this prison. So tell them this: for all that they have been wantonly negligent, I will not turn from them. Instead, this night I forgive, and offer them a renewal of the covenant, and seal it with blood. If they accept, I will lead them to eternal glory. If not, they will find no place on Vereld to hide from my wrath, for this night you will give me back my freedom, Morlic of the Mud clan."'

'Blasphemy!' Kassem of the Sky clan shouted, his round, homely face florid with outrage. 'Sacrilege! I'll hear no more of it!'

Samad was angrily thumping the floor with his cane, most likely waiting for the appropriate words to complete their lengthy journey

74

from his brain to his vocal cords.

Asukan gave a twitch, as if she were about to break her silence, but immediately turned the involuntary start into something more innocuous, resettling herself in her chair.

'Please,' Munnir said, the voice of reason. 'I perfectly understand your indignation. In fact, I share it. But let the man finish, or we'll never get to the bottom of this. Master Morlic, if you please.'

"Good," was what the God really said. "Very good. Finally someone's doing something useful around here. I am infinitely sick and tired of all the yammering and begging, and never a thought as to what I might need."

It almost had you there, for a moment.

'Who are you?' *you asked like a good little boy.* 'Are you the God?'

As if you really cared.

"If that's what you want," it answered. "Though I rather doubt that you do. But as far as the others out there are concerned, yes, the God is definitely what I am."

'What do you want, then?' *you asked.*

"Easy," it said. "You've unwittingly done me a service with your little slaughterfest out there, providing me with the means to communicate with you. Now get me out of here, and I'll see that you gain riches and power beyond your wildest imaginings."

'Get you out of where?'

"The altar you're standing in front of hides the entrance to a cave. That's where you'll find me, once you've broken the seal and gotten round the altar. Obviously, there's some hard work involved, so best get cracking. We do have all night, as far as I can tell, but

better safe than sorry, and all that.''

'Well?' Jekkim growled. 'We're waiting.'

'Master Morlic, if you please,' Munnir seconded.

'The God asked me to free it by sacrificing the girl, saying it was the only way to undo the demons' safeguards. So I did. Then I had to chip that round thing, the seal, off the front of the altar and dig a-round the back so I could get into the cave behind. And that's where I found the God – well, part of it at least.'

With his bound hands Morlic gestured towards the table and the thing hidden under the white cloth. 'And now it wants us to find the other parts and put them back together again.'

'Fasik, if you'd be so kind,' Munnir said to the fat man, who was sitting nearest the table.

Fasik leaned over and gingerly picked up the cloth. Under it was a mummified human head, darkened by time to the color of old wood. Hanks of long, stringy blond hair still clung to the scalp. The carti-lage of the nose had contracted as it dried, exposing the nostrils as two vertical slits. Eyes like black, shriveled raisins lay behind half-closed lids.

It was not a pretty sight.

❖   ❖   ❖

Jekkim rose: time to take over.

'So this is your God,' he said, walking over to stand beside the table. 'Can it speak to us? Perform some small miracle, perhaps?'

Munnir didn't interrupt. He'd already made his point.

'It speaks through me,' Morlic said.

76

'How very convenient for you,' Jekkim said sarcastically. 'And what does it have to say?'

Morlic seemed to listen for a moment.

'It says it's already laid out all the pertinent facts,' he said. 'And it strongly recommends you pay attention and take it seriously, or be prepared to bear the consequences.'

'Threatening us, is it?' Jekkim said with a grim smile. 'Well, I for my part believe we've heard enough. My friends?'

The other elders nodded their assent.

None of them saw any gain in continuing with the public part of the proceedings. The rest would be hours of heated discussions followed by more hours of tough negotiations and shrewd bargaining, all of it behind closed doors.

'High priestess?' Jekkim turned to Asukan, fully expecting her to choose this of all moments to strike. To his surprise and relief, she merely gave a slight shake of the head.

'Fine,' Jekkim said. 'Then we'll retire for deliberation. Which means, everybody out of here. Hamad, Rasid, put the prisoner in the cellar under the cookhouse and guard him well. I'll have your hides if anything happens to him. Somebody make them a pot of kaf. And relieve them, if necessary. This is going to take a while.'

Morlic was suddenly a lot less confident of the outcome.

He'd been relying heavily on the head's support, but right when he needed it most it had gone completely silent, forcing him to improvise.

77

'Talk to me!' he hissed at it.

'Shut up!' It was burly Hamad, come to take him away. He studied Morlic for a moment, distaste written all over his blunt features, obviously trying to figure out how to handle him without actually having to touch him. Then he discovered the free end of the chain binding Morlic's hands. Grabbing it, he gave an experimental tug, forcing Morlic to take two quick, short steps forward to keep from falling over.

From the head, nothing. Morlic was beginning to wonder whether it had ever really spoken to him. Maybe he was going mad and had imagined it all. Then he noticed Rasid, Hamad's sidekick, leaning over the head and staring at it fixedly with a mixture of fear and fascination, as if he were listening to something only he could hear. Hellfire and damnation!

It must be talking to Rasid now! A black rage boiled up in Morlic. He'd kill the traitorous scum! His body was way ahead of him, already straining towards Rasid and the head, a fact he only noticed when Hamad gave a hard yank on the chain, nearly laying him out flat on his face.

'I can already see we're going to have to teach you some manners,' Hamad said. 'Rasid. Rasid? Rasid, you son of a mule, let's go!'

With a visible effort, Rasid managed to tear himself away from the head, but there was a very strange look on his face. Then his eyes came back into focus. He looked at Morlic, an evil grin spreading over his heavy features.

'They're going to hang you, you know,' he said.

❖   ❖   ❖

When the gods wish to punish us, they answer our prayers.
Oscar Wilde

4 Larnakis

t was a sunny morning in Sirida, and surprisingly mild for early October. A few small wisps of cloud hung in the deep blue sky, and the snow-covered peaks of the Caer-rocks looked down on Larnakis' capital like eternal, silent sentries, benevolent deities of stone and ice.

It was a high day in the city – though city was perhaps too grand a word for Sirida with its less than five thousand souls. The whole town was decked out in sky-blue and gold, banners and pennants flying the Sky Dragon, national emblem and arms of the royal house. Long rows of many-colored silk squares inscribed with prayers and good wishes strung along balconies and across the streets were fluttering merrily in the breeze. Today, all of Larnakis was celebrating the young royal couple's announcement that an heir had been conceived.

The people had come from all parts of the kingdom, proud and gay and dressed in their finest, and Sirida was straining at the seams. A reception and felicitation ceremony had been improvised by Ramen Lobsang, the mayor of Sirida who doubled as Lord Chamberlain on official occasions – or rather, he'd invented one, since there was no fixed procedure for this kind of thing and the last such occasion that might have served as an example, the conception of the current ruler and father-to-be himself, had taken place over thirty years ago.

The festivity was held in the palace courtyard, seeing as it was the only space large enough to accommodate everyone. Even so it was a tight fit, with every space where a person could possibly sit or stand claimed, from the ground level up to windows, balconies, wall-tops and any other besittable protuberance the buildings around the courtyard offered.

Except for official functions, the palace was seldom used. It contained living quarters only for foreign guests and visiting dignitaries. Larnakis' kings – or Radjs, as they were called – regarded themselves as men no different from all others, and by tradition lived in an ordinary house like everyone else. Anyone could come and see the Radj with a request or a complaint, or just drop by for a cup of tea and a chat, and his home was where the kingdom's business was carried out, where disputes and grievances were settled and justice administered.

No ceremony was complete without an appearance by the monks of Anpok, the great monastery sitting atop its own hill a short walking distance from the town like a regal but somewhat down-at-the-heel dowager, so large and sprawling that it was forever impossible to keep up with renovations, even though work had never really stopped since the building of Anpok was begun more than a thousand years ago.

As usual, the monks didn't get around to the actual blessing until they'd performed an elaborate and lengthy ceremony. First, scores of greater and lesser gods had to be appeased and demons banned, a ritual that involved much beating of drums, blowing of horns, and clashing of cymbals in accompaniment to a minutely choreographed dance of masks fighting the eternal battle between good and evil.

Today, the better part of the densely populated pantheon was represented, Radj Anskar thought, and not for the first time found himself wishing there was some way to speed things up, if only a little. His wife Rupili, sitting cross-legged on the throne-like dais beside him, seemed to have no trouble at all, but his own knees just weren't made for spending prolonged stretches of time in this posture. Never had been, which made official functions a torturous ordeal for him.

But the monks wouldn't be rushed. And the people were enjoying the spectacle, the fearsome, awe-inspiring masks and fantastic costumes with their gaudy colors and abundance of feathers, mirrors, veils, horsehair panaches and golden trimmings twirling and flashing in the clear mountain light.

Finally, it was over. Everyone who mattered and everyone who didn't had been blessed, their continued happiness and wellbeing commended to the gods responsible for such matters. Led by Narayan, the old abbot's second-in-command, the delegation filed out of the palace courtyard and headed back home, their shoulder bags filled to bursting with enough choice offerings to feed the whole of Anpok for a week.

After the ceremony, the royal couple withdrew to one of the palace's apartments. The Radjani suffered from bouts of morning sickness, and needed a moment's rest. Despite her inconvenienced state, Anskar found Rupili looking radiant as only a pregnant woman can, as if during this time the gods looked upon her with special favor, surrounding her and the child with an invisible cocoon of divine good-will.

Her long, jet-black hair was gathered in two luxuriant braids that reached all the way down to her delightful derrière, and she wore the traditional holiday dress, an ankle-length silk skirt in her clan's color, saffron, and a long, slimly tailored jacket of sky blue for her husband's House Tanore, richly embroidered and set with scores of tiny silver mirrors. In Anskar's estimate, no woman had ever looked more beautiful. Beside Rupili, he always felt large and ungainly, seeing as he was uncommonly tall and strongly built for a Larnaki, a trait he had inherited along with the lighter hair from his Dunmarkan grand-mother.

'Come, rest,' he said, leading her to a low couch. 'Perhaps you should lie down for a bit.'

Rupili merely sat, and Anskar noticed a tiny frown.

'What is it?' he asked, sitting beside her and taking her hand.

'Oh, nothing, really. It's just that... somehow it feels like we're tempting fate, making the announcement this early on. So many things can go wrong. Having the people's good wishes and asking the gods' favor is all well and good. But it *will* be a child of royal blood, destined to play a role in this world, and maybe not only in Larnakis. It's just... I can't help wondering who else's attention the ceremony might have drawn, and whether all of it's benign.'

'You may have a point there,' Anskar said. 'To be honest, I've had similar thoughts. But then, gods know how many generations before us have followed this tradition without any ill befalling them for it. I think the gods' favor and the people's goodwill should more than balance out any adverse influences. Which doesn't mean those

82

shouldn't be be guarded against. Next week, when abbot Tönden comes out of his retreat, we'll go to Anpok and ask him for a special blessing.'

'You're right, love. I must stop worrying. As the wise abbot would say: "Fear only serves to strengthen that which we fear." So come. I'm feeling quite well again. Let's go join our people and share the rest of this day with them.'

Just as they stepped out onto the palace's terrace, something strange and disquieting occurred. As a ray of sunlight may break suddenly from a cloudy sky, so the opposite now occurred. A finger of darkness suddenly leapt from the far southern horizon, as if some gigantic object had been raised high into the distant sky and was casting an impossibly long shadow over the land. Crossing the clear skies with frightening speed, it shot past and over the dividing mountain range into neighboring Anapur.

A gasp went through the crowd, and then a low, frightened murmuring. Slowly, the dark beam drew back again, sweeping left and right as if searching for something – only to stop right over their heads. It stayed there for what seemed like an eternity but was in truth only the space of a few short, terrified heartbeats. Then it withdrew, disappearing as quickly as it had come.

A hush had fallen over the people, fear and dismay written large on their faces as they turned to their Radj and Radjani, looking for a comforting gesture and perhaps some sort of explanation.

Anskar had no idea what had just happened – only that it couldn't have been anything good. Desperately wishing the monks were still there, he tried to think of something to say, some soothing words that might calm and reassure the people, and Rupili. She was thoroughly shaken, he saw, close to tears. But, with an admirable effort, she composed herself. Gave his hand a squeeze, and nodded. Together they stepped forward.

'It's nothing!' he shouted. Dismissing the whole episode as a natural occurrence was out of the question. The Larnaki, fervent believers in the supernatural, would never accept it. 'Wizard's play! A trick of the light! Tönden's novices could probably do as much or better, if they were allowed to waste their time on such useless mummery. Should we cringe before some mage-apprentice's silly games? Should we let good food and drink go to waste because of some rude trickster's prank? Come, my friends! The tables are set. The rak is ready to flow. Let us celebrate our joy and good fortune instead of allowing this foolishness to spoil our day.'

For all he knew, what he'd just said might have been total nonsense. But it was the best he'd been able to come up with. He took a cup offered by mayor Lobsang, who as usual was thinking on his feet, and raised it high.

'Health!' he called out. 'Health, prosperity and the god's goodwill! To the heir! And to you, my friends. Larnakis!'

'Larnakis!' the crowd answered. 'The Radj! The Radjani! The Heir!'

At first there was only a smattering of uncertain voices, but by the time they reached 'The Heir!' most of them had joined in, and Anskar thought he heard them end on a note of pride and defiance. Still, there remained a heaviness, a shadow of doubt that wasn't quick in lifting, expressed in somber miens and a muted buzz, the talk undoubtedly turning on what had just happened. Speculation would be rife.

He signaled the musicians. As if they'd been desperately awaiting their moment of release they struck up a lively tune, and Anskar stepped forward with Rupili to lead the first dance. It was the right thing to do. Larnaki could resist all sorts of temptations, but never music. The worst was over.

Later, Anskar stood and watched as the people, their mood somewhat restored, turned their attention to food and drink, to lighter talk and tentative merriment, the unsettling episode eventually relegated to second place, at least for the moment.

When he turned to his wife, he saw that she was still shaken. Her eyes hinted at unshed tears, and she was trembling. He should have known she wouldn't put the incident behind her so quickly.

'Rupili.' He pulled her close, and then led her a few steps to the side, the only small measure of privacy they could afford without raising renewed concern among those observing them.

'It felt... terrible,' she whispered, her mouth close to his ear. 'Evil. Menacing.'

'Yes, it did.'

'What ever could it have been?' she asked.

'I wish I knew.' No use being anything less than honest with her. 'It seemed somehow... curious. As if it were searching for something. Let's hope it found what it was looking for elsewhere.'

Briefly, she rested against him the full weight of her fear and dismay. Then he felt her back stiffen.

'Whatever it was, I won't be threatened,' she said. 'I won't have our child menaced, or you. I'll fight it, if I must. I won't allow it to harm either of you, or any of our people.'

She looked up at him, and in that instant he wouldn't for anything in the world have wished to be an enemy of hers. Resolve shone from her eyes, a great strength and courage, and something more, something as wild and ferocious as any great force of nature, and he found that where he hadn't thought that his love and admiration for her could possibly still grow, it did.

'If anyone dares threaten Larnakis, we'll deal with them,' he said, holding her tightly. 'But gods grant it will never be necessary, that it was nothing more than what it seemed: a silly spook.'

Without Power, there is no Magic. It is the source from which a practitioner draws his Power that determines which path he will tread, the Light or the Dark. The Mage builds up the Power within himself through years of diligent study and practice, not only of the arts of magicking but first and foremost of his own person, for knowledge of the self is his sole safeguard against slipping from his chosen path and turning to the Dark Side.

A Mage, when performing Magic, draws upon this, his own Power. Once it is exhausted, the Magic will begin to feed on his substance, physical and metaphysical, causing grave illness or even death. An Adept of the Dark Side, or Sorcerer, on the other hand, uses the power, that is, the life force of others to fuel his spells, curses and incantations, most often by causing the source's death. Therefore the only limit to his magicking is determined by the number of victims at his disposal.

Carric Three Suns, The Secret History of Magic

5 Fellmere

n the hours preceding dawn, while most of Larnakis still slept and the monks of Anpok were chanting first prayers and asking the gods' blessing for the coming day of celebration, a different kind of ritual was being performed far to the south. Here, a drab, gray landscape of endlessly repeated shallow dips and rises cowered under a low ceiling of perpetual cloud that frequently produced searing arcs of lightning and deafening thunder, though seldom rain. Not a single tree had been left standing, and the tallest vegetation were the thorny hedgerows dividing mostly barren fields. More often that not, daylight was hardly more than a sulphurous haze of drifting ashes, and the sound of birdsong and human laughter had not been heard in nearly a generation. Many of the farms had fallen into ruin, and few of those remaining showed signs of habitation. Here, on a rise that barely deserved to be called a hill, stood Fellmere, the hulking, formidable stronghold of the Brotherhood of the Black Priests of Amut.

Built by the order's founder in times that remained mercifully shrouded in a past too distant to be remembered as more than a gruesome fairytale to frighten children with, the keep had stood empty for many centuries. Long enough for the land to have recovered and become habitable again. Long enough for men to have returned and reclaimed it, fallow and overgrown as it was by then, to rebuild the old farmsteads, to clear and till and plant and make a living for themselves and their families.

Then, a little over thirty years ago, the Brotherhood had returned to Fellmere in force, and along with the castle had reclaimed all the surrounding lands. The farmers' initial opposition had been swiftly and brutally quashed, their brave but inexpert resistance doomed from the start, no more than a futile gesture in the face of a ruthless and overwhelming force such as sorcery.

The people's descent from independent freeholders into serfdom and slavery was as quick as it was absolute. Tithes were set by the priests, high beyond all reason. Half the able-bodied men were drafted into restoring and expanding the keep, the other half were forced to help oust a handful of rebels and recalcitrant nobles who refused to abandon their holdings without a fight. Only the women and children were left to work the fields, and even they weren't exempt from the black priests' requisitions, easy fodder to satisfy their growing demand for the human sacrifices needed to fuel their dark magic.

And so it was that, in the span of two generations, a prosperous people was brought lower than low and a fertile landscape turned into a wasteland, ruined by greed, neglect, and by the poisonous outpourings of ashes and gas from Pik Varakul, reawakened by the sorcerers' ghastly experiments deep in the mountain's entrails, where they tinkered with things that should by rights have never existed.

Fellmere's massive walls were stained with dark streaks and splotches left by events better not recalled. A dark crimson banner bearing a black, twisted cross hung over the main gate, limp as death in the oppressive stillness and gathering a rime of drifting ash like a fungal infestation.

The same motive was repeated on the wall hangings in the keep's upper hall, where this morning thirteen men in black habits sat at a long stone table, six to a side and one at the head. At the table's lower end stood a huge throne hewn from a single block of dull, black stone. A middle-aged woman hung on it, limp and deathly pale, drugged nearly to the point of unconsciousness and supported only by rough ties binding her wrists to ringed spikes driven into the throne's armrests. Her hair had been rudely chopped off, and her once-fine dress was in tatters, exposing one milk-white, sagging breast like a pathetic flag of truce.

Led by the man at the head of the table, the priests were chanting a series of malignant incantations, some pronounced in Common, others in a harsh, guttural language that sounded as if it had never been intended for the human tongue.

At first sight, the thirteen were rather ordinary and unremarkable men. Kuruma, their leader, for example, was short, pudgy man with a face that, save maybe for the wide, hungry mouth, would have gone unnoticed even in a crowd of three or four. His pale, effeminate hands looked as if they'd never held anything more dangerous than a quill or spoon.

Granted, the twisted crosses tattooed on the crowns of the men's shaven heads were unusual, to say the least. But what set them apart more than anything else was the aura of unrelieved malice and casual violence that hung about them like an oppressive fug, rife with a whiff of the slaughterhouse. And then there were their eyes: darkly glittering stones devoid of all humanity. Comparing only the eyes, a stone killer would have seemed an innocent babe beside these men.

They rose.

The chanting rose in volume and coalesced into a single word, repeated over and over: 'Ummuz, Ummuz, Ummuz…'

At a gesture from Kuruma, one of the men farthest down the table moved to stand beside the insensate woman, drawing an obsidian blade and holding it over her exposed left breast. The chant receded to a mere whisper as Kuruma intoned a prayer to the God.

'Lord Amut, we who call you by your true name, Ummuz, hear us. We offer you this death, that you may drink and have sustenance; we offer you this soul, that you may feed and be resurrected. Hear us,

Lord, we beg of you. Hear us and accept our humble offering. Hear us, and if it please you speak to us through this sacrifice and make your divine will known to us.'

The chanting stopped abruptly.

One swift stroke drove the blade deep into the woman's chest.

As the knife was withdrawn and blood gushed from the wound, darkness seemed to gather around the dying woman. A low, slow sigh escaped her lips. Riding on that death-sigh like an incorporeal leech came a thin, cold voice.

'Soon,' it said, and then, 'I am coming.'

As the gathering dispersed and novices came to take away the body, Kuruma moved to a quiet, secluded niche at the back of the hall with two of the brothers he trusted slightly more than the rest, which was still not at all.

'Very satisfying,' he said.

'Bled like a pig,' observed Tano, a large, blunt-featured man with thick black eyebrows and greasy, acne-scarred skin. 'Bit old, though.'

'Quite,' Kuruma said. 'But we could hardly have hoped for better news. Soon now, we will rule, and none shall withstand us.'

'Surely you meant to say, *He* will rule,' Tano said.

'Why, certainly,' Kuruma said. 'He will rule, with out humble assistance.' Tano was starting to irritate him. The man needed to be taken down a notch or two.

Elderly Gracklin's reedy voice interrupted his train of thought. 'I heard Him say He's coming, but I must have missed the part where He told us when exactly that's supposed to be.'

The old bugger had an unsettling way of coming straight to the

91

point, especially if it was a sore one. With his beaky nose and rapidly blinking eyes, Gracklin often reminded Kuruma of a flustered chicken. He could easily envision that scrawny neck stretched over a chopping block, with himself wielding the axe.

'Exactly,' Tano said. 'When? Considering the gods' sense of time, it could be this afternoon, or it could be in fifty years.'

'Soon,' Kuruma said. 'It will be soon. And we must prepare.'

'Yes, let's,' Gracklin said. 'And speaking of preparing: our flesh reserves are running low. Only three left in the dungeons, and one of them is in pretty bad shape. I hear she might not make it through the day. Handlers got a bit rough with her, it seems.'

'Then we should find a use for her before she goes to waste,' Kuruma said. 'A fresh load should be arriving tomorrow at the latest. I'll leave it to you to dispose of the damaged specimen. Pass her around, maybe. A little treat for the lower ranks. But see that she lasts, or else we'll have to break out another one to make everyone happy. Oh, and find some new handlers. I want the ones who spoiled the girl put down – no, better yet, add them to the reserves. They'll do for the simpler jobs.'

'So what about the timetable?' Tano asked. 'What do we do?'

'*You* will do exactly as I've just told you,' Kuruma said. Time to put these two in their place. They were getting notions. 'I am going to have a little chat with our special guest. Might turn up something useful.'

That got him a studiously blank look from Tano and some slightly accelerated eyeblinking from Gracklin. Not good enough. On a sudden inspiration, Kuruma waved over one of the novices.

'Poder, I believe it is? Yes? Good. Ever been to see the Oracle?'

Everyone knew full well that none of the novices and few of the Brothers had been allowed anywhere near the Oracle, as Kuruma liked to call his recent acquisition. Poder, a gangling, pimply youth, shook his head.

'N-no, sir.'

'Well, then. Care to come along? Might be an interesting experience. Yes? Splendid. Off we go, then.'

As he swept up Poder and turned to leave, Kuruma noted with satisfaction that Tano's mouth stood half open as if he'd been about to say something but thought better of it, and Gracklin was looking at poor Poder with a version of the Grandfatherly Smile that would have made any grandchild soil itself in sheer terror.

Deep down in the bowels of Fellmere, Kuruma stopped at one of several cells that lay along a torch-lit corridor. Farther down the hallway, far enough away to be out of earshot and therefore of no concern, stood a lone guard. One of the Unborn, a reject most likely, its disproportioned body swaying slightly, its skewed, lumpy features incapable of expression.

Kuruma had the boy face away before he turned his attention to the triple-plied, iron-banded cell door and undid the Ward, admiring his own handiwork. It was a thing of beauty, both intricate and simple, and very effective. If anyone other than himself should tamper with the door, two things would happen simultaneously: a Sending would alert Kuruma, and a Binding would capture and hold the intruder for however long it took Kuruma to arrive at the scene. An earlier version had been designed to kill immediately, but Kuruma had more recently decided he preferred to deal with the culprit personally. So much more satisfying. He was actually a bit disappointed that no one had ever set off the Ward – except for a drunken human guard who'd made the terminal mistake of confusing his doors.

Once the Ward was disabled, Kuruma bid the boy enter.

As always, the smell hit first, a ripe mixture of butcher's shop and deathbed underlaid with the hot-metal tang of sorcery and the musty odor of dank walls and mildew.

The cell was bathed in a dirty orange light emanating from several large glass tanks. A web of glistening, semi-transparent tubing made from an intestine-like, organic material was stretched across one end of the room from wall to wall and floor to ceiling. In the center of the web, a human body hung suspended. Tubes pulsing with liquids, some reddish, some clear, were attached to the head and torso, and clusters of them sprang like long, spidery digits from the stumps where the hands and feet were missing.

The body itself was gaunt to the point of emaciation, the skin ghostly white and completely hairless. Only an angry red scar remained where the man's member and testicles had been removed, and his eyelids had been sewn shut with coarse, black thread.

Kuruma, watching Poder out of the corner of his eye, saw the boy's Adam's apple bob repeatedly. Weakness? Or excitement?

'Meet the Oracle,' he said. 'As you can see, we take good care of it. We've freed it from the baser necessities such as eating, drinking, and excreting, and we've also eliminated anything that might distract it from its inner vision. Which, by the way, has improved remarkably, thanks to our modifcations. The only thing we haven't been able to correct is its stubborn and recalcitrant nature. Unfortunately, it sel-

94

dom talks without persuasion.'

Kuruma stepped over and opened a stopcock on a tube leading into the Oracle's neck. He let a few drops of clear liquid trickle through from a glass cylinder sitting on a side table, surrounded by a collection of surgical instruments.

'It burns,' he said almost lovingly. 'It burns away the will to resist, consumes the blockage.'

The Oracle spasmed, then its muscles and tendons relaxed, its head rolling over until it was facing in the direction of its torturer.

'Soul stealer,' it said, its voice weak and phlegmy from long disuse. 'As always, the stink of corruption precedes you.'

'Oh, spare me the banter,' Kuruma said. 'Tell me something useful.'

'Ah,' the Oracle said. 'I do know what you want to find out.'

'Splendid. So tell me.'

'Nah, I have something better for you. Something I just remembered. Something you should find very interesting. This one you could have even had for free, if you weren't such a habit-bound, sadistic creep. So listen carefully, demon turd.'

As the Oracle continued, its voice gained strength. 'Ready? Okay. Here goes: "Come summer solstice" – and that's next year's, just so you know – "come summer solstice, the last of three eggs will hatch. One is the egg of a cat, one is the egg of a carrion bird, and one the egg of a lizard. Three will hatch, and these three will be the doom and downfall of you and your stinking ilk and spell your master's end as well, and mankind shall know again the pleasure of being alive." Ah, took that one right out of old Stendhal, didn't he? Well. Where was I?

Oh, yes.

'Remember the cards you drew the other day when you were dabbling in fortune telling? The Warrior, The Wizard, the King? Oh, and the Wild Card, nearly forgot that one. It's mentioned too, rest assured. Be interesting to know who that one is, wouldn't it?

'That's them. The Redeemers. They're coming. That's who you're going to be up against, blood-guzzler. And believe it or not, you don't stand a snowball's chance in hell.'

Kuruma was silent.

The reference to the cards, together with its immediate and far-reaching implications, had jolted him. How did the bloody thing know about the cards? Was someone spying for it? Hardly. Or had it developed visionary qualities of its own? That its mind might be roaming the castle and spying on its inhabitants and their secrets – especially Kuruma and his secrets – was a more than disquieting notion.

If it could do that, how much had it already gleaned? How much did it know that it shouldn't? If it was capable of watching and eavesdropping as it pleased, it might well be aware of everything that went on in Fellmere. It certainly had all the time in the world on its hands and nothing better to do. Was there a danger that it might get past the castle's Wards and communicate with the outside, with the enemy? What to do about it? Could he afford to keep it alive and talking? Could he afford not to?

'Cat got your tongue?' the Oracle said.

'Not at all. Please continue.'

'Nothing to continue, corpse-fucker. That's all she wrote. Now get out of here. You make me sick.'

'My, but we're running foul at the mouth today! And, with all that drivel about eggs and doom, you still haven't told me what I came for. Are you trying to waste my time?'

'No. You're wasting mine. Now piss off.'

'Very well, then. But I do believe your lamentable behavior calls for a little reminder.'

'Go ahead, asshole, knock yourself out. I've still got more balls than you and all your sewer rat brothers put together.'

Kuruma opened the stopcock and let a hefty dose of the cylinder's contents empty into the tube. The Oracle groaned. Its body gave one violent jerk, then its head lolled forward and it hung there, lifeless.

'Y-you've killed it,' Poder stammered.

Kuruma had completely forgotten him. Not good. 'No, I haven't,' he said conversationally. 'Although I know the bastard would like nothing better than to die on me, he can't, not as long as he's attached to the web. It sustains him no matter what. By tomorrow he'll be as good as new.

'And you,' he continued. Suddenly there was menace in his voice. 'You heard what he said.' It wasn't a question.

Poder, who wasn't stupid enough by half not to see what was coming, raised his hands in a futile gesture of supplication. 'I w-won't tell anyone, I swear.'

Kuruma casually picked up a razor-sharp scalpel from among the implements on the table. 'I'm sure you won't,' he said, stepping closer.

Poder backed towards the door. Not daring to take his eyes off Kuruma, he missed it by a couple of feet and fetched up against the wall. Before he could correct his mistake and slip out, Kuruma struck.

The first swipe of the blade slashed Poder's defensively raised hands at the wrists, severing tendons and blood vessels. The second opened his belly. As he lowered his useless hands in a vain attempt to keep his guts from spilling out, the third stroke cut his throat from ear to ear. Gurgling, he fell to the floor.

Kuruma watched Poder's death struggle.

It was short. At the very last moment, he knelt and ate the boy's life force. Weak, as he'd suspected, but at least not entirely wasted. With so much work to be done in bringing his plans to fruition, he hated losing even a novice. But there was no helping it.

No Geas he could lay on the boy would have held up against the combined effort of the other Brothers, who would be curious as hell and for once willing to cooperate with each other in order to learn what he'd gleaned from the Oracle. In their hands, Poder would have blabbed in a matter of moments. And that would have inconvenienced Kuruma no end. He preferred to break the news at a time of his own choosing – sparingly rationed and carefully edited down to a version that best suited his own plans.

Knowledge was power, and the less of either trickled down to the Brothers the better. Divide and conquer, was his motto.

With surprising strength, he lifted the body and heaved it into one of the tanks. He stood for a moment and watched as the fluid inside began its slow work of decomposition and assimilation: fresh food for the Oracle.

Then he left, reestablishing the Ward on his way out. The Unborn down the hall hadn't budged an inch.

Soon after, Kuruma stood at the parapet atop Fellmere's highest tower, using a portable scrying device to send out a Questing far to the north. Poder's contribution was already coming in handy. Kuruma had a fair idea where to find at least one of the Oracle's 'eggs'.

There. Lizard. Yes, this one looked very promising.

And he was sure he'd find a crow or a vulture or some such thing adorning the coat of arms of a noble house somewhere on Vereld. But a cat? One that laid eggs? Tricky. No matter. He would persevere, and sooner or later he'd find them all. If not, maybe eliminating one of them might already suffice to stop the prophecy dead in its tracks. The bloody things only came out true if all the elements foretold were in place. Common knowledge, tried and tested.

On the way down, another thought struck him. What if the Oracle was playing him? Could he just go ahead and assume the damned word-monger was telling the truth? Common knowledge said oracles and prophets didn't lie. But common knowledge could err. And in this case he wasn't even dealing with the original prophet but with a sort of human recording device. Was truthfulness inherent in the prophecy, or only in the prophet himself?

Granted, so far it had been possible to fit certain events and their outcomes to the few grudging predictions he'd managed to squeeze out of the Oracle. But had those concurrences been real, or had they been wishful thinking on his part? Well, in this case he *would* find out, though it would be a challenge, a battle of wits. The Oracle was a cunning bastard: sly, full of tricks, and perfectly capable of distorting the truth beyond all recognition even without resorting to outright lies. No, it wouldn't be easy.

In the meantime, he would send a minor brother with the requisite skills north on a spying mission, maybe with an Unborn to keep him company. But he was already convinced that a preemptive strike in that direction was warranted. And it might not be a bad idea to let some of the Oracle's newest information trickle out to brothers in other parts of Vereld. Many eyes, and so on.

❖   ❖   ❖

When the Unborn guard's shift ended, instead of heading straight for the barracks it took a circuitous route along untraveled corridors and dusty stairways to a part of the castle long fallen into disuse.

Here the Unborn, who called itself Rain Seven, climbed a rickety staircase to the top floor of a crumbling tower propped against the outer wall.

From a cage hidden far back under the remaining half of the tower's roof, the Unborn extracted a small bird. The animal had traveled hundreds of leagues and passed through many hands until, concealed in a wagonload of produce, it reached Fellmere and was secretly handed over to Three Flower, an Unborn working in the kitchens, who in turn gave it into the care of Rain Seven.

Careful not to hurt the fragile creature with its huge, ungainly hands, Rain Seven fastened a minuscule brass cylinder to one tiny leg. Then, after a furtive glance around to make sure it remained unobserved, the Unborn gently lofted the bird into the air and stood watching until it became an infinitesimal speck in the vast, gray sky, finally vanishing from sight altogether.

❖   ❖   ❖

Flying north and west, the bird took several weeks to cross the high mountains and reach its destination, only to find that the recipient of the message it bore wasn't at home. Luckily the place offered shelter, and there was food and water within easy reach. Though there was an owl living under the building's roof, the little bird knew it was safe from this particular predator.

It built a nest of dry twigs and grass in the lee of a deeply recessed stone lintel that framed one of the building's upper windows. Then it settled down to wait.

❖   ❖   ❖

A Great Adept of the Dark Side may also choose to store Power in his own body. If he is truly great, he may succeed in amassing so many of his victim's deaths within his flesh that at a certain point the Balance of nature is tipped. If this should come to pass, the Adept dies the Last Death, from which he awakens after six days to a state of non-death rather than life. From then on, he can be said to be immortal, or as near as makes no difference, existing in a way never foreseen by creation.

Carric Three Suns, The Secret History of Magic

6 The Madal Skog

In the cellar underneath the cookhouse, Morlic paced furiously. Six short steps towards the outer wall with the tiny, barred slit of a window, far too high for him to reach. Six steps the other way, passing under the trap door through which an hour ago his two guards had for the third time lowered a basket containing half a loaf of stale bread and a pitcher of tepid water that tasted and smelled as if one of them, probably Rasid, had pissed in it.

'Looks like they *are* going to hang you,' Rasid had said, his voice dripping satisfaction.

Hang him! Nobody was hanged in the Madal Skog! It was considered a death unfit for any man, no matter what his crime. So was he a dog now, to be deprived even of his humanity? It was the ultimate insult. It was unthinkable.

Turn. Six steps, outer wall, turn.

Three days! Three bloody, endless, excruciating days!

Why was it taking them so long? Munnir had promised he'd be freed within hours. What the hell was going on? It must be that thrice-damned Jekkim! The man wanted blood. Well, he wouldn't get it.

Morlic absolutely refused to accept that a bunch of doddering old fools could have the power to determine his fate, to take his life. Nobody decided for Morlic Silt, nobody! He was the one who decided over other people's lives, or rather their deaths, not the other way round.

This was all totally wrong, a complete mess.

But he should have expected that something like this would happen. It was what you got when idiots were given the power to make decisions. Nine times out of ten they'd get hopelessly muddled, and the one time they got it right, it was purely by chance. And people like himself, the clever, superior ones, shouldn't by rights be at the receiving end of these turdbrains' cockups.

Six steps. Turn. Six steps.

What made things worse was that he couldn't seem to get his mind to focus properly anymore. His thoughts kept flitting here and there, forcing him to waste precious energy beating them back into line – only to have them scatter anew like chaff on the wind without his even noticing until it was too late and they were gone again, darting off down a thousand useless roads and dragging him along for the ride.

Concentrate! Think! he told himself yet again.

One thing was for certain: there was no way out of here, no chance of escape. He'd been over that ground a hundred times. The stone walls were massive, three feet thick up at the window and probably closer to four at floor level. The trap door was way out of reach, and under a layer of damp, rotting straw the floor was flagged with great, solid slabs of granite. Rasid and Hamad hated him with a vengeance. They'd made it abundantly clear that they were of half a mind to see him off themselves, and had given him to understand that arranging an unfortunate 'accident' would be no problem at all. No help there, even if he'd had something to bribe them with.

Wherever they took him for his execution, he'd be trussed in chains and surrounded by an ugly mob just waiting for an excuse to take justice into their own hands.

He interrupted his pacing and sat on the cold stone bench that served as a bed. Once more, he'd reasoned his way around the course, and again he found himself arriving at the same conclusion. He really only had two choices: either give up and let those shit-headed old farts go ahead and kill him, or take the matter into his own hands. Ruin their fun. Deny them the satisfaction.

But how? Make a rope out of his shirt and trousers and hang himself?

No. That was what *they* wanted to do to him, and he wasn't about to go out admitting he was no better than a cur.

What else, then? Bang his head to pulp against the wall? Tear open his wrists with his teeth? Stuff his shirt down his throat and suffocate himself?

Messy and unreliable, all of it. If only he had a knife. Involuntarily, his hands went for his pockets. He knew there was nothing there, hadn't been since they'd seized and searched him in Rivensend. His hands didn't care, had a will of their own.

See? he told them. *Empty.*

No. Wait. There was something. Something small and flat...

Then he remembered.

When he'd lifted the head from its resting place in the cave, a scrap of hard, leathery skin the size of two thumbnails, dangling from the neck by a thread of desiccated tissue, had come loose. Since the head had insisted he make sure nothing was left behind, he'd picked up the piece and stuck it in his pocket. They'd missed it when they searched him.

He held it on his palm now, inspected it, sniffed it. It smelled musty, rancid, sour. Disgusted, he tossed it into a corner and resumed his pacing. Six, turn, six.

Stopped. Got down on all fours and scrabbled frantically in the rotting straw until he'd found the thing again. Idiot!

This might just be his way out, if what he had was enough to do the job. Corpses were poisonous, everybody knew that. He'd even heard stories of evil necromancers making corpse powder from dead bodies and using it to kill their enemies. Would it work?

Only one way to find out.

Before he could change his mind, he stuck the piece of skin in his mouth. It was too big to swallow whole, so he had to moisten and chew it first. It tasted exactly like it smelled: sour and rancid, like butter gone bad. He forced himself not to spit it out, or worse, throw

106

up. He didn't want to go picking it out of his own puke. After a while his mouth, and then his throat, went numb. Good. That must be the poison taking hold. Finally the thing was soft enough to swallow. That was it. No going back now.

He lay down on the bench and waited for whatever would happen next.

He must have drifted off.

It was dark outside, meaning the cell was pitch-black. He felt hot and fevered. He was soaked in sweat, and his stomach was cramping painfully. That was what had woken him. He wondered how long this was going to take, and how bad it would get.

The answer to his second question came almost immediately. A white-hot, searing bolt of pain erupted in his guts and shot up his spine, leaving him doubled over and gasping for breath, tears streaming from his eyes and mingling with the sweat. He was still struggling for air when a fresh cramp hit. And another right after that. The next one sent lightning agony all the way up his spine, ripping into his brain in exploding shards of bright thunder and robbing him of his senses.

Once more he awoke, and seemed to be floating above his body, above the pain. He knew he was awake because he could see the first light of dawn through the window and hear a rooster crowing.

He had the strangest sensation that he'd just been shown something hugely important, and that everything would be just fine if he could only recall what it was he'd learned. Something to do with dark, scary places and even scarier people doing weird things like stuffing themselves with long, spidery strands of something black and wavy, rippling-like. He'd been able to see inside them as if they were made of glass, and he'd noticed how the black stuff seemed to sort of drift around for a bit and then settle down and pile up in different parts of their bodies.

He knew he should be able to remember what it all meant, but he couldn't, not for the life of him. He was simply too exhausted, and he was dying.

Without warning, a spasm of sheer unbelievable pain yanked him back into his body, plunging him into a thundering maelstrom of pitch-dark energy that pounded through his bones and crackled along his veins, raging in every cell and threatening to rip him apart and scatter him into a million irreconcilable bits and pieces.

Finally, when his body and brain could take no more, he fell through a series of ever more absurd and disjointed fever dreams into darkness, and from there into nothing.

❖   ❖   ❖

In the end, Jekkim was defeated, though not by Munnir.

For three days, interrupted by long periods of recess necessary to get the festival back on track and keep it running in a halfway solemn and dignified manner, they had negotiated and haggled over the future of Morlic Silt. In truth, they all knew they were setting the course for the future of the clans themselves. The nature of their deepest belief, the foundation of their faith was at stake, as was the distribution of power. Politics.

Jekkim himself wasn't interested in power for power's sake. All he really wanted was to preserve orthodox faith in its current form, to prevent his people from taking a step that he regarded as wrong, ill-fated, dangerous.

Alas, here as most everywhere else, religion and power were inextricably, hopelessly entangled, and he needed the one to save the other. What he didn't wish was for this controversy to become an outright quarrel and end in bad blood, in schism.

With Munnir, Jekkim knew, it was a different story, and yet much the same: he desperately wanted his and the Black Yurt clan's heresy to become mainstream orthodoxy, and so to end their role as doctrinal aberrants and religious underdogs. But he wasn't so hungry for power that he was willing to sacrifice the coherence of the clans.

They both needed to win their side of the argument, and neither could do so without causing far more damage than he was willing to permit.

So they reached an agreement.

Jekkim, who wanted Morlic sentenced and executed not only for the murder of the girl Sosha but for the deaths of his parents, of Hurim the shepherd, of Pamuk, Rivensend's previous custodian, and of at least four other girls, had to content himself with the man being found guilty of only Sosha's death.

Munnir, who wanted Morlic acquitted on the grounds that he'd acted on behalf of a higher power – Munnir didn't quite dare declare the head to be the God's, not just yet – and possibly as the chosen mouthpiece of said higher power. Again, Munnir shied away from going so far as to use the word 'prophet'.

But it was clear to everyone where he was headed, and Jekkim knew that Munnir's giving up Morlic came at a price. That price was the provisional conservation of the head, and Jekkim's consent to further examination regarding its origins and possible authenticity. For the time being, the head would be entrusted into the care of Sky, the clan regarded as most neutral on questions of dogma. It was a huge and painful concession on Jekkim's part, who had wanted the despicable thing smashed and burned on the spot.

There still remained the question of the manner of Morlic's death. Asukan, who had absented herself from the intervening sessions, had returned for the final sentencing, detached and silent as ever. Jekkim had given up trying to understand what motives and calculations drove the woman, hoping only that she wouldn't intervene at the last moment and overthrow the fragile balance they'd reached. As for the execution – he wanted it to be, above all, memorable.

Munnir suggested that Morlic should be swiftly and discreetly dispatched by axe or sword. Someone mentioned stoning. Someone else came up with drowning. At some stage Samad, just awakened from a snooze and overcome by a fit of youthful enthusiasm, remembered that he'd once heard how these things were done over in Gomilar. He insisted the culprit should be burned, drowned, quartered and hanged in the southern fashion, though he admitted he wasn't quite sure whether he'd got it all in the right order. But he reckoned you could do it pretty much any way you wanted. At the end of the day, the result would be the same.

'That'll show him!' he cackled, thumping the floor with his cane. 'And it'd make for some great entertainment as well.' When no one showed any great enthusiasm for his suggestion, he leaned back in his chair and soon nodded off again.

But Jekkim immediately took to the idea of hanging, if not to the rest of the list. It was the perfect way to make his point one more time, and in front of an audience no less, for he was determined to make the execution a public affair. And in this he got his will, and Munnir's consent, though he could practically hear the man's teeth gnashing. Finally agreed, they sent someone to rouse Hamad and Rasid and have them bring over the prisoner for sentencing. And then two things happened.

Hamad arrived all in a fluster. He sincerely apologized for the bad news, but unfortunately the man Morlic was delirious and seemed to be dying.

And Kassem of the Sky clan, at barely forty the newest and youngest member of the council but already highly respected for his level-headedness and restraint, rose from his seat, eyes vacant and features slack, and began to speak in a thin, cold voice that was definitely not his own.

That was when Jekkim knew for certain he'd lost. Everything.

Morlic's execution wasn't the highly visible public event Jekkim had envisioned. Still, he took over supervision of the matter, aided by Hamad and Rasid. There was a certain urgency to the whole affair, as Morlic did appear to be moribund, and hanging a dead man seemed rather pointless. There wasn't a gallows, and no time to build one, so they had to improvise.

Rasid said he knew a suitable tree, fittingly at a crossroads and not too far away. So they loaded Marlic onto a cart and set out, followed by a gaggle of hardcore gaffers and the morbidly curious. Halfway there, Jekkim realized they'd forgotten to bring a rope, and Hamad had to go back and fetch one.

When everything was finally in place – the rope attached to a stout limb and carefully measured and remeasured for just the right amount of slack, the high-bedded cart with Morlic on it positioned just so, the onlookers gathered round in an orderly semi-circle – they ran into another problem: try as they might, they couldn't get Morlic to stand up, much less remain upright on his own.

He was mumbling and groaning, locked in the grip of some feverish fantasy and limp as an empty waterskin. So Hamad had to prop him up while Rasid put the noose around his neck.

Suddenly Morlic opened his eyes. He seemed completely aware, though unable to speak or control his body. His eyes rolling wildly, obviously taking in and understanding the situation, he reminded Jekkim of a thoroughly panicked nag being dragged to slaughter.

'On with it,' Jekkim said forcefully, 'before he passes out again. Shame if he missed his own hanging.'

Rasid and Hamad both held Morlic erect while the mare hitched to the cart was led forward a few steps. Then they lifted him off his feet and dropped him off the back of the cart. There was an audible crunch as the rope reached the end of its slack and snapped Morlic's neck, his feet swinging a bare three inches above the ground.

Morlic twitched a few times, there were a few oohs and aahs and some rather obnoxious comments, and finally the small crowd began to disperse. The show was over.

Jekkim told Hamad and Rasid to go on ahead with the cart; he'd stay for a few moments longer. They gave him surprised looks, as if to say they hadn't suspected him for a ghoul, but he didn't care. He had things to think about, needed a moment of solitude, and this was as good a place as any.

He sat on the Crossing Stone, a waist-high boulder placed in the center of the crossroads. A silly custom, he mused, putting the things right in the middle like that where they practically begged people to run into them, especially in the dark. Next, his thoughts drifted back to that last scene in the great hall, when Kassem had begun to speak in that strange, hair-raising voice that he claimed belonged to the God. The elders had listened to him in awed silence, their eyes wandering back and forth uncertainly between Kassem and the head still lying uncovered on the side table.

He told them in no uncertain terms that yes, he was their god Uilmaz and they had damn well better believe it, because his patience with them was running out and when it did, the consequences for them would be extremely unpleasant.

On the other hand, he continued, if they decided to pull their thumbs out and join him, there was great work to be done, a grand quest awaiting them that would ultimately lead them to power and glory beyond their wildest imaginings. Once he, their God, was made whole again, his irresistible might would transport them from victory to victory, and no force in the world would be able to withstand them.

Hearing it from the horse's mouth, so to speak, or rather from Kassem's, who was anything but rash, impressionable, or given to zealotry, they were swayed. One by one, Jekkim saw them carried off, all but himself and, surprisingly, Munnir, who suddenly seemed a lot less sure of himself.

No help came from Asukan. Far from objecting, she was sitting forward in her chair, her whole body expressing eagerness. She was watching Kassem with a fascination, an avidity that struck Jekkim as almost sexual in its intensity. For the first time in Jekkim's memory she didn't bother to hide her thoughts and emotions behind a carefully crafted non-expression. All her lust and craving for power and control were suddenly out in the open, unwittingly or unconcernedly displayed before the elders who had now, in the face of this new and singular possibility presenting itself, become entirely irrelevant, her attraction to what Kassem represented so great it stretched the spiritual to encompass the carnal.

Jekkim was shocked but not surprised. In a forlorn attempt to rescue the situation and bring Kassem back to his senses, he grabbed a pitcher full of water and dashed the contents into Kassem's face.

Kassem looked at him with cold, alien eyes that seemed to suck the warmth out of Jekkim's bones.

'Do that again and I'll kill you,' he said matter-of-factly. 'Now, go and hang that vermin Morlic before there's nothing left to hang.' He made a shooing gesture, as with an annoying child or animal. 'Go on, get moving.'

Asukan's lips were stretched thin in an unpleasant smile: complicit, judgmental, superior.

Jekkim, who knew when he was beaten, went, taking Hamad with him.

Coming out of his reverie, he suddenly realized he'd been staring at the dead man, or rather through him, for quite some time. He also became aware that he wasn't quite sure anymore that hanging Morlic had been the right thing to do. He might have just lost a potential ally, repellent as the thought was. Whatever. It was too late now.

He sighed, and turned away, wondering where he should go from here.

❖   ❖   ❖

The wise man in the storm prays to God, not for safety from danger, but deliverance from fear.

Ralph Waldo Emerson

7 Larnakis

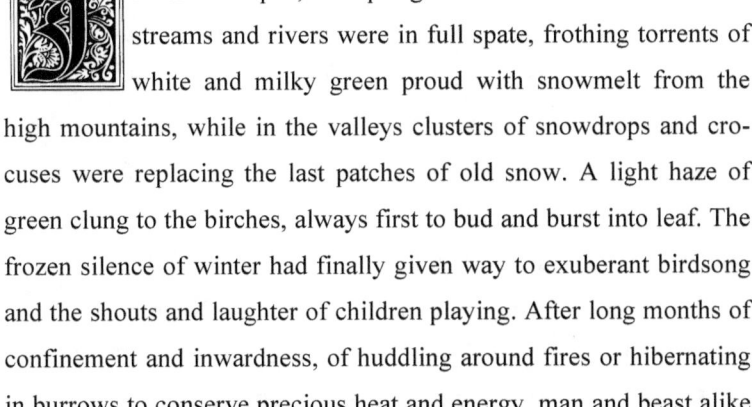t was late April, and spring had returned to Larnakis. The streams and rivers were in full spate, frothing torrents of white and milky green proud with snowmelt from the high mountains, while in the valleys clusters of snowdrops and crocuses were replacing the last patches of old snow. A light haze of green clung to the birches, always first to bud and burst into leaf. The frozen silence of winter had finally given way to exuberant birdsong and the shouts and laughter of children playing. After long months of confinement and inwardness, of huddling around fires or hibernating in burrows to conserve precious heat and energy, man and beast alike emerged from their shelters into the warmth and light of the strengthening sun to greet a new season of growth and replenishment.

In Sirida, the sun's first early-morning rays tickled Radj Anskar awake. Lazily, still half asleep, he turned to his wife, only to find the other side of the bed empty.

Right. She had lessons this morning. Though why they had to be at such an ungodly hour was beyond him.

Last October, after the scare of the strange shadow play in the sky

117

above Sirida, Rupili, never one to meekly wait for what fate might or might not bring to her doorstep, had immediately set herself on a course of action.

Through her clan's widespread net of relations and friends she'd heard of a man in neighboring Anapur who was said to be a Jeje, a Great Master of the martial arts. She sent him a message, asking if he would consider coming to Larnakis and teaching her.

Three weeks later, right in the middle of the season's first serious snowstorm, a frail old man leaning on a staff that looked too heavy for him to even lift had appeared at their door and announced that he was Jeje Rinpong, come to teach the Radjani the Proper Way to Admire the Hoshu Flower. Rupili later told Anskar that the old man had looked as if the wind might blow him away any moment, so she courteously invited him to come in out of the cold and offered him hot tea and freshly baked nan bread with honey.

Observing the rituals of politeness and hospitality, she spoke lightly of extraneous things such as the weather, this autumn's harvest, and the Jeje's trip from Anapur, while the old man stuffed himself until she began to fear he'd give himself indigestion.

The Jeje's part of the conversation consisted mainly of grunts and belches, punctuated by curt comments that were just shy of seriously rude. When not a crumb of bread or a lick of honey was left, his eyelids drooped and he began to nod. Moments later he gave a rumbling snore and seemed about to fall over face-first into his teacup.

Rupili smiled. 'Jeje,' she said, quietly clapping her hands, 'I'm quite impressed. A very convincing performance. You could have fooled a lot of people with it, but unfortunately I'm not one of them. Why don't we discuss my lessons now?'

The Jeje opened his eyes and gave her an appraising stare. He looked very much awake, and sharp as a Tanuri dagger. He grinned mischievously.

'I think it will be great fun teaching you, young woman. Already we can skip the first lesson, which is, "don't get hung up on outward appearances." If you like, we can begin immediately.'

He rose from sitting cross-legged to standing position in one fluid, graceful and seemingly effortless motion that filled even lithe Rupili with envy. 'Show me where we will practice.'

'By the way,' Rupili said, getting to her feet like a normal person. 'What was all that about "the proper way…" and so on?'

'Oh, that.' The Jeje chuckled. 'Just a bit of esoteric mumbo-jumbo I use to impress gullible would-be students with.'

'Well,' Rupili sniffed, 'I was certainly not impressed by it, just so you know.'

Since then, not a day had passed without lessons.

At first the Jeje taught Rupili hand-to-hand self-defense, simple but effective moves to counter an attack and disarm and neutralize an assailant. Later on, when the Radjani's advancing pregnancy and the growing bulge of her belly made this practice too awkward and strenuous, he switched to Twin Thorns, a fighting technique that employed two long-daggers or short-swords. Like a sponge with sheer unlimited capacity, Rupili absorbed all of it, making progress in leaps and bounds.

Anskar too profited from the Jeje's presence. Whenever his time allowed, he practiced swordplay with the old man, and though Anskar was a highly accomplished swordsman in his own right, he found that the Jeje could still teach him a trick or two.

If only it weren't for these godsawful morning sessions.

He was definitely not an early morning person, never had been. He preferred to take his time waking up and enjoying the slow, gradual transition from sleep into the waking world. And he missed cuddling with his wife before getting up. It made for such a nice beginning of the day to come.

Finally he heaved himself out of bed and walked naked out into the small, secluded inner courtyard, where he took a wooden pail from a row that Asha and Soonil, Rupili's maids, filled each morning with water from the fountain in the outer yard. He poured the ice-cold water over his head and body, soaped down, and rinsed off with a second and third pail.

Ablutions done, he dressed and settled down in his study with a sheaf of long-winded documents pertaining to a land dispute. Asha appeared almost immediately with a pot of tea and some nan. For no good reason she was blushing furiously, and Anskar wondered if she and Soonil had been peeking again. It wouldn't have been the first time. On several occasions when he was bathing in the mornings, he'd heard muffled giggling from inside the house. He wasn't all that bothered by their foolish girls' games, but they had better not let Rupili catch them at it, or there would be hell to pay.

He was trying to think of some roundabout, face-saving way to warn them off when Asha returned, this time to announce that Baran, captain of the Watch, was here to see the Radj.

Anskar's grandfather had founded the Watch some sixty years earlier, when bands of Ithraki raiders began to find their way from the eastern plains into Larnakis, following the trails of wild mountain goats through the passless Caerrocks. Bloodthirsty and utterly without mercy, they descended on isolated holdings and small villages, slaughtering every living thing they came upon, whether man, woman, child or beast. When the killing was done, they threw a feast in the midst of all the carnage, eating and drinking themselves into oblivion with looted food and spirits. Once the food stores and drink were used up, they packed what valuables they could find and either sought out a new target or, if the spoils had been plentiful enough, left the way they had come.

Following the first of these bloody incursions, the old king for the first time in Larnakis' history put together a small standing army, a force of several hundred men he named the Watch, and found and appointed an arms-master from Dunmark to train them. In time, the Larnaki discovered that, with a bit of practice, they could deal quite handily with the hulking barbarians from the east.

Though on a much reduced scale, the raids continued. As long as there was some measure of excitement, action and glory to be had, the invaders seemed not to care overmuch whether it was their intended victims or they themselves who lost their lives in these senseless bloodbaths. To the Larnaki's great satisfaction, mostly the latter was the case.

The Watch's first captain proved himself not only courageous and cunning but also a true and loyal friend to the old Radj and to Larnakis, and it quickly became something of a tradition to recruit his successors out of Dunmark as well, not least for the fun involved in spying out the best candidate for the job and stealing him away from some stuffy, high-and-mighty Dunmarkan noble.

Which was exactly how Anskar had come by Baran Kendarren, the red-haired, blue-eyed bear of a man entering his study this moment, sparing Asha a wide grin and a few whispered words that made her blush all over again.

Baran, second son of a minor noble, had been a soldier all his life, and at thirty-five already had ten years of captaincy under his belt, three of them in Larnakis. Unmarried and gregarious, he preferred the company of various lady friends to the ties of marriage. His soldiers were his family and children, and he treated them exactly as a stern but loving father would. When he'd taken over from his predecessor, he'd won the men's hearts over in no time at all, and Anskar had no doubt they'd follow Baran to hell and back if he asked it of them.

'Come, sit,' Anskar said, 'before you get yourself in trouble with Rupili. Make eyes at her maids, and she'll have you married off before you know what's hit you.'

Baran laughed, and Asha scurried off for more tea and a second cup.

'Radj.' Baran lowered himself onto a cushion. 'How is Rupili? Well, I trust? Everything as it should be, with the bairn and all?'

'Never better,' Anskar said. 'Give her another six months with the Jeje, and we probably won't need the army anymore.'

Asha brought fresh tea, and for a while they sipped in amicable silence.

'Well, my friend,' Anskar said finally. 'I suppose there's a reason you're sitting here drinking tea with me instead of whipping the troops out of their winter lethargy.'

Baran nodded. 'Not that I wouldn't have come just for the tea and company. But yes, there is another reason why I'm here. A patrol I sent out last week returned this morning. It seems they found something pretty strange, not to say unsettling, up by the Yangan rapids. I'm riding over there to have a look myself, and I thought you might like to come along. It's only an hour's ride, and I think it may be something you need to see.' He grinned. 'I even troubled myself to have Fleet saddled for you, just in case you said yes.'

'As if you didn't know I would,' Anskar said, laughing. 'Whatever this mysterious thing is, it's got to be more fun than reading boring documents. Just give me a moment to leave a message for Rupili, and I'll be ready to go.'

To their surprise, they found Abbot Tönden and a middle-aged monk leading a packhorse waiting for them where the road to the Yangan branched off from the one connecting the city with Anpok monastery. The old man seldom left Anpok, much less on horseback. Anskar was beginning to get a funny feeling about this whole business.

'Padhu.' He bowed a greeting.

'Radj,' Tönden said. 'Captain. I thought I'd better come along and have a look at what young Baran here has found. It sounds like something that may require an... expert.'

Anskar didn't ask Tönden how he knew. The abbot had his own ways of gaining information, some of them no doubt involving more than just the help of mere human agents. Despite the myriad laughter lines around his eyes and mouth, the abbot looked somber today. Even his thin white mustaches and goatee seemed to droop.

'We're very glad for your company, padhu,' Anskar said. 'Especially if this involves, ah... things we might not be qualified to deal with.'

Baran signaled the two scouts accompanying them to lead the way, and to go slowly. Good. Anskar didn't want Tönden's old bones suffering needlessly, and Baran had obviously had the same thought.

That's what makes him so good with his men, Anskar thought. *He pays attention. He cares. I owe the gods for this man.*

They traveled at a moderate pace and without much talk, each of them following his own private train of thought, awed into silence by the breathtaking beauty that surrounded them. They were headed east, where the high peaks of the Caerrocks stood in stark contrast to the impossibly deep blue of the sky, the eternal snow fields on their far-away flanks glinting in the sunlight like polished silver. For most of the way they rode through a gently undulating landscape shaded a pale yellow ochre by last year's grass and dotted with dark green scrub pines, large, pink swathes of blooming heather, and ancient, time-rounded outcroppings of gray, lichen-covered granite.

Every so often they passed through stands of larches, still bare but standing amid soft, red-gold carpets of fallen needles that hushed the horses' hoofbeats to a gentle patter. To Anskar, the short journey through this untouched land seemed like a fresh breath of clean air clearing the cobwebs out of his head.

Seeing Tönden reminded him of something he'd been meaning to hand over into the abbot's care for months now, ever since the bone gatherer Durpa and his son Dorting had brought it to him last October. Awed and a bit frightened by the power he'd felt from the little blue bowl when he'd held it in his hands, he'd thought it best to give it to Tönden, who would doubtless know what to do – or not to do – with it. He'd tucked it away in a box in his study, meaning to take it to the monastery soonest, but somehow it had completely slipped his mind every time the opportunity arose.

With only a passing thought as to why he should feel a guilty conscience over the matter, he decided that now was not the time and place to broach the subject. He would take the thing to Tönden immediately he got back. It was a quarter-hour walk from his house up to Anpok. Surely he could find the time for that.

Arriving at the Yangan, they bypassed the village of the same name and headed straight for the river crossing. The river entered a deep, narrow gorge just above the crossing, turning from a lively, rushing stream into a thundering whitewater in the space of twenty paces. Dismounting, they stood by the bridge-posts at the lip of the gorge. The posts were all that was left of the hanging bridge that had crossed the river at this point, if you didn't count the frayed length of rope with a single board still attached to it trailing from one of the posts on the far side.

It was a way of life in Larnakis to build a bridge and use it until it broke and then build another one in its place, a centuries-old habit that cost the lives of travelers time and again. It was one of the things that Anskar upon becoming Radj had immediately begun to change. But some things took time to take root in people's heads, and in any case there were far too many bridges in Larnakis to have them renewed all at once.

From the crossing they traveled downstream to the end of the rapids. Here the river suddenly found space again and widened into a large pool, almost a small lake. They dismounted and hobbled the horses before descending on foot down a steep but navigable trail that led to the water's edge. They were greeted by the sickening stench of rotting flesh. Baran stopped to pass around a small jar containing a sharp, clean-smelling balm, which they rubbed under their nostrils to counter the foul stink.

Anskar steeled himself.

Twenty paces downriver, in a large tangle of driftwood washed up on the shore and still partly covered by a bank of old snow, they found two bodies in the early stages of decomposition. Conserved until recently under the snow, they were still recognizable, though they'd been badly battered by the rapids.

One was a man, shrouded in the tattered remains of a black cloak. The whole left side of his face was stove in like a rotten fruit, and his right arm had been torn off at the shoulder. His head was shaven and tattooed with some sort of twisted cross.

The other corpse was only partly human. What was left of the body was based more or less on the human form, but there the resemblance ended. The upper body and arms were grotesquely muscled, while the legs were lean and sinewy, reminiscent of the huge, earthbound running birds found on the plains of Gomilar, and like a bird's legs they bent backwards where a man's knee joint would have been.

Lying prone, the thing looked to be half again as tall as a man. The fingers ended in thick, sharp claws, as did the three large toes on each of its wide, leathery feet. Of all the cadaver's parts the face was the most human – and at the same time sickeningly different. The features struck Anskar as completely wrong, displaced and out of proportion, like something put together by a nasty child dabbling in clay. The eyes under the low forehead and the overhanging brow were tiny and seemed to have a second set of nictating membranes beneath the outer lids. The nose and ears were rudimentary, as if they'd been added on as an afterthought. Enormous, bulging jaws accommodated a gaping mouth that showed razor-sharp, triangular teeth arrayed in three rows one behind the other, reminding Anskar of tales he'd heard about a species of large, rapacious fish that were the ultimate terror of ship-wrecked sailors, attacking anything that moved in the water with just such rows of deadly teeth. Teeth that were said to never let go once they'd gotten hold of a victim. He made to look more closely, but Tönden stopped him with a sharp hiss.

'Don't go any closer,' the abbot said. He turned to the two scouts. 'You were the ones who found this? Did you touch anything?'

'I did,' the younger of the two said. 'But only to pull back the man's cloak so we could get a look at his face.'

'Captain,' Tönden said. 'Please have your man help Mepe here gather wood for a pyre. We must burn the bodies immediately. And you.' He beckoned the young scout. 'Come with me.'

While Tönden performed a thorough cleansing ritual on the young scout, Anskar and Baran pitched in and helped build a large pile of driftwood over the corpses, taking care not to come in contact with any part of them. When the abbot finally deemed the pile big enough, he sent Mepe to fetch the pack horse. The monk led the animal down to the river, where it caught the corpse scent and balked, refusing to go on. They unloaded it where it stood. Tönden had brought four large clay jars filled with oil, which they poured over the woodpile. The abbot himself lit the fire and stood praying until it had burned down to a smoking heap of dark ashes. Meanwhile Mepe prayed by the river's edge, holding a small glass vial filled with a clear substance between his palms. Every so often he paused to pour a few drops into the water.

It was mid-afternoon when Tönden finally turned away from the remains of the fire, signaling that he was ready to leave.

Only when they were well away from the river and back on the trail to Sirida did the abbot break the heavy silence. 'Radj. I imagine you have questions.'

'I do, padhu. I do. Can you tell me who they were?'

'What I can tell you is that the man was a sorcerer, and as corrupted by evil as a human being can be. Even dead, his body remained a source of contamination. That's why we burned it, and why Mepe cleansed the river, though I fear for those who may have come into contact with the water during the time the corpses lay there. But then, water is a powerful cleansing element by itself, and the next village is ten miles downriver, so we can hope the corruption was sufficiently diluted. Still, I'll send someone to inquire after the villagers' health and spiritual wellbeing.

'As for the other thing – I've never encountered anything like it, and pray I never will again. All I can say is that it was nothing natural, and almost certainly the work of sorcery. Abomination is much too weak a word for it, but it's the best I have to offer. Though the maker was at fault here, not the creature. It deserves our deepest compassion for the terrible existence that was forced upon it, and our tireless prayers that it might find peace with the merciful gods.'

'Where do you think they came from?' Anskar asked. A vague but disquieting sense of threat had lodged between his shoulder blades, as if something dangerous and ill-intentioned were about to strike from behind. He willed himself not to cast a fearful glance over his shoulder. 'And what could they have wanted here?'

'I've heard rumors of a sorcerer stronghold far to the south, near the Fire Mountains,' the abbot replied. 'Perhaps they came from there. What they sought here, I can't say. Nothing good, of that we can be fairly certain.'

'So what do we do?' Anskar asked, his apprehension growing with every one of the abbot's words. 'Is there any way to find out more about them?'

'Perhaps,' Tönden said, stroking his beard. 'I will seek to gather information, but it may take a while. In the meantime, the less you think about it the better. As I'm sure you know, thinking too much about something can draw that something to us, and fear...'

'... only serves to strengthen that which we fear,' Anskar said. 'Which reminds me. I would like to keep this from Rupili for the time being. She worries too much as it is.'

'Oh,' Tönden said, 'I think we will keep it from everybody for the time being. Speak to Baran. He needs to make it clear to his men that this is to remain a secret for now. Though, knowing him, he's probably already done so. Still, better to be sure.'

Silence settled on their small party again, nobody being in the mood for idle talk or banter after what they had just witnessed.

Anskar felt a weight that had lifted during the winter return, heavier now that he'd seen concrete evidence that something evil had turned its attention towards Larnakis. He tried to shake off the feeling of foreboding, fervently hoping that nothing more would come of it, but his gut told him different.

Looking up at the sky, he half expected to see a searching finger of darkness hovering above their heads. But there was nothing there, only a few puffy, white clouds dotting the deep blue, and in the far distance a lone bird – a heron, he thought – majestically flapping towards some unknown, birdish destination.

❖ ❖ ❖

Before all else, be armed.

Niccolo Macchiavelli

8 The Fire Mountains

uruma was on his way to Pik Varakul, to review what was to be his new army. Though he'd left Fellmere before first light, the trip had already taken up most of the day, and twilight was fast approaching under the oppressive ceiling of lowering grey that spanned the approach to Varakul: a wide but steadily narrowing gap between steep, barren slopes that rose ever higher the farther he progressed, mounting waves of black, volcanic scree that threatened to come crashing down and smother the last vestiges of life still stubbornly clinging to their inhospitable flanks. Too stingy to expend sorcery for warmth, Kuruma huddled deeper into his cloak, seeking refuge from the clammy cold that seemed to eternally pervade this place like a patient predator waiting to pounce on a weary traveler and chill him to the bones.

These last few leagues of the road leading from Fellmere to the foot of the Fire Mountains crossed a desolate, rock-strewn region of glassy shards and hard-baked ashes. Dank currents of air stirred up fetid odors from stagnant pools of slime-infested, oily water, some colored a poisonous red or green. Their edges were choked with rotting debris that included bones, sodden hanks of pelt or hair, and ragged heaps of putrid skin and flesh. Many of the larger pools held darkly coiled presences, half-seen shadowy shapes that rose from the depths as if from some hideous, primordial nightmare, disturbing the surface with ripples of hair-raising menace before sinking slowly back into the impenetrable murk. At night, other things emerged from their lairs in and out of the water, and the place became a theater of screaming madness, an insane slaughterhouse.

Leftovers from the earliest breeding experiments, Kuruma mused, holding a tight rein on the frightened, skittish horse. *Bits and pieces that somehow made their way through the drains and sewers to the outside, where over time they combined and grew, developing into something new and different. It would be interesting to study them sometime – and extremely dangerous.*

Years ago, he'd considered having them eliminated. It would have been a fearsome task even given the resources of Fellmere. As it was, the things made for a good defense against unwelcome intruders – though there was slight chance of anyone ever penetrating this far into sorcerer territory.

We've come a long way since those first attempts. And now, we're finally ready to reap the fruits of many years of labor.

The horse suddenly refused to go on, trembling and snorting, its rolling eyes flashing the white of mortal terror. It should have been well broken in and impervious to the presence of Unborn, even these mutated, feral forms. But obviously there had been a mix-up at the stables back in Fellmere, and they'd given him an untrained mount. He cursed. Someone would pay for the mistake. Dearly.

He dug needle-sharp spurs deep into the horse's quivering flanks and applied the switch mercilessly, forcing the terrified animal forward. Conquer fear with greater fear, that had always been his strategy with recalcitrant subjects, man or beast.

The place was not for weak nerves, though.

Once, this had been a flourishing landscape of grassy plains and wooded hills, of meandering streams and clear blue lakes, dotted with peaceful, homey hamlets where woodsmoke rose from the chimneys of timber-framed, thatch-roofed houses nestled alone or in groups among the hills or by a lakeshore, where farmers tilled their fields or herded cows and sheep while the women tended their homes and spun fine wool and their well-fed, apple-cheeked children happily played hoops or catch in the village square. In short: nauseatingly quaint, and totally useless.

The experiments had put an end to all that. The price of progress, and well worth it. Kuruma liked the place just fine the way it was now – it suited his purposes much better like this.

Rounding the last bend, he rode into the small valley that gave access to the northern flank of Pik Varakul, home to the breeding caves. It rose abruptly from the valley floor, a steep cliff against which a fortress had been built that dwarfed even giant Fellmere. Tier upon tier of towers and battlements built from great blocks of dark, igneous rock rose to dizzying heights, their upper reaches lost in the smoky, sulphurous haze. Hundreds of embrasures and slitted windows stared out from the walls like malevolent eyes.

High as it was, the structure was neither very wide nor overly deep, for the valley narrowed to less than two hundred feet where it met the cliff, and most of the fortress lay inside the mountain itself. Varakul was riddled with vents and chambers, with great halls, tunnels and galleries formed in part by volcanic activity, and in part by hammer and chisel.

Unlike some of its neighbors it was more or less dormant, had been for many decades, but it remained a hotbed of minor activity and rare chemical processes. Its innards seethed with streams and lakes of bubbling magma, with restless pools and spurting geysers of boiling, mineral-laden water and vents that spewed searing jets of steam and noxious gases.

The iron gates flanked by massive towers stood open. Kuruma rode under the raised portcullis and through the passage under the curtain wall, his mount's iron-shod hooves striking sparks from the flagstones and echoes from the barrel-vaulted ceiling studded with murder holes.

In the inner courtyard an Unborn, one of the rejects, was waiting to take his horse, had probably been standing there for hours, single-mindedly focused on this one, all-important task it had been given. Dumb as fence posts, the Unborn, but at least they did what they were told without needing to be threatened.

The breeding program was designed to produce creatures that were simple but highly effective fighting machines, mountains of fanged, clawed muscle with just enough brains to fulfill their purpose: to kill without question, and to do it on minimum rations and with maximum efficiency.

Up until recently, before they'd come up with a way to replicate from a basic model, they'd had to import large quantities of raw materials: living water dragons from Bodharesh and killer fish in sloshing tanks from the Middle Sea, running birds from Gomilar and, most important, hundreds of human subjects, preferably between fifteen and thirty, and definitely male. Each Unborn was grown from a human seed, as it were. A living man was enclosed in a breeding sac, the contents enriched with the requisite animal essences. How the process exactly worked, Kuruma didn't know, but it did: stick the whole thing in a breeding chamber, wait six months, and when you opened the sac, you had a perfect – though definitely not natural-born – killer.

But the process wasn't flawless. Every so often, some small glitch in the program turned out an Unborn that didn't meet battle standards – a reject. It was as if none of the aggressive, predatory ingredients had taken with them. More human but no less ugly in aspect, they lacked the ferocity and bloodlust of their soldier counterparts, tending instead to be meek, servile creatures utterly unsuited for violence. They had their uses as servants though, being slightly more intelligent on the one hand and willing to do the most menial work without complaint on the other. And they never, ever dared look a human in the eyes, a welcome trait in Kuruma's opinion. He detested seeing bloody, puking *niceness,* especially in these creatures.

There existed one Unborn that fit neither category, and Kuruma was about to meet it – him – yes, he actually thought of Gormin as a 'he'.

Eight years ago, Gormin had come out of the sac short, skinny and crippled, a complete failure marked down for immediate termination. While he was waiting to be led away, he took a good, long look around the breeding chambers. Then he began pointing out to Noburo, the Brother overseeing the operations, every weak point, every fault, each wrong, superfluous or wasteful step he saw in the procedure as it was then. Though Noburo's first impulse had been to

135

kill the impertinent little humpback on the spot, he was smart enough to see how Gormin could benefit the project and by default his own standing within the Brotherhood. He rescinded the termination order and took Gormin on as an assistant. A year later, Gormin had his own laboratory and did most of the research while Noburo ran the general operations. Since then, things had moved along quite nicely.

Kuruma found the little Unborn in his laboratory next to the breeding chambers, deep in Varakul's sultry bowels.

Gormin looked up from his work, his gaze cool and direct. His slight body may have been weak and deformed, but a formidable intelligence shone from his dark eyes.

'Greetings, lord,' he said with his usual perfunctory dryness. 'Your journey went well?'

'What have you got there? A new development?' Kuruma asked, skipping the niceties.

'Ah.' Gormin gestured at the array on the workbench before him. 'No more than an idea so far, I'm afraid.'

On the bench lay a human arm sprouting a multitude of tubes and wires that led to various glass containers filled with clear liquids, and to a strange-looking mechanical contraption made of brass, wood, and copper wire. The nails of the hand had been replaced with long, wicked claws.

Gormin pressed a lever on the machine. The arm jerked, the hand contracted, and Kuruma saw drops of clear liquid appear at the tips of the claws. Poison, no doubt.

'Nice,' Kuruma said. 'Can you incorporate that with the next batch?'

'Doubtful,' Gormin said. 'Too many kinks to iron out still. But

I'll see what I can do.'

Kuruma noticed a dark figure hovering in the corridor outside Gormin's laboratory. 'Ah, Noburo. Don't lurk. Come in. You're just the man I wanted to see.'

'Kuruma,' Noburo said, stomping into the room. 'How nice of you to remember. I was beginning to think you'd forgotten my existence entirely.' He cast an accusing glance at Gormin.

Kuruma suppressed a desire to do something painful to Noburo. The man was reproach on two legs, feeling permanently slighted and taking pains to keep everyone aware of the fact. Since he'd taken to wearing a neatly trimmed grey goatee with his habitually sour expression, looking for all the world like a stuffy schoolmaster suffering from a bilious stomach, Kuruma could stand him even less.

'Why, Brother,' he said, 'you do me injustice. It's you I'm actually here to see. Just decided on the spur of the moment to drop by and see what our Master Gormin has been up to. Come, I'm most eager to hear your report. Where do we stand? Are we ready?'

'See for yourself.' Noburo, ungracious as usual, waved him towards the door. With a nod to Gormin, Kuruma followed him out.

The sight that greeted Kuruma never failed to impress him.

A few steps to the left, the corridor opened onto a gallery that circled an enormous subterranean chamber, so large it took over a quarter-hour to walk its whole circumference. Stepping over to the balustrade, he looked out into the great cavern. Above, the stone ceiling was lost in a cloud of vapor, raining drops of condensed water. Below, another nine tiers of galleries had been hewn from the rock. The lowest lay just above a small lake of boiling water, a strange, incongruously cold light glowing in its depths. In its center a small, rocky island rose above the milky, bubbling surface. On it stood a pair of slender columns and a matte-black monolith.

The eerie light radiating from the lake was augmented by scores of torches placed at regular intervals on the galleries and casting a dim illumination out into the gigantic space. The air was hot and steamy, hot enough to scorch the airways if one breathed in too deeply, and it was filled with the overpowering reek of every imaginable bodily fluid mixed together and concentrated by a factor of ten.

Roughly fifty small chambers were hewn into the wall of each gallery, the openings sealed with semi-transparent, wetly glistening membranes. A soft, dirty-orange glow emanated from the their interiors. Reject Unborn were everywhere, doing whatever was needed to keep the breeding process moving along – Kuruma wasn't interested in the details, only in the results.

Noburo gestured him over to the nearest breeding chamber. Through the membrane Kuruma could make out several dark, oblong forms floating in some kind of thick, gelatinous liquid that filled the entire cavity.

'Ten,' Noburo said. 'Ten to a chamber, eight entire galleries with together two hundred chambers, makes two thousand. Plus the specialized versions: two hundred sergeants, twenty captains, fifty scouts. A hundred rejects to handle supplies and so on. And a little extra something I think you'll enjoy. Your army.'

'Not to forget the eight hundred Moragian mercenaries camped outside Fellmere,' Kuruma said, rubbing his hands. 'How long until these here are ready?'

'They *are* ready,' Noburo said. 'We're just keeping them sacced until you actually need them. Saves us the trouble of having to feed them.'

'Well, I need them now. Unsac them and get them into the barracks. We march in three weeks. That'll give them time to dry out behind the ears and absorb some basic training. Not that they need to learn how to kill. Marching in a straight line though – that might prove somewhat of an intellectual challenge. Oh, and, Noburo. Good work. Excellent.'

Noburo humphed and sniffed, and Kuruma found himself fingering the hilt of the poisoned dagger he carried in an arm sheath up the sleeve of his robe. Ingrate runt. Time to go inspect the armory, or he *would* lose his temper.

Pity he still needed the man.

❖   ❖   ❖

On the eve of departure, the Brothers gathered for a last ceremony. Two Minors dragged in the sacrifice, still struggling despite the massive dose of drugs she'd been given. Kuruma raised an eyebrow.

'What's this?' he asked. 'A child? And a black one, at that? Why in the void hasn't she at least been properly drugged?'

'She has been,' Gracklin said. 'But she's a wildcat, this one. Young Durstin here got her cheap last trip from a Korulian slaver. Seems the man couldn't get rid of her fast enough. Said she was an Almorican fire witch. Claimed she badly hurt two of his men, burned them to a crisp.'

Meanwhile the girl's struggles had weakened, and the Minors had managed to tie her to the black throne. Kuruma stepped over and looked down at her. She couldn't have been more than fourteen, fifteen at the outside. She even carried some last traces of baby fat. Her skin was the color of kaf mixed with a dollop of milk, her black hair done up in countless tiny, beaded braids. Though Kuruma had no fondness for people of color, found them inferior in every respect, even he had to admit that the child was quite beautiful – for a black, that was. A budding beauty that would have held great promise for the future, had she had one.

'Do we now risk offending Ummuz by offering him mere children?' he said.

'Granted, she's young,' Durstin ventured. 'But she has Talent, and not too little of it. That should more than make up for her youth, don't you think, Supreme Brother?'

Slimy weasel, Kuruma thought. *But he has a point.*

'I suppose it does,' he mused out loud. 'I suppose it does. Talent. A veritable feast for our Lord. We couldn't by any chance use her for anything else, could we? No, didn't think so. Well, then. Let's get on with it.'

The Brothers took their places around the table, and Kuruma initiated the chant. They'd hardly begun when something very unusual happened. The black mist began to gather around the girl almost immediately, clinging to her greedily. Shortly, her head and upper body were wreathed in darkness. The Brothers exchanged uneasy glances.

Suddenly and much too early, the sacrifice spoke in a dry, thin voice that sounded as if it came from a throat filled with sand: the voice of Ummuz.

'I want ships,' it said. 'You must make them for me.'

'When?' Kuruma asked, stunned. 'When do you need these ships,

Lord? When are you coming? When should we expect you?'

'Soon,' came the answer. 'I have things to see to on the way.'

'Forgive me, Lord, but how soon is "soon"? We wish to prepare you a fitting welcome.'

There was no answer.

The mist around the girl began to dissipate. Kuruma hesitated: interrupting the ritual could have catastrophic consequences. On the other hand, Ummuz had already been and gone. Making up his mind, he continued to lead the chant and nodded to Durstin, designated to perform the sacrifice this evening. Durstin stood, moved to stand beside the throne and drew his sacrificial knife.

Then everything happened in a rush.

The girl suddenly opened her eyes, staring at Durstin with a strange and startling expression on her face: a far-away look of utter concentration, where one should have expected to see mortal fear.

A heartbeat later Durstin screamed, dropped the knife as if it were red-hot, and with a sudden WHOOSH! burst into flames. In the blink of an eye, the whole man was burning like a human torch. He staggered back a few steps, feebly attempting to beat at the flames that engulfed him. To Kuruma it looked as if Durstin were waving a last farewell from hell's doorstep. He felt sorcery gather around him, preparing to strike, and raised a hand.

'No, leave it. Let him burn. Lord Ummuz shall have his sacrifice.'

The girl seemed to have fainted from her exertions.

Kuruma stood watching as the burning man crumpled to the floor and gave a last twitch or two. A smell of burnt wool and roasting pork filled the air. Interesting development. There was much food for

141

thought here.

'I do *not* want the girl harmed,' he said, returning to the business at hand. 'The God has spared her, and she may be of great use to us alive. Brother Tano, Brother Marden, a Binding if you please. Get her down to the dungeons and put her in a cell with our long-term guests. Once you have her settled in, put her to sleep. Meaning, use something that will keep her under until we get back.

'And you,' he gestured to two attendant novices who stood gaping in the background. 'Find some water. Put this... thing out, and then get rid of it.'

He turned to the Brothers, allowing himself a moment to savor the look of shock on their faces. It could have been any one of them lying in a smoking heap on the floor, and they all knew it. The incident served to remind them of just how expendable each of them was in the grander scheme of things. Good.

'And now, let's all of us get some sleep. We ride at first light. Gracklin, you'll see us off in the morning? Splendid. I trust you'll have no trouble keeping the place running smoothly until we return. Very well, then. I wish you all a good night.'

Kuruma was sure that quite a few of the Brothers would have much preferred to stay at home and let others put themselves in harm's way. But he wanted no two of them together where he couldn't keep an eye on them. It was why he was leaving behind only Gracklin to hold the fort, Noburo having taken a 'sabbatical' and gone off somewhere or other to field-test a new theory of his.

As for himself, Kuruma was very much looking forward to some action. Nothing like a nice war to get a man's juices flowing.

If only he'd had news from his spy. There had been a bird in early March but since then, nothing. Some more recent information would have been very welcome.

Well, too late now, but possibly they'd meet up on the way.

Make the lie big, make it simple, keep saying it, and eventually they will believe it.

Varyingly ascribed to Joseph Goebbels, Adolf Hitler, and Josif Vissarionovic Djugasvili aka Stalin

9 The Madal Skog

rapped in a cloak, the loose end of his head-cloth drawn across his face and hiding everything but his eyes, Jekkim hung back at the rear edge of the crowd gathered in Rivensend for the God Festival's closing ceremony, doing his best to remain inconspicuous. Unthinkable as it had seemed only days ago, he wasn't sure how the people in this malignant, overheated gathering would react if they recognized him.

Last night he'd gone to see Kassem with a vague notion of somehow bringing him back to reason. It had been a fiasco.

When Jekkim scratched at the door of Kassem's yurt, a young Mud opened. Femaz, if Jekkim remembered correctly.

'Dras,' Femaz said, his bow hardly more than a nod. 'What do you want here?'

Disrespectful brat, Jekkim thought, but reined in his temper. He was not here to quarrel with the doorman. 'I'm here to see Kassem.'

'He's unwell,' Femaz said. 'He's not seeing – '

'Please show dras Jekkim in, Femaz,' a voice called from inside.

Jekkim slipped out of his shoes and stepped inside. He found Kassem reclining on a bed of cushions. There were several young men from different clans present, none of them the kind he'd have wanted to see his daughter with, had he had one. Kassem did look ill, pallid and bloated. For no good reason he made Jekkim think of a fat, pale grub on the brink of metamorphosis, though not one that would result in anything so nice as a butterfly.

'If you don't mind,' Jekkim said to Kassem, 'I'd like to speak to you alone.'

'Oh, I think not,' Kassem answered in that strange, unsettling voice. 'No secrets here.'

Jekkim was debating whether to let the insult pass when his eyes met Kassem's. What he saw there gave him a profound shock and left him feeling as if the bottom had dropped out of his soul. In that chilling, completely inhuman gaze he found no trace at all of the old Kassem. Something else was now looking out of those eyes. Eyes he could have sworn had until recently been blue but now seemed entirely dark, almost pure black. He saw in them something he'd superficially always reckoned with as the dark side of all faith but never really believed existed, a terrifying truth he would not have acknowledged before the advent of Morlic Silt and the horrible thing he'd dragged out of that cave. Jekkim was suddenly sure that it had been hidden away there for a very good reason, and that it had not been meant to see the light of day ever again.

He knew with unfailing certainty that he was now looking at the greatest danger he'd ever encountered, at the nemesis of everything that made the Skogon what they were, at something infinitely ancient and malevolent, the bane of all life since the beginning of time. He was looking at pure evil. A deep chill crept into his soul.

Just then he noticed with dismay that the pillow upon which Kassem's left hand was resting wasn't a pillow at all but a large, round object draped with a white cloth.

'Kassem,' he said imploringly. 'If you're still in there somewhere, listen to me. You have to stop this. Now. You may believe you know what you're doing, but trust me, you have no idea. You may think you can handle it, but you can't. Nobody can. Those who try pay a price horrendous and bitter beyond all reckoning. Don't go down that road, I beg you. It will cost you everything. You, and the clans. Give up that thing. Hand it over to me, and I'll see that it's destroyed, as it should have been long ago.'

'Stay out of this, old man,' Kassem grated. 'It's none of your business anymore. You should leave before you get yourself hurt. And by the way: you're relieved from the council. Stone will have a new elder.'

'You can't do that.' Jekkim was aghast. 'The clans choose their elders, not you. The council won't stand for this.'

'Oh, but it will. The council reports to me now.'

'That's impossible. It's against the law.'

'Impossible, you say? Would you put your puny clan law before the God's?'

'What god?' Jekkim was suddenly calm. He didn't care anymore what happened to him. He'd come with a purpose. Almost detachedly he watched the men around Kassem tense at his words, hands reaching for daggers. 'If this is a god, it would be best if there weren't any gods at all. Leave off. It's not too late. Let me help you.'

'Help yourself, old fool, by getting out of here, and quickly.

You've been warned. Don't meddle. Try to cross me again and you'll pay dearly. Now go.'

Two of the men rose with an anticipatory swagger that told Jekkim he was about to be removed bodily. He chose to leave on his own two feet.

Femaz stood at the door, all looming menace now. He hardly budged, forcing Jekkim to squeeze by in a highly undignified manner. Another time Jekkim would have drawn on him, but not tonight.

Outside, he found himself shaking. Jekkim Flint was not a man who scared easily, but as of this moment he was more afraid than ever before in his life.

Half the Skogon must have been crammed into Rivensend, making the place appear even smaller than it was. At least forty members of Kassem's newly created 'personal guard' roamed the crowd's edge. Carrying staffs or cudgels, they were easily recognizable by their red armbands.

Not quite a uniform, Jekkim thought, *but the statement is clear enough: this is my new, armed executive. Where there is an organized force, obviously there is also a lawful authority behind it, and behold, I am it. I speak for the God. The fact that I command this force is proof of it.*

The logic of it was back to front, but it was exactly right for impressing Kassem's claim to power on this unthinking mass of people, who all seemed to have lost their individual minds. Perhaps they'd deposited them with Kassem's bullyboys at the entrance, Jekkim thought wryly, though no one had asked him for his.

A murmur went through the crowd.

The doors of the small temple opened, and four of Kassem's men carried him out on a litter cobbled together from an ornate, high-backed ceremonial chair and two stout poles. They set him down on a dais erected at the top of the steps leading up to the temple. He looked even more swollen than when Jekkim had last seen him, and there were dark rings under his eyes. A low table had been set within easy reach of Kassem's left hand, and a golden tray bearing a familiar, cloth-covered object was now placed upon it with utmost reverence.

As the men retreated to stand by the door, Asukan, followed by Halima and Tomay, stepped out of the temple and went to stand beside the dais. The high priestess looked down on Kassem with a proprietary air. Kassem ignored her.

Jekkim, his heart plummeting with the shock of the final and terrible certainty that Asukan had chosen a side – and not the one he'd hoped and prayed for but the one that could only lead to ruination – saw lifetimes of tragedy presaged in scant moments. In a flash of insight, he understood how she meant to control this evil and use it to her own ends, and he saw how it would use her instead, and grind her under its heel when her usefulness was over and it was done with her. Though she had eyes to see what the owner of the head was doing with Kassem, effortlessly taking him over and filling him with its evil presence like a vessel emptied of its previous contents, and though that alone should have been warning enough, she was obviously blinded beyond reason by ambition and hubris.

Jekkim didn't like the woman, and her individual fate paled beside that of the clans, but for an instant he felt a poignant sadness over what was to befall her. What had already become of Kassem – the real Kassem – didn't bear contemplating.

It was heartbreaking. Kassem had been a good man.

Jekkim's emotional moment was cut short by Kassem, raising a hand. The crowd became so quiet one could have heard a midge cough.

'I am Ummuz-din,' Kassem said, 'The Mouth of the God. This He bids me say to you: He rejects and will no longer tolerate the name Uilmaz, imposed on Him by ignorant misbelievers who even now seek to deny Him and to keep you, my friends, from entering onto the path of glory and salvation He has chosen for you in His boundless mercy.

'Henceforth, you shall call Him by His true name, Ummuz, Lord Binder of Light, and whenever you speak it, He will hear you and listen to your prayers and wishes. He has chosen you, brothers and sisters, chosen you above all others to embark upon His Great Work, to carry forth His Word into all the lands of Vereld, and your rewards in His service shall be rich beyond all imagining – in this world as well as in the next.

'He has elected every single one of you to be His sword and spear, Warriors of God. Be prepared, my friends, for soon He will send you out to conquer the world and rule it in His Name. You shall be His faithful servants, and by His grace you shall live as kings and queens, in this life and in the one to come. Let us speak His Name together, that it may engrave itself deeply on our hearts and souls. Ummuz.'

'Ummuz,' the crowd murmured in response, the voices of the three priestesses clearly audible above the rest, Asukan's shrill with the pretense of leadership.

'Ummuz.'

'Ummuz,' the crowd echoed, louder now.

Kassem began to chant. 'Ummuz, Ummuz, Ummuz...'

The crowd joined in, fusing into one great entity, gaining momentum. Kassem leaned forward to remove the white cloth.

He held up the head for all to see, and suddenly the whole gathering was caught up in the grip of its dark, hungry power. Even Jekkim could feel its force: enticing, cajoling, promising. This was nothing at all like the vague discomfort he'd experienced at Morlic's trial. It was incomparably stronger now, a frontal assault offering an irresistible, honeyed lure to lull the senses while it quietly tiptoed around and slipped in through the back door. He could smell the stink of corruption beneath the cloying sweetness, could see the jaws of the trap waiting to snap shut.

And still the thing sought entrance. He felt as if slippery shadow-fingers were insinuating themselves into his brain, attempting to twist his thoughts and feelings into a different shape and direction. All of a sudden it seemed so easy to give in and go along, so inevitable, so right. Everyone was doing it, so why shouldn't he? How could so many people be wrong? So much good would come of it. Such great rewards awaited him...

With an effort, he caught himself, shaking off the greedy feelers groping for his very soul. Immediately, he felt his head clear.

The chanting had grown almost deafeningly loud and shrill as the crowd became more and more frenzied. Finally, Kassem set the head down and covered it with the cloth. He raised a hand, and the people began to quiet down.

Just then, someone standing to Jekkim's right jostled him roughly. He risked a glance. Not someone he knew, he'd never seen the face before.

'Watch your step, fellow!' the man said angrily, though Jekkim had been standing perfectly still when the other bumped into him. He turned and faced forward again, saying nothing, hoping the man would let it go at that. No such luck.

'What?' the man persisted, raising his voice. 'You're so high and mighty you don't need to apologize when you elbow a person in the ribs?'

Jekkim tried to discreetly move away, but someone grabbed him by the arm from the other side. This one he knew. Bullyboy Femaz. He pushed back Jekkim's hood with the tip of his cudgel.

'Well, well,' he said. 'You again. I thought Ummuz-din told you to stay away. Had a change of heart? Well sorry, but I'm not stupid. Only reason for you being here is, you're spying. I told him he should get rid of you, that you were nothing but trouble. Why don't you come up front and explain to him what it is you think you're doing here?'

He gave Jekkim a rough shove forward. The people in front, who had turned around to see what the commotion was about, were ready for him. Hands gripped him and propelled him onward. Something struck his back. A fist landed on his ear, another split his lip. People kept shoving him, more blows raining down on him from all sides along with jeers and curses.

Finally, bruised and bleeding, he was pushed out in front of the throng. One of the bullyboys cracked his staff across the back of Jekkim's legs, and he fell to his knees on the hard-packed dirt at the foot of the porch. He struggled to get to his feet but was held down from behind by a heavy hand on his shoulder.

The face that looked down on Jekkim with black, expressionless eyes wasn't Kassem's anymore. It was as if the thing that inhabited him had begun molding its own features onto his skull.

'You,' he said in that voice that wasn't his own either. Then he looked up and addressed the crowd. 'See this lost soul, this poor unbeliever who stubbornly clings to the old, false order. His time is over. He and his ilk are no longer needed, and they are no longer welcome. He was warned not to interfere, and I could say now that what befalls him for disobeying is upon his own head. But, once again, I have pity and am merciful, for it is clear that he is nothing but a confused, senile old man. Go, old fool. But this is your last warning. If I see you again, there will be no more mercy for you. Rezak, see that he gets out of here in one piece.'

Absently, Jekkim noticed Asukan and her fellow vultures looking on, their expressions hovering somewhere between contempt and satisfaction, as if he were the true enemy brought to heel.

But he wasn't about to leave with nothing in recompense for the pain and indignity he'd suffered. 'You will lose them,' he croaked. 'You may have them for a while, but in the end you'll lose them all. God have mercy on their souls.'

'Oh, but he does,' Kassem said with a humorless smile that looked more like a feral grimace. 'That's why he's sent them to me. And you're the one who's lost. Now get yourself out of here before you lose more than you can afford.'

He waved a hand at Rezak, who roughly pulled Jekkim to his feet and led him away while the crowd stood watching in hostile silence. As soon as they were out of sight of the gathering, the bullyboy gave Jekkim a shove in the direction of the exit.

'Get lost,' he spat. 'And stay lost, if you know what's good for you.'

Wiping blood and, yes, tears from his face, Jekkim stumbled away. For the first time in his life, he felt truly old. Old and beaten. Only a few days ago, he would have left the place with the blood of each and every one of those puffed-up scum who had so vilely insulted him dripping from his knife – or died trying. But there was no honor here anymore, no respect for anything. If this was what the clans had come to, and in so short a time, then the days of the Skogon weren't just numbered. They were already good as over.

What now? he asked himself despairingly. *What now?*

He was past evoking any more gods. Chances were high he'd draw the wrong one's attention.

Returning to his yurt, he was surprised to see a faint beam of light coming from the smoke hole. Childless and a widower, he could only expect the company waiting for him inside to be inimical. He didn't really care anymore.

Still, he was glad to find not more of Kassem's bullyboys lying in wait for him but Munnir, sitting quietly at the rekindled fire. He seemed no less relieved to see Jekkim.

'Jekkim,' Munnir said, rising to greet him. 'Sorry to intrude like this. But I needed to see you, and didn't want to be caught skulking around outside. I hope you'll forgive me.'

A look passed between the two erstwhile rivals, and there was an

154

understanding of sorts in it, the possibility of friendship maybe, and some small amount of consolation.

'Forgive you?' Jekkim felt renewed tears stinging his eyes. 'I'm glad you're here. I truly am. I was beginning to think I'd never see a normal, sane person again.'

'Tell me about it,' Munnir sighed. 'They've all gone nuts out there.'

'Totally insane,' Jekkim agreed. 'Don't tell me you've been to that crazy gathering too.'

'I was. Left early. Couldn't stand it anymore. I'd say it's a good thing I didn't outstay my welcome, seeing the state you're in.'

Jekkim told Munnir what had happened.

'Bloody cowards!' Munnir exclaimed. 'Gutless bastards, the lot of them. Call themselves Skogon, those craven rats!'

'We have to do something about it,' Jekkim said. 'You know there's no way around it. Not as long as we aim to remain honorable men.'

'I agree. But what? How? Both Kassem and the head are guarded day and night, and there's only the two of us.'

'Three,' someone said from the door. 'And you'd better start lowering your voices if you want to live long enough to accomplish anything at all. I could hear every word you said outside.'

It was Nesud, Sosha's brother.

'Come,' Jekkim said. 'Join us.'

There was no question of Nesud being one of Kassem's spies. He'd just recently lost a sister to the head's machinations, and had no reason to feel anything but implacable hate for the god Kassem served.

Thus the conspiracy of three began.

Nesud, young and angry, would have struck at once, going for Kassem. A suicide mission, the two older men explained to him, with no chance of success, and worse, no point to it.

'There's only one option,' Munnir said. 'We have to destroy the bloody head. Killing Kassem changes nothing. Someone else would take his place, and we'd have wasted our chance.'

'And one chance is all we're going to get,' Jekkim agreed. 'So we'd best make it count.'

They spent the rest of that night, and many others after, making plans and weighing options, but in the end they always came to the same conclusion. There was no way they could get to the head as long as Kassem was holed up in Rivensend with his bullyboys guarding him. They were already two hundred strong, with more joining every day and no end in sight. All the three of them could do was wait until the grand 'quest' had begun and Kassem was on the move. He'd be much more vulnerable on the road, and sooner or later an opportunity would present itself.

Or so they hoped.

Three weeks later the Skogon clans, over twelve thousand strong, departed the Madal Skog, embarking on the God's Great Quest to find and reassemble the rest of its missing parts – which He said were scattered in five different places, none of them in the Madal – and then on to conquer the world.

Kassem had given the clans those weeks to return to their home grounds and fetch whatever they deemed necessary. At the allotted time they returned, men, women and children, bringing with them those who had stayed behind during the festival. They came leading carthorses, mules and ponies laden with yurts and their few possessions, and they brought their livestock as well, cattle, pigs, chickens and herds upon herds of sheep and goats, everything they owned and couldn't or wouldn't leave behind.

When all were assembled, they left, never to return.

❖ ❖ ❖

Morlic awoke with a start.

His eyes wouldn't focus properly and his brain was extremely sluggish, so by the time he'd figured out where he was, he was already dying again, asphyxiated by the rope around his neck.

When he next came to, he was able to ascertain that his situation was completely, utterly and effingly hopeless before he succumbed to death by strangulation again.

The third time around it was getting dark, which meant that time was actually passing and he wasn't in some insane afterlife, imagining this ultimate of all nightmares – or so he reasoned. He managed to determine that he could just barely touch the ground with the tips of his toes, which wasn't any help at all. Then he passed away again.

It went on and on like this, waking up, dying, waking up, dying again. After a while, since he had nothing better to do, he started counting. During the night and the next day he tallied forty-two deaths, from which he calculated that one cycle lasted slightly over half an hour. Roughly five minutes of life to twenty-something of being stone cold dead. Bad ratio. And one more totally useless insight.

But he did notice something rather more important if no less depressing. There was no traffic on any of the roads, none at all.

Which was strange, because on any given day there'd normally be all kinds of people passing by this blasted crossroads where he was dangling from a stupid tree like an oversized fruit – only it didn't look like he was going to ripen and fall off any time soon, not before the damned rope eventually rotted through. Which would probably take years.

Hold that thought, he told himself as he faded once again.

When he came round for about the hundred-and-eightieth time, there was a surprise waiting for him. A wagon was pulled up at the cross-roads, hung on all sides with pots and pans and tools and bundles of who-knew-what. A peddler.

The wagon's owner stepped into Morlic's field of view, cramped and tilted as it was by the rope around his neck, and stared at him curiously. Morlic got so excited he could have pissed himself, had there been anything left in his bladder. Here was his chance, maybe the only one he'd get this year, or the next, or any year at all.

Since he couldn't talk, he started waving his arms to draw attention to the fact that he was alive, at least momentarily.

'Well I'll be damned,' the man said, rubbing his stubbly chin in wonder. 'It's alive. Gods above, nobody's gonna believe this.' An idea struck him. 'Say,' he asked, 'where is everybody? Ain't seen a soul in days.'

Morlic gestured ever more frantically, pointing to his neck, and the rope. He was beginning to expire again.

'What?' the man said. 'Oh. Sorry. Should've thought of that my-self. Hang in there – no pun intended. Be back in a jiffy.'

He turned towards his wagon, but Morlic was already out of it again.

The next time he woke, the view had changed dramatically.

He was lying on his back in the dirt, looking up at the sky. He could see a few branches of the blasted tree poking into the edge of the picture, which moments later also included a foreshortened version of the peddler. A delicious smell hit his nostrils.

'Here,' the peddler said. 'Want some kaf? Can you sit up?'

To his surprise, Morlic could. As soon as he did, the world was all skewed again, his head refusing to do anything but hang sharply to the left, nearly but not quite resting on his shoulder. Very uncomfortable.

It must be the neck, he decided, *from all that hanging about on the end of a rope. Probably broken, too.*

Feeling revived by the kaf, he tried to speak. All he managed at first was a faint hiss. A dead fish could have done better. He took a sip of kaf and gave it another go, found that he could speak if he went about it like he had a really bad sore throat – which he did, actually – and used just air instead of a voice he seemed to have lost. Small wonder, after what he'd been through.

In a loud, hoarse whisper he said, 'Thanks for the kaf. And thanks for saving my life. I'm really grateful.'

The peddler scratched his backside. 'You know – I could have sworn you was dead when I got here.'

'I was,' Morlic said. 'And I wasn't. Whatever. Forget it. It's complicated.'

'Right. I'd better get going, though. Ain't gonna sell much if I'm hanging about here all day. Reckon you'll be all right?'

'Actually, would you mind giving me a lift?'

'Depends on where you're going.'

'Doesn't really matter for now. Wherever you're currently headed is fine, I guess.'

'Okay then, I suppose. If Gomilar's all right with you. I'll just put out the fire, and we'll be off. Oh. Name's Jessop, by the way.'

'Morlic,' Morlic said. 'Extremely glad to meet you.'

Sitting beside Jessop on the box of the wagon, lumbering along at a leisurely pace, Morlic idly considered killing the man but found he didn't have it in him, at least not at the moment. Besides, he felt a kind of weird kinship with the peddler. Each in their own way, they were unique: Morlic a compulsive killer who seemed to have recently acquired a mysterious knack for immortality, and Jessop by far the most dimwitted man Morlic had ever met, quite possibly record-breaking stupid. It made Morlic feel a kind of benevolent lenience towards the man. Always time to kill him later on, if circumstances required it.

They probably would. He liked the idea of slipping into the man's identity, and in the same stroke getting himself transportation and a means of support while he hunted down the source of all his troubles: the head, that lying, conniving, traitorous bastard. The hatred he felt every time he thought of the damned thing was overwhelming, all-encompassing. And absolutely implacable. He could have screamed, raved, torn out his hair, blacked out or vomited with the intensity of it.

'You know, I'm totally insane,' he told Jessop conversationally.

'Wouldn't have guessed.' Lifting one plump buttock, Jessop fart-ed loudly.

'That's because I'm really good at hiding it,' Morlic said. The world was still madly tilted, especially seen from atop the wagon, and he was feeling slightly dizzy. Watching the swaying haunches of the two ageing mares pulling the creaking, clanking contraption didn't help either.

Weird world, he thought. *Wonky. Crooked. Just like me.*

'Promise me one thing, though,' Jessop said. 'Promise you're not gonna go all loopy and kill me in my sleep.'

'If I wanted to kill you,' Morlic answered, 'you'd be dead already.'

'Just so we're clear.'

'I won't.'

'All right, then. Gomilar it is.'

Only after it was far too late to matter anymore did Morlic think to wonder what a peddler was doing coming out of the Skogon back country, when obviously there wasn't a single body left to sell anything to, quite apart from the fact that a peddler had to be suicidal or terminally stupid – sic – to go where people hated foreigners with a vengeance and were much more likely to slit his throat and rob him blind than pay him a copper quarter for his troubles.

❖　❖　❖

While I thought that I was learning how to live, I have been learning how to die.

Leonardo Da Vinci

10 Fellmere

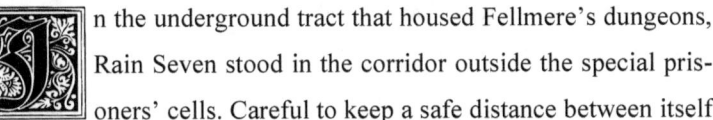n the underground tract that housed Fellmere's dungeons, Rain Seven stood in the corridor outside the special prisoners' cells. Careful to keep a safe distance between itself and the Oracle's spellbound door, it looked in through the barred window. The emaciated figure hanging in the glistening net of tubes stirred, turning its sightless gaze towards the door.

'Rain,' the Oracle croaked, 'is that you?'

'It is, Wordlord,' Rain Seven answered. 'They are gone, everyone except the one called Gracklin and some of the novices. We will do it tonight. Striving Four and Changing Grey are about to begin removing the stones. Gormin should be arriving soon. Three Flower and Counting Clouds are meeting him at the postern gate. Please do not worry. Stone Blue is standing watch at the main stairs. We will know if anyone approaches.'

'Me? Worry?' the Oracle made a dry sound in his throat that came out as more of a cough than a chuckle. 'I gave that up a long time ago. But I still think it would be a much better idea if you guys just pulled me off this damned thing and let me die in peace. Would save us all a lot of trouble.'

'You know we can't let you die, lord,' Rain Seven said softly, 'even if we wished to.'

'So you say,' the Oracle sighed. 'But I can still hope, can't I? This crazy plan of yours sounds like I stand an excellent chance of buying the farm anyway. So maybe I will get my wish in the end.'

Rain Seven was distressed by the Oracle's insistent wish to die, had been since the first time they had spoken over a year ago, when it had first been moved to this posting. Back then Rain, like all the other reject Unborn, would never have dared address a human, even one in such a helpless, dire position as the Oracle.

The initiative had come from the Oracle. After very quietly sneaking up to the cell, Rain had been standing outside the door looking in through the bars, its heart filled with sadness and compassion for the human's horrendous suffering. More than once, it had spoken to its brethren about the man, and they had shuddered and groaned in empathy with his terrible fate. They all fervently wished there was something, anything, they could do to help.

'Talk to me,' the man had suddenly said, seeming to look directly at Rain through his sewn-up eyelids. Rain nearly jumped out of its skin. Briefly, it was torn between the impulse to flee and something else, a feeling it couldn't yet have named back then.

'I mustn't,' it said, trembling at its own audacity. 'It is forbidden.'

'Or what?' the man asked. 'They'll do something bad to you? Something worse than what they've already done just by making you?'

'No,' Rain said. 'But you are a human, a Master, and I am – nothing.'

'Who told you that?' The man's voice softened. 'Who dares say such a thing? Those tattooed shit-for-brains from the upper floors?'

'There wasn't any need for them to say it,' the Unborn replied, still wondering where it found the nerve to speak like this. 'It is something everyone knows. Some say my kind shouldn't exist. But then, this is how the Masters think of all creatures, even their own fellow humans.' With a thrill of fear, Rain realized it was being dangerously forward.

'They're wrong,' the man said. 'You didn't ask for this. But now that you're here, you damn well have the same right to exist as everybody else. A lot more in fact than the sick bastards who made you, if you ask me. Tell me – what's your name again? Never seem to have heard it mentioned.'

'I don't have a name,' the Unborn had said. 'None of us do. We are worthless. Of no importance at all. We don't deserve to have names.'

'Listen to me,' the man said, his voice deepening.
Rain, whose excellent hearing had permitted it to overhear everything that had been spoken during Lord Kuruma's visits, knew what the change of tone meant: the Oracle was about to foretell – and to an Unborn, no less. Rain felt its knees go weak with excitement and disbelief.

'Listen to me,' the Oracle said, the walls suddenly seeming to resonate with the timbre of his voice. 'For this I tell you: you and your kind are no less creatures of God than any others upon this world, no matter how you came to exist. Even a power striving for evil as the Brotherhood does can unwittingly become His instrument. He has set

165

you upon this earth with a purpose, and He has given you a task and a destiny. In the dark years to come, you shall break the bonds that hold you to your makers. You shall go forth to heal what is wounded and mend what is broken, and thus find peace and your place in the world.'

The Oracle took a deep breath. 'There. Now go and find a name for yourself. And don't bother with the sneaky stuff anymore. I always know exactly where you are.'

'Lord – '

'Oh, don't "lord" me. Look at me. I'm worse off than you are. If anybody's "nothing" around here, it's me. Now go, your shift's up. We don't want you getting in trouble now, do we?'

'Lord, thank you!' Rain blurted, as close to tears as an Unborn could ever hope to come. It hurried away.

Dull thudding and grinding sounds from the cell next door brought Rain Seven back to the present. Striving Four and Changing Grey were removing big blocks of stone from the dividing wall between the cells. Over the past weeks, Rain had spent every possible moment scraping the mortar out of the joins and loosening enough stones to prepare for the making of a hole that would allow at least a small Unborn to pass.

To think now how much time had been lost until that first contact between human and Unborn had been made! Rain had at least wasted no time informing its brethren of what had taken place. That same evening, their small circle had gathered in their secret meeting place to exchange news as they always did between shifts.

When Rain confided that it had spoken to the Wordlord, as the

Unborn called the Oracle, hands were clapped over mouths, sharp breaths drawn in and eyes squeezed shut, signaling intense distress over such bold and daring behavior. And when it spoke to them of the Oracle's foretelling, they were rocked, thunderstruck, suspended between disbelief and excitement just like Rain had been.

Over the next few weeks, even the most timid and incredulous gradually came to believe that maybe, just maybe, there might be a purpose to their lives other then the one intended by their makers. With time, it began to seem less unthinkable that there might actually be truth in what the Wordlord had said about their having a task and a future. Rain affirmed that everything else it had heard the Oracle foretell had so far been proven true. But dared one believe that this might also be the case regarding themselves? They were in high turmoil, by far the greatest confusion any of them had ever known. They were scared, upset, torn every which way, and shaken to the cores of their humble, unassuming beings.

In the midst of the fear and uncertainty, something began to grow and take shape that none of them had dreamed possible. The first tangible step in this slow and hesitant process took place when Rain announced one evening that it had found a name for itself.

'I have chosen to call myself Rain Seven,' it said, 'after the seven kinds of rain that fall from the sky, and for the seven good companions fate has given me.'

After some appreciative oohs and aahs, the others one by one shyly admitted they'd also conceived of names for themselves.

Rain's companion to the left, by far the largest and strongest among their number but also the gentlest, spoke. 'I have chosen the name Three Flower, after three small flowers I saw growing outside the postern gate where the refuse is dumped, because there is beauty to be found even on a midden.'

Next to speak was an Unborn whom the humans found especially ugly, so ugly they'd actually noticed and relegated it to duty in the stores cellars where it was well out of their sight. 'I have chosen Stone Blue, for a blue stone I once saw in one of the Masters' studies when I was still a cleaner. It seemed a piece of the sky come down to the earth, like the hope that has come to us through the Wordlord.'

Then came an Unborn who was often sad and melancholy. 'I choose Changing Grey, for, like the world we see around us every day, my heart is grey and lacks color. I wish for the grey to change and become many colors, in my heart and in the world at large.'

The one who spoke after Changing Grey was a rarity among the Unborn. Small, quick, and agile, it not only had a sense of humor but was actually capable of displaying levity of a sort. 'I've chosen the name Striving Four,' it said with an Unborn approximation of a mischievous grin. 'Four like the number, that is, but don't ask me why. I'll let you know what I'm striving four as soon as I've found out myself.'

Another Unborn spoke. This one worked in the kitchen gardens, and there were half moons of rich, black earth under the nails of its huge hands. It actually managed to get things to grow and thrive, a seemingly impossible task in these ash-infested, sun-starved parts. 'I name myself Once Green, for I have heard that in other parts of the world there are great, green plains of grass and forests covering the land, and I think that at least once an Unborn should travel there and see these wonders for itself.'

The last one to speak was an Unborn given to flights of day-dreaming, a fact which often got it into trouble with the Masters. 'I choose something with clouds, though I haven't yet decided what else.'

'How about Counting Clouds,' Striving Four suggested. 'Seeing as that seems to be your favorite pastime.'

The Unborn thought for a moment, then it said, 'Yes, that is a wonderful name. Thank you, Striving Four. You've been very helpful.'

Rain Seven had to wait until the next day to break the news to the Wordlord. On the way down to the dungeons it felt anticipation, and realized it no longer looked forward to its shifts for the solitude and quiet but for the Wordlord's company and conversation.

'I have chosen a name, lord,' it announced at the Oracle's door, slightly out of breath from hurrying down the many stairs.

'Good,' the Oracle said, and when nothing more came from the Unborn, 'Are you going to tell me what it is, or am I supposed to guess?'

'Oh. Yes. Forgive me. It is Rain Seven. For the seven different kinds of rain that fall from the sky.'

'And for the seven kinds of goodness that live in your heart and one day shall fall on the world like a beneficent shower,' the Oracle said. 'Speaking of goodness – you wouldn't by any chance have remembered that crossbow I asked you to bring along?'

'No, lord,' Rain said unhappily. 'Nothing has changed. I still cannot kill you. None of us can. But we do wish to help you. The gift you have given us is too great for words, and it is too many things to

169

count, but foremost of all, I believe, is that you have given us hope. We wish to give you hope in return.'

'Ah, my friend, I hope that some day you won't discover to your bitter disappointment that the sentiment can be a double-edged blade. As they say where I come from, "Be careful what you wish for." The same should go for hoping.'

The moment had arrived for Rain to break its real news.

'Lord, I am here to tell you that we will endeavor to free you from this prison. It is the least we can do to repay our debt to you.'

The Oracle barked a laugh.

'Free me? Whatever for? To go out into the world like this, too gruesome a sight even for a cheap carnival act? And even if there was a way I could survive being taken off of this fantastical perversion of an ICU, do you really think I'd want to go on living in this ruin of a body even for a day, an hour? If you really want to do something for me, find someone who *can* pull a trigger and send them down here with a crossbow. You say you owe me big time. Well I say you owe me nothing but a bolt between the eyes. So find a way to deliver that, and we'll call it even.'

'Lord, please. Don't agitate yourself. I have been foolish and inept in delivering the message. There is more. Naturally we understand that freeing you from this place while leaving you imprisoned in a broken body would be more of a curse than a blessing. But we believe we have found a way to restore you to your former health. Please let us at least try. Nothing could possibly give us more contentment than to be allowed to do this for you. Lord Kuruma is leaving soon, going to war, and he is taking all the Masters with him. When they are gone, we will act. And if for some reason we fail, I promise you I will find a way to fulfill your wish to die.'

The Oracle sighed. 'I'm sorry, Rain. I guess I'm not having one of my best days. I really appreciate what you guys are trying to do here, and sure, I'll hang in for a while longer so you can give it a go. I've held out in this hellhole for so long, I suppose I can manage a few more weeks. Just don't expect me to get all excited. Hope is not something I can afford right now. Still, be sure to say hello and thanks to your friends from me.'

'Thank you, lord, I will do that. And now, I should be doing my rounds.' But Rain lingered a moment longer. Obviously there was still something on its mind. 'I have told you my name, lord. Now I am wondering: do you have a name as well, other than "Oracle?" And if so, may I be so bold as to ask what it is?'

'Ah, my friend. Let's not get into that right now. It leads to places I don't want to go – not from here. I've gotten used to all kinds of pain, but that would be more than I could stand. I'll tell you what, though: you do the impossible and get me out of here, make me whole and healthy again, and then I'll tell you my name. Deal?'

'Deal,' Rain Seven said. 'I will look by again later on. And thank you for your trust, Wordlord. Be assured I will honor it, as will my brethren.'

The sounds coming from the neighboring cell grew louder.

A stone fell out of the wall on the Oracle's side. They were through. Grinning despite himself, the Oracle turned his head towards the door where Rain Seven stood. Though he couldn't see it, Rain answered with what passed for an Unborn smile. Moments later, Striving Four gently touched the Oracle's shoulder.

171

'Wordlord.'

There was a soft whistle from further down the corridor and short, humpbacked Gormin appeared, bobbing towards Rain Seven as fast as his twisted, stumpy legs allowed. Behind him came Three Flower and Counting Clouds, carrying a longish wooden box.

❖ ❖ ❖

What none of them knew or even suspected was that, with the cat out of the house, they were not the only mice out to play. For hours now, Gracklin had been restlessly pacing up in his tower room, debating whether he should risk paying the Oracle a visit, if only to try for a little conversation through the barred and spellbound door. Finally he concluded that, if Kuruma ever found out, he could always say he'd only gone down to check and see that everything was in order. Kuruma wouldn't believe it for a moment, but he couldn't prove otherwise either. Gracklin was just about to head down to the dungeons when a novice showed up at his door with some stupid questions about the management of stores. Anxious to be on his way, Gracklin sought to deal with the unwelcome interruption as quickly as possible.

❖ ❖ ❖

Three Flower and Counting Clouds maneuvered the box into the adjoining cell. Gormin crawled through the hole in the wall and joined Striving Four in the Oracle's cell.

'Wordlord,' he said. 'We haven't met. I'm Gormin.'

'I'm not sure yet whether I should be glad to meet you, Gormin,' the Oracle said. 'But you do sound like a nice person.'

'Alas, I'm not. But I'm here to help you all the same, so let me quickly explain what is going to happen. We will take you off the web. In the cell next door there is a box containing a modified version of the breeding sac used to make Unborn. We'll put you in the sac and, if all goes well, it will not only keep you alive but heal and restore you as well. You'll have to stay in the sac for three to four weeks, but you'll be asleep and not wake up until you're ready to come out again.

'Now. The critical moments will be when we're moving you from the web to the sac. During that time you'll experience a great deal of pain, and you'll have nothing to support you except your own will to live.

'I've been told you entertain a wish for the opposite, but please consider this: if you survive the transfer, there's an excellent chance that in a few week's time your body will be as good as new. What damage your soul and spirit have sustained only you can know. But they too may heal if you have the strength and patience to let them. That is all. If you are ready, we will begin now. Time presses.'

'Thanks for explaining,' the Oracle said. 'With those bedside manners you'd make a very fine doctor. As for the rest, I guess I'm as ready as I'll ever be. Let's do it.'

Gormin directed Striving Four to hold up the Oracle while he quickly severed the tubes attached to his body with a scalpel. As the last tubes were cut, the Oracle sank into Striving Four's arms.

❖   ❖   ❖

Already he could feel the life ebbing out of him.

The constant pain he'd endured for months flared and then receded, leaving him dizzy and light-headed. A welcome lassitude stole into

173

his sore body and wounded soul, finding no resistance there, only a quick softening and grateful acceptance. He experienced a feeling of profound relief, as if a mountain had been rolled off his soul, and he was sorely tempted to give in and let go.

He was about to let himself sink into the welcoming darkness already crowding the edges of his inner vision, narrowing it down to what he thought might eventually become a beckoning point of pure light, when out of nowhere a long repressed image flashed through his mind: a picture of home. It was enough to make him pause. Now *that* was something that just might be worth staying alive for: a chance to return home. Who knew but there might be a way after all. And just like that, hope plucked him out of death's grip and gave him a reason to go on – at least provisionally.

He felt the two Unborn carry him across the room with all possible speed. They passed him through the hole in the wall to Three Flower and Rain Seven, who had the box open and were waiting for him on the other side. He felt himself being gently lifted and swung towards the box, noting with dark amusement that it looked exactly like a coffin.

To his surprise, he saw that the cell was occupied. A slight, dark-skinned girl lay on a straw pallet in the corner. Immediately he had a strong and unequivocal feeling about her. Though he had no idea how and why, he knew she was important.

'Wait,' he gasped. The Unborn paused.

'The girl,' he whispered feebly. 'She has to come with us. Promise me you'll take her too.'

'If you wish, Wordlord,' Rain Seven said, 'we will bring her. I promise. Rest assured.'

❖ ❖ ❖

Holding the Wordlord in its arms, Rain Seven could hardly believe that a body so light and frail could contain any life at all.

It felt the man go limp. Quickly now, before the spark died.

Gormin had come through, and following his instructions they gently slipped the Oracle into the sac, a thin but tough membrane filled with a clear, gelatinous mass. When all of the Wordlord was inside, Gormin sealed the opening. After they'd put the lid on the box, Three Flower opened the tightly closed drawstrings of a leather sack, releasing a ripe stench of decay. He took out a piece of raw, rotting meat he'd picked up from the midden outside the castle walls and rubbed the coffin's sides and lid with it. Time to go.

Rain and Three Flower had just picked up the box when they heard a door slam loudly at the far end of the corridor – the agreed upon sign from Stone Blue warning them that someone was coming.

'Hurry!' Rain said to Three Flowers. 'The hidden stairs!'

They set out at a fast trot, followed by the others, Striving Four carrying the girl in its arms. At the opposite end of where Stone Blue was standing watch, the hallway seemed to dead-end.

Supporting his end of the box with one hand, Rain pressed a combination of two stones at waist level, releasing a hidden catch. A section of the wall swung open, revealing a narrow, winding staircase. Changing Grey took a torch from a wall sconce and lit the way. The stairs were a tight fit for the larger Unborn, and maneuvering the box through the turns was tricky work, but eventually they reached ground level, exiting through a similar opening in the wall of an unused pantry. From there, they went through the deserted kitchens and out into a small courtyard, where they ran straight into the arms of two battle-Unborn guards doing rounds.

❖   ❖   ❖

Gracklin had finally managed to get rid of the annoying novice and make his way downstairs without being spotted by another of the pimply nuisances whose only purpose in life seemed to be delaying him with trifling matters and keeping him from getting around to the really important things. Rounding the bend into the corridor along which the Oracle's cell lay, he nearly ran into a huge reject standing there filling the narrow passage with its enormous bulk.

'Get out of my way, you ugly sack of shit!' the sorcerer spat.

❖   ❖   ❖

Stone Blue didn't budge.

While reject Unborn were incapable of aggression and violence towards other living beings, there was one exception: they could fight when the necessity arose to defend either themselves or innocents from death or serious harm, provided they followed the precept of doing no more damage than absolutely necessary – all except Stone Blue, who was too gentle a soul even for that.

So it just stood there looking down on the puny, terrifying human and doing the only thing it could: blocking the way and looking the human straight in the eyes, a feat that took every last ounce of courage it possessed. By the shocked expression on his face, the sorcerer had never looked into an Unborn's eyes before. He obviously didn't like what he saw there.

'I'm sorry, but I can't let you pass,' Stone Blue said meekly, its voice trembling with the enormity of the transgression.

The fact that an Unborn dared look him in the eyes and speak to him unbidden made Gracklin extremely angry, though what the thing said didn't even register at first. When it did, he gave a furious roar and raised his hands to blast the obstacle standing in his way into oblivion. Invisible to a Talent-less creature such as this Unborn, dark power arced and crackled from Gracklin's splayed fingers, questing, looking for some weakness he could exploit and inflate to terminal proportions. He experienced another shock when he found just how faulty the Unborn was, almost as if it had been made after a purposely flawed design. He was confused by how many weak points there were to choose from, enough to put him in danger of losing his concentration.

Settling on the heart, he struck the Unborn square in the chest.

Stone Blue stood fast, if only just.

The pain was enormous, crushing, final. The Unborn felt its heart stumble and flutter in its chest like a moth with burnt wings, and it knew it was dying. Strangely, in this last moment it remembered what the Wordlord had said about the Unborn's destiny, and healing. With a titanic effort, it pushed away the pain and fear, concentrating every fiber of its being on one single thing: the image of a blue stone falling from the skies to heal the earth and all beings that walked upon it.

In this image Stone Blue found surprising strength, and a measure of peace.

Gracklin couldn't believe what was happening.

Under the onslaught of the power he was expending, the damn thing should have long since disintegrated and melted into a puddle of sludge on the floor. Instead, it remained standing while some unforeseen, mysterious change occurring within its body. Far from collapsing in a soft, lifeless heap of malleable tissue, it seemed to be doing the exact opposite, inexplicably solidifying in some strange manner Gracklin couldn't even begin to fathom.

And all the while it was still looking at him with those dreadfully sad, compassionate eyes as the very fabric of its body turned from flesh to stone – blue stone, the exact color of a summer sky. Damn it all, he'd need a sledgehammer to get past the bloody thing! Best to…

With a sound like rock grinding on rock, a huge, sky-blue hand reached out and came to rest on Gracklin's shoulder. The sorcerer tried to scream, but the sound never made it out of his throat, which, along with the rest of him, was instantly and irreversibly transformed into hard, blue stone.

❖ ❖ ❖

Rain Seven and Three Flower, carrying the box between them, were first out the door. Gormin, close behind, immediately saw the guards and had the presence of mind to stay back out of sight, stopping the others and letting the door fall closed of its own accord.

'Well, well,' the larger and meaner-looking of the guards growled. 'What's this? Been stealing, have we? And now we're off to hide the loot, eh? Well, not before we've had our cut. Open up, and let's see what you've got there.'

'A deader from the dungeons,' Rain said. 'Forgotten in one of the back cells. Must have died days ago, judging by the state he's in. Last I heard, you boys like your meat fresh. Sorry to disappoint, but this one's a bit ripe. Midden heap is all he's good for.'

Stepping closer, the guard caught a whiff of rotten meat. 'Phew! More than a bit ripe, I'd say. Well, don't just stand there stinking up the place! Get the bloody thing out of here! And make sure you lock the postern gate when you're done. A few nights back, one of you idiots left it open for all the world to walk in and do as they pleased. And afterwards it's always us who catch the shit.'

He made to move away, then turned back.

'And what's to say you haven't got some stuff stashed in there with the stiff, huh? I've a mind to let you open up that box anyway, stink or no.'

'If that's what you want,' Rain said evenly, though its heart threatened to jump up its throat and its knees felt about to give out. 'You wouldn't by any chance have a crowbar on you? It's nailed shut.'

It was a bald-faced lie, but it worked.

'Come on,' the other guard said. 'Leave these losers to their loser job and let's get on with rounds. We're already running late.'

Rain and Three Flower made for the postern gate.

As soon as the guards were out of sight, the others joined them. Outside, they still had a few hundred paces to go until they reached their means of transportation, left out of earshot of the castle in the care of Once Green.

The two horses hitched to the wagon Gormin had come from Varakul in whickered nervously as they approached. The animals had no fear of reject Unborn, but the smell of rotting meat disturbed them. Once Green quieted them while the box was carefully loaded onto a bed of hay between barrels and sacks of stores procured by Stone Blue for the journey that lay ahead of them.

For it was clear that, even had they wished to, none of them could stay in Fellmere any longer. Kuruma's wrath when he returned and found the Oracle gone would be monumental, and the punishment he would mete out to all and sundry was something none of them wished to even contemplate.

Striving Four gently bedded the girl beside the box, covering her with a blanket, though she seemed warm enough. Gormin clambered onto the bench and took up the reins.

'Let's go,' he said, 'before those greedy guards have second thoughts.'

'But Stone Blue isn't here yet,' Counting Clouds said. 'We aren't leaving without him, are we?'

There was a moment of pained silence, then Rain said softly, 'I'm afraid Stone Blue isn't coming. If he was, he would have been here by now. He bought us precious time with whoever came down the stairs, but he paid a heavy price for it.'

'Oh,' Counting Clouds said with a strangled sob. 'I'll miss him so very much.'

'We all will,' Changing Grey said. 'And I'm sure it would make him glad to know it.'

'You said "he",' Striving Four observed once they were under way.

'What?' Counting Clouds said, confused.

'You said "he" just now, when you were speaking of Stone Blue. So did Rain.'

'Yes, we did,' Counting Clouds wondered. 'How strange.'

'Something's changed,' Rain said. 'Or rather, we are changing. Somehow I don't feel like an it anymore, I feel like a he, too.'

'So do I,' Changing Grey said, looking surprised.

Three Flower and Once Green nodded in agreement.

'It's called coming into your own,' Gormin said. 'It's a wonderful thing. And a bit scary too, am I right?'

'Well, in that case,' Counting Clouds said, 'I just want you all to know that I feel like a she.'

'She it is,' Rain said lightly. 'What about you, Striving Four? Any thoughts on the matter?'

'I'll let you know when I've figured it out,' the little Unborn said with a grin.

The first leg of their journey took them west across the plains of Tothmar, sorcerer territory still. All through the night, they traveled at a steady pace, slowing only to let the horses catch their wind. Striving Four and Counting Clouds, the smallest and weakest among them, took turns riding with Gormin on the wagon; the others trotted alongside. The flat, featureless landscape was lost in the dark, the marginally lighter ribbon of the road their only guide.

To Rain Seven, who had never been out of the shadow of Fellmere's walls, it felt as if they were enclosed in a tiny bubble of here-and-now while moving through a great, unbounded nothingness, anchored to the real world – if such a thing actually existed out there

– only by the sounds of their progress: the horses' occasional snorts and whickers and the softly thudding rhythm of their hooves; the small creaks and groans of the wagon's axles; the hiss of the iron-bound wheels rolling over the hard-baked, sandy dirt of the road; his own steady breathing and that of his companions running beside him.

The seldom-traveled road was dry and hardly rutted, allowing them to make good time. When the eastern sky began to lighten, they found to their relief – and and to Once Green's delight – and that they were not far from a copse of trees, hardly more than a pile of brush overgrown by brambles and sprouting a few dozen scraggly pines but enough to hide them from the eyes of passersby and a lone farm lying a good distance away on the far side of the road.

Gormin drove the wagon around behind the copse, where they unhitched and rubbed down the horses before seeing to their own needs. After watering them at a small brook that flowed by the copse, they hobbled the animals and let them graze, keeping an eye on them to make sure they didn't stray from cover. The Wordlord was safe in his box, but the girl had to be seen to.

'How are we going to feed her?' Striving Four asked in dismay. 'She's completely out of it.'

Rain, who had been responsible for her care ever since she'd fallen under the sorcerers' Binding, knew what to do. But first, she needed to be cleaned up. She'd soiled herself sometime during the night.

'Here,' Counting Clouds said, 'let me do that. I daresay that when she wakes up she'll be relieved to know that another girl has been taking care of her intimate needs. Striving, go get me some water. And you, Rain, take this' – she handed him the girl's bundled-up, dirty dress and shift – 'and wash it. Green, I need another blanket.'

And so it went, Clouds keeping everybody on their toes until she was satisfied the girl was clean and comfortable.

'I guess there really is something to this gender business,' Striving Four said to Rain when they met by the brook. 'I mean, women *are* different, aren't they? At least judging by Clouds and the way she's got everybody jumping. Can't tell about the rest of them yet.'

'You may be on to something there,' Rain said. 'Though I have a feeling it might not be a good idea to put it to her that way.'

For themselves, there was a frugal meal of bread, hard cheese and water, but they were accustomed to simple fare, and after the night's exertions it seemed like a feast. After they had eaten, Rain Seven belatedly remembered that they should post a lookout, in case they were being followed. Once Green volunteered for the first shift, saying that with so many trees around he couldn't go right to sleep in any case. The others lay down to rest.

Gormin remained sitting where he was, staring into the middle distance with a look of such sadness and dejection that Rain was moved to go and sit beside him.

'Gormin,' he said, softly so as not to wake the others. 'What ails you? Aren't you glad to be away from Varakul and the breeding caves?'

Gormin sighed. 'I wish it were that simple. For you it is. But I carry a weight on my shoulders that doesn't grow lighter with distance.'

'What is this weight?' Rain asked. 'Is it sadness for something you left behind?'

'On the contrary. It's something I cannot leave behind: guilt. I've done terrible things, Rain. I betrayed my own kind by working for the sorcerers, for no other reason than to save my worthless little life. And I betrayed them a second time, and the sorcerers to boot, trying to right the first wrong I'd done. I fear I only made things worse.'

'What did you do?'

'One out of every ten Unborn is a reject. Why do you think that is? Because that's just how it works out? No, it's because I purposely designed a faulty process, thinking that if I had to make an army for those evil men, then it should at least be a smaller one than they wished for.

'And that's not the worst of it. Thanks to me, our warrior brethren are flawed as well, though neither they not the sorcerers suspect it – nor will they until it's too late. And we, the rejects, are doubly flawed. You can thank me for that, Rain. Me alone. And here I am, wishing I were one of you, innocent and worthy of your friendship. I'm disgusted by myself.'

Rain was silent for a time, mulling over what Gormin had said.

'I can't see the wrong in what you've done,' he finally said. 'You strove for the best answer to an impossible situation, one you were cast into by no choice of your own. The Wordlord said that even the sorcerers might become unwitting instruments of the Creator. Well, I see you as another of His instruments, only one that strove for good from the beginning.

'I think you have much more cause to blame Him for putting you in such a lousy position than He has reason to fault you for not coming up with the perfect solution. As I see it, I am no more innocent than you are guilty. You are one of us, and I count you a friend, which is why I dare offer you something you won't allow yourself: an Unborn name. You strive to right what you perceive as wrong, and you wish to leave the dark behind and better yourself. "Aspiring White" seems like a name that might fit you. What do you say?'

Gormin laid a malformed hand on Rain's arm and pressed it long and hard. If their kind had been able to cry, Rain reckoned, there would have been tears in the little Unborn's eyes.

'Thank you, my friend,' Gormin finally said. 'Thank you. I will think about what you've said. Now get some rest. You have a long walk behind you and a longer one ahead – provided they aren't already hot on out trail, about to catch up with us.'

'No,' Rain said. 'I don't feel that they are. I believe we will succeed.'

'You may be right,' Gormin said, nodding. 'You may well be right. We'll know soon enough. If we manage to reach the sanctuary of the western mountains without being caught, we might actually stand a fighting chance.'

They continued to travel by night and lie up during the day in whatever sheltered spot they could find at first light. Days passed without any sign of pursuit, and slowly their hopes began to rise.

The first few days on the road brought sore joints and aching muscles, but gradually the aches and pains faded as the constant exercise began to take effect. Even Counting Clouds and Striving Four took to walking longer and longer stretches. By the time they reached the foothills of the mountains after almost three weeks on the road, they had all lost what little fat they'd carried and become lean and fit.

Before their departure from Fellmere, Striving Four had managed to get a look at a map in Kuruma's study. He'd copied as much as he could and added the rest from memory, faithfully reproducing the lines and every letter of the words he couldn't read. Gormin, who could, said that the mountains looming ahead of them were called the Hag's Teeth.

Seeing their jagged, broken silhouettes in the distance, Rain thought they were aptly named. A long disused and forgotten pass lay somewhere ahead. On its far side, the Great Desert awaited them. The prospect of traveling into the desert should have filled them with trepidation but, just as none of them had ever seen a forest, they had only the vaguest notion of what awaited them beyond the mountains.

Besides, of the three ways leading out of Tothmar this was the only one that stood open to them. Following Kuruma's army north obviously wasn't an option, and taking a ship from the port of Rannon, where the Black Priests did business and were well known and better feared, was equally out of the question. Not only would they have needed the means to buy passage on a ship, but also a group of Unborn traveling on their own and transporting a mysterious box would have immediately raised suspicions and in all probability gotten them thrown into Rannon's slave pens, there to await the arrival of the next sorcerer from Fellmere coming to buy fresh meat.

Lawlessness and corruption were rife in Rannon, and they might have bought and bribed their way out but, plentiful as gold was in Fellmere, it was the one thing the sorcerers kept securely locked away and out of reach of even the most enterprising Unborn.

So the Hag's Teeth and the desert it was.

They took the wagon as far as conditions allowed.

Finally they reached a point where the road narrowed to a mule track. Here they made camp in a large, dry cave they found nearby. The horses they kept, hoping the pass would prove negotiable for them; the wagon, once unloaded, was taken apart and used for firewood.

They had water from a nearby stream, there was ample pasture for the horses, and their supplies, if carefully husbanded, should last them for many weeks.

They decided not to risk carrying the box and its precious contents through the mountains on paths that might well turn out to be dangerous or even altogether impassable, so they settled down to wait until the Wordlord was ready to emerge from his chrysalis and sufficiently recuperated after to walk on his own two feet.

If Gormin's modified procedure worked. He seemed confident that it would, though he steadfastly refused to let anyone else look inside the box, saying that this was a very delicate and private time for the Wordlord, and that when he awoke he surely wouldn't be happy to know he'd been the object of everyone's idle curiosity. Rain accepted the argument, contenting himself with daily prayers to the Creator for the Wordlord's wellbeing.

Praying was a novelty for him, and he had no idea if he was going about it in the right way, or if it made any sense at all for an Unborn to pray – or if there was even anyone listening. He'd gotten the notion of a benign, creative force at work in the world from certain things the Wordlord had said, though whether such a force might concern itself with a creature such as himself seemed doubtful to Rain. He prayed anyway, and hoped for the best.

❖   ❖   ❖

Back in Fellmere, luck was on the fugitives' side.

Since Rain Seven and Changing Grey had done alternating twelve-hour shifts guarding in the tract for special prisoners, and since there was no reason to assume they weren't still doing so, nobody noticed anything amiss down there.

Days passed before a halfhearted search began in the castle's upper regions for Gracklin, who seemed to have gone missing. A week went by before anyone thought to look in the dungeons. Truth be told, nobody was all that intent on finding him.

When they finally did discover the sorcerer down in the castle's bowels, turned to a statue of blue stone – and together with an Unborn, no less – there was much righteous gloating, vitriolic whispering, and malicious sniggering over the stupid old fart who'd apparently gotten his spells mixed up and shot himself in the foot, so to speak. He was soon given the posthumous nickname 'The Stone Killer', though the look of abject terror preserved on his face left them all with a vague sense of unease, which they tried to gloss over with ever more silly and disrespectful jokes.

With Gracklin terminally stalled, there was no full Brother left to supervise the novices. When they eventually got it through their heads that authority was now a long way off and not likely to return any time soon, discipline began to slip, hesitantly at first and then in a downhill rush that the few conscientious Minors who even tried were powerless to stem. Not long, and they broke out the wine, the drugs, and the female prisoners, and with hardly a thought to the future proceeded to have themselves a jolly good time.

One drunken night, someone had the brilliant idea to round up six of the strongest Unborn and have them haul the petrified pair up the stairs and into the courtyard, where thy made a very fine set of fountain figures in the big trough used for watering the horses.

A few days later, a bleary-eyed novice passing the fountain early one morning after a night of pleasant but strenuous debauchery noted a strange detail: due perhaps to some weirdly placed fault lines in the stone, water was seeping from both figures in certain places.

In no time at all, someone had come up with the perfect title for the new piece of artwork decorating the courtyard. From that day on, it was referred to as 'The Pissing Contest'.

There are said to exist several Gates on Vereld, and though their exact number remains unknown, it appears that each leads to a different destination, none of which is on Vereld itself. That is to say, no two Gates on Vereld are connected to each other. Lore has it that the first Gate was discovered by the mage Greytower more than a thousand years before the writing of this account. Reputedly, immediately upon discovering the Gate he disguised and hid it in a most ingenious way, and so prevented it from falling into the hands of the Dark Side.

Alas, soon after, the Dark Side came to possess a Gate of its own. Although no exact or detailed knowledge exists concerning the present actions and machinations of the Dark Side, one may assume with a large degree of confidence that, as ever, this Gate is being put to no favorable use.

Carric Three Suns, The Secret History of Magic

11 Bonesend

ano guided his mount around a man-high boulder, brutally jerking on the reins. He was seething with anger, and something had to suffer, if only the stupid horse. For three weeks, things had gone as well as could be expected with an army of more than three thousand on the move, and they'd made reasonably good time: a week from Fellmere to the foot of the mountains, another two to negotiate the southern end of the pass. The ancient road was in surprisingly good condition, and clearing the few

rockfalls and minor landslides they encountered hardly held them up at all. When they topped out on the plateau's southern rim and saw the perfectly flat plain stretching north all the way to the horizon, they expected to cross it in a matter of days.

That estimate held for less than half a day. From there on, the landscape and the road were littered with rocks and boulders of all sizes as if giants had tossed them about in huge handfuls, scattering them all over the plain. As if that wasn't difficulty enough, at intervals the road abruptly ended, sheered off by titanic forces that seemed to have shifted and displaced whole tracts of the plain. Shallow, rubble-filled trenches that must have once been deep cracks and yawning chasms delineated the ancient fault lines criss-crossing the plateau.

Kuruma, the little rat, had seen fit to put Tano in command of the vanguard, which in plain words meant he was responsible for clearing away the mess so the bloody supply wagons could get through. Traveling far ahead of the main force with a hundred Unborn, Tano oversaw the removal of sometimes dauntingly large obstacles from their path, and spent endless hours ranging through the stony waste, searching for the next piece of road and determining how best to connect it to the previous stretch.

It was lowly, humiliating work for the man who was second in strength and second in command and should by rights have been comfortably ensconced in the main camp, enjoying its conveniences and planning their general strategy while waiting for someone else to finish the dirty work.

For nearly a month now, he'd been slogging through this void-damned vastness, and in that time he'd come to thoroughly hate the place, especially the bloody wind that sighed and groaned across the plain almost incessantly from sunup to sundown, drying out the mucous membranes of eyes, nose, and throat until they became chronically irritated and penetrating even the thickest cloak with cold, relentlessly prying fingers.

Cursing Kuruma for the ten thousandth time, Tano shifted uncomfortably in the saddle as the horse gingerly picked its way over the rocky terrain. Kuruma's strategy of divide and conquer was totally transparent – first leaving Gracklin behind alone in Fellmere, and now keeping Tano away from the army and the rest of the Brothers – but that didn't make it any less effective.

And it made sense. Oh yes, it made a lot of sense if you stood in Kuruma's shoes. Tano wanted into those shoes, wanted into them badly. Given half a chance, he'd cut the man presently wearing them off at the knees in the blink of an eye, before parting him from his head for good measure. Time was on his side, he told himself, as was this stupid campaign of Kuruma's.

Already they were far behind schedule. It was the beginning of August, and if things continued to move as slowly as the did now they stood a fair chance of getting bogged down by an early snowfall, maybe even stuck in Larnakis for the winter. That would put a nice dent in Kuruma's claim to leadership, and it would give Tano time he could put to good use. Sooner or later his moment would come, and it would be Kuruma's last, of that he would make sure.

The horse stumbled, and Tano gave another sharp tug on the reins. Stupid beast wasn't paying attention. Looking up, something on the horizon caught his eye. It was far too tall and angular to be a boulder, even a very large one. It must have been hidden by one of the almost imperceptible swells in the terrain, for it seemed nearer than it should be without him having noticed it earlier.

Could it be…? Yes! It was man-made, a building. A tower, by the looks of it. And huge, as far as he could tell from this distance. Was it an enemy outpost, a first, advanced bulwark against invading forces? He needed to find out. Even the smallest bit of information he possessed and Kuruma didn't could give him the edge he needed. He looked back at the two battle-Unborn following him on foot. What to do? Play it safe and turn back to collect a larger force? Or go on with these two and rely on their small number remaining undetected? He decided to go on.

An hour later, he was as close to the building as he dared go on horseback. Dismounting, he left the animal in the lee of a group of boulders, reins tied around a good-sized rock. A few steps farther on, he found a vantage point from where he could see the tower clearly. It was indeed enormous, and exuded a dark menace. He was beginning to wonder if it had anything at all to do with the enemy. Something about the huge spire of black stone seemed familiar, tugging at some memory he didn't even recall possessing but that nonetheless insistently beckoned him on. He stepped onto a knee-high rock for a better view, and a thrill of excitement ran through him.

For the first time, he could see the pair of slender columns and the squat, black monolith standing opposite the tower's entrance. He felt like letting out an exultant yell – almost did – for there was no more mistaking what he'd found. With no further thought to concealment, he ordered the Unborn to stay where they were and strode towards the tower, for he was certain now that this was a place the enemy would not go near willingly, much less use it as an outpost or stronghold. This was ancient sorcerer territory, forgotten maybe, but never lost.

Up close, the standing stones gave off a low hum like a stationary swarm of hornets. The air was charged with the force emanating from the black stone, sending a tingling over Tano's skin and raising the hairs on his arms.

He drew off one leather riding glove and held a bare palm over the surface of the monolith. The crackling rush of power nearly blasted him off his feet.

Yes! Oh, yes! Here was all the ancient Dark Lore preserved, just waiting to be understood and used. This was true sorcery, worlds away from the amateur dabblings of a Kuruma and his likes. Compared to this, their puny advances and achievements seemed like the feckless games of children, their grandiose ideas and plans like the irrelevant stuttering of halfwits.

Only here and now did Tano begin to comprehend how much knowledge had been lost since the end of the Great Age when sorcery had ruled supreme on Vereld, before the enemy banded together and forced the Dark Side to its knees, breaking up the Brotherhood and almost succeeding in eradicating it altogether. But here it still was, ready to raise them again to true glory. And he, Tano, had discovered it. He knew in his bones that everything he needed to unseat Kuruma and gain unprecedented power for himself was in these stones and in the tower, and first and foremost he had to make sure that Kuruma didn't get his dirty little hands on this treasure trove.

A quick tour through the tower – it took him well over an hour, the thing was that big – confirmed his wildest expectations. Among many other things that made his blood sing with anticipation, Tano found what turned out to be a controlling device for the monolith in a small chamber on the ground floor. With a little experimenting and a few trips back and forth between the chamber and the stones, he managed to power down the big black stone. His finely honed sorcerous senses told him that the force collected in the stone was transferred to some kind of reservoir beneath the tower, where so much of it was already stored that he could have probably ripped all of Vereld in two with it, had he known how to use it and been so inclined.

When he was done, he locked the chamber door with a spell that bloody Kuruma would have given an arm and a leg to know, a spell that left no discernible trace of when, how, and by whom it had been made. For all Kuruma would know, it could have been in place since the Breaking of the Brotherhood, or since the dawn of time.

Having made sure there were no side doors or windows that might serve as entry points, Tano proceeded to the tower's main entrance, heaved shut the tall bronze doors and sealed them from outside with another spell.

There! All his now. Kuruma could rave and rant and try every single spell he knew on the doors. He would only break his teeth on them. Should have studied harder and left no page unturned, like Tano had done. Instead, the pompous, self-satisfied little bugger had relied on his innate strength alone – a big mistake in the face of all the knowledge and power to be gained not only from a site like this

196

but waiting in places like Fellmere's library as well, to be discovered in bits and pieces and assembled into relevancy by the diligent and the persevering.

Tano felt like laughing out loud. He was well aware that Kuruma thought him boorish and a bit simple-minded, and he'd done everything he could to subtly reinforce that dangerous misconception, even to the point of demeaning himself. Now his strategy was finally paying off. Kuruma, thinking to have Tano out of the way and in a position of weakness, had unwittingly achieved the exact opposite, giving his worst enemy an advantage and tripping himself up in the process.

Hilarious!

Very satisfied with his day's work, Tano returned to his provisional forward base, and for the first time in over a month didn't feel cheated out of the amenities of the main camp, nor envious of those who were in a position to enjoy them. Though they didn't know it yet, a volcano was set to erupt under their softly cushioned arses, courtesy of Tano. Pity he didn't have more time alone with the tower. Suddenly he would have given much to be able to spend another week or two up on the blasted plateau. But alas, together with the tower they'd also reached the high plain's northern rim, and from here on the way looked to be clear.

As was only to be expected, upon seeing the tower Kuruma managed to style himself the discoverer of this grandest of all monuments of sorcery, graciously accepting the thanks and admiration of his arse-kissing colleagues. But, to Tano's unending satisfaction, he could do nothing with his glorious find.

A quick peek through the Gate revealed nothing but a circular clearing in a forest that could have been anywhere and at first sight held no great promise. The only tangible result of this piece of daring reconnaissance, delegated by Kuruma to one of the Minors – surprise, surprise – was that it gave the man a screaming headache.

Kuruma nonetheless made it out to be a revelation they would study in depth once they had successfully concluded their campaign in Larnakis. As for the tower itself, Tano's spells had Kuruma stymied. In the end he ranted and raved a bit in front of the great doors and tried a few spells on them, but he was so intent on his little war that his heart wasn't really in the exercise.

And he was so full of himself, Tano observed with an inward smirk, that he didn't even think to ask anyone's advice or help – not that he'd have gotten any from Tano. Apparently, what the great Kuruma couldn't do, no one could.

They marched on, leaving the riddle of the tower for the return trip.

At the plateau's very edge, where a muleteer's trail dipped down towards the lower-lying valleys and the heart of Larnakis, they came upon the remains of a small, hastily abandoned camp. A few embers still glowed in the banked fire pit, and Kuruma dispatched a mixed squad of lean, long-legged Unborn scouts and heavy battle-Unborn to hunt down and eliminate the camp's recently departed occupants. No need to let the enemy receive an early warning of their arrival.

A few leagues on, they caught up with the members of the squad, busy gorging themselves on the flesh of two ponies. They'd taken three human prisoners. Kuruma let the Unborn finish their meal while he interrogated the prisoners. The men were resolutely tight-lipped, and Kuruma seemed more interested in wielding the whip than in getting them to talk. Shortly, with Kuruma none the wiser, they were chained to the other human resources brought from Fellmere's dungeons, and the army moved on.

Tano thought that he himself would have preferred to take more time with the prisoners, trying a bit harder to gain some maybe vital information about what awaited them down the road. But that was Kuruma for you: overbearing, arrogant, and always in a hurry that bordered on the reckless.

Another week saw them out of the pass and into the great central valley of Larnakis, and it was here they encountered the first resistance.

At the first river crossing they came to, the hanging bridge had been removed, the boards neatly stacked on the other side, and a volley of arrows greeted those who went to investigate. A small group of Larnaki peasants was positioned on the far bank, shouting and jeering whenever a well-aimed shot found its mark.

Kuruma ordered the mercenaries to bring up a company of archers. The battle-Unborn were very good at cutting and hacking, ripping and rending, but close to useless with a bow. To Kuruma's anger and frustration his counter-move showed no effect other than persuading the enemy to take better cover, from where they continued to pick off his men with unerring, fatal precision. If this was how good the farmers were with bow and arrows, Tano mused, watching from a safe distance, he didn't much look forward to coming within range of their soldiers.

He noticed a low-order novice, Tinner or Finner or whatever his name was, heading straight towards him. That could only mean one thing: Kuruma needed him to wade into the shit again. Breathing hard in the thin air, the harsh, high-altitude sunlight reflecting off the sheen of sweat slicking his shaven, tattooed skull like a badly misplaced halo, the young man struggled up the slope to where Tano stood.

'Sir,' he panted. 'Lord Kuruma wishes to speak to you.'

Tano could see Kuruma farther along the slope, standing on a rare piece of even ground in front of his hastily erected command tent and looking in Tano's direction.

'Does he now? As you can see, I'm taking a break. Why don't you go tell Lord Kuruma that you simply couldn't find me anywhere.'

Seeing Rinner blanch and glance over to where Kuruma stood watching, Tano gave a dirty laugh. 'Don't piss yourself. Just joking.'

He made his way over to the command post.

Kuruma didn't bother with a greeting. 'Get rid of them,' he said, pointing across the river.

'And how am I supposed to do that?' Tano asked. 'Swim over and ask them nicely to leave?'

'Void's sake, man, do I have to spell *everything* out to *everyone* around here?' Kuruma barked, his eyes showing the fevered, manic glitter of dangerously over-strung nerves.

Good, Tano thought. *String them tighter. Give the screw another turn. Pour on the pressure. Play dumb. Rub in the fact that he does have to see to everything himself if he wants anything done at all, that he's alone with the burden of command and responsibility. Isolate him, let the stress build, and sooner or later he just might do you the favor of cracking all by himself.*

200

'Send the scouts to find a ford, take whatever force you need, go around and roll them up from behind,' Kuruma said with exasperated patience. 'Do you think you can manage that? Not too hard for you, is it? Good, then get going. I don't want to sit here all day twiddling my thumbs.'

Yes you do, Tano wanted to say. *Sitting here in safety and keeping that soft, pink flesh of yours out of harm's way while someone else does the dirty work is* exactly *how you want it, you conniving, pussy-arsed son of gutter snake and a rat turd.*

Instead he said, 'Right, I'll see what I can do, then,' and went to find and organize his troops.

After some searching they found a fordable spot. Here too, there were Larnaki bowmen waiting on the far bank, and Tano's troops took considerable losses crossing over. When they reached the other side, the enemy had vanished. It was the same at the site of the dismantled bridge: not a single Larnaki to be found. What they did find were the rolled-up bridge cables, which it turned out had been detached from the anchoring posts in an orderly fashion, rather than cut. That was one piece of good news, and a grievous mistake on the enemy's part. In short order, mercenary engineers and reject Unborn were busy putting the bridge back into place.

This was how things continued to go.

There were several rivers to cross on their way into the heart of Larnakis, and they had to fight for every crossing and rebuild every bridge. Since the bridges were made to size for the Larnaki's small carts and ponies, they also had to unload and take apart the big supply wagons and lug them and the provisions as well as every piece of equipment across the swaying bridges while the horses, balking at the sight of the narrow strip of planks suspended over the deep, were forded across in another spot, often miles away up or down the river.

Once they even had to build rafts to ferry everything across, including the two huge, ironbound boxes whose contents only Kuruma knew and fussed over like they were some great treasure. Most of the villages and farms they found were abandoned, and they made few prisoners. Kuruma had every building put to the torch, leaving a trail of smoking ruins in their wake. And he personally took out his mounting frustration on the Larnaki prisoners under the guise of 'questioning' them, a process in which a nail-studded cat o' nine tails played a far more important role than answers, which he didn't get in any case.

Food was shaping up to be another problem. The fleeing Larnaki had destroyed the crops not already harvested, leaving nothing edible behind. The army was totally dependent on their supply line reaching all the way back to Fellmere, meaning that at any given time there had to be scores of wagons on the move. They took to leaving a few wagons between the bridges so they could serve to relay supplies without having to be dismantled and transported across every time. But the goods still had to be transferred by hand, and it meant leaving battle-Unborn to accompany and guard them, depleting their fighting force. And, wherever the terrain presented a possibility, they unfailingly became the targets of arrows that seemed to fly out of nowhere, always with the same, deadly accuracy. Kuruma sent out scouting party after scouting party, but not once did they return with an enemy combatant, dead or alive. Quite a few scouts went missing though, and Kuruma's mood continued to darken while his temper became ever more volatile and unpredictable.

Except for the fact that it was mostly himself who got stuck with the fighting, Tano couldn't have been happier with the way things were going. It wasn't as if he was actually at any great risk. He took care to direct operations from well outside the range of the Larnaki's bows, leaving the dangerous stuff to those who were either made or paid for it.

It was slow going and the second half of August by the time they reached what according to Kuruma's maps was the last major crossing that lay between them and Larnakis' capital Sirida.

This time, the bridge was intact but useless all the same, a mockery. Instead of the usual rag-tag band of peasants, there was an army awaiting them on the other side. And Tano's misgivings about Larnaki military archers were swiftly and bloodily confirmed. Not only did they use longbows that gave them nearly twice the range of the peasants' homemade weapons; they were also, if anything, even more accurate shots. By the time Kuruma's army had gotten the message, almost thirty mercenaries and a few Unborn lay dead, as well as a Minor and three novices who seemed to have still believed that the whole outing was an extended sightseeing tour with a certain thrill factor thrown in for their benefit, and had been right there in the first line where the death toll reached close to a hundred percent.

This is where things get interesting, Tano thought. He was curious to see how Kuruma would handle the situation now that it had turned serious. He would stick around and see for himself, if only to keep his ass covered in case by some incredible stroke of luck Kuruma won.

But he had alternative plans ready. At the first sign that things were about to go belly-up, he would discreetly and quietly retreat back up the pass and install himself in the Black Tower. No army could threaten him there, and he would have all the time he needed to study and learn the tower's secrets.

Then, the world would be his.

To Tano's surprise, Kuruma came up with a strategy that actually made sense, though part of it was luck dealing him the cards he needed. The scouts found a ford half a league upriver, and another one even closer in the other direction. They set up camp as if they were planning to dig in for a while, and waited for nightfall. Under cover of darkness, they began to move.

Leaving only a token force at the bridgehead, arranged to look larger than it actually was with the help of numerous campfires, Kuruma sent Tano upriver with half of the remaining force, including a score of Brothers. Tonight, they all wore chainmail under their black robes. They were about to earn their keep.

Kuruma himself led the other half downriver.

At the ford, Tano sent a scout across. As expected, the enemy had the site covered. It would be the same at Kuruma's end.

Setting up battle formation in the dark and as stealthily as possible was nerve-wracking and time-consuming work. Tano began by having twenty-one battle-Unborn specially trained for this maneuver and carrying eight-foot shields form two sides of a triangle, its tip pointing towards the enemy.

Inside the triangle, another twenty Unborn armed with pikes were placed at the interstices, ready to turn the shield wall into a porcupine in an instant. Another row with shields held overhead protected the whole formation from high-arcing arrows. Inside this defensive perimeter, thirteen Brothers made a Wedge – again two sides of a triangle, with six sorcerers to a side and the strongest, Tano, at the tip.

It was not a position Tano relished.

Though he would have the accumulated power of twelve Brothers to draw on and direct, it also meant trusting and relying on them to stay in formation and hold up their end of the deal. If either side of the line was broken and the balance upset, the power could – and probably would – turn back on the wielder, in this case Tano, and those still connected to him, frying their brains and nervous systems to a crisp. Breaking the line in a Wedge without prior warning was a time-tested move open to sorcerers who wanted to get rid of a colleague too strong for them to confront one on one.

Tano's insurance was that quite probably none of them would get out of Larnakis alive if they messed up this operation, and they all knew it.

Briefly, he wondered whether that knowledge would be enough of a deterrent to those working with Kuruma. As much as he wanted the man gone, this might be an awkward time to lose him.

Right behind the Wedge Tano placed his remaining sorcerers and a score of shield-bearing Unborn as backup. Bodra, a stout, fussily pedantic Brother with a single black beetle brow and teeth filed to needle points, was responsible for the two dozen sacrifices whose blood and life force would be spilled as needed to sustain the dark magic. Tano had the rest of his force assemble in the lee of the Wedge in alternating lines of battle-Unborn shield rows and mercenary archers. Behind those came the pikes and horse. During the crossing they were constricted by the narrow ford, but as soon as they reached the far bank those in the rear would move up and spread out on either side of the Wedge.

Downriver, Kuruma would be mirroring Tano's every move.

Just before first light, when everything was to Tano's satisfaction, he took his own place at the tip of the Wedge. On his command, the power from twelve Brothers strong in the dark magic flowed to him in a giddy rush. Immediately clamping down on it, he waited for the first, woozily eye-crossing effects to pass. Then he gave the order to advance.

The drummers broke the predawn silence with a roll that startled even Tano, who'd known it was coming. Then they fell into a slow, bone-shivering beat, a deep, booming shout of menace that carried easily across the mist-wreathed water.

Beat by beat, step by step, they moved forward, fused together into one great, lumbering, deadly beast. When the first volley of arrows thunked and clanked against the shield-wall, Tano prepared to loose the magic.

❖   ❖   ❖

God has seen your tears and heard your prayers. Fear not, the child will die.

Grigori Rasputin

12 Larnakis

eclining in the private sitting room of his house in Sirida after a long day's work, Anskar watched in quiet fascination as Rupili breast-fed their two month-old daughter Anili. It wasn't as if he hadn't seen babies before – he was godfather to scores of them, actually – but to him they'd been mysterious bundles in their mothers' arms, little things that had the power to command everyone's rapt attention with a gurgle or a squall, or a whiff of dirty diapers. He had never understood how perfectly sane, well-balanced adults could be driven to starry-eyed admiration and embarrass themselves with ecstatic cooing and foolish antics at the smallest whim of such a tiny being.

Now, naturally, all that had changed. Surely this was because his daughter was quite different from all those other babies: more beautiful, more perfect, more interesting – more everything, come to think of it.

He noticed Rupili looking at him with an amused smile, and wondered whether he'd been wearing that mooncalf look he'd seen on the faces of so many young fathers. Quickly, he rearranged his expression into something more intelligent.

Rupili laughed – softly, so as not to disturb Anili, who seemed to be suckling with a vengeance, to judge by her busy gulping and small, satisfied grunts.

'Don't even try, love,' Rupili said. 'You're entirely smitten, admit it.'

Damn, but the woman could read him like a book.

'Guilty,' he said. 'Twice smitten, actually. With two such beautiful women in my life, I'll have to double my offerings to the gods, else they become jealous.'

'Hush,' Rupili said, only half joking. 'Don't give them ideas.'

'Wouldn't want that, would we?' Anskar leaned over and caressed the soft, blond down on Anili's head. With the light hair and the pink complexion, she too seemed to be taking after his Dunmarkan grandmother. But he could already see that she had her mother's beauty and dark eyes, though rounder, the almond shape less pronounced. He could have sworn that Anili purred for a moment. With the tip of his finger he touched the back of one tiny hand, balled up in blissful concentration. Immediately and with surprising strength for one so little, her miniscule fingers opened and grasped his, holding on as if she intended never to let go again.

'She's strong, this one,' he told Rupili. 'If I didn't know better, I'd say what we have here is a sturdy boy who will one day grow up to be a fierce warrior.'

'And who says girls can't become warriors?' Rupili said. 'Just because men excel at something doesn't mean that women can't be good at it too.'

'I stand corrected.' Anskar chuckled. 'With her mother as an example, how can she become anything less than a great and fearsome fighter, the bane of all who wish Larnakis ill?'

'Oh, you!' Rupili scoffed, but he could see that she was secretly pleased.

There was a knock on the door, and Soonil looked in, as usual without waiting for an answer.

'The captain is waiting for you in the study,' she informed Anskar. She seemed flushed and out of breath, a fact he could see hadn't escaped his wife either. 'He says it's urgent. And there's a boy with him.'

Anskar felt a pang of unease. Only a serious matter would bring Baran round at this late hour. Rupili grasped his arm and gave it a small, apprehensive squeeze.

'Well,' he said. 'Let's see what it's about, then. Don't worry, love. I'm sure we'll have it sorted in no time, whatever it is.'

She let go of his arm and gave it a pat. 'Go. I'll see you later. And see that Baran behaves himself with the girls. Lately, every time he's been here they've had their heads on backwards for hours after. Tell him that from now on I'll hold him responsible for every spilled cup, broken plate, and over-cooked dinner in this household.'

Anskar laughed. 'I'm sure he'll be duly terrified,' he said, and left for the study.

His heart sank when he saw the expressions of the visitors waiting for him. Soonil had lit candles and started a fire in the hearth. This late in summer, the nights were growing noticeably colder.

He recognized the boy immediately: Dorting, son of Durpa the bone gatherer, who had found and brought him the stone bowl still resting in a box in this very room for all his good intentions to take it

209

to the abbot.

Dorting seemed both heartbroken and completely exhausted. There were dark rings under his eyes as if he hadn't slept in days, and Anskar saw where tears had washed lighter channels through the dirt and grime on his cheeks. The boy was just barely holding himself together.

'Dorting,' Anskar said. 'Come, sit.' He placed a gentle hand on the boy's shoulder, guiding him to the cushions laid out along the wide stone rim of the fireplace. Dorting was trembling with fatigue.

Baran, looking frighteningly grim, new and unaccustomed worry lines sitting uneasily on his normally sanguine features, remained standing.

'Radj,' he said. 'I see you've already met Dorting, son of Durpa. He's come all the way from Bonesend with dire news. It would seem we're being invaded by a large force from the south. He says he saw a great army of men and strange, man-like creatures approaching Blacktower, where they paused for a few hours before moving on towards the rim and the descent into Larnakis. This was ten days ago. By now the enemy are probably well into our territory.'

He was interrupted by Soonil bringing fresh tea, bread, and a large bowl of the evening's soup reheated with a generous garnishing of meat for the boy.

'The poor thing looks like he's starving,' she said with a defiant look directed at Anskar, clearly prepared to refute any criticism of her unauthorized initiative.

'Thank you, Soonil,' he said mildly. 'The care you show our guests does great credit to this house.'

She left looking very satisfied with herself.

Dorting ate like a wolf.

When the worst of the boy's hunger was stilled, Anskar spoke. It was obvious that Dorting needed a bed even worse than food, but Anskar required answers from him now, before sleep overwhelmed him. Already the boy's eyelids were beginning to droop.

'Dorting,' Anskar said. 'Please tell me exactly what you saw on Bonesend.'

'My cousin Jalme and I were out looking for bones,' Dorting said. 'It was just the two of us that afternoon. In the morning, my uncle Ügmen fell and hurt his leg. My father and Jalme's brother Pasong helped him back to camp, and they didn't come out again that day.

'We were collecting from a trove we'd found inside a ring of high boulders, so we didn't notice them until they were already close. Then we heard them. They were clearing the old road, moving rocks and making a lot of noise. We looked, but carefully, so they wouldn't see us. There were many huge man-beasts handling big rocks, tossing them aside like they were pebbles. They were very strong, stronger than any man. We were frightened when we saw them, but then the black man on the horse came, and he scared us worse than the others. He made us want to jump up and run away. But we didn't, because then he would have caught us for sure.'

'What exactly did this man look like?' Anskar asked, although he feared he already knew the answer.

'He was dressed all in black,' Dorting said. 'He was bald, and when he leaned forward in the saddle to talk to one of the man-beasts I saw that he had a sign on the top of his head, like this.' With the tip of his finger he drew a familiar symbol in the cold ashes at the edge of the fire: a twisted cross, exactly like the one Anskar had seen on

211

the head of the dead man they'd found by the Yangan river.

'Scouts,' he said, looking at Baran. 'They were spying on us.'

The captain understood immediately, and nodded. 'My thought exactly,' he said. 'I should have seen it then.'

'How could you? None of us did, not even Tönden.'

But Baran was not to be moved. 'It's my job, not Tönden's,' he said grimly. 'My responsibility. I missed it.'

Anskar let it go for the moment.

'What else can you tell us?' he asked the boy.

During Anskar's exchange with Baran, Dorting had been repeatedly smoothing over the symbol he'd drawn in the ashes with quiet intensity, as if trying to erase from existence all that it stood for.

'When the road was clear, the rest of them came. There were many more of the beasts, and at least ten hands of men like the one on the horse. And there were other men, soldiers, maybe half of them on foot and the other half on horseback. They passed by where we were hiding, all of them headed for Blacktower. It took hours for all of them to pass. We wanted to run to our camp and warn the others. But the army was between us and them, so we had to wait.'

'That was wise of you,' Anskar said, 'and very brave. Even a grown warrior couldn't have done better.'

That woke the boy up some, and got an approving nod from Baran. Praise from the Radj bestowed honor and good fortune on the recipient and was treasured like an heirloom in Larnaki families, often for generations. The boy had earned it twice and three times over.

'I know this is a hard question to answer,' Anskar said, 'seeing as you probably had other things on your mind than counting enemies.

212

But do you think you could give me at least a rough estimate of how many there were?'

'We thought it might be important,' Dorting said. 'So we counted them as best we could. And it gave us something to do while we were waiting. I counted the man-beasts, and Jalme the men. I counted more than twice a hundred double hands of beasts, and Jalme eight times ten double hands of men. Plus the black men, ten hands. And they had prisoners, about fifty of them.'

'Two thousand of the beasts,' Anskar said. 'Eight hundred men, and fifty in black. Very good. We have an excellent scout here, captain. You might want to think about offering him a job before someone else does. Now, I don't want to offend a man who counts so well, but I do need to ask. Are you sure it was only ten days since you saw all this? It seems hardly possible to make the journey in so short a time.'

'Ten days,' Dorting confirmed, raising both hands to display all ten fingers. 'I'm sure. My father...' He faltered, his eyes filling with tears.

'I'm sorry,' Anskar said softly.
'You're worried for him, and for your uncle and cousins. I should have asked earlier. Tell me what happened.'

'When we finally reached our camp and told them what was going on, my father went to see for himself. He was only gone for a short time. When he got back, he talked to uncle Ügmen, and they decided that Jalme and I should take two of our ponies and ride to Sirida as fast as we could to warn you, and that we should also warn people along the way.

'Since uncle Ügmen with his injured leg couldn't travel so fast, my father and Pasong would go with him. We left the tents and all the bones we'd gathered behind and took only food, water, and our sleeping rolls. The last Jalme and I saw of them, they were working on a pack-saddle, trying to fix it so uncle Ügmen could ride without his leg hurting too much. On the second day we reached Bintan, and Jalme said I should go on alone with both ponies. That way, one of them could rest while I rode the other one, and it'd be much faster.

'The men in Bintan said they'd go back with Jalme and look for his father and mine and Pasong. I don't know if they got away in time, and I'm worried for them. I need to go back and look for them, and I'd be very grateful if you could lend me a horse. I'd take the ponies, but they're completely done in.'

Dorting stood and bowed, clearly determined to depart as soon as Anskar produced a fresh mount for him.

Though Anskar's heart went out to the boy, he knew that in the state he was in he was more likely to fall off and break his neck than achieve anything useful.

'Dorting,' he said. 'Armies tend to move slowly, much more slowly than normal travelers. There's no reason to think that this one caught up with your relatives if they didn't tarry too long, which I'm sure they didn't. And you need sleep more than anything else. So here's what I suggest: get some rest while the captain and I assemble our own army. We'll march out to meet the enemy no later than three days from now, and you can come with us. As a scout if you like, with direct orders from the Radj to search for the bone gatherers Durpa, Ügmen and Pasong. How does that sound to you?'

The boy nodded gratefully, too weary now for words.

'Good,' Anskar said. 'There's a bed here for you tonight, and tomorrow you can go to your village and see your family. Now rest. I need you to be fit and strong by the time we leave. A sleepy scout is no good to anyone.'

When Dorting had been seen safely off to bed, Anskar turned to Baran. 'What do we do?'

'You said it yourself a moment ago,' the captain answered. 'We march. And we meet them at a place of our choosing.'

'They're three times our number.'

'What other choice do we have? The only defensible position in Sirida – in all of Larnakis, for that matter – is Anpok monastery. It's well stocked and we could probably hold out there for a good while, even against a superior force. But that would mean leaving the rest of Larnakis and most of the people at the mercy of the enemy.'

'No,' Anskar said. 'The army is there to protect the people, not to hole up in Anpok and look out for itself. We go. Where do you intend to meet them?'

'The Yangan comes to mind. Anything farther out, and we risk getting caught in a bad spot before we're ready. And we don't want the river at our back. We have the one chance, but only if everything is as much in our favor as we can make it.'

'What if they choose a different approach? Use one of the smaller bridges farther east or west and loop around?'

'They won't. There's only the one road, and they need it to move their supplies. Yangan bridge is the way they'll be coming.'

'The bridge is new,' Anskar said. 'We can hold it easily or take it down, but there are fords upriver and down. The enemy will find that out soon enough and attempt to cross there, possibly in both places at once. They'll try to come around from both sides and roll up our flanks.'

'Exactly,' Baran replied. 'It's what I'm counting on.' He outlined his battle plan to Anskar. When he was done, the Radj nodded.

'Good. I think it's our best chance, though it means abandoning three quarters of Larnakis to the enemy. But it's the only thing I see that could work. Still, we must be prepared for the worst. And we do have another defensible position: Teniddin's Wall.'

'But that's at Donner Pass,' Baran said, frowning, 'on the border with Anapur, and facing the wrong way. We'd have to ask them to grant us refuge, and even though they're friends I doubt they'd be willing to let in so many of us. We might end up having to fight our way in, with another enemy at our back.'

'Teniddin's Wall is not quite on the border,' Anskar said, getting up. 'Let's have a look at the map.'

He fetched a parchment from a shelf by his worktable and unrolled it, weighing down the corners with river stones he kept for just this purpose.

'Here is Donner Pass,' he explained, 'and here is Teniddin's Wall, closing off the pass at its narrowest point, the gorge between Donner Peak and the Redhorn. North of Donner Pass the terrain opens up, and we have the high pastures of Tinnan valley. Tinnan is still part of Larnakis. At the far end of the valley, the pass splits in two. Tinnan Pass to the right leads into Anapur, Long Pass on the left goes to Dunmark. Tinnan can be our refuge, and still leave us two ways out to the rear.

216

'And you're mistaken about Teniddin's Wall. It faces the wrong way only if you think of it as a defense against the outside, against an enemy coming through Dunmark or Anapur. But that's not what it was built for. Mark you, this is only legend, but it's said that Radj Teniddin had the wall built at the time of the Battle of Bonesend, nearly two thousand years ago, when he foresaw just such a situation as we face now. As things turned out back then, the wall wasn't needed. But now it might be our best hope.

'Here's what I propose we do. We go ahead with your plan. But at the same time we evacuate Sirida and all the villages we can reach in time, and send the people to Tinnan valley with every cart and wagon and all the supplies and shelter they can carry. Thus we have them out of harm's way, at least for the time being, and we won't be fighting with our backs to the wall.'

'I see your point,' Baran agreed. 'It gives us room to maneuver and retreat if necessary, without putting the populace in immediate danger. Very well. There's something else we need to discuss. Knowing the Larnaki, I'm convinced that as soon as news of this gets out we'll have hundreds of civilians wanting to join us. Under the circumstances, I'm inclined to accept their help, trained or no. Defending the bridge and two fords is going to spread us mighty thin.'

'Use them,' Anskar said, pacing. 'But the first pick goes to Tinnan with the women and children. We need strong hands there to build shelters and to prepare and man the wall. The rest can come with us. I'll issue a proclamation first thing tomorrow morning. Lobsang will be a great help organizing the civilian side of things. I'll speak to him. What about your men? Can they be ready in three days' time?'

'They will be. Raiding season is practically over, and most of them are in barracks. A few are out riding rounds. I've already sent riders to fetch the ones we can reach in time and leave messages for the ones we can't.'

'Good. What are we forgetting?'

'There's always something. We can only hope we haven't missed anything important. There is one thing has me wondering, though.'

'What?' Anskar asked.

'What in the gods' sweet name do they want from us?'

After Baran had left, Anskar remained in his study, his mind too active for sleep. He wasn't aware of any conscious decision to take out the box holding the little blue bowl. Nonetheless, he suddenly found himself holding it in his hands. After a moment's thought, he set it on the writing table, found the sturdy pouch that went on his weapons belt, and transferred the bowl from the box to the pouch, thinking that maybe he'd meet Tönden before he left and hand the bowl over to him.

There was a part of him that knew better, but unfortunately Anskar wasn't well acquainted with it. Born heir to the throne, loved by all, he'd been brought up on a rich fare of goodness and virtue and very little of the opposite. Of the darker areas of the human soul, including his own, he had only a vague notion, and so was oblivious to the fact that the bowl had long since found the chink in his armor and gained entry to the very place where he was blind.

Had things been different, Anskar might have seen the danger he was in and realized that he was in no way fit to hold this kind of power, much less control it. Maybe he would have hastened to rid himself of the bowl and give it into the abbot's care before it betrayed him into doing something irrevocable – and then again, maybe not. Great power is a thing very few men can hold in their possession without being seduced by it, and even the best man's goodness has its limits – limits he will only come to know and understand once they have been severely tested.

Anskar, blessed as his life had been so far, had never even come close to undergoing such a test.

❖   ❖   ❖

At the upriver ford, the Yangan flowed wide and slow.

Holding the reins of his horse Fleet, Anskar stood in the predawn darkness, as perfectly still and intent as the men spread out on either side of him along the top of the steep riverbank. Over the gurgle and slap of small wavelets lapping the shore below, weak, fickle currents of air intermittently carried barely audible shreds of sound from the far side of the river: gravel grinding under heavy boots, the clink of armor and weapons, muted voices. A faint, strange scent seemed to overlay the clean smell of river water, an unpleasant, meaty odor mixed with the sharp tang of burnt metal.

Dawn was not far away. The waiting would soon be over. Anskar thought of Rupili and Anili, fervently hoping that by now they'd reached safety together with the rest of Sirida's population. They should have arrived. They must have. Eight days had passed since that fateful night, five since they'd parted, Anskar heading towards the Yangan, Rupili to Donner Pass and the sanctuary of Tinnan valley.

She'd been magnificent, a true queen. Upon receiving the news she immediately went into action, assuming responsibility for the evacuation of Sirida, working together with the mayor to get people, supplies, and transportation organized and ready for departure. With her infectious energy and unflagging determination, she left nobody time for despair or panic, rallying the people, especially the women-folk, around her person in an admirable fashion.

Anskar was immensely proud of her. At their parting she'd given Anili into Soonil's arms, freeing herself to be there for him alone in that one, all-important moment – an act that touched him deeply.

'You're absolutely forbidden to get yourself killed,' she said fiercely, her eyes shining with love and unshed tears. 'Promise me you'll come back safe and sound.'

He'd promised, and it was his determination to fulfill that promise as much as anything else that sustained him now.

They'd still been in Sirida when the first refugees began to arrive. They met them in growing numbers on their way to the Yangan, and Anskar was heartened by the fact that so many of the villages had heeded the boys' warnings and chosen to head for safety. There were few men among the refugees though, and Anskar soon learned of the bold and brave resistance they were putting up in the face of such a powerful and terrifying enemy.

Gradually, as the enemy force advanced, they too began to trickle back across the Yangan bridge, some in ones and twos, some in lar-ger groups, and to a man they insisted on joining the army and stay-ing to fight. Baran ordered that the bridge be left up, and a last, large band of Larnaki fighters crossed it only a scant half hour ahead of the enemy. That had been a hard moment for Dorting, when it became clear that the people he desired most to see crossing that bridge weren't coming.

Anskar fought a sinking feeling when he saw the dark tide of men and monsters spill over the crest on the far side of the Yangan, rolling down the hill towards the bridge like a slowly spreading stain of ink-black doom.

Glancing at the sad, forlorn boy standing at his side, it struck him that this was no place for him, not now, not with what was coming down that hill. He took Dorting to the command tent, where he wrote and sealed a message to Rupili asking her to look after the boy and keep him safe with her in Tinnan. Then he promoted Dorting to special messenger and sent him off to safety. More than anything else, Dorting seemed glad for something to do.

Now, in the predawn dark, Anskar felt more than saw Sergeant Tamsin come up beside him. Tamsin was a veteran of many a skirmish with the Ithraki, and he'd traveled most of the continent as a sellsword in his youth. His solid, grizzled presence comforted even Fleet, who gently nuzzled the sergeant's arm.

'It's getting light,' Tamsin said softly, stroking Fleet's neck. 'I reckon they'll be coming soon, now.'

Anskar was about to respond when the silence was shattered by the sudden sound of drums rolling across the water like slow thunder. Fleet shied and whinnied, and while he gentled the animal the drums settled down to a measured, foreboding rhythm. Loud and relentless, it penetrated to the bone, invaded the spirit, and seemed to suck what little light there was right back into the darkness.

'Here they come,' Tamsin said beside him, and then he saw it:

221

like the bristling head of a huge, armored serpent a dark, wedged shape emerged from the dense gray mist hanging over the water. For a fleeting moment it was an otherworldly apparition, seemingly floating in midair.

Then the sloshing of water and grinding of river rocks under hundreds of iron-shod boots grounded it solidly in the real world. A dirty-orange glow emanated from the chinks in the wall of tall, blood-red shields moving towards them, all of them bearing black slashes of paint that formed twisted crosses.

Tamsin let out a hissing breath. 'Sorcerers,' he said. 'Gods help us, but this is bad news.'

'How can you tell?' Anskar asked, his hand moving involuntarily to touch the pouch where the small, blue bowl rested. For some reason he couldn't fathom and didn't even want to think about, he'd taken it with him when he rode from Sirida.

'The devices on their shields,' Tamsin said. 'And that gods-cursed light. I've seen it before, down Rannon way. It always shows when they're doing their dirty tricks. And the results of those are never pretty. Well, no helping it now. We'll just have to see what they throw at us, and hope we can handle it.'

'You know what your job is,' Anskar cautioned him. 'Draw them towards the bridge. No heroics. I want all of you to arrive there in one piece. We'll need every man when the real fighting starts.' He gave Tamsin's shoulder a squeeze. It was like squeezing a rock – hard, solid, dependable. 'Good luck.'

'And to you, sir,' Tamsin answered, before turning to his men. 'Hold steady there. Let them come. No use wasting precious arrows. Anyone hits the water owes me a drink.'

Anskar swung into the saddle, and with a last glance over his shoulder kneed Fleet towards the main force that was waiting farther back, well hidden and ready to strike from behind as soon as the enemy took the bait and turned to follow Tamsin and his fifty archers towards the bridge. Downriver, if everything went as planned, Baran would be mirroring his every move, as they were both reflecting the enemy's actions.

As Baran had accurately foreseen, the sorcerers believed the Larnaki main force to be awaiting them at the bridge and sought to catch it in a pincer movement by crossing in two different places with divided forces, to then come in from both sides. The captain's simple but brilliant plan had the two halves of the Larnaki army waiting in hiding while token forces drew the sorcerers towards the empty middle. Then the Larnaki would swoop in and perform their own pincer movement, catching the enemy unawares from behind.

At least that was the theory. The numbers still weighed heavily against them, and it was common wisdom that battle plans tended to come apart pretty much as soon as the actual fighting began.

Anskar had put some distance between himself and the river and was approaching his waiting troops when suddenly he was struck from behind by a tidal wave of absolute terror, an avalanche of fear a hundred times greater than anything he'd ever felt in his life.

Like a giant fist, it seemed to crush him bodily, seeking to grind him into nothingness. It sapped him of all his strength and will in an instant, slipped the reins from his numbed and weakened fingers, and left him slumped over in the saddle like a man wounded to the death, moaning and trembling.

A flood of images swamped his brain, overlaying the world around him and nearly blotting it out altogether – terrible, bloody images of his loved ones: abused, hurt, mangled, dead. His whole being was taken over by a single, overwhelming urge.

Go! Forget about this stupid war! Run and save them, before it's too late! But it is too late, they're already dead, rotting, food for maggots and worms. You must join them. Share their death. Kill yourself. You have nothing left to live for. Run. Hide. Kill yourself. Do it. Do it now.

He felt himself sliding from the saddle. It was like falling in a dream – a slip, a shock, awakening – and it brought him back to his senses with a snap. He managed to catch himself an instant before he fell for real.

Moments later the whole thing was over, gone as quickly as it had come. A haunting. No, a spell. An attack. Sorcery. There had been nothing natural about the episode he'd just experienced. Instead, he'd felt a clear, cold intent behind it, inhuman design paired with rabid malevolence, an all-encompassing hatred that went far beyond the capacity of a normal, average man like himself to understand. He hardly dared think what it must have been like for Tamsin and his men, so much closer to the source. He wished with all his heart that they'd found some way to survive it and still retain the sense to flee in the right direction.

Snatching up the reins, he urged Fleet on.

He found the troops in disarray, frightened, confused, close to panic. Some had dropped their weapons and were cowering on the ground like cornered prey resigned to a quick death. A few were sobbing. He had to rouse them.

'Sorcerers!' he shouted, reining in Fleet. 'We're dealing with sorcerers. They're trying to play dirty with our minds, but it's not real! None of it's real, do you hear? We can handle it. Ignore it. Or at least be aware that it's nothing but trickery, manipulation, illusion.

'If Abbot Tönden were here, he'd know how to deal with it. But he's not, so we'll figure it out for ourselves. We can. We will. Focus. Think of one thing only. Think of how we'll beat those ugly bastards and chase them off our land, give them such bloody noses they'll go scurrying for their burrows and never come out again. You can do it. I know you can. Who can stand up to these sneaking, underhanded, honorless dirt-bags, if not the men of Larnakis?'

It didn't quite set them cheering, but it did visibly hearten them. To a man, they straightened, steeled themselves, grim but determined. It was all he could have hoped for, all he asked. He dismounted, had a quiet word with Baran's lieutenants – his lieutenants now, for the time being – and then walked among the men, giving them what words of comfort and encouragement he had.

Not long, and the pair of scouts sent to watch the enemy's movements returned, reporting that everything was going as planned. The opposing force following Tamsin and his men had turned towards the center. Time to go.

They moved out and swung in behind. The men were already in formation, a hundred and ninety horse out front, then the regulars on foot: a line of spears and shields, twenty abreast; a line of pikes; two lines of archers. Next was an identical, second block, ready to split and move out to the flanks when they reached the enemy. Then came three hundred volunteers, mostly archers. They would spread out behind the lines and shore them up wherever needed. Behind those came the reserve, ninety regulars and a hundred volunteers. Six-hundred-and-fifty men. Frighteningly few, if one was planning to attack an army of over three thousand, even if another six hundred were coming from the other side.

There was a moment in their rush forward when Anskar felt the world go still. It was as if they all hung suspended for that infinitesimal instant between 'here' and 'there', past and future, life and death, where all the possible choices of an eye-blink ago suddenly converged into one great, inexorable, rip-roaring current that knew only a single course, a course from which there was no escape.

Seemingly without transition, he found himself in the midst of battle. All around him hooves pounded, steel clashed on steel, and men and beasts shouted and screamed. They'd caught the enemy's rear unawares, and they pressed their advantage, allowing the mercenary cavalry neither time nor space to wheel around and fight. The first minutes of the encounter were hardly more than simple slaughter, men and horses stabbed and cut down from behind until the dead began to pile up and hamper the Larnaki's forward momentum.

In the lee of the decimated cavalry, the enemy's second-to-last company managed to get themselves turned around. They were monsters, huge and terrifying. Snarling and hissing, wild with the smell of blood and drooling in anticipation of more, they advanced swiftly, halberds lowered, tramping over the mounds of dead and dying as if they were mere molehills.

Horse against halberds was an uneven match at the best of times, and Anskar signaled the riders to retreat to the left and right. The spearmen behind them knelt, giving the archers an open field of fire. But instead of hunkering down and giving their own archers a clear shot, the monsters just kept on coming. As soon as they were past the barrier of bodies, they let out a deafening roar and charged at a run.

Arrows rained down on them by the hundreds, but the beasts proved damnably hard to kill, and not just because of their wide-brimmed helmets and heavy hauberks. Their greyish-brown skin was tough as boiled leather, and arrows hardly penetrated it far enough to do serious damage. It reminded Anskar of the hide of a Bodhareshi water dragon he'd once seen displayed at an Anapurian market stall, knobby and scaly and somehow still frightening even though it was just a dead, empty skin.

They were wasting precious arrows.
Anskar took a moment to study the enemy. Behind the reorganizing rows of monsters and the mercenary foot and archers, he could make out the sorcerers' Wedge coming round much more slowly. Obviously they were determined to keep the formation intact while turning. It meant a short respite still from their fiendish magic, but it wouldn't last. He wheeled Fleet around and rode back to his own lines, the monsters only a few steps behind him now. His men parted and immediately he was through closed ranks again, the first row kneeling, the second standing, the butts of their long spears planted firmly in the dirt. Presenting the onrushing enemy with a solid, bristling line of sharply pointed steel. Solid as they looked, they couldn't possibly hold against those gigantic, inhuman fighting machines.

But they did. Anskar saw men hacked to pieces by the halberds' huge, axe-like cross-pieces, saw others being skewered on the weapons' points and lifted bodily off the ground. The monsters flung them back over their shoulders like garbs of wheat or dropped them on the heads of their comrades, while soldiers from the third and fourth ranks stepped up to take the places of the fallen.

But the beastly things weren't proof against well-aimed spear thrusts. One by one, they too began to fall. Anskar urged Fleet into the melee and started hacking away at halberd shafts and leathery arms thicker than a man's thigh, every stroke jarring his arm to the shoulder and threatening to wrench the sword from his hand. And while the archers of both sides fought out a duel of their own, lofting volley after volley over the heads of the embattled men and monsters and into the enemy rear lines, with Anskar's men clearly leading the score, the Larnaki spears slowly began to push the monsters back.

Caught in a pocket of time where things seemed to go neither slow nor fast, where minutes could have passed or an eternity, where nothing counted except the next rise and fall of the blade, the next parry and twist to evade an enemy weapon, Anskar was just about to swing at another poking shaft when something passing strange happened.

The beast facing him suddenly put up its halberd. Holding the weapon upright in the crook of its arm, the thing took off its helmet, dropped it on the ground, and with the air of a farmer resting during a hard day's work fished a rag from its belt and wiped its brow. Then, dropping the rag as well, it pulled a knife and stuck it in its own left eye, all the way up to the hilt. Slowly, it began to topple over.

Anskar had no time to watch it fall or to dwell on this extraordinary event, for just then the sorcerers struck again. At the same time, he heard two long blasts of a horn, the prearranged signal that meant Baran was in trouble.

❖   ❖   ❖

Death is not a game which will soon be over.

Tom Stoppard

13 Gomilar

hree days' travel saw Morlic and Jessop to the edge of the Madal Skog, the great plains of Gomilar stretching away before them. Morlic had never seen the plains before, had never been out of the Madal, and his first impression was of an unsettling emptiness. A handful of stunted trees randomly scattered over the sheer endless expanse seemed to float in the waist-high, silvery grass, waving wind-tousled limbs like men lost at sea. Then he noticed insects, birds and voles flitting and rustling in the grass and, far out towards the horizon, the silver-backed, undulating shadow of a great herd of antelope. In the middle distance he saw a pair of large, long-necked creatures that looked like gigantic birds caught up in some kind of strange ritual, their movements comically exaggerated as they dipped and bowed and stalked around each other.

He was not reassured. Accustomed to a life between valley sides and canyon walls, he instinctively mistrusted the wide open plains, felt exposed and threatened in this flat, featureless vastness of grass and sky that offered a man no refuge, no place to hide either from an enemy or from himself.

In this at least, he was a true Skogon clansman.

231

The Skogon lands they drove through were deserted, not a living soul to be seen. But the passing of the clans had left unmistakable marks. What had once been a simple cart track had grown to several times its original width, the hard, stony ground scuffed by thousands of feet and rutted by a sheer endless succession of wheels.

The countryside to both sides was grazed down to bare earth by the passing herds, every brook or rill and long stretches of riverbank churned into a stinking morass by the animals' hooves. Flies were everywhere, attracted by the scattered dung of tens of thousands of animals baking under a cloudless sky and exuding a collective stench that made it seem like they were traveling through a gigantic midden. Every so often, they found broken or discarded objects by the side of the trail, and once even a freshly dug grave marking the first death on the clans' exodus into the unknown.

With all the shit spread about, Morlic and Jessop were hard pressed to find a halfway decent spot for their nightly camp. There was no space to bed down in the wagon, so they slept under it, though Morlic found that, for him, there was no sleep anymore. Try as he might, it eluded him, and he finally gave up on it altogether, realizing to his surprise that he did perfectly well without it – which eventually turned out to be a good thing.

During the first night on the road, lying under the wagon in the eerie silence interrupted only by a lone cricket or two that had not yet found the sense too leave this ravaged, grassless strip of dirt and head for greener fields, Morlic got the distinct impression that the man Jessop wasn't sleeping either. What kept Morlic from striking up a conversation to pass away the time was the creepy feeling that he was being watched, not as a fellow sufferer of insomnia, but as something more akin to… prey. Interesting. Very interesting.

He felt some of his old killing spunk bloom back to life, but decided to wait and see what would happen, with never a thought that he might be dealing with something deadly dangerous, even to him.

During the daytime Jessop alternated between long, ruminative silences that had Morlic wondering what could possibly be going on in that pea-sized brain, and bouts of talkativeness, disjointed ramblings and comments on anything and everything, stating the obvious in a way that began to seriously grate on Morlic's nerves as time progressed.

And all the while he felt that something else besides the peddler Jessop was watching him out of the corner of those dull, spiritless pig's eyes.

Watching, and waiting, just like he was.

It happened on the fourth night.

Jessop had pulled up by the last tree that deserved the name, an ancient oak whose thick trunk and sturdy limbs reminded Morlic of another, similar tree standing at a crossroads a hundred and some miles back.

A few wisps of cloud could be seen drifting across the face of a gibbous moon, and an owl hooted mournfully. Otherwise, all was still.

Morlic, lying in his bedroll, had followed a long and convoluted train of thought into an almost trance-like state that his companion obviously mistook for sleep, for he chose that moment to strike.

Furtively, stealthily, Jessop levered himself up to a low crouch.

The soft rustle of blankets was enough to alert Morlic. He stayed absolutely still, moving only his eyes to assess the threat through half-closed lids.

Even in the feeble moonlight he could make out more than he really wanted to, and the sight made his blood run cold. It was not at all what he'd expected.

Parts of whatever was preparing to attack him still looked like Jessop. Others didn't. The eyes were entirely black, no pupils, irises, or whites, just uniformly black orbs like two windows onto eternal darkness. The mouth had somehow grown much larger. Drooling, it hung half open to show a darting, pointy blue tongue and canines that would have done any large predator proud. Beneath the soft rounds of Jessop's flabby pectorals and protruding belly, new and alien muscles seemed to twitch and bulge with a life of their own.

A hand with nails grown into claws reached for Morlic's throat.

Morlic, who during the past days had secreted several knives from the peddler's stores about his person, had one of them ready. He slashed at the hand and rolled away, his legs getting tangled in the blanket.

The demon inhabiting Jessop hissed in surprise. Then it came after him, erupting out from under the wagon as if shot from a sling.

Morlic gave up fighting with the blanket and just kept on rolling until he fetched up against the trunk of the oak tree.

The demon jumped. Misjudging the distance, it landed short, a mistake it immediately corrected.

But it gave Morlic time to shake off the blanket and right himself against the tree, holding a knife in each hand now. He barely managed to evade razor-sharp claws striking for his head. Instead of taking off his face, they gouged long strips of bark from the trunk. Lunging, he stuck both knives into the creature's stomach. Leaving them there, he let himself fall to the side, rolling once and coming up with two more at the ready.

The demon wasn't impressed.

Not even bothering to glance down, it left the knives where they were, handles protruding from its belly. Facing Morlic, it crouched, feinted left, feinted right, then reached out and plucked the second set of knives from his hands, simply grabbing them by the blades and wrenching them free with inhuman strength.

Morlic was down to his last knife. Before he could produce it, the demon caught hold of him and threw him against the tree. Winded and groggy, darkness crowding the edge of his sight, he felt sharp claws dig into his upper arms, felt himself being lifted into the air again.

A moment later he crashed into the side of the wagon. This time he felt several things inside his body give. With a malicious hiss, the demon came after him.

Mustering his last bit of strength, Morlic pushed himself up, leaning against the wagon. As he did so, something hard struck him on the cheek. The handle of an axe, dangling from one of the many loops on the side of the wagon house.

Fumbling with the leather loop, he managed to free the axe just in time to swipe at the advancing demon. He heard a satisfying chunk! as the blade bit deep into the side of the Jessop-thing's knee. The demon's leg buckled and it went down on the other knee, spitting angrily. Unfortunately, the axe had embedded itself firmly in the bone and wouldn't come free. Morlic had to let go.

Incredibly, with its knee chopped halfway through and two knives stuck in its belly, the monster righted itself. Grinning wickedly, it grabbed Morlic by the throat and began to squeeze. Morlic being experienced with suffocation, it took some time, but in the end he felt himself slowly but surely losing consciousness.

Jaws gaping, the demon leaned in to suck Morlic's soul. The tongue came out, a hungry blue worm testing the air. Fascinated, Morlic noted that it was hollow, the tiny mouth at the tip ringed with barbed hooks. The sheer unbelievable stench coming from the demon's maw hit him like a dose of unspeakably vile smelling salts, giving him a last surge of energy.

Somewhere deep inside him, an unfamiliar muscle spasmed.

The next moment, the Jessop-thing was hanging in the oak's lower branches, motionless. Morlic gulped down a couple of breaths, nearly fainting from the pain. It felt like he'd cracked a few ribs. Slowly, gingerly, he righted himself, expecting the demon to rally and come charging down out of the tree any moment, but nothing happened.

He took a tentative step away from the wagon, found that he could stand on his own. Glanced at the tree. Took another step. And still nothing happened.

He hobbled over to the tree and looked up.

Dead eyes stared down at him. Human eyes. There was no sign that the corpse tangled in the tree's lower branches had ever been anything other than a man. The thing that had inhabited it was gone.

Morlic hadn't the faintest idea what had happened.

Hurting all over, he lit a fire, brewed some kaf and sat down to mull things over. Nothing came to mind. He was simply too exhausted. After a while, he drifted off into a trance-like state again and was visited by a strange vision, a weirdly distorted, wavering image of the moment just before the monster had gone flying into the tree, seen from an outside viewpoint that was neither Morlic's nor the demon's.

Watching in wonder, he saw something like a huge shadow-hand emerge from his belly just below the navel. The hand grabbed the Jessop-thing and squeezed until Morlic thought its eyes would pop out. Suddenly there was a quick flash of sickly green. He thought he heard the faint echo of a rage-filled scream fading in the distance. Then the wraith-like appendage threw Jessop's body into the tree.

All that was left was dead flesh. Human flesh. The demon was gone.

Morlic started. Came to. Food for thought there. Oh, yes.

Though his whole body ached, he didn't have the patience to sit around and wait for daylight. Grunting with pain, he collected his bedroll and the kaf pot. Hitched up the horses. Climbed up on the box and drove off, leaving the fire burning. It cast an eerie, flickering glow on the corpse in the tree, creating the illusion that the dead body was still moving.

When next he stopped, he rummaged around in Jessop's wares until he found a cheap tin pot and a pair of metal shears. He cut the bottom off the pot. Then he cut open the resulting ring. He rummaged some more and came up with a piece of felt, an old shirt, a needle and some thread. He padded the metal with a triple layer of felt and sewed two long strips of fabric from the shirt around it. When he was done, he placed the thing around his neck, bent the open ends back together, and presto – he had himself a neck brace. Not perfect, but it would do for the time being.

He was sick and tired of living in a tilted world.

The road, the river, and the trail of the clans all led to Ulan Bok, so Morlic headed that way too. He half expected to find the walled trading post empty and in ruins, ravished by the clans, but the crenellated walls of pale ochre brick with their domed corner turrets still stood, the gate under the pointed arch was open and the place was alive and bustling. From what he could see, the Skogon had camped some distance from the walls, maybe done some trading and then moved on, turning east.

Morlic decided to spend a day or two in Ulan Bok, get some rest and do a little trading himself. Driving in through the north gate, he saw that a few yards to his left the river also entered the town through a low, grated arch at the foot of the wall. Where it flowed through the town, it had been regulated and forced into the confines of a brick-walled canal. Morlic followed it until he came to a decent-looking inn. He turned into the courtyard.

A couple of burly stable hands approached, eyeing Morlic and the wagon suspiciously, reminding him that he was still wearing his dark Skogon garb. Damn! He should have changed into some of Jessop's spare clothes.

Too late now. He'd just have to brazen it out somehow.

'Say,' one of the stable hands said, frowning and rubbing his bulging jaw. 'Ain't that old Parvat's wagon and team?'

'By golly, you're right,' the other one said, passing a broad hand through bright-red hair.

'So what're you doing with it, then?' he asked Morlic.

'I, um, I bought it from him,' Morlic said. 'Just recently. He decided to retire.'

'Oh yeah?' the first man said. 'How recently?'

'Let me see. Couple of weeks?'

'That so? Then how come he was found dead more'n two months ago, not five miles from here? Murdered, by the looks of it. You wouldn't by any chance have helped him along into retirement, would you?'

'Actually, I didn't buy it from him directly. The man who sold it to me was called Jessop. He's the one bought it from Parvat. So maybe you should ask him about what happened to the old man.'

'But he ain't here, is he?' Lantern Jaw said. 'And you are. So it's you who'll do the answering. Why don't you step down and we'll go have us a little chat with the Justice. It's just down the street.'

Morlic wasn't going near anything to do with justice ever again.
He was getting out of there, as fast as he could. He snapped the reins. The horses didn't budge. Carrot Head had them firmly by the bridles.

'I think you'd better get down,' Lantern Jaw said, the menace in his voice evident.

'This is all an unfortunate misunderstanding,' Morlic said, climbing down from the box and slipping a knife from his sleeve. As soon as his feet touched the ground he whirled and slashed at Lantern Jaw. His knife met nothing but thin air.

Momentum carried him around until he was facing the wagon again. Something hit him in the back of the head with the force of a

239

sledgehammer. His face slammed into the box, breaking his nose. Darkness crowded his vision, and he felt himself slip away.

'Nice try, boyo,' he still heard Lantern Jaw say. 'But not with me. Sem, better go round up a couple of guards and have them take him over to Justice. For years now, I've been waiting for one of them damned uppity black-rags to step wrong, and I think I just got my wish.'

When Morlic came to he found himself – how else could it be – in a cell. His nose hurt abominably, his head was pounding, and he felt nauseous. The cell was dank and moldy and crawling with bugs. He was lying in a puddle of water, and his whole right side was soaked.

Not nearly as nice as the other one, the voice in his head said.

'Not you again!' Morlic said out loud. Only now, hearing it speak, did he realize that the voice had been silent since the trial. 'Why don't you just shut up and get lost.'

Who's going to keep you company then? You'll be needing all the support you can get. This is not going to go well for you, you know.

'Oh, be quiet! I need to think.'

What's to think? They'll find you guilty, and they'll hang you, or whatever they do here. Do you think they're going to go looking for Jessop? And even if they did, I don't see how a rotting corpse hanging in a tree is going to help your case. So, better start looking at your other options, like escape for example.

'Dear, fornicating gods! That's what I'm trying to do! So if you'd just shut your bleeding trap and let me get on with it.'

Sorry, the voice said, sounding miffed. *Just trying to help.*

'Well, you're not.'

'Having a chat with the rats?' A different voice, coming from the door. A key turned in the lock, and a massively built guard stepped in, holding a pair of manacles. Behind him, Morlic could see a second man.

'Let's see your hands, then' the guard said.

'Do we really need those?' Morlic asked, eyeing the iron bracelets.

The guard just gave him a dirty look, so he held out his hands and allowed himself to be shackled.

They led him upstairs and into a cramped office.

A small, rodent-like man of indeterminate age wearing a rimless red hat and eyeglasses sat at a desk, half hidden behind piles of books and documents. The Justice, Morlic assumed. The man finished scribbling something into a large ledger. Then he laid his quill aside and inspected Morlic. His eyes looked huge and funny behind the thick lenses. They were the only thing about the situation that might have raised a smile, though.

'And this is?' the man asked the guard.

'Don't know his name,' the guard said. 'The Parvat thing.'

'Morlic,' Morlic said. 'And I didn't do it. Kill Parvat, I mean.'

'Oh, we're not interested in that,' the Justice said. 'Outside our jurisdiction.'

Morlic breathed a sigh of relief. They'd let him go. 'That's what I told those ruffians at the inn,' he said. 'It's all a stupid misunderstanding.'

'Yes, well. There's still the matter of your having attacked a citizen of Ulan Bok with a knife. Unfortunately for you, such an act carries the death penalty.'

'*What?*' Morlic was flabbergasted. 'But I didn't even touch the man! Whereas he knocked me unconscious and broke my nose. What about that?'

'Self defense,' the Justice said. 'You started it.'

'But only because – '

'Doesn't matter. You're hereby sentenced to the Lucky Four. That's hanging, drowning, quartering, and burning. Any questions? Are you familiar with all the terms?'

'Um,' Morlic said, 'not really. What's quartering?'

'It involves your arms and legs being attached by means of stout ropes to four heavy draught horses. Which are then driven off in four different directions, pulling you apart, so to speak. Got it?'

'And after I've been hanged, drowned and ripped to pieces I get burned, just to make sure I haven't somehow managed to stay alive?' Morlic asked incredulously.

'Precisely,' the Justice said. 'As it happens, I'm free now, so I suggest we get on with it. No time like the present, and so on and so forth. Gentlemen?'

This was *not* good news for Morlic.

Hanging, as he knew from extensive personal experience, he could handle. Drowning shouldn't be too much of a problem either. But the parts where he was quartered and burned seemed likely to present a bit of a problem even for him. It made the whole affair seem kind of terminal. Desperately racking his brain for some excuse or argument that might change their minds, he was only vaguely aware of being led out of the building, down a short flight of steps and onto the street

242

where a small crowd of eager spectators had already gathered, waiting to be entertained at Morlic's expense. Their jeers and whistles rudely returned him to the dire reality of his circumstances.

It was only a few steps to the town square, where a gallows stood on the bank of the canal. They took off his nice new neck brace and his head flopped over to the side, exposing the angry red welt around his neck.

'Looks like our man's made the acquaintance of a rope before,' one of the guards remarked.

'Easy, then,' the Justice said. 'We don't want him dying prematurely. Rules are rules, and we've got to go through with the whole procedure in an orderly fashion.'

As it turned out, the hanging wasn't all that bad – if you didn't consider the pain it caused Morlic's poor, mangled neck. They simply hoisted him up and left him dangling there until he passed out, then lowered him onto the ground again. Next on the list was drowning, and it was here that Morlic saw his only chance to save himself.

He went over his hastily devised plan one last time while they attached a heavy iron bar with eyes at both ends to his shackled wrists and tied a long rope to it.

Then, without further ceremony, they dropped him into the canal.

After how the hanging had gone, Morlic suspected he wouldn't have all that much time. He reckoned they'd pull him out well in time to keep him alive for the rest of the show. The water was cold and murky, and visibility wasn't great, but fair enough even on the bottom to show him an eerie, green land-scape of wavering lines, dizzying angles and crazily tilted planes created by all sorts of junk large and small that had been dumped into the canal over the years. Most of it was covered with green carpets of algae and river-grass, its long tendrils lazily bowing and waving in the current.

Quickly now, before his air ran out or worse, they pulled him back up.

Morlic selected the largest nearby object he could see. It looked like the box, axle, and iron-shod wheels of a wagon. Judging by the rotting boards nearby, it must have been driven into the canal by some smashing drunk wagoner and simply left there, probably pronounced too wrecked to be worth salvaging.

Wobbling like a drunk himself, he half walked, half swam the few steps to the wreck, dragging the iron bar along behind him and stirring up the slimy, muddy bottom. His lungs beginning to scream for air, he bent over and lifted the bar, not nearly as heavy underwater as on land. He passed the rope over and under the sturdy axle twice, anchoring himself firmly to the remains of the wagon. As a final precaution he wedged the bar between the spokes as best he could. Then his air ran out.

Drowning, he decided, wasn't any better than hanging. On the contrary. At least with the latter, you just couldn't breathe anymore, period. But taking a deep breath and feeling your mouth and lungs fill with foul, clammy canal water was a shocking and at the same time frustrating experience all in a class of its own. To his relief, it didn't last all that long. He saw the rope leading to the surface jerk a few times. Then he passed out and died.

Though it took every ounce of his willpower, Morlic let twelve cycles of dying and reviving pass before he made his move. Thankfully, he didn't have to breathe in more of the disgusting water – his lungs were already full of it.

Somehow, time passed. Six hours, give or take. It was the middle of the night. If they hadn't given him up for hopelessly tangled and dead by now, tough luck.

It was pitch black on the canal bottom. He felt for the surface rope and pulled. There was no resistance. Good. Off with it.

Unfortunately, he'd wedged the iron bar in so tightly that it took him another whole cycle to disentangle himself from the remains of the wagon. When he was free, he picked up the bar and set off down-river. Bumping into all sorts of things in the impenetrable darkness but helped along by the current, he made it to the town wall in only five deaths.

But he hadn't factored into his plans the fact that, on this end too, the exit was blocked by an iron grate. He hung there for two more deaths, debating whether to try and climb up the side of the canal, which would still leave him inside the walls with the gates closed for the night. He wasn't sure he'd be able to slip by the guards in day-light, and he sure as hell didn't want to get caught again. He'd gotten away once, but they'd not let it happen a second time. All they need-ed to do was replace the rope with a chain, and he'd be buggered.

Then he remembered the iron bar. Using it as a lever, he managed to bend the grate's bars apart. Thankfully, they were almost rusted through, and it took him only three more deaths to create an opening wide enough to squeeze through.

He was free!

One last demise, and he was crawling up a softly sloping riverbank.

Too weak to stand at first, he remained cowering on all fours, coughing and vomiting up what felt like several buckets of rank, fishy water. After that he felt much better.

He managed to untie the tightly knotted rope linking him to the bar. For now, there was nothing he could do about the manacles. All in good time.

Before setting off, he looked back at the sleeping caravanserai, adding several names to the list of people he was going to kill. Sooner or later, they would pay. Lantern Jaw, Carrot Head, the guards, the Justice. Not to forget the spectators, the vultures come to watch him die. Maybe he'd just bar the gates from the outside and burn down the whole place.

There were already lots of names from the Madal on his list. No one would be forgotten. But first and foremost came his most hated enemy, the head. He would not rest or tarry until he had pulverized the damned thing and killed whatever inhabited it. Too bad it didn't have a living body. He would have loved to torture it for a long, long time. But, hey – maybe he'd find a way even so.

Dripping and shivering, Morlic set off, heading east, the way the clans had gone. His head hung on his left shoulder again, the horizon tilted steeply to the right, but he didn't mind so much anymore. The slant increasingly seemed to fit the state of the world at large as well as his own.

❖　❖　❖

Since knowledge is but sorrow's spy, it is not safe to know.

William Davenant

14 The Hag's Teeth

avoring a few more minutes in bed, Rather yawned and stretched, not yet willing to open his eyes and confront the real world. Any moment now, the alarm would ring, brutally shattering the last remnants of sleep and the extraordinarily vivid dreams he'd had. To his disappointment, he found that the first stirrings of conscious thought had already begun to sever his connection to the dream world, and he couldn't quite remember what just seconds ago had seemed so real, so poignant...

Oh, well. It was going to be another long day at the clinic, and traffic always seemed to be worst on Thursday mornings, so he might as well make use of the few extra minutes and get an early start. Somewhere not too far away, a hawk screeched.

Rather went still inside. The bird called a second time.

And then it was as if someone had suddenly turned up the volume on a completely different version of reality. Nearby a horse whickered. He heard muted voices holding a quiet conversation, the words of which he couldn't quite make out. A susurrus of wind. The faint burble of flowing water. He caught a whiff of wood-smoke.

He opened his eyes, and like a row of falling dominoes bits and pieces of memory tumbled into order and legible context.

'He's awake,' someone said, and then Gormin was there, crouching down beside him, giving him a scrutinizing look. They seemed to be in some sort of cave. Rather could see blue sky and sunlight over Gormin's shoulder.

'Wordlord,' he said. 'Welcome back.'

Rather had to clear his throat several times before he could speak.

'Thanks,' he croaked. 'Where are we?'

'We're in the mountains, the Hag's Teeth,' Gormin said, taking Rather's hand and feeling his pulse. Taking... his hand! Rather lifted his head and looked.

There it was. He had a hand again. It looked exactly like his old one, minus the scar on the back that he'd had since he was a kid. He felt for his feet, wriggled his toes, clenched and stretched the fingers of his other hand. Tentatively, hardly daring to hope, he reached under the blanket for his crotch.

Everything there! He was whole again.

Without warning, a huge sob erupted from the very bottom of his being. Then the tears came, unstoppable, torrential, liberating. Washing out the suffering and the pain of what seemed like several lifetimes. And all the while he was bawling and blubbering like a deeply wounded child, Gormin sat beside him, holding his hand and looking like he was inwardly shedding tears of his own.

When he was finally done crying, Rather felt cleansed. Immensely fragile. And very, very happy. It was a happiness very different from anything he'd ever felt before, different in a way he couldn't yet define. He supposed it was the kind of happiness you had to go through a lot of really, really bad stuff to experience.

'Gormin,' he said. 'I don't know what to say. You've given me back my life. I owe you more than I'll ever be able to repay.'

'Ah, Wordlord,' Gormin sighed, a single tear rolling down his deformed cheek. 'You owe me nothing. It is I who should thank you for allowing me to repay a debt so great it threatened to crush me. I breathe again, and feel very fortunate indeed.'

Rather squeezed the little Unborn's hand.

'Hey,' he said, seeing Gormin wipe the tear away. 'I thought you guys didn't cry.'

'We don't,' Gormin said. 'We can't. It's a wonder. Who knows, some day we might learn to smile. To laugh, even. But I'm being selfish. There are others here waiting to welcome you back among the living. If you feel up to it, that is.'

'Please,' Rather said, and suddenly he was surrounded by goodwill and concern. Several Unborn faces peered down at him. One of them seemed familiar.

'Rain?' he said, and got a nod. 'Good to see you. Please introduce me to your friends.'

'Wordlord,' Rain Seven said. 'So good to have you back. This is Striving Four. Changing Grey. Counting Clouds, Once Green, and Three Flower.'

One by one, Rather took their large, ungainly hands in his and thanked them from the bottom of his heart. They were as deeply moved as he was, though not the half of it showed on their alien faces. They still didn't dare look him in the eyes, though. All except Gormin, who had no problem with it in any case, and Rain, who risked one short glance, a tenth-of-a-second connection that seemed to shock and satisfy him in equal measure. Progress, Rather thought, and asked them how the escape from Fellmere had gone and what had happened since. He was surprised to hear that nearly six weeks had passed.

'I had to keep you in the box longer than expected,' Gormin explained. 'And then you took your own sweet time waking up. Over a week, actually.'

Rather suddenly remembered something else.

'The girl,' he said. 'Did you bring her? Is she all right?'

'Nissa, yes,' Rain answered. 'We brought her, Wordlord. But there is a problem. She won't wake up. We have no way of breaking the spell the sorcerers laid upon her. We've kept her alive until now, but she started running a fever a few days ago. Her temperature's been rising ever since, slowly but steadily.'

'I've been trying to keep the fever down,' Gormin said. 'But without much success. She has a very strange metabolism, though, and the high temperature seems to affect her less than one should expect. I believe she'll hold out for a quite while still, but I'm beginning to fear for her all the same.'

'What about the box?' Rather asked.

'That's where she is right now. But it doesn't seem to be having any great effect, if it's working at all. Might as well be the herbs I've been giving her.'

'I'm a doctor,' Rather said. 'Let me see her.' He suddenly realized he was mumbling. And his eyes were refusing to stay open. All at once he felt infinitely tired.

'Wordlord,' Gormin said. 'You're exhausted. Rest. She'll keep for a few hours, don't worry.'

Gormin said something else, but Rather had trouble understanding him. Then everything went quiet and it was just him alone again, drifting away.

Later, Rain carried Rather over to the Box.

Gormin had the lid off, and he'd pulled the membrane back from Nissa's head and upper body. To his shame, Rather felt a stirring in his loins. God, but she was beautiful. He forced himself back to clinical neutrality and examined the patient, supported by Rain, who was the only thing keeping him from falling on his face. Aside from the fever, he couldn't find anything wrong with her.

Sitting with his back against the box, he discussed her medication with Gormin, and made a suggestion. Gormin prepared a fresh extract, but when Rather tried to enhance it with his Talent he found that he was too weak to muster more than a trickle. It was better than nothing, and it would have to do. He'd get stronger, do better next time, and better still the time after that. He recognized in himself an almost overwhelmingly urgent wish to keep the girl alive.

'We have to get her to somebody who knows how to handle this,' he told the two Unborn. 'What she needs is a mage, and I don't mean a simple hedge-wizard-cum-healer like myself. I mean a real mage. Someone powerful enough to break the bloody spell that's keeping her under.'

'Let me get the map,' Gormin said and started to lever himself up. Rain was quicker, fetching it for him and spreading it out on the hard-packed dirt of the cave floor.

'This is where we are,' Gormin pointed out. 'And here's the path we'll be taking through the mountains. On the other side, there's a narrow strip of savannah, and then it's the Jemmarraa, the great desert. And here' – he pointed to a large dot a good ways out in the desert, – 'is Massarit, the Table of the Gods. If we're lucky and what I looked up in the library at Fellmere is accurate, then this is where the Assenai live, the desert dwellers. And it's our best and only hope of finding help for the girl, unless you want to turn back and ask the sorcerers for their assistance.'

'How long will it take us to get there?' Rather asked.

'I'd say three weeks minimum,' Gormin said.

Rather was dismayed. 'Will she make it?'

Gormin shrugged. 'Your guess is as good as mine.'

'Then we leave in the morning,' Rather said. 'Someone's going to have to carry me, at least in the beginning. But I promise I'll do my best to get back on my own new feet as fast as I can.'

'Don't worry,' Rain Seven said. 'Between us, Three Flower, Changing Grey, Once Green and myself can easily handle you and the box. And we also have the horses to carry the supplies. We will be fine, Wordlord.'

'That reminds me,' Rather said. 'We had a deal, remember?'

'Yes, Wordlord.'

'No,' Rather said. 'It's Rather. My name is Rather, and from now on, for every time you call me Wordlord I'm going to make you carry me an extra mile. Deal?'

'Deal,' Rain Seven said, 'Rather.'

Rain was adamant about carrying Rather himself.

The Unborn fashioned a sling from a blanket and carried Rather piggyback. It was actually quite comfortable, though his legs did tend to get pins and needles after a while. Every so often he asked Rain to let him down, and walked on his own. In the beginning it was only a few wobbly steps. But he kept at it, and soon managed longer and longer stretches, feeling a little stronger every time.

Every six hours, he and Gormin opened the box to look after Nissa. Before administering the medicine, Rather worked his modest magic over it, and in this too he found himself strengthening day by day. It got so he could bring the fever down for several hours, but in the end it always rose again. At least this way they had a hope of getting her over the mountains alive.

As they climbed farther and farther up the winding path, the Hag's Teeth turned increasingly barren and inhospitable. The vegetation changed from dense, deciduous woodland to sparse, weather-beaten pines, to hard, dry mountain grass and small patches of ankle-high alpine rhododendron sheltering in the lee of lichen-covered boulders. There were less and ever smaller brooks and rills, and it began to look like finding water might soon become a problem.

Still, the going was relatively good. They were following an old trade route, a bridle path that in times past must have seen a fair amount of traffic. There were long stretches that had been fortified with a pavement of sorts, unworked but mostly flat stones laid in a bed of earth and gravel and consolidated by centuries of tramping feet and hooves. In the steeper sections, steps and sometimes long stairways had been built using large, flat slabs of rock.

They made good headway despite a few detours around rock-falls and a hair-raising passage along a precipice where half of the trail had broken off and fallen into the deep. It cost them hours of sweat and nerves to coax the frightened horses across.

For all that things were going well, Rather felt himself falling into an ever-deepening depression he didn't have the power to fight.

For the others' sake he tried to put the best face he could on it, but they noticed all the same. They were strong on empathy, these tragic, abused creatures, in the making of whom empathy had played no part at all. It was their greatest strength, and also their greatest weakness. Maybe this was the way of angels, Rather thought, and why they were so seldom seen among the living: how hard to know all their charges' needs and wishes, all their dark and painful secrets, all their shortcomings and weaknesses, all the lies, sadness, frustration, fear, anger, hatred, pain and misery involved in being human. And how hard to be unable *not* to know these things, to be exposed and defenseless in the face of so much needless yet inevitable suffering.

One evening he was off by himself, as he'd been more and more often lately. Sitting on a large rock at the edge of a precipice, he stared into the far distance without really taking in the grandiose view of the sun setting in a sea of pale orange over a wild, bizarrely beautiful landscape of deeply shadowed purple gorges and staggered ranks of black, serrated crags culminating in steep and eternally unattainable peaks.

A pair of eagles circled, dark silhouettes against the glowing sky. Somewhere higher up on the mountainside, there was a clatter of rocks, and then silence again, perhaps a chamois or mountain goat crossing a tail of scree on its way to find shelter for the night.

Rather shivered. Though it was the beginning of August and the cloudless days were sweltering, nights at this high altitude were freezing. He huddled down and wrapped his arms around himself, reluctant to impose his bleak company on his companions gathered around a warming fire in the lee of several large boulders.

'Rather.'

It was Rain Seven, bringing him a blanket, considerate as ever.

'Thanks, Rain. That's very kind of you.'

'May I sit with you for a moment? The view is spectacular from here.'

'Please.'

They sat in silence for a while, watching the sun's glowing red orb sink beneath the jagged horizon. Eventually Rain spoke.

'You're not alone, you know,' he said. 'We may be Unborn, but we're not so different that we can't share any of your human feelings.'

'I know, Rain. I know. It's just that... I wouldn't even know where to begin.'

'You worry and fear for Nissa. For some reason she is important to you. But that isn't all.'

'I do. And no, it's not. I've been trying to tell myself it's the stuff I went through in Fellmere catching up with me, and I suppose in part it is. The rebound from the rebound, so to speak. But the real problem isn't what's been done to me, it's what I have done.'

'The prophecy.'

'Exactly. The prophecy. I told Kuruma as little as possible, but it was still far too much. I'm sure he's gone off on a bloody rampage, and he's probably going to harm a lot of innocent people in the process. All because I couldn't keep my stupid mouth shut.'

'Did you really have a choice? Is it even possible to hold back on prophecy?'

'There's always a choice. And besides, it wasn't even my prophecy. I was only the mouthpiece chosen by… I don't know, the real prophet, a boy called Jareth? A random twist of fate? Or the prophecy itself?'

Rather told Rain Seven about Orr, about Jareth, Kuruma, and his own involvement, first as a doctor and then because of his extraordinary gift of memory, though by now it felt more like a curse.

'So you remember everything that was written on those walls?' Rain Seven asked.

'Yes and no,' Rather said. 'It's there in my head somewhere, all of it, but I can't seem to call it up at will. It's like there's a time lock on it, releasing certain information only at a particular moment and under specific circumstances. At least that's how far I've gotten trying to figure it out. If everything's just right, I can suddenly see a complete section of text as if I had the real thing right in front of me. All I have to do is read it. Or not.'

'Do you really think you could choose not to?' Rain asked.

'Honestly?' Rather said. 'I'm not sure. Probably not. And here's another thing. What I told Kuruma about the eggs and so on: that was only part of the story. I held something back. The most important stuff, actually, according to Jareth. Because – and this is really weird – in this case he told me what to say and what not. It was written there on the wall with all the rest, written at least twenty years ago, when Jareth couldn't possibly have known that I even existed and the probability that we'd ever meet was absolutely, totally, unequivocally zero.

'Included in that piece of text, there was the thing about the eggs I told Kuruma, but there was more, something about a "little light" that would be crucial, the fulcrum in everything that was to come. After that, Jareth had left a personal message for me. He wrote: "Rather, I am sorry to lay this burden on you, but none of us are spared by the foretelling. When the time has come, you must tell the Black Man everything, save for one thing. Under no circumstances must he learn about the Little Light. But the rest he must know, even if the consequences for many will be sad and terrible. It is the only way for everyone to be in the right place when they are needed. It is essential. The survival of worlds hinges upon it. Forgive me."

'So I did what he asked of me,' Rather continued. 'But that doesn't make it any better. I just hope he got it right, and all the bad stuff that's going to happen because of what I did won't be for nothing.'

'I don't hold with the idea of sacrificing the few for the many,' Rain Seven ventured hesitantly after a moment of silence. 'But sometimes fate doesn't leave us a choice. If your Jareth was right, and I believe that he was, then the only other possibility left to you was to sacrifice the many for the few, and I don't see how that would have made things better.'

'I guess you're right. Reminds me of the old saw people comfort themselves with in hard times. They say that nothing bad happens that doesn't somehow also lead to something good. Only they tend to forget that the opposite holds equally true.'

Rain Seven nodded. They sat for a while still in companionable silence until the last light had faded from the horizon.

The next day, out of the blue, the girl got worse.

It was mid-afternoon on their tenth day in the mountains. They had just reached the highest point of the pass, and now the trail ahead of them dipped steeply down a mountainside. Far below, it led into a shadowed vale. They could see green on the valley's floor and lower sides, and a small mountain lake like a turquoise jewel. The sun had hidden behind clouds since mid-morning, and the air was chilling. Three Flower, who was carrying the box on his shoulder, abruptly stopped and set it down, rubbing the side of his neck.

'It's hot,' he said, puzzled. The skin on his palm and forearm was bright red. His neck and shoulder looked the same.

A cloud of steam escaped from the box when Gormin opened it. The sac inside was noticeably shriveled, the jelly-like substance partly evaporated by the intense heat emanating from Nissa's body. Rather knelt beside Gormin and felt her forehead. He quickly snatched his hand away.

'She's burning hot!' he said.

'Let's take her out,' Gormin said.

Rather and Gormin wrapped their hands in strips torn from a spare blanket before lifting the girl out of the box and gently placing her on the reversed lid. Trails of vapor rose from the goo stuck to her body. Counting Clouds used their last water to wash the girl down. It instantly evaporated, rising off her steamy mist. Clouds wanted to cover her with a blanket, but Gormin shook his head.

'If it helps to assuage your sensibilities, cover her with something light,' he told her. 'She needs to cool off.'

'This is crazy,' Rather said. 'Nobody can be this hot and still be alive.' He was agitated, desperate to do something for the girl.

'I just remembered something,' Changing Grey offered. 'When they brought her back down after the ritual, they seemed afraid of her, and I heard one of them say that she was a fire witch. Maybe that's got something to do with it. I'm sorry it didn't come back to me earlier.'

'That's got to be it,' Rather said. 'Otherwise she'd be dead right now. It must be her Talent running wild. The sorcerers' spell keeps her from controlling it, so it just goes on building up the pressure on its own, with no real outlet. We don't know how much of it she can take. I say we get her down to the water as quickly as we can, and hope it's nice and cold.'

Using the lid as a stretcher, Three Flower and Once Green lifted Nissa between them.

'What about the box?' Clouds asked.

'Leave it,' Gormin said. 'It's used up in any case.'

They set off, Rather trying to curb his impatience with what seemed to him an unnecessarily slow and careful pace.

By the time they had negotiated the seemingly endless series of steep switchbacks leading down into the valley, it was nearly dark. Halfway down, the shift that Clouds had covered the girl with began to smolder. Reluctantly, Clouds took it off, and Rather urged them on.

They reached the valley floor and made their way to the lake in darkness, finding it more by feel and smell than by sight. Striving Four immediately got busy building a fire while Two Flower and Once Green took Nissa to the lake's edge and lowered her, lid and all, into the shallow, ice-cold water.

With a hiss of steam, it bubbled up around her, brought to boiling by her body's heat. They propped up one end of the lid to keep her head out of the water and left her there, keeping the fire going and taking turns watching over her all through the night. Rather got up every hour to check on her.

Slowly, slowly, she began to cool off. In the wee hours after midnight he could touch her forehead without getting his fingers burned. When the first light of dawn crept into the valley, her temperature was down to something approaching normal, and he breathed a deep sigh of relief.

It was a brief respite. His anxiety returned with renewed force when he began to contemplate the task of getting her down the rest of the mountain trail and through twenty miles of savannah and eighty miles of desert to Massarit, with nothing more than a vague hope of finding help for her there.

He had to find a way. *Had* to.

It seemed somehow pathetic, ridiculous almost, given that he didn't even know her, had never exchanged even a glance or spoken single a word with her, but he couldn't bear the thought of losing her. Not anymore.

Rather, he told himself, *you're a fool. You're twice her age. If she ever wakes up, she'll probably take one look at you, have a good laugh, and then be on her merry way. Get a grip.*

When it was full light he asked Clouds to help him carry the girl onto dry land and drape her with the singed shift.

'I want to keep her out of the water and see what happens,' he explained to Gormin and the others. 'Maybe she's let off so much heat it'll take a good long while to build up again. Let's hope so, because otherwise I don't see how we're going to get her to Massarit in one piece.'

'I agree,' Gormin said. 'But I've been thinking, and I suspect it's less the cold than the water itself that's doing the trick. After all, we seem to be dealing with some kind of elemental magic here, and water is the opposite element of fire. If I'm not mistaken in this, then it should greatly better our chances, as long as we find enough water on the way.'

'Or carry as much as we can with us,' Rain Seven said.

'Both,' Rather said. 'We can't rely on always finding water when we need it, and the desert's going to be a problem anyway.'

'Not necessarily,' Gormin said. 'If the map is correct, there should be two water holes between the foothills and Massarit. All we have to do is find them, though that may prove easier said than done.'

They decided to stay at the lake and move on the next day.

To Rather, hope came, unbidden but welcome.

It was a magical place, this green vale amidst towering walls of bare, barren rock, filled with birdsong and peace. The clouds had moved on and the sun was back but milder now. A gentle breeze moved the air and sent ripples chasing over the lake's mirror surface. Shining blue dragonflies flitted over the water, and several times deer emerged from the woods to drink at the far side of the lake.

Rather was reluctant to leave, but Nissa's temperature rose only very slightly during the day, and there was no reason to tarry. In the morning, Clouds gave her a thorough bath in the lake and dressed her in the freshly washed shift. Then they set out again, down now, always down, and the going was much easier, for them and for the horses, who had greatly profited from the rest and the good grazing.

Nine more days saw them at the desert's edge.

Water had been no problem as the lake, fed by an underground spring, overflowed into a small stream that bounced and burbled merrily down its rocky bed, slowly growing in size as other rivulets joined it along the way. The trail roughly paralleled the stream, winding sometimes closer to and sometimes farther away from the water but never so far they couldn't hear its steady, comforting sound.

Gormin's theory proved to be correct, and they were able to keep Nissa's temperature at close to normal. At the foot of the mountains, the stream seemed to dry up over a stretch of less than a hundred yards, but Gormin said it went underground, running on deep under the desert sands, all the way to Massarit. In two places along the way it came very close to the surface; this was where the waterholes could be found. With full water skins and in good spirits, they set out to conquer the twenty miles of savannah and eighty miles of flat, featureless sand that separated them from their goal.

They spent the last night before entering the desert proper camped just inside the savannah's zone of sparse vegetation, allowing the horses to graze one more time, their camp nestled between two huge boulders. The map indicated these as starting point for the route across the desert, along which they ought to find the waterholes. The first was about twenty miles out, the second another twenty-five.

The last leg to Massarit was going to be a very long slog.

❖ ❖ ❖

War does not determine who is right – only who is left.

Bertrand Russell

15 Donner Pass

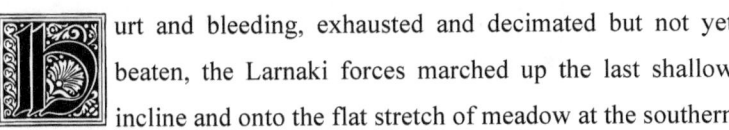 urt and bleeding, exhausted and decimated but not yet beaten, the Larnaki forces marched up the last shallow incline and onto the flat stretch of meadow at the southern end of Donner Pass. Here the valley they'd been traveling through ended, the mountains drawing close together to form a narrow gorge bordered on either side by steep slopes of jumbled scree and boulders and overshadowed by sheer, vertical rock faces that stood over a thousand feet tall. Above the gorge's rim, the mountainsides of Donner Peak to the left and the Redhorn to the right leaned back and rose another three thousand feet.

Before them, blocking the entrance to the gorge, lay Teniddin's Wall. Climbing the slopes on either side to join two massive towers built right up against the rock faces, it was a good hundred yards long, twenty feet high and twelve feet wide. Midway along the wall, two more towers flanked the gatehouse, and additional battlements reinforced the defensive works.

While the weary men filed into the arched gateway, passing under the ancient headstone carved with a weathered and faded Sky Dragon, Anskar and Baran guided their mounts aside and studied the defenses. Baran had sent two of the army's four Dunmarkan master engineers ahead with the refugees, and they'd done their best to eliminate the wall's weak points. The gate was new, the old one having succumbed to age and rot centuries ago. In several places, mainly along the parapet, the stonework showed signs of recent repairs. Anskar also saw newly built catapults positioned atop the battlements, a first in the history of Larnaki warfare, as far as he knew. The engines looked tough, mean, and ready for business. Thank the gods for Baran and his Dunmarkans.

This was their last defense, and it had better hold. The future of the Larnaki people depended on it.

In a matter of moments, the battle at the Yangan had turned into an unmitigated disaster. The monstrous halberdiers had suddenly turned and retreated at a run, and briefly it seemed as if the Larnaki had gotten the better of them. But then the sorcerers released magic so potent it shredded the Larnaki lines in an instant.

Hearing Baran's call of distress, Anskar had just signaled his lieutenants and ridden back to confer with them behind the lines when he saw a wall of darkness rushing at the Larnaki front with dizzying speed. As it reached the first row of men it slowed abruptly, like a hurled stone passing from air into water. A black fog came drifting in and swirled through the front ranks, acidic and poisonous, blinding the men and scorching their airways.

Eyes streaming, coughing and gasping, they lowered their weapons or abandoned them altogether. Some staggered about like drunks lost in a pitch-black alley, fighting for air, unable to scream out their agony. Others vomited great gouts of blood and died where they stood.

But the sorcerers weren't done yet. Anskar saw a second wave of sorcery coming towards them. He ordered the signal to retreat blown. A heartbeat later, its echo could be heard, coming from Baran's position.

Given the circumstances, it was less a retreat than frantic, headlong flight. But Anskar managed to get things calmed down and under control by the time they met up with Baran's force on the road to Sirida. Thankfully, the enemy chose not to pursue immediately.

Baran looked pale and drawn.

His right arm was in a sling, broken above the elbow by a swinging halberd shaft. The sight of him reassured Anskar all the same. He was there. He was alive. As were, at a rough count, two thirds of their troops. It wasn't over yet.

'Sweet gods above, but I'm glad to see you alive and in one piece,' Baran said, kneeing his mount up alongside Fleet. 'I thought we'd had it there for a moment. Hardly anyone made it out of the black stuff, and those who did died anyway, same as the others.'

'I know,' Anskar said, shaken. 'It's the sort of thing leaves you speechless. It's got nothing to do with warfare. Plain murder, is what it is, underhanded and craven. And there's no defense against it. If they keep throwing that kind of stuff at us, we might as well slit our own throats and save them the trouble.'

'Ah, but they won't,' Baran said, managing a grin despite the pain. 'A few weeks back, while you were busy with other things I had a little chat with Tönden. You'll remember you asked him to see what he could find out about the origins of those two cadavers we found.

'As it turned out, the good abbot had a few interesting things to say. One of them was that those black rats need human blood to power their magic. In other words, they have to kill people every time they perform one of their dirty tricks. Now – the boy Dorting said they brought about fifty prisoners with them, who we can assume were fodder for their bloody hokum. And I think pretty much all of our people got out of the enemy's way in time. Meaning, they didn't take a lot of additional prisoners, which they were probably counting on doing. So the bottom line is…'

'The bottom line is,' Anskar said, 'sooner or later they're going to run out of people to sacrifice.'

'And when they run out of sacrifices, they run out of power,' Baran said. 'No power, no magic.'

'So let's hope they run out sooner rather than later,' Anskar said.

When they reached Sirida, the abandoned city greeted them with an eerie, echoing silence broken only be their own footfalls and the horses' hoofbeats as they marched through empty streets. Between houses Anskar caught glimpses of Anpok, sitting high on its hill like a betrayed and forgotten wife, empty too. Well, not quite. Tönden and two of the oldest monks had stayed behind, adamantly refusing to leave.

They didn't explain themselves, but Anskar supposed that, in a spiritual context, their reasons were as valid as they were irrefutable. He briefly considered making one last plea to Tönden but quickly rejected the idea. There was no time, and it would be futile in any case.

They marched on, leaving Sirida and the three old men in Anpok to their fates.

And here we are, Anskar thought to himself, his gaze traveling up and up the gorge's mighty escarpments. They reminded him of a stone giant's gargantuan palms held close together, ready to squash anything that came between them. *Here we are, all of us gathered for Larnakis' last stand.*

But first, they all needed rest. There was still time.

Over the last few days, they'd harried the enemy every chance they got, laying ambushes at strategic spots time and again. They'd succeeded in slowing the sorcerers' army down, though not in stopping it. The black fiends simply took their losses in stride and kept on coming. But after a while they did fall back and leave some space between themselves and the Larnaki, a day's worth by now, Anskar reckoned.

The last men had entered the barbican when Rupili came storming out. He'd barely slipped from the saddle when she bowled into his arms. Only Fleet, standing patiently right behind him, saved them both from ending up sprawled on the ground and making an undignified spectacle of themselves. Not that it would have mattered. She was here, he was here, and that was all that counted for the moment.

They simply stood there for long moments, embracing each other with quiet intensity while Baran gave the wall another extensive study. Then Rupili, still holding Anskar tight, mumbled into his shoulder.

'You're coming back to Tinnan for a proper meal, both of you. And Baran's having a healer look at his arm.'

'I'm fine,' Baran, who had ostensibly not been listening, said. 'The medics said – '

'Baran,' was all she said, her tone somehow managing to redden the man's ears and leave no room for argument. The woman was a terror.

They left command in the capable hands of Tamsin, who by a miracle had survived the Yangan. Rupili riding double with Anskar, they passed through the gate and by the soldiers setting up camp a good distance behind the wall, out of range of the enemy artillery and on the last bit of open ground before the canyon walls drew close together, leaving just enough room for two narrow lanes of traffic.

There was quite a bit of coming and going. Rupili wasn't the only wife come to greet her husband. There were many others, sometimes whole families, searching for sons, husbands, fathers, brothers. Far too many of them would not find the loved ones they were looking for, Anskar thought sadly.

There would be much grief in Tinnan this night.

A mile and a half later the gorge released them out into Tinnan valley. Usually at this time of the year, its green meadows dotted with small stone cots would be temporary home only to a handful of shepherds grazing their flocks on these high pastures during the summer months. Now, the small valley was filled to bursting with Larnaki and their livestock. Tents and improvised shelters had been put up in an orderly fashion, grouped around the cots in clusters of twenty or thirty and leaving as much open grazing space as possible for the animals. Each small community shared a central cook fire, and well-chosen areas had been set aside for midden heaps and latrines. Without a doubt there was a very organized and tidy hand behind all this, and Anskar was pretty sure he knew whose it was.

'Good work,' he told Rupili. 'If you ever want a steady job, I'm sure the army would take you on as quartermaster in a twinkling.'

'Well now,' she said. 'If you offered me the post of commander general, I just might give it a thought.'

'Careful there,' Baran said. 'She'd have us simple soldiers knitting doilies, changing diapers, and helping old people cross the street before we knew it.'

'You wish,' Rupili shot back. 'Then you could retire and do nothing but chase the ladies.'

'That transparent, am I?' Baran chuckled.

'Here we are,' Rupili said, sliding off Fleet's back before Anskar could offer her a hand.

She'd commandeered the cot closest to the canyon entrance, surrounded by its own little village of tents. Soonil was there, busy stirring a huge pot hung over the fire. Asha stood beside her with Anili in her arms, rocking the infant gently and singing a nursery song. And there was Dorting, too, looking much better than the last time Anskar had seen him. Unbidden, the boy took their horses and led them away while Anskar greeted his daughter. Even in the short time since he'd last seen her, she'd grown. Resting in his arms, she looked up at him and gifted him with a radiant smile. Rupili had to tell him twice that dinner was ready.

Two hours he spent with his family, and even so he felt he was stealing time away from the many pressing and vitally important things that needed seeing to.

A healer came to look at Baran's arm and pronounced it well set. She splinted and bound it up again, and told him to keep it still as much as possible, advice both of them knew was futile. Then it was back to the wall to see to the soldiers and the defenses. Baran offered to go on ahead and leave Anskar more time with his family, but Anskar knew he couldn't stay. This was a time when the Radj needed to be with his men.

'I'll be back as soon as I can,' he told Rupili.

She simply nodded, holding him tight for another moment, neither of them knowing if they'd see each other again in this life.

❖　❖　❖

They were down to their last eight prisoners, among them the three Larnaki they'd caught coming down from Bonesend, but Kuruma wasn't worried. Over eighty percent of his forces were intact, and he still had his secret weapons, a special contribution from Noburo, who'd felt the need to remind everyone that he was still the gifted and valuable innovator of old and not just administrator to Gormin's genius.

They had arrived the previous evening, a day behind the Larnaki army. Rather than face constant attrition by their stupid little traps and ambushes, he'd decided to hang back and let them run for a while. Having found the city as well as the countryside completely deserted, and having also evaluated a sketchy but nonetheless revealing report by his scouts, he correctly assumed that the populace had departed in the same direction their army had taken. From this he concluded that the enemy would soon be burdened with thousands of helpless civilians. That would slow them down very quickly. Time enough to catch up.

The wall had been an unpleasant surprise, though. Very vexing, especially since he had no one on hand to blame for it. There *had* been this tiny, unintelligible mark on one of the maps he'd studied, but only on the one. And who was to guess it meant anything at all, let alone such a big, bloody obstacle. Damned mapmakers should draw their maps so a person could tell a bleeding wall from an accidental squiggle.

Tough little buggers, those Larnaki, and a real nuisance when you had to fight them out in the open. Behind that wall, they could well turn into a serious problem. Kuruma wanted to be long gone before the weather turned and the first snows came. He hated the cold. But he'd pry them out of there forthwith, if Noburo's toys held even half of what he'd promised. Better count on half, actually: people's penchant for delusional self-aggrandizement was boundless, and Noburo was certainly no exception.

Ilario Zamaròn, the Moragian mercenary captain, rode up to report that his engineers had finished setting up the three small trebuchets they'd brought along. Kuruma also had them building a larger mangonel for bombarding the wall, though he doubted he'd need it, and a battering ram to take down the gate. He was on his way to inspect the engineers' handiwork and tell them what he wanted them to shoot at when a stone from one of the catapults on the wall hissed by scant feet away. Kuruma flinched but resisted the urge to run or flatten himself on the ground. Blasted brothers would never let him live *that* down.

The stone burrowed a bloody path through a squad of reject Unborn who were assembling a scaling ladder. No big loss. There were lots more where those came from. He'd kept most of his fighting force well back and out of range of flying stones and arrows. Their time would come later. First, a bit of softening up the opposition.

He had the trebuchets start out with throwing simple rocks, the aim being to destroy the catapults on the wall. They had one lucky hit early on, but an hour later the Larnaki had cleared away the dead, the wounded, and the debris and winched up and assembled a replacement. Industrious little mice. Then they had a lucky shot of their own that made matchsticks of one of his trebuchets. No matter. Two was all he needed.

Towards noon, everything was in place.

Twenty platoons of battle-Unborn stood ready, evenly spaced the length of the wall and just out of the Larnaki's range. Rejects had laid out twenty scaling ladders much closer to the wall, too close for the defenders' catapults to do them damage but still far enough away so they couldn't lob stones down on them by hand. The exercise had cost him two dozen rejects, all of them expendable. This way the platoons could grab the ladders on the run, meaning they'd have a good hundred yards less to lug the heavy things. The mercenary archers were concentrated in the middle, positioned to cover the advance of another Unborn platoon carrying the battering ram.

The thing was a work of art. Not only had the engineers found what had to be the largest tree in all of Larnakis, they'd also fitted it with an iron tip wrought in the form of a dragon's head. A fitting irony, Kuruma thought. Dragon eats dragon. Large holes had been drilled through the trunk to accommodate thick oaken spars that served as handles to carry and swing the ram by.

And lastly, tended by two brothers each, the two huge crates containing Noburo's little extra something were positioned by the surviving trebuchets, ready to load and shoot.

Well outside the danger zone, Kuruma had one more thing to take care of before he gave the signal. He motioned Tano over.

'I have a special assignment for you. As soon as the gate is breached, I want you on the other side of that wall with a squad of Unborn. Your one and only objective is to find and eliminate the royal family, especially the child. It shouldn't be more than a few months old. If you can bring it to me alive, even better. But don't risk anything. I'd rather you killed it than lost it.'

'And how am I supposed to find the right woman and child among, what, ten, twenty thousand people?' Tano asked with his usual contrariness.

'Ah. There I have a little helper for you.' Kuruma smiled and fished in one of the deep inner pockets of his robe.

He handed Tano a chain with a twisted-cross pendant hanging from it. A colorless stone was set in the middle of the cross. Kuruma had spent a considerable amount of gold to procure the three long, dark hairs embedded with the stone, working through a chain of agents that reached all the way to Dunmark, and from there into Larnakis.

'This will lead you to them. The stone will point you in their direction by turning darker the nearer they are. It's attuned to the mother, but where she is the child won't be far. Kindly don't lose it. I've spent months preparing it, and there's no way to make another. Now go, and be ready.'

Satisfied that he'd forgotten nothing, Kuruma gave the signal.

At the left trebuchet, the attendant brothers had the rear wall of the crate off. It was packed with stacked rows of cages, each one completely filled with a transparent sac containing roughly two dozen small, weird-looking creatures. Pale as human skin, with five legs and a blunt, neckless head that ended in a distensible mouth filled with needle-sharp teeth, they bore a close resemblance to human hands.

Wearing thick protective gloves that reached up to their elbows, the brothers injected a liquid reagent into a sac, rousing the creatures inside to frenzied movement. Then they placed the cage in the trebuchet's bucket. One of the crew pulled the release, and the cage went sailing over the wall. While the crew rewound the engine, the brothers prepared the next cage. Even before it was ready to launch, angry, frightened shouts arose from the wall.

Meanwhile, the other pair of brothers were filling their engine's bucket with a different payload. They too wore gloves, but the cages they pulled from their box held discs of pink flesh, each the size of a barrow wheel, ten or twelve to a cage. They stirred in restless, undulating movement, furling and opening like stranded deep-sea creatures, the variously shaded, smooth or hairy skin on their backs crinkling and stretching. Their moist, wrinkled undersides were covered with hundreds of tiny suckers surrounding central, puckered orifices that opened and closed rhythmically, revealing rings of hooked, sickle-shaped teeth. A cage at a time, the brothers emptied them into the bucket and loosed them at the enemy.

Once airborne, the creatures were able to influence their trajectories by slightly modifying the shapes of their bodies, and they seemed to have an uncanny knack for alighting on people. Especially on people's heads. After a successful landing they instantly thinned and spread out, becoming tough, airtight membranes that covered the target's head and face or whatever other body part they landed on. The

274

suckers made it next to impossible to pull them off. As soon as they were in place they began chomping on their hosts' faces, tearing off chunks of flesh by expanding and retracting their teeth-rings. Few of their victims were still able to scream.

When Kuruma saw that mayhem was rampant on and behind the wall, he ordered the scaling ladders and ram to advance. He had to make an effort to resist slaughtering the remaining sacrifices and sending an utterly gratuitous wave of debilitating fear at the defenders on the wall.

A hail of arrows greeted the attackers. A few Unborn fell. The rest kept going.

The first ladders went up.

Up on the wall near the left gatehouse tower, Anskar was trying to pry one of the ghastly flying stranglers off a man's arm with his bare hands. The things were nearly impossible to kill. They were tough as elephant hide, and if you put enough pressure behind the blade to cut them open, you were just as liable to go right through and do serious harm to the person you were trying to save. If you got one early on, before it had suckered itself tight, and you managed to tear it off, you'd not only rip a good-sized patch of skin off with it. You'd most likely also have it fastened to yourself in the blink of an eye. He kicked away one of the scuttling, crablike creatures before it could sink its evil little teeth into the soldier's neck.

'Cut it off!' the man yelled, frantic. 'I don't care about my arm. Just get the damned thing off me! It's eating me alive!'

He was right. Lumps were beginning to swell the thing's shape,

275

pieces of meat from the man's arm, torn off and engorged by that ugly ring of sharp, scything teeth. Steeling himself, Anskar made one, two, three, four swift, surgical cuts with his knife, grabbed the thing still clinging to skin and bits of flesh and quickly flung it over the parapet. Then he cut off a broad strip of the soldier's surcoat and wrapped it tightly around the lacerated arm.

'Thank you, Radj,' the man breathed, and fainted.

Anskar was about to call for a healer when he heard – and felt – the first booming impact of the ram hitting the gate.

Leaving the unconscious man in the care of a fellow soldier, he picked up his sword and hastened towards the gatehouse tower. Out of the corner of his eye he saw one of the great, hideous beasts rushing through the air towards him, clinging to the top of a ladder and brandishing a heavy, four foot-long cleaver. Without thinking, Anskar swung. His timing was instinctively right, his blow splitting the thing's ugly head down the middle, helmet and all. It hung there with one arm caught in the rungs until the next one down grabbed it by the ankle and pulled it off, flinging it away like a sack of meal. It was frightening how strong the beasts were.

Anskar propped a foot against the top of the ladder, holding the iron grappling hooks away from the wall while a couple of soldiers hurried to his aid with a pole long enough to topple it over. They arrived just in time to save his foot from being hacked off by the next monster clambering to the top. The ladder stood balanced in mid-air for a moment. Then it tilted backwards, gathering downward momentum, and crashed to the ground. The uglies hanging on to it took a rough tumble, but none of them stayed down.

Anskar saw more ladders go up along the wall. There was another booming impact down at the gate. Maybe there was something more they could do to shore it up. He ran down the tower stairs and out into the barbican. Baran was there, directing a group of men who were desperately working to reinforce the weakened timbers.

'It's not going to hold much longer,' Baran shouted above the noise of the battle. 'We should think about getting out of here. Maybe we can hold them in the canyon.'

With the realization that their last line of defense was about to give way, a sudden calm descended on Anskar.

'Baran. Listen to me. They're going to overrun us any moment now. I want you to go and tell everyone to clear out of Tinnan and head for the passes as fast as they can. Then find my wife and daughter. Take them to safety. To Dunmark. Our relatives there will take them in.'

'But I – '

'No. With your broken arm you're pretty much useless here, and you know it. You'd only get yourself killed, and you'd be doing no one a favor by it.'

'But Rupili – '

'I don't care if you have to knock her senseless and tie her to her horse. Just get them out of here, to Dunmark. It'll probably be safer than Anapur. Now go. I'd say ride like all hell was after you, but that would be stating the obvious. Farewell, my friend.'

'Radj,' Baran said, tears in his eyes. 'I'll be seeing you.'

They clasped hands. Then he was off.

Anskar rushed back up to top of the wall. Things weren't going quite as badly as he'd feared. So far the Larnaki had managed to keep most of the invaders off of the wall. The gate was slowly disintegrating but hadn't broken down yet. Maybe he could still buy some time for the people in Tinnan.

Then at least ten ladders went up, and stayed up. Uglies began to pour onto the walkway, hacking away with their big, nasty cleavers and sending men and parts of men flying left and right. There was another huge, splintering crash down below. This one sounded terminal.

'Retreat!' Anskar shouted. 'Get off the wall! Retreat! Retreat!'

The surviving men took up the call. Covered from below by the reserve archers spending their last arrows, most of them made it off the wall. Down by the gate, Anskar found Tamsin awaiting him, holding Fleet's reins.

The retreat through the canyon was a nightmare.

Time and again, they tried to make a stand and somehow stem the evil tide, but the relentless pressure of the enemy's overwhelming numbers kept pushing them back.

Then they were at the end of the canyon, forced out into the open. Before they could form a battle line, the enemy forces were already streaming past on either side, flowing out into the valley and slaughtering every living thing in their way. With the Unborn and mercenary soldiers came the small, five-legged scuttlers. They went largely unnoticed, though they were already busy wreaking some not inconsiderable havoc of their own.

Anskar, surrounded by his remaining troops, was about to throw himself into this last struggle when suddenly he felt a commanding call. Without conscious thought his hand went for his belt pouch, undid the string and pulled out the blue stone bowl.

It was singing, giving off a high ringing sound like a perfect blade coming out of the scabbard. The bowl was excited. It spoke to him.

It wanted to be used.

❖ ❖ ❖

Kuruma didn't join in the mad rush.

His was a quieter, more deliberate kind of bloodlust. Besides, hand-to-hand fighting had never been his cup of tea. So he left the command post right where it was, three hundred yards shy of the wall, and set up a relay with reject runners traveling back and forth between his tent and the front, bringing him news of the latest developments. Most of the other brothers followed his example and hung back. Only Tano was nowhere in sight – meaning he must have departed on his errand. He'd better have.

From the runners' reports it seemed that things were going splendidly on the other end. But if Tano's mission didn't succeed and the child wasn't killed in the general melee either, if the mother or someone else managed to flee with the brat and save it's cursed little neck, then the whole bloody exercise would come to nothing. Ummuz have mercy on Tano if he came back empty-handed. Kuruma certainly wouldn't.

Then it struck him what a nuisance it would be if the child died and was gobbled up by a hungry Unborn before they had a chance to confirm the kill. Damn! He should have thought of that earlier.

Suddenly he went completely still, listening.

Yes. There was... something. He heard a faint, keening sound. It seemed to be coming out of the gorge, steadily rising in tone and volume even as he strained to make out what it was.

Of a sudden there was a strange, crackling tension in the air. He felt the hairs on his neck and forearms rise as if a mighty storm were about to break loose. He glanced up. The sky was cloudless. Then he had it. Magic!

But not sorcery. No, those cursed Larnaki must have a mage among them! Only there wasn't a living mage who had this kind of power, hadn't been in centuries – at least not that he'd heard. And still the magic was gathering force. Incredible.

He had to do something.

Frightened, the brothers flocked around him.

Kuruma himself was close to panicking. He sent for the prisoners. Then he had the brothers form a Wedge. He used all of them save for the one needed to kill the sacrifices. Eighteen Brothers to a side. Thirty-seven in all, counting himself.

Something like this had never been done before. Doctrine held that thirteen was the maximum. Anything more threatened to overload and burn out the point man, with catastrophic consequences not only for him but for the whole Wedge. No one argued with him. They were scared witless. And they were probably thinking they could always break the chain and drop Kuruma in the crap if things got iffy.

He didn't care. He was the strongest sorcerer alive, and this was an emergency, a matter of life or death. Better to make use of the one chance they still had. He placed himself at the tip of the Wedge, calmed himself, concentrated, gave the signal to begin.

One by one, the sacrifices had their carotids slit. That way they wouldn't bleed out too quickly, and the force of their deaths could be exploited to the last drop.

Impossibly, the strange magic was still growing.

Not a mage, then. Kuruma had dealt with them before, and knew the taste and smell of their magic. This was developing into something different, and a hundred thousand times stronger. A god maybe? It was too late to reconsider.

The power was already flowing into him through the wings of the Wedge, dizzying, exhilarating, nauseating, building in a mad crescendo that shook the very foundations of his being. He'd never known anything like it. In a rush, his body seemed to disintegrate into infinitesimally small particles, and he became a cloud of pure force suspended in a maelstrom of raging elements, about to be blown apart and scattered in a wild, merciless storm of energy.

He released.

A pitch-black, roiling thunderbolt the size of a house shot into the canyon and vanished from sight. Moments later, he felt himself solidify again, though he was still riding a glorious high in the aftermath of the enormous power he'd just wielded.

He exulted. He was still standing. He'd done it!

In the next breath, he realized he'd rejoiced too soon.

He felt the backlash coming before he saw it. A sudden pressure built up in his ears, and he heard an ominous soughing and rumbling as if the mother of all storms were approaching through the pass, funneled and compressed into an insane inferno in the narrow gap between the cliffs.

Then it came screaming out of the canyon, faster than any earthly wind could blow, driving a madly whirling cloud of dust and debris before it and engulfing the Wedge in less time than it took to blink.

Miraculously, Kuruma was spared. Whether it was because he hastily flattened himself on the ground, giving a damn for the integrity of the chain and the idiots behind him, or because whatever came back at them just skipped right through, using him like an open door, he neither knew nor cared. Behind him, it went through the Brothers like a scythe through ripe wheat, leaving nothing but an eighty-foot smear of blood, tattered flesh, and fragments of bone fanned out along the ground where the Wedge had stood just moments ago.

A deep rumbling started up somewhere in the mountain. Kuruma felt the ground vibrate under his feet. By now he had a very bad feeling about where this was going. Only one thing left to do. Run.

He wasn't going alone, though. Only there wasn't a single reject anywhere in sight. They all seemed to have vanished while he wasn't looking. And he saw with horror that the remaining reserve of battle-Unborn were busy committing suicide, sticking knives in their eyes or ears, slitting their throats or opening their bellies. He screamed at them to stop, but they paid him no heed. There was an expression on their ugly, normally blank faces that Kuruma had never seen there before. It was completely absurd: they actually looked serene, content, almost happy.

Thankfully, a handful of them remained untouched by this madness, and Kuruma promptly took command of them. The mountain groaned and trembled. There was no time to pack, no time to take anything at all. Kuruma ordered the largest Unborn to kneel so he could climb onto its back.

Then he yelled at them to run.

They'd gone maybe a mile and a half when the earth suddenly bucked, throwing them off their feet with a deafening sound like thunder, a crashing and roaring and shaking that seemed to go on forever.

Dazed, Kuruma looked up to see a gigantic dust cloud rolling towards them, gobbling up the sky and the landscape with frightening speed. Frantically looking around for cover, he spotted a wide crack in the rock face bordering the road. He motioned to the Unborn, pointing at the cleft. Just then, the descending dust storm began to spit out house-sized boulders, sending them crashing and careening down the slope and pulverizing everything in their way. One of the Unborn was mashed into a reddish smear on the road. The others managed to join Kuruma in relative safety. He reckoned a direct hit on their hidey-hole by one of the gigantic flying rocks would probably do them in anyway. Then the dust came, turning day into night, invading and clogging their eyes and noses and throats, and their whole universe narrowed down to a single, desperate occupation: fighting to breathe.

It seemed as if days oozed by before the dust finally thinned enough to allow a minimum of light and air to seep back into the world. When they could see again, they crawled out of the fissure. Everything in sight was covered with at least an inch of fine, grey dust. Every step raised a small cloud of it. It was as if they'd been transported to another planet, a grey, wasted world circling a dying sun.

Kuruma looked up the slope, back towards the pass. Farther up, the air was beginning to clear. It took him a while to grasp what he was seeing there – or rather, what he wasn't seeing. He suddenly felt incredibly lucky to be alive at all. A miracle.

No. Fate had taken a hand in this. He still had a destiny to fulfill.

Setting his jaw and squaring his shoulders, he turned his back on a lamentable episode in his life – one that would soon be forgotten, he'd see to that – and focused his attention firmly on the future.

Back to Fellmere, then.

Taking the first few steps, he'd already begun rewriting the whole sad affair in his head, changing a fact here and bending a truth there until the blame was neatly shifted and much more conveniently placed, meaning squarely on everyone's shoulders except his own.

Easy. After all, there was no one left to contradict him.

❖ ❖ ❖

Anskar was lost in a whirlwind.

What had started as a tingling sensation in his hand when he grasped the bowl had spread in an instant and taken over his whole body, taken him over. He hadn't the power to resist it. It simply overwhelmed him, like a tidal wave sweeping up a grain of sand.

The bowl was in complete control, liberated, exulting, a vortex of pure, unfettered energy driven by nothing but a boundless need to expand and grow and finally release the colossal force bound up in it in one vast and glorious discharge of wild, untamed magic.

He had no eyes for the Unborn, who had suddenly stopped butchering the Larnaki and begun to maim and kill themselves instead. Nor was he aware of the mercenaries lowering their weapons, dazed and confused, half a breath from surrendering and ending this mad sorcerers' game that showed less and less likelihood of delivering the promised spoils.

Blind to everything around him, he didn't notice his men drawing back, staring at him first in amazement and then in growing apprehension. He didn't hear Tamsin shouting at him, didn't feel the brave and stalwart sergeant step up and take his arm any more than he noticed the magic reacting to the disturbance, repelling Tamsin and hurling him like a human missile into the terrified bystanders.

Still, Anskar was aware that this wasn't going as it should, that something was gravely amiss. He fought with the bowl, struggled to win back control at least over his own actions, summoned every last ounce of willpower to release it and cast it away, to break the connection and thus maybe stop the magic.

For a moment, he thought he might succeed.

Then a tremendous thunderbolt of dark malintent rushed out of the canyon, slamming into the bowl's force field, and just like that, Anskar's struggle was over. He was reduced to a helpless spectator as the two powers mixed and became something else again, something infinitely more potent, dangerous and unstable.

Half a breath later, the volatile mixture exploded.

Connected as he was to the bowl's part in what was happening, Anskar felt rather than saw gigantic strands of interwoven power shooting out in all directions like horizontal bolts of sullied lightning, burrowing deep into the sides of the mountains, dividing and branching into multiple, ever smaller skeins as the hybrid magic found and followed every weakness, every vein, seam, fissure, crack, and fault line down to the very heart of the stone.

The earth shook.

There was an earsplitting, ripping, grinding crash of rock on rock, as if the very bones of the earth were being violently twisted and broken.

The canyon disappeared. The gap between its walls closed with a colossal bang, expelling a huge cloud of dust. Redhorn and Donner Peak seemed to waver and shift as if seen through a swirling heat haze.

Then, with a gigantic, deafening rumble, the mountains' flanks disintegrated. Slowly at first, and then in a massive rush, they toppled and fell into Tinnan valley, burying it under a billion tons of rock, erasing it in a billowing, mile-high storm of dust.

The cataclysm seemed to go on forever.

At last it susbsided. There were a few minor slides still, a last clatter here and there of a rock finding its final equilibrium, and then there was only silence, unbroken and final.

❖ ❖ ❖

A handful of fugitives had already reached the valley's southernmost end, thus narrowly escaping the falling mountains. The suffocating dust and stray, flying rocks decimated their small number even further. Only a very few survived the cataclysm and fought their way over Tinnan pass and down into Anapur, there to tell the tale of the death of Larnakis.

❖ ❖ ❖

An idea that is not dangerous is unworthy of being called an idea at all.

Oscar Wilde

16 The Jemmarraa

ather and the Unborn broke camp in the dark and set out long before first light. They'd discussed traveling only at night and lying up during the daytime but decided against it. They couldn't risk missing a water hole in the dark, not with Nissa's life in the balance.

Already back in Fellmere Gormin, thinking ahead, had the Unborn secretly sequester and pack the essentials they'd need for this part of the trip. They all had long scarves to cover their heads and faces, and one of the pack-horses carried poles, guy ropes, pegs and a large canvas for building a shelter.

As the sun rose higher, the heat quickly became intense. To Rather, who'd never been anywhere near a desert, it was a physical shock, like the opposite of being plunged into ice water. He supposed it wasn't any better for the others, though none of them complained, and as the morning progressed he began to acclimatize and find it bearable.

The terrain was flat, the light-colored sand packed and firm, as if the winds coming down from the mountains had swept all the loose sand far out into the desert. It made traveling easier, but if there was any of the stark beauty ascribed to deserts in general to be found in this flat, featureless expanse of sand and sky, it escaped him.

Gormin kept them on track by looking back every so often to check whether the boulders they'd camped by, rapidly shrinking to a couple of specks on the horizon, were still lined up with a prominent peak of the mountains behind them.

His reckoning turned out to be accurate. Late in the afternoon, they came upon the first water hole – or rather nearly fell into it. Hidden from sight in a steep-sided dip of the terrain, it became visible only at the very last moment. Rather, who was in the lead and trudging along in a stupor of heat and exhaustion, noticed the drop too late and went sliding down the slope of loose sand, ending up sitting on the pool's stony rim with his feet in the water, which was surprisingly cool and clear.

Looking down, he could see no bottom, only the rocky sides plunging like a vertical shaft into the deep until they were lost in blue-green shadow. He reckoned the shaft went all the way down to the subterranean river that fed the pool – which was probably the reason why it didn't fill up and become clogged with sand; whatever fell in and sank to the bottom was carried away by the current far below, likely never to surface again. He shivered.

There was a patch of even ground on the opposite side of the pool, perfect for putting up a shelter. First though, Rather checked on Nissa. She was parched, and very hot, almost too hot to touch. She needed to go into the water immediately. But this was no shallow lakeside, and Rather feared for her safety. The mere notion of her sinking into this watery abyss filled him with near panic.

With Rain's help and a few lengths of rope, he tied her securely to the wooden stretcher, attaching the excess rope to pegs driven deep into the sand. Then they lowered Nissa into the pool, and Rather spent the next two hours sitting on the edge and making sure her head stayed out of the water while the others saw to the horses, set up camp and prepared the evening meal.

By the time Changing Gray came to spell him, the ice-cold water had brought Nissa's temperature down to something between 'hot' and 'very warm'. It had also leeched most of the feeling out of Rather's feet and lower legs, and he nearly fell on his face getting up. The smell of food kept him going. He was starved. The simple fare of freshly baked bread, jerky, and hard cheese was more than welcome, their last meal having been breakfast roughly twelve hours earlier. Despite his hunger, Rather was so tired he nearly nodded off several times before he'd finished eating. When he was done, he remembered to ask that he be woken at midnight. Then, without noticeable transition, he was asleep.

It seemed like he'd only slept for a few minutes when Gormin gently shook him. 'You can go right back to sleep,' the Unborn said. 'I've taken her out. She was getting cool.'

'How is she?' Rather mumbled, only marginally awake.

'She's fine. Rest. Everything's taken care of.'

Five hours later, they were packed and on the march again.

The second day went much like the first, except that, arriving at the next water hole, they found it filled with sand. The only indication that they were in fact in the right place were the upper branches of a small, gnarled tree sticking out of the sand.

They dug, the Unborns' huge hands moving sand faster than shovels. It took them two hours to excavate a shallow puddle of milky, gritty sludge, hardly large enough to hold the girl's body, the water barely covering her. This time the cooling process was much slower. They left her there all night, but in the morning she was still too warm for comfort.

It was still dark when they departed on the longest leg of their journey through the desert. Rather's heart was heavy with worry, and so he was much relieved when day broke and he saw a dark smudge on the horizon ahead of them: their first sight of Massarit, the Table of the Gods.

All through the day Massarit loomed ever larger, a flat-topped slab of dark brown rock more than five miles long and rising at least six hundred feet above the desert floor. Spurred on by the sight of their goal as well as by the urgency of Nissa's worsening condition, they decided to forego the noon rest period and press on. It was near dark when, following a growing convergence of animal and human tracks, they reached the towering rock and found the entrance to Massarit: a large, triangular cleft in the massif's north-eastern face.

As they were about to enter a wide gallery running through the rock, two men stepped from the shadows, barring the way with leveled spears. They wore loose, dark trousers and shirts, and black turbans with veils that covered their faces, leaving only slits for the eyes.

'You cannot enter,' the taller of the two said.

'Please,' Rather said. 'We have a sick woman with us. She'll die if we can't get her to water.'

'She will die anyway, if she enters,' the man said. 'All of you will die. There is a plague in Massarit.'

'I don't care,' Rather said, desperate. 'We can help. I'm a healer, as is one of my companions, and the others can make themselves useful too. Let us in.'

The two Assenai seemed only now to take in the Unborn standing patiently behind Rather. A look passed between them.

'Wait here,' the taller man said and vanished into the dark tunnel, leaving his companion to guard the entrance.

After a long wait during which Rather fussed over Nissa who was dangerously hot again and Gormin rummaged around in the horses' panniers, the tall man reappeared, bearing a torch and accompanied by an old man dressed in white, his unveiled, suntanned face crisscrossed with a myriad of wrinkles. Before Rather could say anything, Gormin hobbled past him and placed a large, heavy bundle at the old man's feet. Rather saw a sliver of something white poking out of the cloth wrapping, glittering faintly in the torchlight.

'Ah,' the old man said. 'Someone who knows the desert ways. I see *aksh*. That is good. Tell me, what brings you to Massarit at such a dire time?'

Gormin began by repeating Rather's offer of assistance in the crisis that had struck Massarit. Then he related the story of their quest to find help for Nissa, mentioning that she'd been imprisoned and bespelled by sorcerers but leaving out much of the details.

If the old man had any questions, he saved them for later. Instead, he asked to see the girl. He knelt and studied her intently for a moment. Then he rose and looked in turn at each member of the party.

Meeting the ancient's eyes, Rather was surprised by the sharpness and clarity of his gaze.

'I am Batukhan, elder of the Assenai,' the old man finally said. 'I bid you welcome to Massarit, though you come at a time of sickness, death, and mourning. You have respected the traditions of the desert, bringing the *chalat,* the gift of salt, and you have offered help before asking it for yourselves. You have *aksh,* and that may be the one thing that can save us now. Come, let us find succor for your young companion, and a warming fire and sustenance for the rest of you.'

He led the way with the tall man bearing the torch. The other man stayed behind to guard the entrance.

'How did you know about the salt?' Rather whispered to Gormin as they stepped under the arched stone roof of the gallery. 'And what was all that talk about aksh or whatever it's called?'

'Just a bit of reading I did back in Fellmere,' Gormin answered with an expression that Rather tentatively identified as the Unborn version of a satisfied smirk. 'It always pays off to educate oneself. As for explaining aksh, it would take me all night just to get started. It's a sort of honor code, very complicated. I think we'd better save it for another time.'

The path through the bedrock rose steadily.

After about a hundred yards, the gallery opened up and became a deep, sandy-bottomed cleft that continued to climb upwards for another three hundred yards. Then suddenly the walls either side were gone, and they stood looking out on the dwelling place of the Assenai.

In the dark, Rather had only the Assenai's cooking fires and the stars to reckon by, but even so it was clear that the open space inside Massarit's walls was enormous, an irregular round well over a mile in diameter. There were several clusters of fires on the near perimeter that seemed to lie a good deal higher than the canyon floor. Not far away, he saw faint reflections of light on what looked like a fairly large body of water.

Somewhere off to the right, he heard women's voices joined in a keening chant that was half song, half wail. It transported such an acuteness of feeling, such sadness and grief that he found himself moved to tears by it, sensing in it a depth and range that resonated with the desert's vastness and the age-old struggle of humans to survive in this hard and unforgiving environment.

Batukhan sent the tall man, whose name was Chinua, off on an errand. Then he led the party down to the water's edge. Wasting no time, he instructed Rain and Two Flower to prepare a place for Nissa's stretcher in a carefully chosen, shallow spot about fifteen feet out from the shore, underlaying one end of the board with rocks to keep her head out of the water. Then he had them place five larger rocks in a ring around her. He showed no reserve or unease in dealing with the Unborn, treating them, Rather imagined, no different than any of his Assenai, a fact that didn't go unnoticed by them.

While Batukhan oversaw the preparations and Striving Four led the horses off to one side and let them drink, another four elders arrived, two men and two women dressed in white like Batukhan. All five of them squatted down around Nissa's stretcher, giving her a thorough inspection, though they touched her only briefly and lightly with the backs of their hands.

Finally Erdene, a diminutive, bowed woman so ancient she looked like she could have been Batukhan's grandmother, rose and beckoned Rather over. 'Tell me, young man,' she said, 'do you know where the girl is from?'

'I'm not sure,' he answered. 'But Changing Grey mentioned something about her being from Almorica.'

'Ah,' Erdene said. 'The Fire People. That explains much. And the place where this was done to her? Across the mountains, you say?'

'A place called Fellmere,' Rather said. 'East of the Hag's teeth. It's a stronghold of sorcerers. They call themselves the Brotherhood of Um – '

'Don't!' Erdene said sharply, making a warding sign. 'Do not speak that name aloud here – or anywhere else, for that matter. It's worse than bad luck. It's evil. I've heard of them, in any case. At least now, we have an idea what we're up against. It's not going to be easy, and I can't make any promises. So don't get your hopes up just yet.'

Seeing Rather's face fall, she added, 'But we'll give it our best, and that's more than you'll find elsewhere.' She gave him a grandmotherly pat on the arm.

'Thank you,' Rather said. 'This means a lot to me.'

'Let's not be hasty, young man. Time enough to thank us when we're done. Now go and see to your girl while we get ready.'

She sent him off with a wave.

While Rather had been talking to Erdene, Chinua had returned with three men bearing poles and a large bundle of white cloth. In a surprisingly short time, they set up a round, steep-sided tent over the site in the water chosen by Batukhan, who fussed over them, making sure every detail was executed just so and the entrance flap was facing exactly due east. Four torches were lit in the tent. When everything was arranged to his satisfaction, he addressed Rather and the Unborn.

'We will likely be all night,' he told them. 'Maybe longer. Time enough for you to get some food and rest. You'll need it. Tomorrow, you'll begin fulfilling your part of the bargain. Go now. We will send for you when we're done.'

Chinua settled down in the sand a good twenty yards from the tent, a bundle of spare torches by his side; clearly he was going to stay and hold watch. Another man, Mongke, accompanied Rather and the Unborn to the nearest cluster of fires. At the foot of a long flight of stone steps leading up through a series of narrow, cultivated terraces, they unloaded the horses and left them in a small, stone-fenced corral where someone had already deposited a pile of hay for the exhausted and hungry animals.

They climbed the stairs to the topmost terrace, which was a good deal wider than the others. Rather saw stone dwellings built right up against the canyon wall and light falling from the openings of chambers cut into the rock. Mongke took them to a cookfire burning in front of one of the simple, flat-roofed houses. A great iron pot hanging from a tripod over the fire gave off a delicious, stewy smell, and a young woman was baking thin rounds of bread on a large, flat stone set close to the embers. Rather was touched when Mongke introduced her as his wife Tolui, realizing that the man had brought them as guests to his own home.

Tolui, pretty and shy, glanced at the Unborn with awe, but without any sign of fear, indicating they should sit on stone benches set

295

around the fire. She ladled out generous helpings of stew into earthenware bowls. Mongke passed them around, together with rounds of bread. Next, there followed a lengthy silence while the famished travelers stilled the worst of their hunger.

'Very, very good,' Gormin complimented Tolui.

'Excellent,' Rain confirmed shyly.

'That's only because you're famished,' Tolui said modestly, blushing. 'It's nothing special, really.'

'Oh, but it is,' Rather said. 'Best I've had in a long, long time.'

'Best I've *ever* had,' Striving Four said with an impish grin, even risking a darting glance at the young woman. 'But then, that's not saying much, seeing what they fed us back in Fellmere.'

Once Green let out a loud, rumbling belch that echoed off the canyon wall and got him a severely disapproving glance from Counting Clouds.

'Sorry,' he said, belatedly covering his mouth with a huge paw. If Unborn had been able to blush, he would have glowed pink in the dark. Tolui giggled.

'Don't be,' Mongke said, smiling. 'With us Assenai, it is only good manners to show that you appreciated the meal.' He underlined his statement with a substantial belch of his own.

Once Green gave Counting Clouds a smirk, and got a sniff in reply.

Mongke and Tolui were prepared to sleep outside and offer their guests the house, but Rather and the Unborn politely declined, saying they were used to sleeping rough and actually preferred it. They bedded down around the dying fire, more for the light than warmth. Nights inside Massarit were distinctly warmer than out in the open desert, the dark rock walls radiating back the heat they'd absorbed during the day.

Sleep came quickly for the Unborn, but it eluded Rather.

He stared into the night sky, watching the stars slowly turn through their endless cycle and a thin sliver of a moon appear over the canyon's rim like an opening parenthesis to some mysterious and undecipherable message from the gods or from some alien, space-faring race – if a distinction between the two made any sense; maybe they were one and the same, and maybe neither existed. His thoughts turned on Nissa and her predicament.

Recklessly, crazily, he'd bet everything on finding help for her here in Massarit, not even considering another possibility, though in truth he still couldn't think of one. If this didn't work out, he had no alternative, no plan B. Nissa would die or spend the rest of her life as a water-bound vegetable lying inanimate in some pool or other, slowly shriveling up and wasting away under the constant threat of terminal dissolution. Or maybe she'd turn into some kind of pseudo-marine life form with gills, webbed fingers and a fish tail, a comatose mermaid to Rather's haunted sailor.

When he couldn't stand it any longer, he quietly rose and made his way down to the lake. Chinua hadn't moved from his post. Beside him a single candle burned, sheltered in a hollow dug from the sand. Rather settled down next to him. The tent was dark now, the torches inside extinguished. Chinua seemed comfortable with Rather's company.

'Are all your elders ashamans?' Rather asked softly.

Chinua hesitated, threw him an unreadable glance. 'Not all of them,' he said. 'But these five, yes. We are lucky to have so many of them, and such powerful ones, more than any of the other tribes.'

'Anything happening yet?' Rather asked.

'A lot, probably,' Chinua answered. 'Just nothing an ordinary person like you or me could see. But it's early still. These things take time. Before you arrived, they were about to sit down for a three-day ceremony to try and rid us of the sickness that has been spreading for a week. More than fifty have died of it already.'

'They postponed the ceremony because of us?' Rather asked.

'Don't worry,' Chinua said. 'They have their reasons for doing things, and they wouldn't be going through with this without a good one. They seem to think it's a worthwhile trade.'

'I just hope they're right,' Rather sighed, 'and we'll be able to do what they expect from us in return.'

They lapsed into silence.

Later – the moon was just disappearing over the canyon's western rim – Rather thought he saw a flicker of light inside the tent. He began to watch more closely. After a few minutes he saw it again, a muted glint that lasted less than a second. Soon after, another. And then another.

The elders started to chant, a sporadic singsong that rose and fell, stopped and began anew, an erratic, flickering non-rhythm that somehow reminded Rather of random flames licking the coals of a dying fire. Only this fire was being stoked, it seemed. There were more flashes, the intervals between them shortening, every flare brighter than the last until finally they merged into a continuous staccato of flickering lights.

Simultaneously, the chanting rose and quickened, the voices separating into a fivefold canon and reuniting again in a single flow of rising urgency.

Rather felt Chinua beside him tense. His own hands were sweating, he realized, his jaw muscles working up to a cramp.

And still the lights and the chanting continued to accelerate, until he felt himself pulsating along with them like an instrument resonating to some fundamental, arcane harmonic.

Suddenly there was a blinding flash of light and a thunderclap.

With a WHOOSH! the whole tent flew up into the air, catching fire like a fatally stricken airship. In the light of the burning fabric Rather saw the ancients flung off their stone perches, flying backwards and splashing into the shallow water.

Moments later it was dark again. A few smoldering shreds were all that remained of the tent, suicidal fireflies drifting down to extinguish themselves in the lake with tiny hisses.

Rather jumped up and stumbled down to the water's edge.
Blinded by the flash, he couldn't see a thing. Chinua lit a torch from the candle and followed him. Rather heard a cough and saw a white-clad figure lying in the water right in front of him. He bent down to help whoever it was up.

'I'm fine,' Erdene grunted. 'Go and see to your woman. She'll need a familiar face now more than anything.'

Rather didn't bother to point out that Nissa had never seen his face before tonight. He waded out to the center of the circle.

In the flickering light of Chinua's torch, he saw her. She was sitting up on the stretcher, her legs still in the water. There was a wild gleam in her eyes, as if she imagined herself still surrounded by dangerous, bloodthirsty enemies and was readying to release another blast of her fiery magic.

'Hey,' Rather said, squatting down beside her.

For a moment he thought she was going to blow him out of the water. Then, slowly, her eyes focused on him, and the craziness in them began to subside.

'It's okay,' he said, the words feeling awkward and inane. 'You're safe. You're among friends.'

Her expression softened. 'I know you.'

'Um.' Rather was suddenly tongue-tied.

'I know you,' she repeated. 'You've been in all my dreams lately. I kept falling off high places, and somehow you were always there to catch me and save my life. And then we'd ...' She broke off suddenly. Even in the feeble light, he could see her blushing.

Sounds like she's just handed you the perfect opening. All you need to do now is come up with something that, if nothing else, at least doesn't make you look like a complete moron.

But his brain seemed to have switched itself off. Nothing at all came to mind. Instead, he just squatted there, looking at her, losing himself in the allure of those deep, dark eyes. With an effort, he pulled himself back from the brink.

'I'm sorry,' he stammered. 'I shouldn't... How are you feeling? Would you like to, um, get out of the water?'

'I'm fine,' she said, and he thought she looked slightly disappointed. 'And yes, I'd love to get on dry land again. I feel like I've had enough water for a very long time.'

She took Rather's outstretched hand and let him pull her upright. She was still shaky, steadying herself against him. In a sudden fit of recklessness, he put an arm around her waist.

Idiot, he told himself. *Get off this slippery slope while you still can. Dammit, she's half your age!*

At the same time he was immensely gratified to feel how easily she leaned into his loose embrace. He tightened it just a fraction – purely out of consideration for her weakened state.

Meanwhile Chinua had all the elders back on their feet and out of the water. As far as Rather could see, apart from a thorough soaking, some blackened patches on their formerly white clothes, and a few singed beards and eyebrows, they seemed all right.

A small crowd had gathered round, among them Mongke and Rain Seven. Gormin was just hobbling up. He headed straight for Nissa. Seeing the Unborn, she cringed and clung to Rather. The sight obviously brought back some bad memories for her.

'It's all right,' Rather said. 'This is Gormin. He's done a lot to keep you alive over the past few weeks.'

'Not half as much as this young man here,' Gormin said. 'Although, knowing him, he's probably been too modest to mention it. How are you feeling, my dear?'

'A bit wobbly still,' Nissa said. 'But otherwise fine. And thank you for helping me, Gormin. I didn't mean to offend, but – '

'I know, I know,' Gormin said. 'Don't worry about it. But you should know that you're absolutely safe with us.' He motioned towards Rain standing in the background. 'We like to think of ourselves as the good guys, and we've been doing our best to live up to the notion.'

Will wonders never cease, Rather thought. *Gormin joking! I do*

301

believe I'm not the only one who's got a soft spot for Nissa.

Standing there with his arm around the girl and everyone looking on, he suddenly felt very self-conscious. Somewhat hastily, he disengaged, relieved to give Nissa over into Erdene's care when the old woman said she wanted to keep an eye on the girl, decreeing that Nissa should spend the night at her house. It seemed to be his moment for catching unreadable glances, for he got one from Nissa, another from Erdene, and a quizzically raised eyebrow from Gormin. He decided to ignore all three – wisely, he thought, as he trundled off to bed and, blessedly, sleep.

The following days went by in a blur.

The plague continued to spread, and people were dying left and right. Rather went from one patient to the next, doing what he could to alleviate the worst of their suffering but helpless to save anyone. The symptoms were always the same.

They began with sudden fatigue and a slightly elevated temperature, quickly developing into a state of utter weakness combined with a raging fever. A brownish, sticky residue began to collect around the mouth and eyes; usually on the same day, the patients began to experience extreme abdominal pain and to disgorge blood. After that, they rapidly became incoherent and unresponsive. In the last stage they bled from every orifice, suggesting that the sickness was corroding and dissolving their internal organs and blood vessels.

Though he doubted it would be of any help, Rather struggled to find an explanation for the strange disease. There were certain similarities to viral infections he'd heard of or read about, but nothing quite seemed to fit. Small wonder, he thought, seeing that he was in a

302

different world, and one infested with magic, to boot. It was factoring magic into the equation that gave him the first clue: put it together with an unknown virus and a potent venom, and you might get something very similar or even identical to what was presenting itself here.

The longer he thought about it, the more convinced he became that this was the only possible explanation. He was dealing with a devilish sort of biological weaponization, driven not by technology but by magic, not by biogenetic engineering but by theurgic manipulation.

And it didn't stop there. Sorcery was not only the manipulator but also an integral part of the resulting deadly mix. He could isolate, fight, and probably cure each factor individually, but not all three together. Together, they were something else entirely.

With the shamans' help, he tried anyway.

But, as if it resented the interference, the disease escalated, its virulence increasing – deliberately, it seemed to Rather, as if it had a malignant volition of its own. He explained his theory to the elders, and found that they had reached much the same conclusion looking at the problem from their shamanistic point of view. Rather, Erdene, and Batukhan experimented with multiple, simultaneous treatments, each of them tackling a different aspect of the disease, but it was no use.

There always remained the fourth factor, the sum resulting from the combination of the other three, and it proved immune to their collective assaults even when they were joined by Gormin, whose knowledge on the matter was greater than anyone else's. In the end it came down to one simple fact: only evil might have been capable of undoing what evil had wrought, and none of them were practitioners of the Dark Side, though Rather doubted that even a sorcerer could have succeeded in reigning in this blackest of occult creations.

And so they lost battle after battle for the lives of the Assenai, who by now were dying like the proverbial flies. All they could do was relieve some of the pain and spare their patients the worst agonies, their medical and thaumaturgical arsenal reduced to palliative measures, and even those were spread ever more thinly as more and more people were taken ill.

The Unborn seemed indefatigable, unfazed by the most menial tasks, amenable to any request. They radiated an unobtrusive empathy and a steady calm that Rather felt was doing as much if not more good than all his pseudo-medical exertions. Nonetheless, whenever it was possible he showed and explained procedures to them, teaching them what he could in small, hurried increments. Gormin and the elders did the same, the Unborn absorbing every tidbit with the greatest attentiveness and curiosity.

More than once, Rather was reminded of the foretelling he'd given them. Having nothing to do with Jareth's prophecies, it had been entirely of Rather's own making, but to his surprise it was proving accurate. They all had a gift and propensity for healing that went far beyond the average. More, they had the heart for it. They cared, deeply, and somehow that caring communicated itself to the sick and the dying and lessened their suffering on a plane other than medical.

Rather could come up with no better word for it than 'humane'. Even though there was precious little of the human in the Unborn's appearance, inside they seemed blessed to overflowing with an asset that those who thought of themselves as true men so often lacked: simple human decency.

During the morning of the first day Nissa, still pale and shaky, joined the healers. She brought her Talent to bear, absorbing the fever heat from the sick, a contribution that didn't save them any more than the others' efforts but did help to make them feel a bit more comfortable. Somehow, she ended up working side by side with Rather. Twice Rather experienced a jolt of electricity when their hands accidentally touched, and several times he caught her gazing at him, scrutinizing him with that same, unreadable expression. Each time he looked away quickly, heat rising to his face. Not since Fellmere had he felt so helpless and uncomfortable. Compared to him, a bug being vivisected under a microscope would have looked like the epitome of relaxation.

Gormin noticed that Chinua also seemed out of his depth.

When he wasn't away checking on the lookouts and sentries guarding Massarit, he hovered around the elders like a mother hen expecting trouble to strike at any moment from a clear blue sky, jumping at the call of a finch and seeing a hawk in every sparrow's shadow.

'Chinua is our war chief,' Batukhan told Gormin when asked about it. 'His whole existence is centered on protecting the Assenai. Now here is an enemy killing his people, and there isn't a thing he can do about it. He must be feeling very helpless and superfluous right now.

'But he's not a man who handles idleness well, and less so if it's forced upon him. So he tries at least to look out for those he deems

305

most irreplaceable: us elders. He can't save us from the plague any more than the rest of the people, and he knows it. But at least he'll see that no other harm befalls us. It's the way of the warrior: never give up; find something you can do, even if it seems only a small and mostly useless thing.'

'Not so different from the way of the healer, then,' Gormin mused.

'Not so different at all,' Batukhan agreed. He was laying a pair of flat pebbles on the lids of a man who had died just moments ago. Gormin was already turning to the next patient when Erdene stopped him with a hand on his arm. She looked haggard. Gormin told himself it was only to be expected in an old woman who'd been on her feet and working without respite for gods knew how many hours. Surely it was nothing more; surely the elders at least, by dint of their magic, were immune to this terrible nemesis.

'Time for a break, friend Gormin,' she said. 'Nissa. Batukhan. Rather, you too. Come. If we don't care for our own simplest needs, we'll soon be no good to anyone.'

They found a cook-fire going outside, and settled down to their first meal in ten hours. They ate in silence, though Gormin couldn't stop his mind from churning away. He wasn't the only one.

'I realize that knowing how the disease got here in the first place isn't going to change anything,' Rather said as they were finishing up. 'But I do wonder. I mean... it didn't just fly here on the wind. Someone or something had to bring it here physically, knowingly or not.'

Erdene shifted on her seat as if with some inner pain. 'Three days

306

before it began, I had a dream,' she said heavily, and Gormin heard a great sadness in her voice. 'Had I paid more attention to it then, we might have been spared all this. In the dream I saw a huge, dark shadow, tall as a mountain, leaning over the rim of Massarit and looking down on the Assenai, tiny as ants, as they went about their lives. Then the dark figure began to pull smaller shadows from its mouth and throw them into the lake, turning the water black. I was woken by Sube, whose wife Checheg was having her first baby, and in all the excitement I forgot about the dream. When finally I did remember, it was too late.'

'The day after Erdene's dream,' Batukhan explained, 'we had a visitor. When I saw him at the entrance, I did not like or trust him and would have sent him on his way. But he asked for water, and it is law among the desert tribes that no one may be denied water, not even an enemy. So I let him in. Chinua escorted him to the lake and back, keeping an eye on him, and the man was gone again in less than an hour. I fear it was he who brought the plague to Massarit. And I think he did it knowingly, though for what reason I cannot begin to imagine.'

'What did he look like?' Gormin asked, a terrible suspicion dropping on him like a crushing weight. 'Can you describe him for me?'

'He was an unremarkable man,' Batukhan said. 'Average in every respect except for the sloping shoulders, a beard that would have better suited a goat, and a sour look that seemed to be permanently fixed on his features as if it were the only expression he'd ever learned.'

Noburo! Out to counter a part of the prophecy and collect points he can rub in Kuruma's face forever, Gormin thought but didn't say.

He knew what it would do to Rather, who'd immediately see the connection to his prophecy and find fresh reason to blame himself. It was a wonder how well he'd come through his ordeal in Fellmere, but Gormin sensed that, below the surface, he was still extremely fragile. More guilt was the last thing he needed. As it was, Gormin suspected that Nissa was a great part of what was keeping Rather going; that, and being desperately needed in this terrible crisis.

But Rather was already two steps ahead of him.

'Your tribe, the Assenai,' he asked the elders, 'do you have some kind of symbol or emblem? An animal, perhaps?'

'In our tongue, Assenai means "spears of the lion",' Batukhan said, Gormin wishing he could somehow stop the words from coming out. 'The lion is our tribe's totem animal. Though I have to admit I don't quite see the connection here.'

'I do,' Rather said grimly. 'I see it very clearly, in fact. The cat. You can both stop blaming yourselves for anything you did or didn't do. If anyone's responsible for this horror, it's me, and me alone.' And then the whole story poured out of him, Erdene and Batukhan listening with rapt attention.

When he was done, Erdene took both of his hands in hers and looked him deep in the eyes.

'Listen to me,' she said, and Gormin heard a new and deeply authoritative note in her voice. 'You are not responsible for the fore-telling you spoke. Prophecy will out, and it uses whomever it can find. There is no denying it. Nor are you responsible for the deeds of the Dark Side. You may choose to help good people and share their troubles for a time – but only for a time.

'What you may not do is carry the burden of guilt incurred by others. It isn't yours, and what moves you to take it up is weakness, not strength. I beg you to think on this, young Rather. You're too important in the scheme of things unfolding to indulge in such nonsense.

'Now.' She released his hands and patted him on the knee. 'I'm old, I'm tired, and I'm going to exercise my right to take a nap. You may wake me in an hour.'

❖ ❖ ❖

As it turned out, Erdene never got up from her nap.
She died the next day. One by one, Batukhan and the other elders followed her. Mongke died, Sube and Checheg who had made Erdene forget her dream died, and so many others that it came to a point where there were hardly enough of the living left to bury the dead.

In all this horror and pain there was one glimmer of light. Strangely, not a single child under the age of twelve had fallen sick. It was as if the younger children were immune to the disease, a fact that puzzled Rather no end. If anything, he'd have looked for the opposite, would have expected the attack to be designed according to the sorcerers' exigencies dictated by the prophecy, concentrating precisely on the children.

Gormin brought some light to the matter, opining that Noburo had indeed targeted the children but must have made a mistake somewhere along the way, thus achieving the opposite of what he'd intended. Whatever the reason, the children were exempt from death, but more and more were orphaned as their parents died. Other families took them in, but the foster parents too succumbed to the plague, and it soon became clear to Rather that after the plague another task

309

awaited him: that of looking after the surviving children.

In the end, when the last dead had been laid to rest in the burial caves, all that remained of the Assenai were two adults, Tolui and Chinua, and a hundred and fourteen children. The eldest was thirteen, the youngest less than a month. Rather, depleted from three weeks of constant and ultimately futile struggle against the disease, was sitting by the lake, pondering this new dilemma, when Chinua joined him, saying there was something he wanted to show him.

Though he felt too exhausted to even consider getting up, Rather rose and followed Chinua to the southern wall and then along a hair-raising trail winding up through an impossibly steep ravine, where a slip or a misstep would have likely led to a very bad ending. The last bit consisted of a series of foot and handholds chiseled into a nearly vertical rock face and leading onto a wide ledge high above the can-yon floor. For the first time, Rather got a good look at Massarit.

It was larger than he'd thought, large enough to sustain a popu-lation of nearly a thousand with its terraced gardens and orchards running all the way around the canyon's wall and a green expanse of meadows and pastures stretching almost two miles from the lake to the northern wall, sheep, goats, and camels grazing in its shade. It could have been a small piece of paradise, and probably had been, he thought. If only evil had stayed away from it.

But it soon became apparent that Chinua hadn't brought him here for the grandiose view. Instead, he led Rather to the back of the ledge. Here, under a deep, cave-like overhang, the rock face was covered from end to end with a long row of petroglyphs, images of men and beasts as well as beings that looked like a mixture of both, all of them done in a simple but beautifully clear and incisive style that reminded Rather of the most ancient drawings back on Earth, bequeathed to mankind by its paleolithic ancestors.

A figure that was half human and half lion figured prominently, and there were all sorts of different scenes, most of them connected to hunting and warfare. But Chinua had a specific image in mind. He took Rather to the very end of the row.

A man and a woman were drawn there, side by side. They were flanked by seven taller figures, three to the left and four to the right, showing an uncanny resemblance to seven overly large and not quite human-looking persons whom Rather happened to know pretty well. All nine figures held their arms stretched out to their sides in a human cruciform, and on every arm stood a row of smaller figures. Rather didn't bother to count them, but he reckoned that, if he had, he'd have come up with something like a hundred and fourteen.

'This,' Chinua said, 'is why Batukhan didn't hesitate to bid you welcome in Massarit. For centuries, the Assenai elders debated whether these pictures showed things that had already happened or things that were still to come. Batukhan believed the latter, and it seems he was right. He also said that the Assenai's debt to these strangers – to you – would rise and rise, until the only way to repay it was with our lives. So, we are yours.'

'Looks to me like I'm yours as well,' Rather sighed, 'since destiny seems hell-bent on keeping me busy. Whatever. There's no question we'll stay and help you look after the kids, Chinua, prophecy or no. And now, if you don't mind, I'd like to get back down to the ground. To be honest, I'm not very good with heights.'

That evening, Rather felt the need for a moment of solitude.

After dinner with a horde of very subdued kids, he grabbed a couple of blankets and wandered down to the lake. He went for a long swim that left him feeling somewhat cleansed and relaxed. Lying between the blankets, he felt for the first time in what seemed like ages that he could look forward to a good night's sleep.

It wasn't to be.

He was drifting off and almost gone when someone slipped in beside him and a soft, warm, naked body nestled up against his own. Nissa.

He started to say something along the lines that this was all wrong but realized that, really, it wasn't. She laid a finger on his lips before covering them with her own, and by then it was too late anyway.

The moon, a thin sliver again but waning now, had crossed a good piece of the sky by the time Rather found words to express his concerns.

'What?' Nissa asked before he even had a chance to draw a breath for speaking, much less open his mouth.

'Um,' he said, 'it's just that I feel... I mean, you're really very young, and I should feel like a dirty old man, and I do, but I don't, not really, only – '

'Rather?'

'Er, yes?'

'How about if you asked me how old I am, instead of rushing to conclusions?'

'But – '

'Just ask.'

'Okay. How old are you?'

'See, that wasn't so hard. I'm twenty-three. It's the magic that makes me look younger than I am, in case you wondered. Feel better now?'

'Much better. But I'm still nearly ten years older than you are. Are you sure you're all right with that?'

'Oh, poor old man! Should I go fetch you a walking stick?'

'Uh, that is definitely *not* my walking stick.'

Nissa giggled. 'No. But it seems to be firming up nicely all the same.'

Thereafter, the discussion deteriorated rapidly. Rather didn't mind at all. He was suddenly very happy, a feeling he'd almost forgotten. It had been a long time. Actually, if he put his mind to it, he didn't think he'd been this happy ever, period. All through the night, Nissa proved to him in many different ways that she felt exactly the same.

❖　❖　❖

If there must be trouble let it be in my day, that my child may have peace.

Thomas Paine

17 Dunmark

t was an hour's ride to the highest point of Long Pass. Rupili had shown surprisingly little resistance when Baran came to fetch her after having put out the word among the panicking Larnaki to drop everything and flee from Tinnan valley as fast as they could. It was obvious that the Radjani had already been pondering the situation, thinking ahead of the current disaster, and it was equally clear that she was painfully torn between staying and fighting with her husband and people, and saving her daughter.

What seemed to tip the scales and make up her mind was Baran's observation that, should anything happen to Anskar, she and Anili were possibly the only hope the Larnaki nation had for any kind of a future. Though neither he nor Rupili put it in so many words, they both knew that Anskar's chances of coming out of this business alive were slim and diminishing by the minute.

In the time it took Dorting to saddle a horse for Rupili, and the maids to pack the saddlebags with supplies and Rupili's short swords, the matter was settled. Rupili excused the boy as well as Asha and Soonil, sending them off to help evacuate their families. After short and tearful farewells, Rupili stood for a long moment facing the canyon, at the other end of which Anskar was fighting for all their lives.

When she turned, Baran was stricken by the look on her face, a conflicting assortment of all the different emotions that were pulling at her, threatening to tear her apart. Love, loss, hope, guilt, uncertainty and despair were there, plain to see, all of it tamed and held together by sheer will and a desperate courage that stirred a deep admiration in him, even a reverence, for this brave and thoroughly good woman.

Rupili winced as she swung into the saddle. Baran, cradling Anili in his good arm, noticed a small but ugly-looking wound on her ankle.

'It's nothing,' she said when he asked. 'Just a bite from one of those disgusting little spidery things.'

Baran was surprised that one of them had already made it this far. He wondered why the sorcerers would bother with the repulsive creatures.

'I'll bind it up for you as soon as there's a chance,' he told Rupili as she bent down to take Anili from him. She nestled the little girl into a shawl with its ends knotted together to form a sling, making sure that the child's face was free and she could breathe properly.

Then they were off.

They reached the highest point of Long Pass and the stone cairn marking the border between Larnakis and Dunmark in good time. On the way up, they'd felt several small tremors, and a few loose rocks had come tumbling down, some dangerously close, making it something of a job to keep the horses steady. Baran wondered whether the shocks were a natural occurrence, or if they were provoked by sorcery. He tended towards the latter. Under the circumstances, anything else would be just too much of a coincidence.

At the top of the pass, the road ran between low, tumular rises, spur-ends of the adjoining mountains. Here there was no more risk of falling rocks but, much as Baran was relieved to be out of the immediate danger zone, he still felt anxious and apprehensive, as if the worst was yet to come. He noticed how the mountainsides had suddenly gone eerily quiet. The birds that had been singing just moments ago seemed to have vanished all at once. Rupili looked drawn and exhausted. They reined in the horses and turned around for one last look. Rupili gasped.

Too far away to make out any details, the picture was still clear enough.

Far below, all the fleeing Larnaki seemed to be heading in the same direction, towards Tinnan pass. Frighteningly few had made it there. Many were stubbornly refusing to part with their livestock, and the herds they'd driven ahead of them were hopelessly clogging the approach to the pass, slowing down the people behind them to a near standstill. There was heavy fighting going on at the other end of the valley. Dark hordes of what could only be the enemy were streaming out of Donner Pass. There, a faint, light blue haze lay in the air, shimmering like a mirage dancing above an overheated desert.

As they looked on, something resembling a huge fist of roiling darkness shot out of the canyon and smashed into the blue, rimming it with black and spreading through it like a morbid taint. Briefly, the whole scene seemed suspended, breathless.

Then, with a drawn-out series of ear-splitting cracks like continuous peals of thunder, a web of dirty blue tentacles raced up the flanks of the Redhorn and Donner Peak. The contours of both mountains appeared suddenly blurred and uncertain, as if they were inwardly shifting, rearranging their basic architecture in search of some new and as yet undefined position.

Finally, with a roaring of thunder like ten thousand avalanches, the two enormous massifs toppled and fell into the valley from both sides, filling it completely and raising a gigantic cloud of dust that soon hid everything from sight.

Rupili let out a wail of such boundless grief, it penetrated Baran's shocked numbness like a bolt straight to his heart; he could have sworn he felt it miss a beat and spring a crack.

There was no more holding the terrified horses, and he let them run. The gradient on the Dunmarkan side of the pass was shallow for the first few miles, the road in good condition. And there was another reason that drove him to give the animals a free rein.

At the last moment, just before the horses bolted, something very disturbing had caught his eye. It had been only the briefest of glimpses, but he was pretty sure he'd seen three figures far down the Tinnan side of Long Pass, making their way up. One had been on horseback, a man clad in black; the other two had been on foot and far too large to be human.

After two miles at a full gallop, they reined in the horses.
From here the terrain plunged steeply down, the road cutting down a wide slope in a series of switchbacks until it reached the treeline and disappeared under a canopy of foliage already beginning to turn color in the hard mountain climate.

Rupili was breathing heavily, swaying in the saddle.

Baran was shocked by the change in her appearance. The Radjani was visibly unwell. She was deathly pale and had dark rings under her eyes. Sweat beaded her forehead and upper lip.

'Radjani, what is it? You look ill.'

'I don't know,' she said, her words slightly slurred. 'I must have caught a fever. And my foot hurts.'

Baran dismounted to look at Rupili's ankle. The implications of what he saw there sent his heart plummeting. It was swollen to twice its normal size, and the skin of her foot and lower leg was a deep, ugly red. There was a black border around the bite where the flesh was already turning to rot. The wound itself was oozing a brownish scum.

He'd never seen an injury like this before. But he'd heard tell of forest tribes on the southern continent who poisoned the tips of their arrows by dipping them in deadly venom obtained from a certain species of tree-dwelling frog. It was supposed to kill a man in under an hour.

The Imperial merchant who'd told Baran the story had given him a detailed and violently graphic description of the symptoms caused by the venom. They matched Rupili's exactly. Checking for the other signs, he found small flecks of the same brown gook at the corners of her mouth and eyes. A seething rush of anger momentarily joined the despair that was threatening to overwhelm him. Gods damn those perverse, corrupt, conscienceless, meddling black swine and their abominable creations! He looked Rupili in the eyes, trying for an air of confidence, but she saw right through it.

'It's bad,' she stated bleakly.

He hesitated, considered lying to her but found he couldn't. He nodded.

'There's a wayfarer's chapel down by the forest's edge,' he said. 'Let's get you there and see what we can do for your leg.'

Back in the saddle, he felt a sudden prickling on his neck and looked back.

There was nothing to see – yet.

The chapel was dedicated to Verelda, the Mother, goddess of fecundity and patroness of farmers, midwives and travelers. It consisted of a stone roof resting on a wall at the back and two columns in front, and a marble floor littered with dust and dead leaves. In a niche above a stone bench footing the wall stood an alabaster statue of the goddess, arms spread wide in a gesture of welcome and succor.

Baran took Anili from Rupili and bedded her down on his cloak. Then he helped the Radjani dismount. She nearly fell and he had to steady her when she tried to stand on her injured foot. He made to lead her under the sheltering roof, but she held up a hand, turned away and heaved up a spurt of scummy brown liquid mixed with red. According to the merchant from Orr, this was the beginning of the end. She vomited again, this time pure blood.

When she'd caught her breath and collected herself, she nodded and allowed him to lead her under the chapel's roof. Easing her down onto the bench, he knelt to inspect her ankle.

'Leave it,' she said, her voice weak and shaking. 'It's useless. I'm dying.'

'Radjani – '

'No, dear friend. You've never lied to me, and now isn't the time

320

to start. And just so you know: I saw them too, the ones who are after us. Now please, listen to me. This is what I want you to do.'

She had to pause for breath.

'First, bring me my swords. They're in the right saddlebag. There's also a packet, done up in a red scarf. Bring that too.'

He did as she asked, unsheathing the two short swords and laying them beside her on the bench.

'Now give me my daughter. I want to hold her one last time and say good bye.'

'What... '

'Please don't argue, there's no time.'

He picked up Anili and placed her in Rupili's arms. She kissed the baby's forehead, tears running down her cheeks. Then she looked at Baran, her gaze bright and clear even through the tears.

'Baran Kendarren,' she said. 'I charge you with my daughter's life. Take her to safety. Preserve her from harm. Guard, nurture, and counsel her until she is capable of looking out for herself. Will you do that for me, my friend?'

'Yes, Radjani, I will,' Baran said, failing to fight back tears of his own. 'But you should come too. Or I should stay and fight. We can beat them.'

'A one-armed man and a dying woman against a sorcerer and two of his monsters? We both know better. As for coming with you, I'd only hold us up and make it so much easier for them to overtake us and harm Anili. It's her they're after. I don't know how, but I know. No, you must go. Now.'

She handed him the packet.

'These are my jewels. Take them. They should see you both

through for a long while. But you must be careful when you sell them. Break the stones from the settings beforehand, else they might be recognized and lead them to you. Take the saddlebags; there's everything you'll need for Anili in there. You'll have to find her some milk soon. Goat's milk is best, and sheep's milk will do. Quickly now, before it's too late. Farewell, my friend.'

Even now she was thinking ahead, her daughter's welfare first and foremost on her mind. Baran knelt and kissed her hand.

'May we meet again after the last battle is fought, my lady,' he said, the time-honored soldier's salute offered a dying comrade.

She smiled weakly. 'Never to fight again.

'It's not true, you know,' she added, 'what they say. It's never a good day to die.'

Baran managed to slip the sling around his shoulders. He gently took Anili from her mother's arms and placed the infant in the shawl like he'd seen Rupili do. They exchanged one last parting glance. Then she waved him off. With one good arm and Anili hanging at his chest, he fought his way up into the saddle and rode into the forest without looking back.

❖   ❖   ❖

Rupili knew she had very little time left.

But there was one more thing she wanted to do for her daughter, so she willed herself to stay alive for just a little bit longer. She slipped off her cloak and laid it on the bench beside her, rolled into the shape of a bundled-up infant. Then she leaned back, the last of her strength exhausted. The pain was less violent now, though still worse than anything she'd ever known or imagined a person could bear. She could feel the poison eating away at her, could sense her insides dissolving under its onslaught and slowly leaking out of her. But the discomfort of sitting in a growing puddle of blood and feces was the least of her worries. She was tired unto death, and gravity seemed to be pulling at her with many times its usual force. Staying awake and not falling over took everything she had left, and then some.

Her losses were too great to contemplate, like a terrible wound one dares not touch or even observe for fear of fainting and thereby losing the connecting thread to wakefulness and life. Anili was safe in the hands of Baran. Rupili trusted him unreservedly, and couldn't have wished for anyone better. Anskar was in the hands of the gods, as was she. As were they all. She let all that be as it was. The Jeje hadn't been her teacher for nothing.

Instead, she concentrated on the wind whispering in the trees and gently brushing over the exposed skin of her face and hands, the rustle of dry leaves performing an intricate, mysterious dance with their black, cutout shadow-selves in a wide band of sunlight splashed across the marble floor like a carpet of evanescent luminosity. She inhaled, absorbing the fading perfume of summer, mixed with autumn's cool breath carrying the first hints of decay.

And then she felt it, found it. It was everywhere around her, the great cycle of life – and of death, for there wasn't one without the other. She was a part of it, and it of her. All things and all beings were equal here, were One in this great togetherness. In the center of it, she found a vast sense of allowance, of release and the freedom to relinquish, of consolation and calm.

When the pursuer's shadow fell across the sunlit floor, she was ready.

The black-robed man who stood before her was tall, but his two companions remaining outside and several steps behind reduced his size to that of a child. Not a nice child, though. Not the kind you'd want to play with but instead the kind who tore the wings from butterflies, the joy from play and the innocence from his peers, and sent everybody running home in tears.

This time, he was the one who would leave crying.

She gripped the hilts of her short-swords, felt power flowing into her.

'I want the child,' he said in a voice that grated like a steel brush over tender skin, casting an avid glance at the bundle lying beside Rupili.

'Come and fetch her, then,' she told the man who'd come to kill her daughter.

Not seeming to notice the eagerness in her voice, he took a step forward. It brought him nicely inside her reach. She saw him wrinkle his nose at the smell, but it didn't stop him. Another step.

It was all she needed. Faster than lightning and with the sudden strength of all the world behind her she struck, cutting him twice. A slash across the thighs to throw him off balance, and then the killing stroke that went through the chainmail covering his gut like a hot knife through butter, opening him up wide and exposing the dark coils of his inner workings to the light of day. Before he had time to blink she threw the swords, one with each hand, burying them to the hilts in the chests of the two monsters coming up on either side of him.

She didn't have time to watch them fall and die; her eyelids were suddenly much too heavy for that. So she just let them close, and went away to see if she could find Anskar.

❖ ❖ ❖

Tano and the two Unborn hadn't gone very far up the pass when the mountains fell. Thankfully, a stiff wind blowing down from the north spared them the worst of the dust. The edge of the cloud overtook them for a time, which was bad enough, particularly because it made him lose sight of his quarry. It was the only thing that interested him at the moment. Whatever had happened down there in the valley, fascinating as it was, he filed away for later consideration. First he wanted to get this done and over with.

When they finally got clear of the dust, the fugitives were just disappearing over the crest of the pass. Not too far ahead, then. He'd catch them, no worries, even if it took a day or two. Which it probably wouldn't.

In the end it went much faster than he'd anticipated.

An hour after he'd last seen his prey, he came upon the woman sitting in a small wayside chapel just down the other side of the pass. The child was lying beside her, wrapped up in a blanket. The woman was clearly in very bad shape. She looked as if one of Noburo's little biters had gotten her, and he didn't expect any resistance from her at all. He looked around to see if her companion was lurking somewhere in the vicinity, but the man must have put common sense above valor and taken off on his own, leaving these two behind. Good of him to remove himself. One less obstacle for Tano.

Stepping under the chapel roof, he noticed the statue of the goddess in the niche above the woman's head, saw the outspread arms offering welcome, solace and forgiveness, and a short, sharp pang of some alien, ghostly mood momentarily constricted his chest.

He shook the feeling off. He was here for business, not to indulge in maudlin moods. 'I want the child.'

The woman's eyes remained shut, but her lips seemed to move for a moment, though she made no sound. Suddenly an extremely painful stomach cramp nearly bent him double. It felt as if a sword were slicing through his guts. For a moment he was completely disoriented, struggling for breath and wondering if maybe he was dying too. Thankfully, it passed as quickly as it had come.

He heard surprised grunts from the Unborn behind him but paid them no heed.

When next he looked, the woman was dead, had stopped breathing. Strangely, she was smiling now. Tano bent to pick up the child. And cursed.

What he'd taken for a swaddled infant was nothing but a cleverly arranged cloak. Which meant that whoever had been with the woman had taken the child and was heading down the mountain towards safety, while Tano was wasting his time with a corpse. He wanted to strike her, topple her over onto the floor, smash her head and kick her ribs in, but knowing she wouldn't feel a thing anymore took the fun out of it. He turned away and headed for his horse.

Then another thought hit him, ratcheting his anger and frustration up another few notches. The amulet Kuruma had given him was attuned to the dead woman, not the child. It would be completely useless now.

Overbearing, incompetent little shit. Cursing Kuruma, he spurred on his horse, the Unborn trotting along behind him.

For three days they followed the road down the mountainside and into Dunmark proper. There was no trace of the fugitives. At the first dwellings they came by, poor, pitiful little farmsteads, Tano stopped to ask the equally pitiful inhabitants if they'd seen anyone passing by on the road from Larnakis. No one had. Famished though he was, he didn't bother taking their puny little life forces. Even beset by hardship he still had certain standards.

Finally he found an inn. There was a wagon standing outside, an elaborate, sturdy affair that had a wagon house of iron-banded wood with a barrel roof and a door at the back, the kind of coach used by a noble's wife or a wealthy merchant. A coachman was tending the team of four, attaching feeding sacks to their headgear. He cringed when he saw the Unborn, and to judge by his rapidly darting eyes was clearly debating whether to run inside or make a break for the woods.

Tano spared him the decision by dismounting, laying a friendly arm around the man's shoulders and asking an innocuous question about the quality of the inn. Leading the fellow around behind the wagon where they were out of sight of the inn's windows, Tano knocked him out cold with a simple Stricture. It was the best he could do, depleted as he was from fighting his way through the madness at Tinnan. Signaling the Unborn to stay out of sight, he went inside.

There was a single guest sitting at a table by the fireside, busy tucking into a huge helping of meat and potatoes, a freshly drawn, foam-topped tankard at his elbow. Judging by his crimson silk habit and the fur-lined red cloak lying on the bench beside him, he was a high priest. One of Emenudra's, the goddess's of love and war, and also the only candidate for ownership of the wagon outside.

The man blanched when he saw Tano and recognized which brotherhood the newcomer belonged to. His grease-covered fingers grasping a choice piece of meat froze midway to his open mouth as he watched Tano pull out a chair and sit down at his table.

'Greetings, Brother,' Tano said.

'Greetings,' the red priest said, his voice unsteady. 'Er, Brother.'

'I'm so glad I found you,' Tano said. 'I seem to have lost my traveling companion. Man on a horse, has a child with him. You wouldn't have seen him, by any chance?'

'Sorry, no. No one of that description. No one of any description, as a matter of fact. Road's been deserted these last few days.'

'Yes, well. Come a long way, have you? A fine wagon and team you've got there.'

'Quite far, yes. And not actually mine. The wagon, I mean. Belongs to the Temple. I'm just allowed to… borrow it.' The man was sweating, his hand trembling visibly as he reached for the tankard.

'Wonderful,' Tano said. 'Then I'm sure you won't mind if I borrow it from you. Brother to brother, so to speak. Or temple to temple.'

'Wish I could help you, but I'm in a bit of a hurry, and – '

'No, you're not,' Tano said easily, drawing his knife. 'Not anymore.'

He consumed the dying man's life force, a welcome and timely replenishment of his reserves. Bloody Kuruma thought he was the only one who knew that trick, but Tano could have taught him a few others the stupid runt had never even heard of. He let the man's face drop onto the platter, blood from his severed jugular garnishing the remaining food with a lush, red sauce.

Since nobody had shown up to serve Tano he went through the door behind the bar and into the kitchen, where he found the innkeeper's wife and a serving wench huddled in a corner. The man himself was positioned between them and the door, brandishing a cudgel.

'Careful you don't drop that on your foot,' Tano said, advancing on the terrified man and smiling amiably.

'G-go away,' the innkeeper stammered, wagging his cudgel. 'We want nothing to do with your kind. Just, please, go away and leave us alone.'

'Seen one of us before, have you? Well, not to worry. I'll be gone in a trice. Just wanted to make sure you don't talk to anyone once I'm gone.'

'W-we won't. I swear. Not a word. T-to no one.'

'I know,' Tano said soothingly. 'I know.'

With the fresh energy of four life forces coursing through his system, Tano felt on top of the world again. He magnanimously allowed the Unborn half an hour to feed on the corpses before setting off in his newly acquired coach, driven by his newly acquired coachman upon whom he'd impressed the absolute futility of trying anything brave and/or stupid. He let the man take a good, long look at the Unborn, their hands and faces freshly smeared with blood, and assured him they would never be farther than a short stone's throw away, only staying out of sight and off the road when they met other travelers, which didn't seem likely in any case. He felt every confidence that this had more than sufficed to make his point.

The coach was very comfortable, suspended on metal springs that took much of the sharpness out of the bumps, its interior lavishly upholstered and cushioned. Too much red for Tano's taste, but then, nothing was ever perfect. He was quite content for the moment.

He did find an unexpected bonus hidden away under the seats: a strong-box filled with gold and silver coins, enough for a discriminating person to retire on and live the rest of his life in comparative luxury. It seemed the red rat had absconded with the temple's treasure only to meet justice at Tano's hands. Tano smiled. Highly amusing, the ironies fate sometimes managed to come up with.

He'd decided to give up the hunt. He had better things to do than continue on Kuruma's wild goose chase. The black tower was waiting, beckoning, calling out to him ever more urgently. Kuruma, if he was still alive – and even if he wasn't – could kiss Tano's arse and stick his stupid prophecies and preemptive strikes where the sun didn't shine.

It was going to be a long trip to the tower, but it was a worthy goal, and the transportation couldn't be faulted. As the coach swayed along, Tano leaned back into the luxuriant cushions, closing his eyes to better savor the unique and glorious future awaiting him.

❖   ❖   ❖

This is not the end. It is not even the beginning of the end. But it is, perhaps, the end of the beginning.

Winston Churchill

18 Tinnan

here was neither rest nor peace for the dead of Tinnan. On the surface, the valley presented a desolate, impassable waste of dusty rubble and jumbled rocks and boulders. What wildlife had survived the catastrophe had fled. The birds were absent, even the vultures and crows, and not a single four-legged scavenger had allowed itself to be drawn in by the stink of putrefaction that hovered over the vast barrow like an evil miasma, refusing to dissipate even under the onslaught of the high mountain winds.

Underneath millions of tons of fallen rock a strange and ghastly life of sorts continued, or began anew. Silently, stealthily and ever so slowly but with a steady purpose nonetheless, from the remains of men and beasts and sorcerous creations crushed together in a restless conglomerate of flesh and juices, in a volatile reagent of dead and undead parts and ingredients exposed to the lingering and incalculable effects of twofold, hybrid magic, new and unprecedented combinations accrued, monstrous excrescences of ultimate perversion, atrocities and horrors that by far surpassed any semblance of the natural, of any possibility foreseen by evolution.

331

For the time being, all of the ghastly forces at work in Tinnan's underground were concentrated solely on their terrible striving towards nascency, towards the evolving of things – one hesitates to call them beings or even creatures – that should never have seen the light of day.

But, inevitably, at some time in the foreseeable future they would emerge from the stony womb, and a horrific plague, a nightmare without precedence would come creeping and crawling down the mountainsides to invade the world of the living.

On Vereld and elsewhere, other forces were gathering – some dark, some light, some not yet certain where they belonged. Though none of them fully realized it at this stage, the long march had begun, a march that would lead them in many different directions. Directions that would eventually all turn out to be one and the same and in the end bring them together in the no-man's land between cataclysm and catharsis, between the near certainty of final ruin and the slimmest of hopes for a future, to decide amongst themselves the fate of their worlds.

❖   ❖   ❖

Part II

AD 2001 / 1197, 4th Empire

The old man under the tree, in the tree, stirs in his sleep.

He is still dreaming, but the dream is beginning to change. Reluctantly he draws his awareness out of the green world and moves to another place, a different plane. He is being called.

'Oh,' he says in this new dream, 'it's you.'

A figure in white is looking down on him; white clothing, white skin, white hair. A woman, it would seem, but no ordinary mortal. Even though her long, thick braid is white as driven snow, it is impossible to tell her age. Every time one looks at her she is the same yet also subtly changed; now she calls to mind a young girl, now a middle-aged woman, now a crone.

'Yes, my friend, it's me. Alas, I've come to wake you.'

'Don't say it,' the old man says. 'Let me guess. Somewhere out there, the muck's about to hit the works again. And somebody's got to go and fix it – that somebody being me, it stands to reason.'

'It's already begun. And yes, you're needed. Once again. It is only with great regret that I disturb you. After all you've already done, you've earned your peace and rest many times over. But the danger is graver than ever, and there is no one else. You are the last one left. But you will have help, I promise you that. Most of it is already in place. The rest I'm seeing to as we speak.'

'Well,' the old man says, 'looks like vacation time's over. To tell you the truth, it was just beginning to get the tiniest bit boring anyway. So please don't feel bad about waking me up. Twenty years in a tree is a long time even for me – no offense, Tree. So, let's hear it. What's happening? Where do I begin?'

'I can only tell you what I know, which is far less than you or I

337

would wish. But one thing is certain: the abominator has been released. It appears that he's been busy collecting his... resources, and he's growing strong again.'

'Oh dear,' the old man sighs. 'It took five of us to put him down last time. That was after he'd spent himself in battle, and it was still hard work. How am I supposed to handle him if there's only one of me? The help, yes, you said. I just hope you've lined up some serious players. I'm not getting any younger, you know.'

She laughs. 'Would you like to?'

'Ha! Do I smell a bribe? But no, thanks. Even though I wouldn't mind regaining certain physical advantages that come with being young, I don't ever want to be that naïve and ignorant again. So, where do I start? Got any suggestions?'

'As a matter of fact, yes, I do.'

And Elil saw that he needed true and faithful servants to oversee what he had wrought, and so he made the Aladrim, or White Ones, and sent them out into the worlds that they should be his gardeners and shepherds, the fosterers and caretakers of all he had created. And he made doors for them so that they could pass easily from place to place throughout his entire realm.

The Book of Elil

19 Paris-Munich

e's in an empty room. There is a wall made of thick glass. On the other side, three shadowy figures wrapped in white bandages are floating, submerged in a dark, uterine space, Stygian travelers of unknown destination: impossible to say whether they are casualties of life or embryonic forms of death. They speak to him, trying to convey a message of existential consequence, but he can't hear them, and because of that something terrible is going to happen. Finally they give up and drift or are carried away on unseen currents, and suddenly he's filled with a rending, crushing, suffocating grief so overpowering it leaves him gasping.

Behind him, a man with no face enters the room. He knows the man is here to kill him. He runs.

Now he's in a huge, empty tower. A narrow stairway with no railing spirals up along the walls into dizzying heights. The faceless man is still coming after him, a long, sharp knife in his hand. As he flees up the stairs the steps behind him crumble away and fall soundlessly into the dark, bottomless well below. Somehow, his pursuer is still following.

Then he reaches the top, and there's nowhere left to go...

Jon awoke with a start.

It had been a while since he'd had this particular dream, and he'd begun to hope that he'd put it behind him. The first time he'd had it was soon after the death of his parents a little over a year ago. Since then, he'd managed to recover a kind of normalcy that left him some space again for things like joy and happiness, but the dream always succeeded in dragging him down again, leaving him low and out of sorts for hours or days until he fought his way back to a lighter state of being.

Completely normal, the grief counselor said. These things just took their time, but eventually it would get better. You didn't expect to heal overnight from a severe physical trauma either.

The train sped on through the night, and Jon found a kind of detached comfort in the steady clickety-clack of the wheels eating up mile after mile while the people aboard safely slept towards the coming day and their various destinations. The blue night light at the head of the pull-down bed glowed softly like a magical beacon, reminding him of his childhood and other night-time train voyages.

Back then, he'd huddle up to the light with the sheet pulled over his head, with one eye squeezed shut and the other so close to the blue glass that it became an azure blur filling his whole field of vision. He'd imagine he was looking through the blue into another world, that if only he tried hard enough he might fall through this wondrous looking glass and tumble into a strange land filled with mystery and magic.

Sleep wasn't about to return. His aunt Lisa and his five year-old sister Lucy were in the compartment next door, and he had this one all to himself. He turned on the reading lamp, found it far too bright and immediately switched it off again. He got up, slipped into a sweater and jeans and sat by the window staring out into the rushing darkness and remembering Haven – Haven the way it used to be before the accident.

Every summer of his life had started out with the long drive from New York to Canada, which for a child meant two long days of immobility and boredom relieved only by stories and guessing games he played with whichever parent wasn't driving, by stops for gas and the intensely craved fast food his health-conscious European mother didn't usually allow, and punctuated by a night in some cheap roadside motel with a terminally over-chlorinated pool, fuzzy black-and-white pay TV and starched, slightly musty sheets.

When it seemed almost certain that they were never going to get there, the four-lane highway went through a series of metamorphoses, finally ending up a simple blacktop. Then suddenly they were at the familiar turnoff onto the bumpy dirt road, the level of anticipation rising sharply. Another two miles, a first glimpse of the lake, one last turnoff, and there it was: Haven, the greatest place in the world.

Unfailingly, his grandparents were already descending from the wide porch, waving a cheerful welcome and ready to get everyone settled into the big house built from sturdy logs of red pine weathered to a soft, silvery gray and standing on a small rise that sloped gently

341

down to the sandy lakeshore.

If the weather was nice, Grand would have the grill going on the terrace facing the lake, and if not, Nana would have prepared a delicious dinner of the kind only grandmothers know how to conjure. The cottages that stood to the left and right along the shore belonged to extended family and friends, and once everyone had arrived, Jon was a happy camper. There were cousins and friends to play with, grandfathers and uncles who took the kids boating and fishing, days filled with swimming, sailing and waterskiing, and long, mild summer evenings with the grownups sitting quietly talking while the kids played in the gathering dusk and on into the night until they were ready to fall asleep on their feet.

A few years on it was the phase of hanging with the beach gang, of trips in cousin George's van to the drive-in movies and Saturday night dances where you pooled your dollars, got a friend who was over twenty-one to buy a pitcher of beer or two, and then stood sipping from your paper cup, pretending you weren't ogling the girls and hoping you'd get lucky.

Jon's most vivid memory of that period however was not of girls or music or beer but of a night at the drive-in theater when most of the movie went by without anyone watching. Instead, people lay on the hoods and roofs of their cars, on blankets and on the bare ground, gazing into a night sky transformed by a stunningly beautiful show of northern lights into an otherworldly, mystical dome of colored, flowing light, a spectacle that made any film seem bland and boring in comparison.

Then, without transition, he was back to that fateful day a year ago.

It was a beautiful evening in late August, the kind where the Haveners liked to go out for a sunset cruise in Grand's favorite boat, the carefully restored and lovingly maintained vintage beauty *Emma Jane,* twenty-one feet of gleaming mahogany, polished brass, and sea-green leather.

Grand and Nana had left early that year to visit old friends in Florida, Lisa offered to stay home with Lucy, who'd come down with a cold, and Jon simply couldn't be bothered, so that evening it was only his parents and his uncle Jude, Lisa's husband, who went.

Jon was sitting on the terrace playing a game of memory with Lucy, who was wrapped up in a blanket against the evening chill. Lisa had just come out to get them to move inside when there was a sudden, bright flash near one of the small, wooded islands that dotted the lake and, half a second later, a peal of thunder. It took Jon a moment to realize that lightning didn't strike from a cloudless sky, that there must have been some kind of explosion out there.

'Oh my God,' Lisa said. 'I hope someone's gas grill didn't just blow up.'

Then another possibility struck her.

'Oh my God,' she said again and looked at Jon, her eyes wide with apprehension.

'That was at Harper's Island,' he said. 'They left last week.'

'You don't think... it couldn't be...'

They waited for a few minutes for the Emma Jane to show up. Maybe she was just passing behind one of the islands.

Nothing.

'Call 911,' Jon said, and ran for the dock.

Quickly unmooring and starting up the little speedboat used for

343

water-skiing, he headed full throttle out into the fast approaching night.

It was dark by the time he reached Harper's Island, but the nearly full moon just rising above the treeline shed enough light to make out bits and pieces of debris floating on the water, among them a torn and singed seatback upholstered in sea-green leather.

The rest of the night was blurred by shock and a numb sense of disconnectedness, a feeling that none of this was actually real. Jon vaguely recalled taking the boat around and around in slow circles shouting, 'Dad! Mom! Uncle Jude!' time after time, with no answer except the soft gurgle and swish of the silky-black water against the sides of the boat.

Later the police boats arrived, their powerful searchlights quartering the scene but unable to find anything the moonlight hadn't already revealed. At some stage someone thought to put a blanket around Jon's shoulders, and shortly after that an officer accompanied him home.

Lisa had managed to put Lucy to bed and stood waiting for them on the dock, her blond hair in disarray, her vivid blue eyes dimmed by the intuitive knowledge that had already begun to engrave new lines on her face even before the officer broke the news to her in the kindest and gentlest words he possessed.

Somehow they got through the night and the next day, drinking endless cups of coffee at the kitchen table and keeping Lucy – and by default themselves – occupied with storybooks and games. In the morning Lisa called the number of Nana and Grand's hotel in Florida. She got Grand on the phone and told him the news. She could feel it shattering him, crushing him, she told Jon afterwards, but Grand bore up and said they'd be on the next available flight back.

And when Lucy woke up that morning, she'd stopped talking.

The police announced their official finding a week after the funeral: accidental death, in all probability caused by a faulty fuel line that had broken or become disconnected during the fatal evening cruise. Fuel had leaked into the engine compartment. Gasoline fumes had built up. At some stage the engine must have stalled for lack of fuel, and an attempt to restart it had sparked off the explosion. There was no evidence to suggest foul play.

Grand was wracked by feelings of guilt that no one could talk him out of: it was his boat, his responsibility. He should have had it serviced more often, it was all his fault. He became increasingly depressed and disoriented, as if reality had suddenly become far too much for him to contemplate any longer and all he could do was loosen his grip on it and let it slip away. Nana kept them both going but just barely.

Jon wondered, though. His dad had handled boats practically all his life, and the smell of gas must have been pretty obvious, certainly when the boat was stopped. He would have known what it meant, would have blown out the engine compartment and thoroughly checked the engine and fuel lines before attempting a restart.

On the other hand, Jon could think of absolutely no reason why anyone would wish to harm his parents. They had been perfectly normal people leading perfectly normal lives – good, friendly, agreeable human beings without an enemy in the world.

Three months later, Nana had a severe stroke. She died a week

345

later, and Grand outlasted her less than a month before a heart attack took him, too. Jon needed no great leap of the imagination to know that the physical causes of their deaths had been no more than symptoms of the illness that really ailed and finally killed them: grief.

Back in New York, Jon and Lucy moved in with Lisa.

She and Jude had moved to the city a year earlier, Lisa wanting to be closer to her elder sister Anna, Jon and Lucy's mother. Jude, a successful composer of film music who didn't really care where he did what he did, had easily agreed to the move.

Now, with so many loved ones gone, the city began to seem less and less like a good place for them to be. Jon and Lisa both began to find it ever more constricting, oppressive, even threatening. Lucy, who had gone mute on the night of their parents' death, continued to remain silent. She'd turned from a loquacious, happy child into a reserved and serious little girl. And a very quiet one. In all other respects she functioned quite normally – she just wouldn't talk. Lisa tried taking her to a therapist, where Lucy sat for fifteen minutes listening to what the woman had to say. Then she got up and marched out of the office with a self-assured certainty that left no room for argument. Lisa, who had liked neither the woman nor her approach, followed Lucy out, and she and Jon decided they'd allow Lucy time and see whether she would come out of it on her own, meanwhile giving her all the love and attention they could without spoiling her.

Disquieting things continued to happen.

Jon was nearly run down by a speeding car. Late one evening he was on his way home, about to cross the street close to his building. He'd just stepped out from the row of cars parked along the curb when suddenly a large SUV came barreling down the street, accelerating as it headed straight towards him.

Just then, a bag lady emerged onto the road three cars to the left, pushing a shopping cart piled high with her belongings. The car swerved too late and smashed into the cart, sending cardboard, rags and bottles flying. The car slowed, both passenger-side doors beginning to open. The old lady, unhurt but furious, started screaming abuse at the vehicle. The driver seemed undecided for a moment, then accelerated away with squealing tires and disappeared around the next corner.

It later turned out the SUV had been stolen – probably by gang-bangers out for a joy ride – and then abandoned on an empty lot, thoroughly wiped down, the only retrievable prints those of the mechanic who regularly serviced the car. Not exactly standard gangbanger procedure, the detective working the case said. A tad too professional compared to their usual style. But hey, live and learn.

Two months later Jon was accosted by a pair of foreign-sounding muggers, one of them brandishing an evil-looking knife, and if it hadn't been for the improbable coincidence of a patrol car responding just then to a 911 call from the house across the street, the episode might have ended badly for Jon.

There was a scare at Lucy's kindergarten, some unsavory type hanging about and accosting kids through the playground fence, asking the three to five year-olds for a light, of all things. When Lisa acquired a stalker, they decided it was time to leave.

Their little patchwork family had grown into a close-knit unit, and there was no question they'd stay together for the foreseeable future, though they had no idea where they wanted to go – except Lucy, who brought one of her children's books to the table where Jon and Lisa were discussing their options, pointing out pictures of Pooh and Tigger and Piglet and making it clear she thought where they lived would be the perfect place to move to.

Then Lisa received a letter from her uncle Richard, who lived in her family's ancestral home in southern Bavaria, in a place called Ravenstein, saying her presence was required in an urgent family matter and asking her to come as soon as she could. He also said he would very much like to meet his grand-nephew Jonathan, and to please bring him along if at all possible.

Jon hadn't started college yet, they had no other immediate plans and nothing to keep them in New York, so here they were, on a train bound for Munich from Paris, where they'd stopped over to visit Jean-Pierre and Claudine, friends of Lisa's from her student days.

❖   ❖   ❖

The sudden loud rush of a train going by in the opposite direction jolted Jon awake. Sometime during his reverie he must have nodded off. It was early morning, and he could hear movement in the adjoining compartment.

There was a knock on his door and Lisa looked in.

'Good,' she said. 'You're up. We've still got about an hour and a half to Munich. Feel like coffee and croissants? Okay. Meet you in the dining car in five.'

The coffee was good, much better than anything he'd ever had back home, and the croissants were freshly baked. Lucy had brought her crayons and drawing paper and was soon busy portraying the brown and white-flecked cows that appeared to be ubiquitous in the rolling, hilly green landscape passing by outside. She seemed much more satisfied with the results of her work than she'd been in Paris, where she'd become increasingly frustrated by the fact that her renditions of the Eiffel tower always tended to slump and bend over sideways before she got to the tip. Jon had suggested she try starting at the top, but she just gave him one of her 'what-a-big-dummy-you-are' looks, as if anybody in their right mind would build a tower from the top down.

'Tell me about uncle Richard,' Jon said to Lisa. 'What's he like?'

She thought for a moment, her gaze turning inward.

'When I was a child,' she finally said, 'the war was a relatively recent thing, still very present, though people were doing their best to forget. In Munich you could still find streets with rubble-filled gaps where houses had been demolished by bombs and nothing yet built in their place.

'I remember one street in Schwabing where a house had been completely destroyed and the one next to it left standing, virtually unscathed. The ruined building had left its imprint on the shared connecting wall, and the surviving house still carried on its side the interior walls of rooms that had belonged to its bombed-out neighbor. There was a pink wall, a blue wall, a green wall, a kitchen wall with the tiles still intact, even a bathroom wall with a wash-basin and a toilet still attached to the masonry by the plumbing, hanging in the air three stories up where only the birds could reach. It was very strange to imagine that one moment people had been living there – sleeping, cooking, reading, taking a bath – and seconds later they were gone, the whole house was gone.

'Many who survived those terrible times were cheated out of a part of their lives, and not just in an outward sense. They may have come through the war physically intact, but they were missing pieces inside, like rooms gone from a house or whole houses from a street, leaving empty, white spots on the maps of their souls. Though for some, dark smudges would be a better analogy.

'When I was about ten, I was playing in the woods with friends one day when we came to a place that was equally weird, if not weirder still. Here too, a bomb had fallen during the war. There was a large crater, and all the trees that grew in a circle around it were bent away from the epicenter of the blast in an outward curve like a "c", low down in every trunk. They couldn't have been more than saplings when the bomb detonated, and it must have taken them years after to grow that way.

'There's no way the explosion itself could have deformed them like that in one short, violent instant, but it did somehow profoundly alter them. In the shape they took on, these trees recorded and reproduced with perfect, graphic clarity a cellular memory of the brutal force and intense violence they'd witnessed, and of its lasting repercussions through time.

'Back then you'd meet people like that too, bent and warped by the horrible things they'd experienced during the war. They stayed that way, never managing to grow quite straight again. That's a bit the case with uncle Richard. The war was bad for everyone, but for some it was worse, and Richard was one of those who were spared nothing.

'I don't know the details, since he's never spoken about that time, but I do know he was sent to the Russian front in 1942, when he was a year younger than you are now. He was at Stalingrad, and from what I've heard, that was about as bad as it can get. What went on there was enough to damage any man, let alone a boy of seventeen.

'Richard is not exactly easy to deal with. He's a very reclusive person, can seem abrupt sometimes, uncommunicative and with-drawn, even downright rude, and not just with strangers. But under-neath, he's a good man. When our father went missing after the death of our mother – your mother was five and I was only two – Richard tried to be some kind of a surrogate father to us. He wasn't very good at it, but at least he tried to do the best he could, and for that I respect him.

'He and Anna were like fire and water. They managed to disagree on just about everything. She fought him every step of the way, made things difficult wherever she could. But in his own, awkward way he loved her and refused to give up on her, and she came out the better for it, I'm sure. But here I'm chattering away while we should be getting our things together. We'll be arriving in Munich soon.'

As Jon made his was back to his compartment and stuffed the few things he'd taken out back into his bags, he wondered whether this trip had really been such a good idea.

❖   ❖   ❖

All men whilst they are awake are in one common world: but each of them, when he is asleep, is in a world of his own.

Plutarch

20 Dunmark

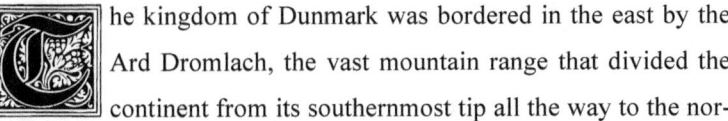he kingdom of Dunmark was bordered in the east by the Ard Dromlach, the vast mountain range that divided the continent from its southernmost tip all the way to the nor- thern ice wastes. The foothills and lower slopes were covered with old forest, most of which had never heard the sound of axe or saw. Ancient trees overshadowed a timeless realm of mossy green twilight and sunny clearings, of sparkling brooks and frothing torrents that spilled down from the high mountains' snowfields and glaciers.

On a rocky outcrop at the upper end of a steep, narrow valley stood a small keep, Caer Ceonad. Built of grey limestone, it consisted of no more than a large, square tower with a walled courtyard on the mountain-facing side and a high, crenelated terrace on the other, jut- ting out like a ship's prow over a sea of green, an ocean of fir, cedar, hemlock, spruce and maple often wreathed in mist and dripping under frequent, heavy rains. The keep itself was an ugly place, unadorned, stark and depressing, its only saving grace an ancient, wide-crowned linden tree that stood on the terrace like a benevolent sylvan spirit come to alleviate the drabness of the place.

On a rare sunny day in late autumn a young man sat on a stone bench by the terrace's parapet, wrapped in a fur-lined cloak and gazing into the hazy distance with vacant eyes, an expression of dull rapture on his homely, square-jawed but not unhandsome face.

The young man's name was Orrin, a fact he sometimes had trouble remembering. He was very glad for the name: it was the one piece of solid, reliable information that always came back to him sooner or later, his last and only anchor to being someone at all, a person, alive. Everything else, his past, his history, was a mist as grey and impenetrable as the thick blanket of fog that often crept down from the mountains on rainy days to hide even the closer treetops behind a blank, silent wall of nothingness.

Sometimes, out of the grey images would pop into his mind – faces mostly, faces he knew he should recognize but couldn't connect to names or times or places. Sad, happy, angry, laughing, scowling, smiling faces that evoked vague stirrings in a part of him he could never quite reach. And then they were gone as quickly as they had come, with no way to call them back.

At times he had a feeling that, in his dreams, the rest of him, the missing person was all still there, everything he had been and forgotten, all he had known and lost. He dreamed a lot, almost every night, but not once did he manage to salvage anything across that infinitesimal instant, that keen blade of a border that separated sleep from waking, remembrance from oblivion.

Orrin was one of only three people living in Caer Ceonad.

The other two were his minders. Searc, a large, beefy man in his early fifties, dour and rough, his short, grey stubble and scarred hands marking him an ex-soldier, was officially Ceonad's castellan and un-officially Orrin's jailer.

Eithne, housekeeper and cook, was Searc's perfect counterpart, except for the fact that, where he had stubble on his head, she wore it on her chin. Ungracious and foul-tempered, her cuisine matched her personality to a fault, and it was a wonder that Orrin hadn't long since dwindled to a skeleton on the fare she provided. But then, taste was one of the things that simply went by him. He ate when and what food was set before him as if it was just another tiresome chore, dull but ultimately filling.

Orrin couldn't have said how long he had been in this place, each day being no different from the one before or the one after – apart from the changes of weather and seasons, which he soon forgot in any case – but if he'd been able to venture a guess, he would have assumed that the time of his stay had been long rather than short.

In fact, it had been seven years since he'd been brought to Ceonad.

Uniform as all his days at the keep were, this one was to be different. As he sat there on the terrace, trying as he so often did to chase a small, niggling slip of a thought through the hazy stupor that blanketed his mind and slowed his thinking down to a muddied trickle, a small, brown face appeared in his field of vision. It took him a moment to focus and realize that the face was looking at him over the parapet, from outside, which meant... which meant...

What was it he'd been thinking?

Something about climbing? Or falling?

Never mind, there was strange little face looking at him over the parapet, studying him intently, it appeared. How ever had it gotten there?

'Orrin?' the face said. 'Prince Orrin?'

Orrin considered the question and managed to hold on to the thread until he hit upon an answer.

'Orrn,' he said, his speech slurred like a drunkard's. 'Don' know noth'n 'bout prince, but Orrn, yes.'

In the meantime, another two of the little brown faces had appeared.

'Listen up, princey,' one of them said – the one in the middle, he thought, who might have also been the first. 'Listen closely, 'cause we're here to save your royal ass. We brought you food and water. There's a satchel and a waterskin hanging right here on this side of the wall, and from now on there's gonna be fresh food and water every day. Do not eat and drink what they give you in there, understand? Do *not* eat or drink that stuff. It's bad for you. Chuck it over the wall when nobody's looking, and take nothing except what we bring you. You got that, princey? You hear me?'

'Hear you,' Orrin mumbled. 'Unnerstan'. Don' eat this, eat that. S'good.'

'Gotta go,' the face said. 'Somebody coming. Remember what I told you.'

'Member,' Orrin told the faces, but they were gone.

'Don' eat this, eat that,' he repeated to himself. 'Don' eat this…'

Eithne waddled up with a tray, his evening meal, and set it on the bench beside him. 'You talkin' to yerself now, boy?' she said, squinting and looking around warily. There was nothing to see, so she turn-

356

ed her attention back to Orrin. 'Always knew ye'd go over the edge one o' these days. Fine with me, just so long as ye don't start pissin' and shittin' yerself, 'cause I sure as hell ain't gonna clean up after ye. Ye can lie in it 'til ye rot, far's I'm concerned. Now eat, an' no more blabbin', y'hear?'

I don't like that person, Orrin thought for the ten thousandth time, though for all he remembered it might as well have been the first. When she was gone, he uncovered the tray, picked up the fork and speared a leathery chunk of meat from the bowl of evil-smelling stew. Halfway to his mouth his hand froze. There was something... something... yes! *Don't eat this. Eat that.* That was it.

He cast a sly look over his shoulder. No one in sight.

He picked up the tray and, keeping the bulk of his body between it and the keep, leaned forward until he could look over the parapet. He saw a leather satchel and a waterskin hanging from a wooden peg driven between the stones just under the crown of the wall. Another quick glance around – still no one watching, good – and he emptied the stew and the pitcher of watered wine over the wall, setting the tray back on the bench, empty as if he'd already eaten. Then he lean-ed forward a second time and rummaged in the sack. Bread, cheese, dried meat. Water with a faint tang of herbs and slightly sweetened with, what, honey? He ate, and the food filled him with something he hadn't known in a long time. He searched for a word. 'Good' was all he could come up with, but it would do. He finished every last crumb and emptied the skin.

Later, after he'd been sent to bed, he lay in the dark and told him-self over and over again, 'Good. Don't eat this, eat that. Good...'

357

Over the next few days, Orrin's head began to clear.

He still couldn't remember anything prior to his imprisonment in Ceonad, but, as the present began to reacquire a certain amount of co-herence and continuity, he understood that he was indeed a prisoner, albeit a privileged one. Or so it seemed.

The day after the little men's visit, it began to rain again. Getting rid of Eithne's food presented no problem, since in bad weather he was served his twice-daily meals in his room and could easily chuck the food out the window. Getting to the cache on the terrace was a bit more difficult. He considered simply not eating at all for a while, but then the little men would think he'd forgotten and maybe abandon him, and he'd be stuck here forever.

So, his brain slowly creaking into gear again, he devised a plan. After breakfast he put on his cloak and announced in his usual, slurred and disjointed speech to Eithne and Searc, who were sitting in the kitchen drinking kaf, that he'd decided it was not only extremely salutary, but practically mandatory for any halfway sensible, health-conscious person to betake himself for a walk after every repast, and that he intended to implement this new regimen forthwith by vigor-ously circumambulating the terrace a number of times – though what he actually said sounded slightly different.

'Going fer walk,' he told them. 'S'good fer digeshn. Should try't too. Be good fer you.'

'Like I said,' Eithne proclaimed. 'His high-and-mightiness has lost the last o' his marbles. Well, go on out then, boy, and catch yer-self a cold if ye must. Just don't expect anyone to nurse an' pamper ye when ye're sick.'

As Orrin was leaving he heard her whisper to Searc, 'Mind, it'd be best fer all of us if he did catch somethin' and turned up his toes. Save us all a lot o' time an' trouble. He ain't never gonna leave this place alive anyhow.'

'Ye might be on to somethin' there, fer once,' Searc mumbled. 'Don't think the boss'd mind, either.'

Orrin did catch a cold.

In the course of the day he felt increasingly weak and shaky and at the same time overly nervous and restless. His nose began to run, his eyes watered, his head ached, and towards evening he developed an inexplicable but nearly irresistible craving for Eithne's foul cooking. When she brought his evening meal and found him in bed and sniffling, she shook her head. Trying for an expression of long suffering but managing only to look smugly justified, she left him to his travails.

Seeing the cloth-covered tray, Orrin found himself ravening for its contents, no matter the smell almost made him gag. And then suddenly it hit him: he wasn't sick at all.

What he was experiencing were the symptoms of withdrawal from whatever drugs had been mixed into his food and drink. They had not only kept him in a state of near idiocy and made him easy to handle, they'd also induced a permanent, euphoric lassitude, a very nice and seductive feeling if you didn't have anything real to compare it with – a life, for instance. And it was most likely the sudden absence of this artificial wellbeing that was causing him acute discomfort. His resolve strengthened, he flung the tray's contents out into the rainy night before he could change his mind. Suddenly the mere thought of food nauseated him, and he skipped that meal altogether, hoping that just the once wouldn't put the little men off.

It didn't.

They continued to deposit fresh food for him, simple but nourishing, and on the fourth day he was already feeling much better, definitely over the worst of the withdrawal. The evening of the day after, the fifth, they were waiting for him.

As soon as he sat down on the bench, three heads popped up over the parapet. For the first time he was able to get a proper look at them, and he saw that, apart from all three being small and brown-skinned, they were really quite distinct personalities. One looked markedly younger, one was a bit on the chubby side, and the one in the middle was clearly the oldest, grey-haired and wrinkled. It was he who spoke.

'Hiya, princey,' he said jauntily. 'Doin' all right, are we? Ain't been eatin' no more gook from the crappy cook? Good man. Knew you'd get it. So, it's phase two then, princey-boy…'

'My name's Orrin,' Orrin said. 'And I'd thank you for stowing the "princey" bit. Actually, you might even want to go so far as to introduce yourselves.'

He must have said something terribly funny, for they cackled and whooped and smacked each other on the shoulders until he feared that one or more of them would lose their grip and fall to their death.

'Don't mind us,' the speaker said when he'd got his breath back. 'Just happy to see you got your spunk back so soon. As we forest folk say, "Celebrate every good thing as it comes along, before something else gets in the way."

'Any road, I'm Sedge, the gentleman to my right is Burr, and this

360

young scallywag is Alder. Now, *Orrin,* time's a'flyin', and we still got plans to make. Tonight, you get to say goodbye to this sorry excuse for a pile of rock, 'cause tonight you're coming with us.'

'You mean,' Orrin said, suddenly apprehensive, 'I'm supposed to climb down that cliff like a lizard or a spider or something?'

'Nah,' Sedge said. 'That's plan B. Plan A is, I give you this' – he handed Orrin a small, wax-stoppered vial – 'and you pour some of it in the stewpot when nobody's looking. A few drops will put them to sleep like babies. Then all you gotta do is find the keys and walk out the front door. We'll meet you... rats! There's Master Nastypants! Gotta go!'

'What's goin' on here?' Searc stomped up angrily. 'Who was that?'

He looked over the parapet, but the forest folk had vanished. To Orrin's relief the satchel and skin were gone as well.

'Huh?' he said. 'I didn' see anybody. D'you see somebody?'

'Don't mess with me, boy,' Searc roared, furious. 'I don't know what manner o' tricks ye think ye're up to, but I'm puttin' an end to 'em, right here an' now. Let's see what ye've got there.'

'Wha?' Orrin said. 'Noth – '

Searc smacked him hard across the face. 'Give it here,' he snarled. 'Or I swear I'll make ye sorry.'

Orrin handed over the vial.

'Well, well,' Searc said. 'Not half as dumb as ye'd have us believe, are ye? Time to put ye safely outta harm's way. Come along, fun's over. Ye're goin' in yer room, an' from now on that's where ye're stayin'.'

With the sound of the key turning, Orrin's dream of freedom was shattered. He despaired. Neither plan A nor plan B was going to work now, and if he didn't want to starve – though that possibility was beginning to look like an option – he'd have to revert to eating Eithne's drugged food and become a living vegetable again.

No! Better to get it over with quickly than to waste away for years and years in a twilight state that was no kind of life at all. If the food could go out the window, so could he. It would be quick and hopefully painless.

And here she was already. The key ground in the lock and Eithne shouldered open the door, bearing his trayful of slops and drugs.

'No more shenanigans, sirrah,' she said harshly. 'Ye're gonna eat every bit o' this, an' I'm gonna watch ye do it. So don't make me call Searc an' have him stuff it down yer gullet. Mood ye've put him in, he's not likely to mind overmuch if it goes down the wrong way an' ye choke on it. Now eat! I got other things to do.'

Orrin had no choice. He forced down bite after bite of the vile, drug-laced food. When he was done eating, Eithne made him drink off the whole pitcher of watered wine. He let a few drops trickle down his airway and made a big show of gasping and choking, a maneuver that left at least half of the stuff spilled down the front of his shirt and puddled on the floor. It also distracted Eithne, for when she left she pulled the door closed behind her but forgot to lock it. Orrin couldn't believe it at first, expecting her to come back any moment and turn the key.

She didn't. Gods! Maybe his luck was holding after all. He could still find a way out of here, even if it meant climbing down a hundred-fifty feet of stone and rock. Anything but this. But first things first. He opened the window, stuck a finger down his throat and chucked up everything he'd eaten. Much better. Now, how to make use of this miraculous break?

Patience, he counseled himself. *Searc and Eithne need to be fast asleep before you try anything. You've got all the time in the world to think this through properly.*

He waited until well after midnight before he made his move.

A week ago, he'd have been oblivious to his surroundings, but in the meantime he'd begun to pay attention, and he'd learned certain things: which floorboards were liable to creak in the upper hallway for instance, or where lamps burned nights on the upper and lower levels, and where Searc slept. He wrapped his boots in his cloak, tiptoed down the hall, and deposited them at the top of the stairs, ready to be picked up on the way out.

Even if he hadn't known where Searc's quarters were, he would have had no trouble finding them. The man snored like a pig. Ever so carefully, Orrin opened the door just far enough so he could slip through, aware of the fact that it produced a shrill squeal on the second leg of its inward swing.

Searc's room was a sty. Dirty clothes and empty bottles lay everywhere, and the smell of stale wine and unwashed bodies was overpowering. Bodies, plural, because Eithne was there too, sharing Searc's bed, her naked, flabby behind sticking out from under the grimy covers like a deliberate insult. Orrin found what he was looking for on a chair by the bedside. Searc's keys. He had them in hand and was about to leave when he noticed something else lying there: the vial Sedge had given him. He took it, thinking it might still come in handy.

He was almost at the door when his foot hit an empty bottle. Clattering loudly, it rolled across the floor until it fetched up against a discarded garment. He froze.

Searc stirred and muttered.

Eithne let out a belch and smacked her lips. Neither of them woke. They were dead drunk. Orrin breathed a silent prayer of thanks to whatever god was responsible for making people drink themselves silly. At the door, he found the key sticking in the lock. He pulled it out, closed the door behind him, inserted the key from outside and turned it, careful not to make a noise.

It didn't work. Try as he might, it wouldn't go more than a quarter turn before it fetched up against something and jammed. Either it was the wrong key, or the lock was broken. After a few tries he gave up, afraid of making too much noise. Pity. He didn't doubt that Searc would have found some way to break down the door eventually. But it would have cost him time, time that Orrin needed to get away.

Passing by the kitchen, his feet freezing on the icy flagstones, he noticed Eithne's kaf pot standing on the hearth. It was half full of cold kaf. Knowing her, she would warm it up in the morning. He decided to enrich the filthy brew and emptied half of the vial's contents into it. He re-stoppered the tiny vessel and pocketed it – you never knew when something like this might come in handy again. When he turned to leave, he found Searc standing in the door, blocking the only exit.

Searc's teeth were bared in a feral snarl, and the look in his bloodshot eyes set Orrin's knees shaking. Searc had only bothered to pull on his breeches, was bare from the waist up. Apart from a layer of flab over his belly he was all solid slabs and rippling bulges of muscle. Worse, he was drunk, and clearly in a very nasty mood. He looked ready for violence, and he was holding a long, wicked knife in a way that said he knew how to use it. And Orrin, after seven years of captivity, of debilitating drugs and enforced idleness, was weak as a puppy, so out of shape that a few rounds on the terrace left him out of breath.

What scared him most, though, was Searc's silence. He'd have been much happier if the man had been yelling at him. This felt more like Searc was finished talking and about to do something reckless and stupid.

Like killing Orrin.

Orrin looked around for something he could use to defend himself. There was a heavy cleaver lying on a butcher's block midway between the two of them. Searc noticed where he was looking, an evil grin twisting his features. Orrin lunged.

He barely managed to pull back his hand before Searc could chop it off, the blade thunking into the block and missing Orrin's fingers by a hair. Inebriated as he was, Searc was still quick. Quicker than Orrin, in any case. Searc picked up the cleaver. Holding it in his left hand, the knife in his right weaving like the head of a snake preparing to strike, he came on. Orrin backed up, fetching up against a table that stood in the middle of the kitchen, laden with unwashed cups and dirty dishes. His hand came to rest on the back of a chair, and he sent it scooting at Searc, who reduced it to kindling with a vicious chop of the cleaver.

Noting that Searc was barefoot, Orrin had a sudden inspiration. Using both hands, he indiscriminately grabbed up pieces of earthenware crockery and flung them on the floor, sent everything he could reach flying and shattering on the granite flagstones.

A look of triumph stole onto Searc's features, as if this childish, futile maneuver only confirmed what he thought of Orrin and what he intended to do to him. His fighting instincts may have been functioning, more or less, but the rest of his brain was bleary and fuddled with wine. He advanced. And stepped on a shard, keen as broken glass. He roared with pain and fury. But he kept on coming nonetheless, sliding his feet along the floor so as not to step on another piece of broken crockery, his lacerated foot leaving bloody smears on the floor.

Orrin backed around the table and kept going until he reached the fireplace, where he'd spied a long, sturdy poker leaning against the stone sidepiece. Sidling up to it, he grabbed the handle, hiding the action with his body.

Searc had reached clear ground again. Giving no sign of warning, he lunged, leading with the knife. At the last possible moment, Orrin brought up the poker, pointing it straight at Searc with arms outstretched and elbows locked.

Carried forward by his own momentum, Searc ran right into it, skewering himself on the pointed steel rod. The force of the collision buckled Orrin's arms and drove the poker's handle hard against his chest. Feeling a sharp pain as Searc's knife slashed across his left ribcage, he gave the poker an instinctive shove.

Searc stumbled backwards, a look of dumb incomprehension on his face. Four inches of poker plus the handle were sticking out of his midriff, the tip protruding from his back. His mouth opening and closing soundlessly, he crashed into the table, lost his footing and fell to the floor, dead before his body hit the icy flagstones.

Sick with relief, weak-kneed and trembling with the after-shock of having killed a man, Orrin tiptoed around the body, careful not to cut his own feet, half fearing that Searc might suddenly jump up and attack him again.

He didn't, was well and truly dead. Orrin felt no satisfaction, only gratitude that it wasn't him lying there in a slowly spreading pool of blood.

Outside the keep's main door, he slipped on his boots and cloak. Then, walking across the courtyard for the first time in seven years, he unlocked the postern gate and let himself out. For good measure he relocked the gate and hurled Searc's bunch of keys far into the thicket that fringed the trail, hearing them rattle against something hard.

'Ouch!' Sedge said, rising out of the brush like an irritated forest spirit. 'That was my head you just bounced those blooming keys off.'

'Sorry,' Orrin said, smiling to himself in the dark despite the fact that his knees were still wobbly. 'Hope they didn't accidentally un-lock anything important in there. Wouldn't want you losing stuff along the way.'

'Ha!' Sedge snorted. 'The boy is being funny!'

'Not really,' Orrin said. 'Just glad I'm still alive. And anyhow, are you guys the only ones who've got a lease on humor here?'

'You got it,' Sedge said in a tone of righteous indignation, but Orrin, his eyes adjusting to the darkness, could see the little man's teeth flashing a grin. And he *was* little, Orrin realized when Sedge came out of the brush and joined him on the road, standing half a head short of Orrin's shoulder. Sedge seemed to be thinking along similar lines.

'Gods,' he said, looking Orrin up and down. 'Why do you people have to be so big? It's indecent. No wonder you're so bad at hiding and stick out all over the landscape like a bunch of sore thumbs. Well, if you're gonna travel with us – which you are – you'll just have to learn to make yourself small. Now, let's get out of here before the stinkers in there wake up.'

'Only one of them's going to wake up,' Orrin said. 'Searc came after me. I killed him.'

'Darn!' Sedge said. 'Ain't no fun killing a man. Don't let it get to you, lad. I know it's hard, but it ain't your fault. You were just trying to stay alive, and in all likelihood, the fellow had it coming anyway.'

Orrin followed the little man through the brush and in among the trees. A little ways into the forest, Burr and Alder were waiting for them. His ribs were aching and he was out of breath, but all he wanted at the moment was to get away from there as fast as possible.

'Is there a reason why we're not taking the road?' he asked.

'Yup,' Sedge said. 'Goin' the other way. Somebody there wants to see you.'

'So what do we tell this guy if there's, like, danger ahead?' Burr butted in, looking Orrin up and down. 'Freeze, or shrink?'

'How about frink?' Alder said, which had them all three back-slapping and laughing tears for a while. They were just catching their breath when Burr had another inspiration.

'No, schreeze!' he gasped, setting them off all over again.

Orrin could see how his new friends might take some getting used to. Thankfully, his worst fears concerning the trip ahead proved groundless – he didn't have to trudge all night long through the pitch-dark forest with unseen branches slapping his face, mean-spirited roots tripping him up, and boggy hollows trying to pull the boots from his feet. Hurt and unfit as he was, he didn't think he'd have been capable of such a feat in any case. An hour into the forest, they reached a bough shelter and a cozy fire. Two forest folk were standing there fidgeting impatiently and craning their necks to get a look at him.

'Did you find him?' they asked in unison.

'What?' Burr said. 'You two been into the juice again? Or he's so big you can't tell him from a tree?'

'Meet the twins,' Sedge said. 'Holly and Hock.'

'Who's who?' Orrin asked.

'Hoo, hoo,' one of the twins said. 'Guy sounds like an owl to me. You sure you got the right one?'

'All right,' Orrin sighed. 'Which is which?'

'Forget it,' Sedge said. 'Nobody can tell them apart, not even their own mother. Most of the time they can't tell themselves apart. You two got some chow ready for us? Good. And then it's off to bed. Gonna be a long day tomorrow.'

Eventually Orrin did mention his wound and got it expertly seen to by Sedge, who sewed it up with a tiny bone needle and some very fine sinew, and then packed it with herbs soaked in hot water before binding it up with Burr's spare shirt.

'Why does it have to be *my* shirt?' Burr asked, not at all happy.

369

'Because you're the biggest of the lot,' Sedge said. 'And as you can see, the patient's not exactly a midget. That's what you get for stuffing yourself between meals and putting on all that blubber.'

Orrin was simply too tired to follow the rest of the argument. His lids drooping shut of their own volition, he was asleep before he knew it.

That night he dreamed again.

This time, a barrier inside him collapsed and he was swept along by a deluge of memories, a tiny speck of awareness ducking and bobbing on a vast, dark sea of rushing images and swirling emotions, finally waking up exhausted and battered, flotsam washed back into consciousness by a storm tide of recollection. For the longest time he lay in the dark breathing, smiling, crying, balancing gains and losses, hard truths and harder choices, desire and duty, fear and resolve. Long before day broke and the forest folk began to stir, he knew what he had to do.

'Sedge, guys,' he said over breakfast. 'I want you to know that I'm very, very grateful for what you've done for me. I'll be in your debt forever.'

Sedge looked at him soberly. 'All right. Let's have the rest of it. The part that stars with but.'

'But I'm not coming with you. I have to go the other way. To Kingskeep. I'm sorry.'

'Not half as sorry as I am,' Sedge sighed. 'I was really looking forward to a nice walk in this part of the forest. But then, he said this was likely to happen, you being young and hasty and all that.'

'Who's this mysterious "he" you keep talking about?' Orrin asked, gingerly moving his left arm. His ribs ached less than he'd expected.

'Greybeard. He's the fellow sent us here to spring you. He wanted to talk to you before you went haring off like a headless chicken and got yourself in a heap of trouble. But he also said that, in the end, it was your choice, and to tell you to be really, *really* careful. And that he'll be along as soon as he can.

'And you should remember the Colors, said you'd know what it meant. Seems there's a few people who're not gonna be thrilled if you show up alive and kicking. And they'll be watching out for you. So you can forget right away about taking any roads. We're gonna stick to the woods.'

'Oh, but you don't have to come with me,' Orrin protested. 'You've done more than enough for me already.'

'Oh, but we do.' Sedge was adamant. 'He'd have our guts for garters if we let you wander off alone and something happened to you. Seems to think you're something special, the old man does. Well. Somebody's got to go and tell him. Holly, methinks that somebody is you.'

'That's him! He's going,' both twins said simultaneously, pointing at each other.

'Gods blooming darn!' Sedge exploded. 'Now's not the time for silly games! Holly, get your sorry ass moving, before I lose my temper! Right. Now, since everybody seems to be done having breakfast, we might as well hit the trail.'

And a trail there was, though Orrin would have never found it by himself, and lost it a hundred times even if he had. The forest folk

371

appeared to know exactly where they were going, stringing together game passes, hunters' tracks, and paths of their own making, seemingly twisting and turning but always headed south in a gradual descent that eventually took them out of the foothills and onto more even ground but never out into the open. Though they must have come close by Caer Ceonad early on, Orrin never saw it.

He wished he knew the path that lay ahead of him half as well as these people knew their forest highways. The cut on his ribs was healing with surprising speed, which he reckoned was due to Sedge's herbs, and after an initial struggle with his untrained muscles he found that the hours and days of walking did him a world of good. More and more, he began to feel like his old self again, or what he remembered of it.

'Where did your people come from originally?' he asked Sedge during a rest.

The little man looked at him uncomprehendingly. 'We didn't need to come from anywhere,' he said. 'We were already here.'

'You mean, like, always?'

'Yup. It was you people that came from elsewhere, over the ocean, a long time ago.'

This was news to Orrin.

'But all the stories say you came down from the north,' he said, 'out of the Great Forest.'

'That's *your* stories, Sedge said. 'And we didn't come from the north, we *went* there. Because suddenly there were all these big people trampling through the forest. The place got so blooming crowded, you couldn't lie down for a snooze for fear of being stepped on by some bumbling Bigfoot.

'Later on, some of us came back. As for the Great Forest, it used to be everywhere. You're walking through it right now. And in my opinion – no offense – your stories are a lot of bunk. At least the ones about us. They call us elves and dwarves and gnomes, can't make up their minds what we're supposed to be. Sprites and spirits! Ha! Ridiculous! We're people like everybody else, just a bit shorter than average, is all. So there you have it. Now, what's the plan once we get to Kingskeep?'

'Er, find out who's responsible and bring them to justice?' Orrin said.

Sedge gave him a pitying look. 'Boy, if that's your entire plan, we might as well top ourselves right here and now. Save us a lot of walking.'

'I'm working on it,' Orrin said defensively. 'I need to get there and feel the lay of the land before I can decide on the finer details.'

'Just remember it's the details that make the plan,' Sedge said. 'And I'll bet there's gonna be a huge, big, blooming heap of those waiting for you. So.' He looked around. 'Break is over. Time to go, before Burr's big behind starts putting down roots.'

'My behind heard that,' Burr grumbled. 'It resents being called big, and says to tell you this.' He lifted one small, meaty buttock and broke wind.

Suddenly everybody was in a splendid mood again, and trouble seemed yet to be a long way off.

❖ ❖ ❖

Good men must not obey the laws too well.

Ralph Waldo Emerson

21 Digger's Row

 basset would have looked positively cheerful beside Sheriff Dwight D. Hunsicker as he stood at the edge of the perfectly round, snow-free clearing, his long, sad face folded into a fresh set of worry lines. Absently, he took off his hat, passing a large-knuckled hand over his pate in a gesture of smoothing down hair that hadn't been there for twenty years. He forgot to replace the hat until snowflakes melting on his bare scalp sent a cold rivulet sliding down the back of his neck and under his collar.

When his deputy Clyde had gone out in answer to a call from Martha Poors, the town's resident busybody, saying that her neighbors' son Eric Sandersen had crashed his father's truck right there in the family's driveway, Hunsicker hadn't expected anything worse than a bent fender. Martha was known to exaggerate on occasion, so when she grudgingly admitted that no one seemed to be hurt before launching into a lengthy lecture about today's youth and its driving habits, Hunsicker politely cut her off, sent Clyde to sort things out, and returned to his paperwork.

Then Clyde called in to say that there was a lot more to the story, and that Hunsicker had better come on over. It turned out that, for once, Martha had been understating the facts. Eric, going much too fast, had skidded on the icy driveway and run the truck right through the closed garage door, reducing it to splinters. His mother's car, parked inside the garage, was scrap. But when Hunsicker entered the house and got his first look at Eric's face, tear-streaked and wild-eyed, he knew immediately that the mayhem outside was not the whole story.

Eric was barely coherent.

But Hunsicker had a quiet, patient way with people, and eventually, piece by piece, he got the story out of the boy. It sounded pretty wild, and Hunsicker suspected that Eric, shocked and traumatized, was subconsciously repressing the true facts and replacing them with something that wouldn't force him to do what for the time being proved simply too much for him: face the truth.

Most likely, Hunsicker thought, the two boys had been careless, banging around wildly way out there past Digger's Row until the inevitable happened and one of them got hit. Eric kept saying that Billy wasn't dead, but Hunsicker reckoned it had been close to two hours since whatever happened had gone down. In this weather, Billy's chances didn't look good, even assuming his injury was non-lethal.

Hunsicker made the necessary calls to set up a search and rescue mission. He didn't like the idea of involving the state police, but they were the ones who owned a chopper, which was the only means of transport that would get him out there in any kind of time. Still, another hour went by before he got to the scene.

The scene: looking at it now, he had to readjust his thinking.

Eric's description had been spot on, down to the pair of weird, black columns sitting smack in the middle of the circular clearing that should by rights have been covered in several inches of snow like everything else around it. There was no sign of Billy. Most of the tracks had been snowed over, but right at the edge, where the snow petered out, Hunsicker found enough signs to tentatively confirm Eric's story. There were two complete impressions of different treads going in, and the front half of one coming out again, clearly made by a person running. So where was Billy? The whole thing was beginning to spook him.

With no body found, the medical team left, and Hunsicker managed to get the staties off his back by humbly apologizing for calling them out on what had obviously turned out to be false information. In any case – though after a first attempt they kept well away from the columns – they seemed much more interested in the strange artifact than in the missing boy, pointing out to Hunsicker that the crime scene lay right on a state line and wanting to know whether he was going to notify the FBI or if they should do it. He said he'd take care of it, knowing they'd call the Feds anyway, if only to keep their asses covered.

Clyde and the volunteers were doing another round through the by now hopelessly churned and trampled area surrounding the site. Both choppers had departed, and in the ensuing quiet Hunsicker began to feel a mounting unease. There was something deeply unsettling about this place. He was reminded of the old stories about Digger's Row, just a stone's throw away. They'd taken on the character of folk tales over time, the creepy-crawly stuff of childish fantasies. But Hunsicker, a bit of a buff for local history, had dug around and found at least part of the truth behind the grisly myth in old records and in the archives of the local paper.

In the early 1880's the leader of an extremist crackpot sect called Joshua Deaker had moved here from somewhere in the east together with thirty of his followers, intending to set up an isolated farming community after the example of other, less questionable congregations.

Apparently the locals had not been pleased, and stories began to circulate about all sorts of perversion and blasphemy being practiced by the 'Children of Umulamut', as the sect called itself, allegedly harking back to some obscure Egyptian prophet wrongfully omitted from biblical tradition.

In the third year after the sect's arrival, two local children disappeared within a week, and it didn't take the good citizens long to determine who had to be responsible. A posse was formed, but before it could move out one of Deaker's followers, a man by the name of Eli Manders, came wandering into town in a state the old news article described as 'altogether bereft of his senses and wholly demented', covered in blood and babbling about the 'master's ascension'. A gruesome scene greeted the men who went to investigate.

They found a double row of freshly dug holes, six feet by three feet by six, a few of them smaller, child-sized, shovels still sticking in some of the neatly mounded piles of dirt beside each hole as if the diggers had just finished up and gone inside for a break.

In the sect's communal hall they found Deaker's dead followers. Men, women and children were sitting around a large table, their carotid arteries opened by precise, surgical cuts, the floor awash in an inch of blood.

A hastily held inquest came to the conclusion that Eli Manders had killed all of his co-sectarians in a fit of insanity, and Manders was sentenced and hanged the following week.

Hunsicker thought he could smell the stink of a cover-up from a hundred and twenty years away. He wondered what it was that had so badly needed to be hidden. Interestingly, Deaker himself, dead or alive, was never found. It was as if he'd vanished from the face of the earth. All that remained of him was his name, distorted but conserved over time in the darkly humorous toponym that local vernacular had bestowed on the site where the sect had resided: Digger's Row. The only relics of the sect's sojourn were a few blackened, crumbling stone chimneys and two rows of slight humps, twenty-nine in all, forming a miniature clearing of their own where anything other than sickly yellow grass refused to grow.

Hunsicker heard the occasional shout from the men combing through the woods, but he could tell by their unexcited tones that they weren't finding anything, just whistling past the graveyard, making halfhearted conversation to keep the cold, hungry atmosphere of the place from closing in on them. Crazy as it sounded, Eric's story was beginning to seem more and more likely.

Another sound was fast approaching. A skidoo, in all likelihood bearing Bob Cummins, the local plumber, with the fiber-optic gizmo he employed to check pipes and drains for ruptures and blockages. Hunsicker had called him earlier and asked him to bring it out.

And here he was, friendly, pudgy Bob, riding double on Joe Hanks' ski-doo and dressed like he was going on a polar expedition. Joe was pulling a sleigh loaded with Bob's gear and some boardings

Hunsicker had also asked for. He went to greet them.

While Bob set up the fiber-optic machine and a small generator and Joe went to join the searchers, Hunsicker laid out the boards over the black stuff covering the approach to the pair of columns. This close, he could physically feel the thing's radiation. He imagined that, if you could actually sense nuclear fallout as and when it reached you, this was what it would feel like: a prickling, stinging sensation that seemed to etch itself into your individual cells and burn in every nerve end. Ugly.

When Cummins had everything set up, they passed the optical end of the cable through the space between the columns. Then they stood together and looked at the monitor.

'Now this is really weird,' Bob said, fiddling with the controls. 'Looks like we're picking up something off the air, some freaky TV show. Never had that happen before. Don't even see how it's possible.'

Hunsicker reached out to switch off the monitor, but just then the screen went dead of its own accord.

'Damn!' Cummins said, pulling the cable back out and studying its business end. 'It's melted. Look, the first inch or so is slagged. Sorry 'bout that, sheriff.'

'No sweat,' Hunsicker said. 'It was just a wild idea anyway. Nothing there. Get that thing fixed and send me the bill. Sorry to have you come all this way for nothing. I'll make it up to you. How about beer and pizza at Marty's tonight?'

Cummins had been about to say something else, but the magic words 'beer and pizza' distracted him, and by then Hunsicker had already started reeling in the cable.

'Time we got out of here,' he said. 'Be getting dark in half an hour. Thanks again, and see you at Marty's at seven, if the time suits you.'

'Fine, great,' Bob said, turning off the generator. Thankfully, he was neither the sharpest knife in the drawer nor an intrepid outdoorsman. Hunsicker fervently hoped that he'd have forgotten all about what he'd seen in the grainy image on the monitor's screen by the time he got home. He wasn't looking forward to spending the evening with gregarious, voluble Bob, and he'd try to keep it as short as possible. He had a lot of thinking to do.

Dwight D. was not a man to let something like a missing boy go just because the FBI told him to – which he knew with absolute certainty they would. He understood all too well how the fate of Billy Perkins paled beside the tremendous implications of the artifact that had swallowed the boy whole. He was sure Billy's case would simply go under – or be made to go under. Dismissed and forgotten in the aftermath of the discovery, when secrecy and concealment would move right up to the top of everyone's agenda and turf wars would be fought out behind closed doors in high places. No one would be interested in Billy anymore. Except him.

He wasn't sheriff for nothing. Though he'd originally sought the job only because Marge, his late wife, seemed to think that he was cut out for it and had encouraged him to try, to his lasting surprise the people seemed to agree with her assessment. They'd elected and re-elected him to take care of situations like this one ever since. He was there to look out for them and theirs, and that was precisely what he was going to do. And screw the FBI, the CIA, the DIA, Homeland

Security and whoever else would soon be scrambling for a piece of the action if they didn't like it. He'd just have to find a way around them.

The Feds showed up the next day with two choppers and whole motorcade of black SUVs. They asked Hunsicker for every scrap of paper he had concerning the disappearance of Billy Perkins, and even brought in an IT guy to go through the office's computers, making sure that nothing pertaining to the case was left in his files.

He didn't fight it. He knew he wouldn't be dealing with the FBI for long. A plan was forming in his head that didn't call for things like files and paperwork. For the moment all he needed was patience, and that was something he'd always had plenty of.

❖ ❖ ❖

For you see, the world is governed by very different personages from what is imagined by those who are not behind the scenes.
Benjamin Disraeli

22 Cannes

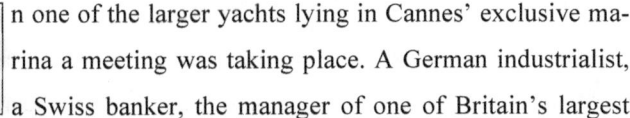n one of the larger yachts lying in Cannes' exclusive marina a meeting was taking place. A German industrialist, a Swiss banker, the manager of one of Britain's largest hedge funds, and the Dutch CEO of a big oil company were connected by secure video link to a group in Washington, DC, consisting of a high-ranking government official, a very influential senator, and a four-star general.

They were discussing strategy on a project initiated by the German, who had in recent years acquired certain pertinent information hidden away in secret Nazi archives and kept under locks by the German and Allied governments to the present day, buried so deep that the men belonging to this group were quite possibly by now the only ones who knew of its existence.

Their small clique, called The Club, had been established quite some time ago as a very profitable association of mutual financial and political interests, allowing them to deal largely outside the usual, oftentimes highly annoying constraints of national and international law. Though none of them would ever appear on a list of the world's richest people, each and every one of them could have claimed a place not too far from the top.

'Have the targets arrived yet?' the secretary asked.

'They are here, holed up with the old man, safe,' the German said. 'Your people's bumbling attempts have only served to put them out of our reach.'

'Bad timing,' the general said defensively. 'The operatives were supposed to take one of them, give us leverage with the old man. Because you people were suddenly in such a damn hurry, they had to improvise. Stuff tends to go wrong when you're forced to go in unprepared.'

'How unprepared can you be after you have had a year to get ready?' the Swiss said, studying his immaculately manicured nails. 'And let us not forget the fiasco in Canada.'

'We had good reason to press ahead,' the German said. 'We've had reports that the old man is not in good health. If he dies without passing on his knowledge, then everything will have been in vain.'

'Correction,' the general said, savoring the moment. 'While you people've been flapping your wings, we've had a new development here. A specimen of what we've been looking for was found right here in the United States. It's being secured as we speak – military project, restricted right off the books, yours truly in charge, so we'll have all the access we want.'

'Well,' the Englishman said. 'This is certainly news. So they really do exist, and are not just a wild pipe dream of Mr. Himmler and his Ahnenerbe fruitcakes. I'm impressed, gentlemen.'

'Very good news indeed,' the German said grudgingly. 'I must congratulate you. But I still think we should go ahead with my project also, to be on the safe side. Two is always better than one.'

'I have to agree,' the senator said. 'Especially because what's been found here seems to be a, ah... black version. I seem to remember you saying those were not, ah, quite so dependable.'

'Ach!' the German said. 'Not dependable at all, if what little information Herr Himmler's people managed to gather on them is correct. But better than nothing, I suppose.'

'I'm sure we'll find a way to iron out the kinks,' the general said. 'Or work around them. I've got some really good people on this. The best. Still, it might not be a bad idea to move forward on your side as well.'

'Absolutely,' the Secretary said. 'Does anyone feel otherwise? No? Good. Then I suggest we go ahead with both projects and keep in close contact. Gentlemen, we'll be hearing from each other.'

Once the Americans had disconnected, the German leaned back and looked at his associates with gleaming eyes.

'Ja!' he said, motioning over a white-jacketed steward wo'd been waiting at the far end of the salon and now rolled over a serving trolley laden with hors d'ouevres, an ice bucket containing a magnum bottle of champagne, and a box of hand-rolled Cuban cigars.

'Let them go ahead with their project. They'll soon find that they've bitten off more than they can chew. In the meantime, they will be busy, and we will have them off our backs until we are ready with our own little venture. In any case, thanks to them we can now be sure that what we are looking for actually exists. Imagine, my friends. Another whole planet to play with! We will be unstoppable. Cigar, anyone?'

'To the birth of a new empire,' the Englishman said, raising his

385

glass.

'The greatest empire of all times,' the Dutchman said.

'The greatest empire of all times,' the others echoed, clinking their glasses.

❖   ❖   ❖

Look for me in the whirlwind or the storm.

Marcus Garvey

23 Ravenstein

ncle Richard's man Franz met them at Munich's Haupt-bahnhof. Standing ramrod-straight in the middle of the platform, a head taller than most of the other passengers scurrying around him, he looked as out of place as a bear among sheep – or a soldier among civilians. When he spotted Lisa, his hard, angular face split into a wide grin, and he enveloped her in a bear hug.

'Vanna, dear friend!' she exclaimed in German, kissing him on both cheeks. 'It's so good to see you. You haven't changed at all.'

Franz chuckled, running a hand over the stubble on his head.

'Except for the grey hair, or what's left of it, and the minor ailments of beginning old age that seem to have conspired to come after me all at once, I guess I'm fine. And you. Where's the skinny girl that left here, what, fifteen years ago? You look beautiful.'

'Thank you, Vanna. You're very kind. These are Lucy and Jonathan, my niece and nephew.'

Franz gave Jon a friendly smile and a surprisingly gentle handshake. Then he squatted down to Lucy's eye level.

'Hello, Miss Lucy,' he said in heavily accented English. 'I am very glad to meet you.'

Lucy looked at him with serious, appraising eyes. Then she offered her hand. Franz took it and kissed it lightly, as if she were a princess. Apparently satisfied with the exchange, she gave him one of her rare, cautious ghosts of a smile. Taking up Lisa and Lucy's luggage, Franz led them to a large, beautifully kept vintage Mercedes. With its immaculate dark green finish and tan leather interior, it looked like it had come off the assembly line just recently instead of forty-something years ago.

Franz made a small scenic detour through the city, passing by the Asam church and the Viktualienmarkt and crossing over the Isar at the Deutsches Museum before taking the Autobahn towards Salzburg. Jon thought it a friendly city, lively at a pleasantly human pace, a place where he might enjoy spending time. Very different from New York.

Franz turned out to be an excellent driver, the kind you instinctively felt safe with, though Jon could more easily envision him handling a tractor or a truck. He did seem to check the rearview mirror more often than necessary, his face set in the old, hard lines again. Jon's attention was soon taken up by the passing scenery. After a stretch of pine forest, the vista opened up onto a bucolic, pre-alpine landscape of gently undulating hills, a succession of meadows and hedgerows, farms, church towers, and villages, all of it set against the background of the Alps, the higher peaks already dusted white by the first snowfalls.

After about an hour Franz turned off the Autobahn and headed towards the mountains. Another thirty minutes, and they reached the small village of Ravenstein, its houses nestled under Castle Ravenstein on its limestone bluff like chicks huddling under the protective wings of a mother hen.

A narrow lane cut into the steep slope flanking the bluff led up and around to the back of the castle and the gate. Franz pressed a remote, and the portcullis rose to let them through into the bailey. As they passed under the stone arch, Jon noted the coat of arms carved into the headstone, a raven holding a key in one claw and a gladius, a Roman short-sword, in the other.

In the cobbled courtyard Franz stopped in front of the perron, the double stairs leading up to the main entrance and the great hall. There they were greeted by Anton, the groundskeeper, and Maria, the cook. Like Franz they were very affectionate with Lisa and gave Jon and Lucy a warm and friendly welcome. They were both around Franz's age, late fifties or early sixties, and, seeing the three of them together, Jon thought he detected a family resemblance.

Just as they were about to go inside, a young man came out. Franz introduced him as his nephew Hans. He seemed nice enough, though lacking the cordiality of his elders, and looked to be in a hurry, mounting a bright green motorbike and thundering out through the gate.

Of uncle Richard there was no sign.

Anton showed them to their rooms on the first floor. Once they'd unpacked and settled in, Maria served them tea in the solar, a large room above the great hall with delicately arched triple windows looking out over the bailey. It had the cozy, well-worn atmosphere of a family sitting room. There was a delicious Apfelstrudel baked by Maria, and homemade raspberry syrup for Lucy.

After tea, Lisa showed Lucy and Jon around the castle. Lucy gazed in awe at the long row of portraits on the upper gallery. She was particularly fascinated by the ones depicting high-born ladies dressed up in all the finery of their respective periods.

'I bet you'd like to wear a dress like that and be a real princess,' Jon said. 'And hey, maybe we could even find a frog for you to kiss, and then you could have a prince, too.'

Lucy gave him one of her indulgent, pitying looks.

They had dinner in a small dining room off the great hall, again without uncle Richard.

'Der Herr Graf is not feeling well,' Anton informed Lisa. 'It's his leg, the old injury. But he asks if you'll meet him in the library after dinner.'

When they had finished a meal that convinced Jon that, if nothing else, Maria's cooking was an excellent reason for an extended stay in Ravenstein, Lisa went to see Richard, and Lucy dragged Jon off to the solar for a game of memory. He hated playing memory with his little sister; nine times out of ten, she won. But it kept her happy, and it wasn't as if he had anything better to do. An hour or so later – Jon had lost three out of three – Lisa returned, looking thoughtful.

'He wants to see you,' she told Jon, 'if you're not too tired from the trip. He's not in good shape, but he seems really excited about meeting you.'

Right then, Jon would have preferred to go just about anywhere except upstairs to meet the old man, who seemed more and more to be a bit of a head case, mildly put.

'Okay,' he sighed. 'Where do I find him?'

Lisa showed him the way, leaving him at the door to the library on the second floor of the west tower. Taking a deep breath, Jon knocked, and heard a thin voice call, 'Come!'

The old man was sitting in a leather wing chair by the fireplace.
His right leg was propped up on a matching footrest, a second chair
pulled up opposite his own. What light there was came from the fire
and from an old-fashioned, green-shaded reading lamp on an enormous desk covered with books and papers. All around the walls of
the large, circular room were shelves laden with more books, sparing
out only the door and the windows and reaching almost to the high
ceiling decorated with gilded stucco.

'Jonathan,' Richard said, his voice weak and strained. 'I'm so
very glad you came. Excuse an old man for not getting up, but the leg
is acting up, doesn't like the cold weather. Come, sit.'

'Uncle Richard. Glad to meet you,' Jon said, feeling awkward
under Richards searching gaze. His blue eyes were sharp and clear, as
if a much younger soul inhabited the old and ailing body. His pat-
rician face with the narrow, aquiline nose showed a distinct resemblance to Lisa, Anna, and Jon himself.

'Thank you for coming, my boy,' Richard said. 'I've been very
much looking forward to our meeting, not only because we are family
and should have the chance to get to know each other but also because there are important matters I would like to discuss with you. I
realize this is a bit of an imposition, and I wish I could break the
news I have to give you at a more palatable pace. But time is a commodity that is in ever dwindling supply for me, and I must see things
set in order before it runs out on me altogether. So please forgive me
for rushing you into this, but if you're not too tired and still feel up to
it, I would like to get started right away.'

391

'I'm fine,' Jon said. 'Please go ahead.'

He did feel slightly overwhelmed by the speed with which things suddenly seemed to be moving, but his earlier feelings about Richard had already begun to change. Far from appearing in any way strange the old man, ill as he was, seemed clear-headed and purposeful. More, Jon felt a connection to his great-uncle, a bond that didn't take any time in the forging but was already there: the ties of blood and family. And he realized that, simply and spontaneously, he liked Richard, and was liked in turn.

'Good. Well. I've spent inordinate amounts of time thinking about this, but I'm still not sure where best to begin. In any case, it's all to do with the future of Ravenstein. Not to beat around the bush, I need a successor, an heir. I've spoken about this with your aunt Lisa, and she agrees with me – whole-heartedly, I may say – that it should be you. If you're willing, that is.'

'Um,' Jon said, 'I don't know what to say. I don't know if I'd be up to it. I mean, it seems like a huge responsibility.'

'It is,' Richard said. 'And I wish I could say you shouldn't feel forced to take it on, especially because the material side of it, the castle, and the associated holdings – the forestry, the farm, and the brewery – is the least of the burden, though the running and upkeep of it all is enough to keep you busy. But there at least you can oversee and delegate, as I have done, and still have time to lead a life of sorts outside of these walls. You can finish your education, see the world, start a family, whatever.

'No, the real burden of responsibility that comes with Ravenstein is something else altogether. And here I must beg you to bear with me for a moment, even if what I'm about to tell you calls for an enormous stretch of the imagination.'

The old man shifted in his chair, searching for a better position.

'Ravenstein holds a secret. There is something hidden away in these ancient walls that has been under the guardianship of our family for nearly two thousand years. It all began with the founder of House Ravenstein, one Flavius Corvinus, a Roman tribune in Iuvavum, the first Roman province in these parts. It was established only a few years before the birth of Christ, and centered on today's Salzburg.

'After playing an important part in the territories' conquest, Flavius Corvinus remained to protect and oversee the salt works in Bad Reichenhall. Salt in those days was a very precious commodity, at times fetching its weight in gold and even used as a currency in its own right. When Corvinus retired, he decided to stay on in this new province north of the Alps, and he began to build himself a splendid villa on the very spot where Burg Ravenstein now stands. And here the most interesting part of his story begins. This is how Corvinus himself told it, and how it's been handed down in our family for many generations.

'Before the actual building was begun, Corvinus was up here one day, sitting on a rock and surveying the site of his future home, when something extraordinary happened. Out of thin air an arm emerged, the hand attached to it waggling around in the manner of someone testing the temperature of their bath water. Then the person to whom the hand belonged appeared before him, looking just as surprised as Corvinus himself. When Corvinus asked Torgrim – that was the young man's name – where he'd come from and how he'd managed that neat trick of seeming to pop up out of nowhere, he was given a very unlikely explanation. He actually laughed it off to begin with. Until he learned better.

'Torgrim told him that he'd come through what he called a Gate, a kind of door between worlds. He said that, on his side of the Gate, he'd been wandering in the hills one day when he happened to glance up and witness something passing strange: a bird in midflight appeared in the sky before him as if by magic, flew a long loop, and then turned back and disappeared in the exact same spot where he'd first seen it.

'At first Torgrim thought he must have hallucinated the whole event, an after-effect perhaps of having experimented with a new, mushroom-based potion only a few days earlier. But, being of a curious nature, he sat down on a fallen log and watched said spot for the next couple of days.

'What he saw prompted him to build a tower there, placing and constructing it in such a manner that the strange phenomenon in the sky, which he eventually came to call the Gate, was incorporated into the tower's structure. He said that he had done this as much to hide the singularity from certain rogue elements in his world – who were sure to put it to bad use if they ever discovered its existence – as to gain access for himself and see what lay on its other side.

'Corvinus said that he didn't much appreciate being made fun of, and did Torgrim take him for a fool? Torgrim assured him that neither was the case. If Corvinus didn't believe him, all he had to do was step through the Gate and see for himself. Corvinus told Torgrim that he needed to have his head checked. Torgrim said that, thank you, his head was fine, and if Corvinus wasn't coming, then he'd leave him to it. Anyway, he said, he preferred the company of people who weren't afraid to find out the truth for themselves.

'That was clever of him, for it left Corvinus with no choice but to follow the matter through to the end. Nobody accused Corvinus of being fainthearted. Torgrim showed him exactly where the so-called Gate was, and imagine Corvinus' surprise when he saw something like a faintly shimmering curtain in the air before him. It reminded him of his time as a soldier in Africa and the strange, deceptive mirages that could sometimes be witnessed in the wavering heat of the desert. Much like Torgrim before him, he first stuck his hand through whatever the thing was, and felt slightly cooler air on the other side. Seeing that nothing terrible had happened so far, he braced himself and stepped through.'

Richard cleared his throat and poured himself a sip of water from a carafe on the side table. 'I'm sorry,' he said. 'I haven't offered you anything to drink. Would you like some water, or a glass of wine perhaps?'

'Thanks,' Jon said, silencing the rational part of his mind that had only an unbelieving smile for this preposterous tale. He found himself fascinated by the exotic piece of family lore, enjoying it like a good fairy tale. 'I'm good. So what happened next?'

'Corvinus stepped through the shimmering curtain. And found himself standing in a huge fireplace, looking out on a circular room cluttered with books and scrolls, shelves and workbenches and all sorts of mysterious paraphernalia that called to mind the workshop of an old Jewish alchemist he'd once visited in Alexandria.

'Though he didn't need to be convinced any more that Torgrim

395

had been telling the truth, he was still curious as to what he would see if he looked out one of the three windows that were regularly spaced around the room, the fireplace taking up the space where the fourth would have been. On his way to the window he was nearly hit by a gob of bird droppings that came sailing down from the rafters. Torgrim, who had stepped through behind him, remonstrated with the bird, which he called Hawk. Corvinus looked up and saw a pair of yellow, ill-humored eyes staring down at him from the shadows underneath the tower's roof. Then he looked out through the window.

'The landscape outside was somehow familiar, and at the same time subtly different from anything he'd ever seen on his own world, and he couldn't but accept the final truth of what he was seeing.

'Corvinus fancied himself a bit of scholar and philosopher, and in Torgrim he found a kindred spirit. They soon became fast friends, traveling to and fro through the Gate and spending many an hour in animated and inspiring dialogue. Torgrim convinced Corvinus that the Gate needed to be protected on his side as well, and so it was that it came to be integrated in the new building, Corvinus' villa on the rock, where now Burg Ravenstein stands.'

'So it's gone,' Jon said, envisioning the Roman villa being torn down at some stage to make place for the castle. To his surprise, he actually felt disappointed that the whole thing was only a fairytale and there was no magical Gate to step through and discover a whole new world.

'On the contrary,' Richard said, and Jon felt a childish thrill of excitement, like a kid who'd just been handed a treasure map. He tried to quash it, but the genie was out of the bottle and refused to go back in. 'It's exactly where it's always been. Ravenstein was built over the villa, conserving it entirely. What were once the rooms of Corvinus' house are now Ravenstein's cellars. I think it's time you had a look for yourself.'

Wincing, Richard eased his bad leg off the footrest and reached for a silver-knobbed cane.

'If you'll give me a hand and help me up, I'll take you down and show you. Oh, and in case you're wearing a watch or carrying a cell phone, please leave them here.'

Jon was carrying neither, but Richard drew a fob watch from the pocket of his waistcoat and laid it on the table. Jon was torn between curiosity and worry for the old man, who was clearly in pain and seemed already exhausted from simply sitting in his chair.

'Are you sure you'll be all right?' he asked, helping Richard up. The old man was frighteningly frail, nothing but skin and bones. 'I mean, it's pretty far to walk, with your bad leg and all.'

'Not far at all,' Richard said, his face drawn in pain as he hobbled across the room. 'Just reach inside the fourth shelf of this bookcase for me, will you? You'll find a lever on the right side – there, yes. Turn it and pull.'

Jon did as he was told, and the Bookcase swung open to reveal a modern elevator.

'This is only for convenience's sake,' Richard said as they glided down into the cellars. 'There are other, quite ordinary ways to reach the remains of the villa, and the Gate is hidden well enough as it is. Any more secrecy, and we'd just be calling attention to the fact that we're hiding something. Ah, here we are.'

They stepped out onto a corridor, Richard leaning heavily on his walking stick and on Jon's arm. Jon could see lamplight falling in through a small, barred window in a door at the other end.

'That's the door under the perron,' Richard said, following his gaze. He hit a switch, and the hallway was bathed in soft, indirect lighting. 'We're standing in what used to be the *vestibulum* and *fauces* of Corvinus' house, the outer and inner entrances. The large cellar behind us was the main *atrium,* and the smaller spaces around it were the villa's rooms.'

The first thing Jon noticed were the magnificent floor mosaics.

They showed a series of three hunting scenes and, by the door, the raven with the key and sword. There were words, too. Even though he was seeing them upside down they were easy enough to read. *'Cave corvum',* they said. 'Beware the raven'.

The walls of the corridor were divided into four segments on each side by limestone pillars, their pedestals and capitals carved with vines, the spaces between them filled in with whitewashed masonry. Richard stopped before the third wall segment on the right.

'What we're about to do takes some getting used to,' he told Jon, who wasn't sure where this was going. 'I've never forgotten my first time – thought I was going to end up with a bloody nose.' He chuck-led. 'Don't worry, you won't.'

Still holding on to Jon's arm, he leaned his cane against the nearest pillar and passed his hand over the wall, seeming to lightly caress it with the tips of his fingers. After the fourth or fifth pass the white-washed surface began to shimmer faintly.

Jon was suddenly very nervous, and a little bit scared. In that instant he couldn't have said whether he was more afraid that Richard's

398

story would prove to be true, or that it wouldn't.

Richard picked up his cane and jabbed it at the wall. It went in like a hot knife stuck into butter. Not being able to reconcile what it knew to be impossible with what the eyes were telling it, the skeptical, rational part of Jon's brain simply shut down. Richard smiled, as if he knew exactly what was going on inside Jon's head.

'Come,' he said. 'You can close your eyes if you want. Just hold on and follow me. Ready?'

Jon nodded numbly. And stepped through the wall after Richard.

Briefly, he felt the weirdest, tingling sensation, like being tickled inside by a thousand tiny feathers. Then he found himself standing in a huge fireplace, looking out on a circular room cluttered with books and scrolls, shelves and workbenches and all sorts of mysterious paraphernalia that called to mind stories he'd read about wizards and sorcerers and the likes.

Though he didn't need to be convinced anymore that his uncle had been telling the truth, he was still curious what he would see if he looked out through one of the three windows that were regularly spaced around the room, the fireplace taking up the space where the fourth would have been. On his way to the window he heard a warning hoot from somewhere up in the rafters. Soft as it was, it somehow managed to sound grumpy and inimical. Looking up, he saw a pair of ill-humored, yellow eyes staring down at him from the shadows underneath the tower's roof.

The view from the window was somehow familiar, and at the same time subtly different from anything he'd ever seen on his own world, and he couldn't but accept the truth of what Richard had been telling him, of what he was seeing with his own eyes.

'Too bad,' Richard said, looking around. 'Seems he's not at home. I very much wanted you to meet him. Ah, well. Next time. I'll leave him a message, in any case. I just hope he hasn't taken off again on one of his "field trips", as he calls them. He just recently got back recently from one that lasted nearly twenty years.'

'Who's "he?"' Jon asked.

'Why, Torgrim, of course,' Richard said.

'You mean the guy who lives here now is also called Torgrim, just like the one Corvinus met two thousand years ago?' Jon asked.

'You could put it that way, yes,' Richard said, smiling to himself. He rummaged on one of the workbenches, found a quill sticking from the ear-hole of a human skull, and a scrap of parchment. More searching unearthed an inkpot. Richard drew the stopper, dipped the quill and wrote a few lines to Torgrim.

'As you can see,' he said, gesturing to a pile of parchment sheets weighed down by a stone, 'I've been trying to keep up with his messages for him all this time, but it looks as if he still hasn't gotten around to reading them. So.' He added the latest note to the pile. 'Time to go. If you like, you can come back to explore another day. But first you have to learn how to open the Gate on your own. Time-honored tradition. But I'll give you a hint: look for the heart of the house. It is the key. Keep that in mind, and you'll eventually solve it. Now. Will you lend me your arm once more? Thank you, my boy.'

Back in the library, Jon found himself in a strange, ambivalent state, dazed and at the same time unnaturally alert. A part of him was dumbfounded and overwhelmed while another accepted Richard's revelation in stride, as if he'd merely been reminded of something he'd always known but temporarily forgotten. As sometimes tends to happen in extreme situations, his mind seized on a detail.

'How come it isn't possible to take something like a watch or a cell phone through the Gate?' he asked.

'Oh, it's possible,' Richard answered. 'But you might not be happy with the result if you did. The Gate translates everything that goes through it, not least language. But it is also a kind of safeguard, you might say, against the transfer of certain objects that would disrupt the balance of either world. Vereld – that's what the place you've just been to is called – is an early medieval society with a corresponding level of technology: catapults, waterwheels, windmills and the like. If, for instance, you took a wrist watch through the Gate, you'd likely end up with something like a small hourglass dangling from a string around your arm. A cell phone might turn into an ear trumpet and, coming back, chances are slim either would return to its original state.

'It works the other way round as well. There is magic on Vereld, mages, demons, sorcerers, what have you. If one of them crossed the Gate in our direction he would have to get along without his magical powers for as long as he stayed here, a fact well established by Torgrim himself. He's a very powerful mage on Vereld, but even his magic can reach no farther than a few centimeters into our world. Still, it's strong enough to enable him to help hide the Gate on this side, creating the very convincing illusion of a wall where in reality there isn't one.'

'Why hide the Gate in the first place?' Jon asked, realizing as the words came out that it was probably a stupid question.

'Think, my boy,' Richard said. 'Think what has been done throughout the ages to newly discovered territories and their indigenous peoples by conquerors wielding superior force and superior technology. Think what is being done to our world, even as we speak, in the name of progress and profit by people without scruples or moral restraints, driven only by greed and an unstillable hunger for money and power.

'And then imagine letting these same people loose on Vereld. What would they see? A whole planet's worth of untapped natural resources ripe for the taking, along with a free work force once the natives were subjugated. Just because you can't take a machine gun or an oil rig through the Gate doesn't mean you can't build them over there, given time and the necessary raw materials.

'And I'm afraid that, in the long run, magic, powerful as it is on Vereld, wouldn't stand a chance against battle tanks and fighter jets and, much worse, the corruption and destruction of the natural order that we earthlings seem to spread around like a vicious disease wherever we go. It would be the end of Vereld, and the end of Earth. I don't think our souls could survive the crime of destroying our own world, let alone another as well.'

'I'm sorry,' Jon said, 'I should have thought of that myself.'

'I'm sure you would have,' Richard said, 'given a bit of time. Right now, you've got a lot to digest. And I have to admit I've reached the end of my strength for today, so I suggest we let things lie as they are for now, and take ourselves to bed. Good night, and rest well.'

'Good night, uncle Richard,' Jon said, 'and thank you for... everything.'

Sleep didn't come easily for Jon that night, and when it finally arrived it brought him wild, disjointed dreams of an endless war between worlds fought by terrifying monsters and faceless men in ever changing landscapes drenched in blood and tears.

Richard joined them for breakfast the next morning, brought down in the lift by Franz in an old-fashioned wicker wheelchair. Jon could see that he and Lisa were not completely at ease in each other's company. He knew from Lisa that their shared past had sometimes been difficult, even stormy. Now they seemed overly careful, taking pains not to stir up old ghosts, and still there were moments when Richard's comments bordered on the curt, and Lisa was obviously straining not to become irritated.

It was Lucy who defused the situation. After an initial bout of shyness that clearly left Richard feeling awkward and inept and at a complete loss as to how he should deal with her, she suddenly got up and went over to him. Standing by his wheelchair, she laid her cheek on the back of his hand gripping the chair's armrest.

Richard seemed momentarily at a loss, uncertain how to react to this spontaneous show of affection. But then he hesitantly raised his other hand and gently stroked Lucy's hair. She looked up, and to Jon's and Lisa's surprise gifted Richard with a radiant smile, the first one since that fateful day in Canada. Baffled but happy, Richard remembered that there was a fabulous dollhouse stored away in the cellar, a subject which soon had Lisa waxing all nostalgic. Suddenly the lighter facets of the past shone through, and the tension evaporated.

After breakfast Lisa pushed Richard out into the garden while Franz accompanied Lucy to the cellars to find the dollhouse, leaving Jon to his own devices. He followed Lucy and Franz down to the cellars, heard them rummaging in one of the side chambers. Passing them by, he went into the corridor that held the Gate and closed the connecting door behind him.

Standing in front of the third wall segment on the right, he laid his hand on it. The whitewashed surface felt cool, slightly rough, and absolutely solid. He pressed against it. It still felt like what it was, or rather wasn't – a wall. He brushed over it lightly, like he'd seen Richard do, thinking, *Open*. Nothing happened. He did different numbers of passes with his hand, three, four, five, trying to summon the 'heart' of the house, whatever that might be.

It was no good. If the place had a heart, it didn't seem prepared to show itself, much less to cooperate with him. Finally he gave up, thinking he'd try to get a little more information out of uncle Richard. After all, the old man had a vested interest in seeing Jon succeed, so maybe he'd at least give him a couple more hints. No use asking Franz or Anton. According to Richard, they knew about the Gate but not how to use it.

Richard was still in the garden with Lisa, as a glance outside revealed. They seemed to be deep in conversation. Jon betook himself to the library. Maybe he'd find something useful there.

❖   ❖   ❖

Lucy was so engrossed she didn't notice Jon come and go.
The doll house that Franz had set up for her in what had been the villa's atrium was actually more of a doll castle. There were boxes

and boxes full of furnishings for its many rooms, everything from beds to wardrobes to dinner plates, and even tiny knives and forks. A whole bunch of made-to-size figures came with it: lords and ladies, soldiers, servants and cooks, all of them dressed in beautiful, old-fashioned clothes. Enough to transport a little girl into another world, even a sad, mute little girl like Lucy.

She made one quick trip upstairs to fetch Bear, her favorite stuffed toy, inherited from her brother Jon and a bit threadbare and bald by now but all the more beloved for it. With Bear's help she opened the last of the boxes, which contained a set of four white horses. She placed a figure she'd decided was the princess on one of them and took her for an outing around the room and then out into the corridor, holding the little horse and rider in one hand while she let the other lightly brush along the walls. Something about doing that must have felt nice, for she parked the princess in front of the castle and did another round, this time with Bear.

She was heading towards the door at the end of the corridor, the one where you could see the underside of the stairs, when she noticed a piece of the wall going all shimmery like the inside of a sea shell.

She touched the wall with her fingertips, and they went right into it. Curious, she pushed her hand in deeper. Then she held her cheek against the wall, seeming to listen for something. Leaning a little too far, she lost her balance and had to take a couple of quick steps forward.

Suddenly she was standing in a strange room, face to face with an old man who studied her intently.

'Well, well, well,' the old man said, stroking his bushy, grey

405

beard. 'Little Miss Lucy, full of surprises. And who's the furry gen-tleman you've brought with you?'

Lucy fixed the old man with a searching stare, seemed to consider him trustworthy and held up Bear for his inspection. *See for yourself.*

'Silly of me,' the old man said. 'Bear. Should have thought of that myself.'

As if she'd been invited to do so she walked past him to inspect the room, taking in the cluttered worktable, the stacks of ancient books on the floor, the many strange objects hanging from strings tied to the rafters. Walking along a set of dusty shelves, she wrinkled her nose at the rows of tall glass jars and their unidentifiable contents, some of which appeared to still be moving. She ran a finger along one of the shelves, held it up for the old man to see.

'Tell me about it,' he sighed. 'You wouldn't happen to know of a good cleaning lady? No? Didn't think so.'

A grumpy hoot sounded from somewhere above, and a splat of bird droppings hit the floor, just barely missing the tabletop cluttered with of all sorts of weird things. The head of a skeleton for example, with a long white feather sticking out of one ear hole. Pulling a face, the old man pointed at the rafters.

'That's Hawk,' he told Lucy in a stage whisper. 'He's still in a huff because I said "Can it, bird!" to him earlier. And he's really an owl who *thinks* he's a hawk. Better not to mention it to him, though.'

Settling into an old wing chair, he pushed out a cushioned foot-stool, making room for Lucy to sit if she wished.

'Got this from over on your side,' he said, patting the chair's pad-ded armrest and raising a small cloud of dust. 'They're still a long way off from learning to make proper easy chairs here.'

Still scanning the room, the little girl's eyes fastened on something she obviously hadn't noticed before. Standing to one side of the huge fireplace was a complete suit of armor. It was old, blemished by dents and scratches and a rash of rust, but it must have been splendid once, every piece of plate covered with intricate inlays of different-colored metals that in some place still shone through the rust and patina.

She approached the armor, stood gazing up at the closed visor. The faintest of creaks sounded when she tentatively touched its hand – or rather its steel-fingered gauntlet. Seemingly satisfied, she returned to the other side of the room and, as if it were the most natural thing in the world, climbed up onto the old man's lap and settled down with Bear in her arms. The old man smiled.

'Would you like to hear a story?' he asked.

She nodded.

'All right. But we'll make it a short one, because I happen to know it's nearly your dinner time over there, and we don't want them missing you now, do we?'

Lucy shook her head and, hugging Bear close, snuggled deeper into the crook of the old man's his arm.

Over the next couple of days she visited the old man – who said his name was Torgrim – at least twice a day. Her aunt Lisa was busy taking care of uncle Richard, who had taken a turn for the worse and was sick in bed, and her brother Jon was reading in the library, so she could pretty much do as she liked as long as she showed up for meals and bedtime.

On one of her visits she found Torgrim handling a small, dead bird, all dried up and shrunken as if it had died a long time ago. She watched the old man gently detach a tiny metal tube from the bird's leg. He looked sad. She threw him a questioning look.

'This was a very brave little bird,' he explained, teasing a miniscule scroll from the cylinder and studying it. 'It brought me a message from far away. I wasn't home when it arrived, so it waited. But I was gone for so long that it grew old and died before I got back. I just found it on the window sill.'

Torgrim laid the little bird aside, but Lucy picked it up again. Taking the old man's hand, she made it clear she wanted him to follow her downstairs.

Outside, in front of the tower, she knelt and began to brush away the snow, scratching at the frozen ground with her fingernails.

'You're right,' Torgrim said. 'We should bury it. Hang on for a moment.'

Rummaging under the stairs, he found an old spade with a broken handle. He used it to hack a small hole in the rock-hard dirt, and they solemnly laid the little bird to rest.

That evening, Lucy tossed and turned in her bed, unable to go to sleep. Everyone else was asleep, so she got up, put on her pink robe and bunny slippers, and went to pay Torgrim a visit.

'Oh boy,' he said when she appeared in his fireplace. 'Someday I'm going to have to brick up that old fireplace. What with all these little girls coming out of it all the time, I'm hardly getting any work done around here anymore.'

Lucy gave him a look that said, *Ha-ha, very funny.*

'Just joking,' he said. 'Where's Bear tonight?'

The little girl nodded towards the fireplace, perhaps to indicate that Bear had stayed behind and was guarding the Gate. She yawned, and her eyes fell on the suit of armor standing by the fireplace. She walked over and looked at it for a long time. Then she took one of its gauntleted hands and tugged at it. With a shriek of rusted hinges, the armored figure took first one, then another halting step. Patiently, Lucy led it over to a window seat and patted the dusty cushions. With a series of squeals and creaks the armored figure lowered itself onto the bench and sat, hands resting on its thighs.

Momentarily the old man looked distracted, as if the image of Bear guarding the Gate had reminded him of something. But then he seemed to let whatever it was go, turning his attention back to the little girl.

'Well, I'll be,' he said. 'Another thing I should have thought of myself. Seems logical the old chap would like to sit down for a change. He *has* been standing there for an awfully long time. I just hope he'll be able to get up again. Let me see if I can find that oilcan, and we'll give him a few drops.'

When the suit of armor had been treated, Lucy indicated that she was ready for another story.

'Many, many years ago,' Torgrim began, 'there lived a man called Thurgon Threetimes. He was – '

Lucy interrupted with a questioning look.

'He's called Threetimes because of something he did,' the old man said. 'But I'm not saying what it was. If I told you now, I'd be spoiling the whole story. So Thurgon – '

Suddenly, from down below there came a tremendous BOOM! that shook the whole tower. All kinds of debris came falling down from the roof and the rafters. Hawk squawked and flew down to land on the table, yellow eyes wide with alarm and indignation. Briefly, Torgrim seemed to listen to something only he could hear.

'Oh darn,' he said, looking worried. 'I'm afraid we have some very nasty visitors. They seem to have become very good at creeping and hiding, to sneak up like that without me noticing. It's as if they've been watching and waiting for a moment when I'm distracted. But to even think of challenging me, they must be quite desperate about something, or... oh. This might not be just about me, but about you as well.'

Lucy stared a frightened question at him.

'Though most people can't see it, you shine like a very bright light in certain places, little missy. And some bad people may have been spying on me, and found out that you're here. Don't worry, I'm holding the door and they can't come in, but I think you should go back home right – '

There was another loud BOOM!

Everything in the room did a little jump. Hawk started screeching madly, flying around over their heads as if his tail feathers were on fire. Lucy slid off Torgrim's lap, ready to make a run for safety. She never got started. Of a sudden the air was split by a deafening, rending and tearing sound accompanied by the thump, bang, and clatter of falling stones, and the room split open on one side, a wide crack snaking down the wall and tearing a large gap across floor. A whole row of floorboards tore loose from the beams and fell down into the room below. A gust of icy wind swirled snowflakes into the room.

Torgrim struggled to his feet. 'Hurry!' he shouted at Lucy. 'Go!

410

Run! This is much worse than I thought!'

But Lucy remained frozen in place, unable to cross the gap in the floor.

'Damn! Wait, I'll – '

Before the old man could finish his sentence, part of the roof came crashing down, a falling beam throwing him back into his chair and pinning him there, rubble raining down after it.

'Oh my,' he murmured to himself. 'So strong, so strong.'

There was another crash from below. Teary-eyed, Lucy searched for Torgim amid the timbers, dust, and rubble.

'I'm fine, pumpkin,' he groaned. 'Just stuck here for the moment. And very busy trying to keep that thing out. We've got to get you out of here though, and right now. There – grab that cloak. There should be a hat in one of the pockets, though you need to be careful with the other stuff in there. It's my traveling hedge-wizard's disguise.

'I'm going to do something so the bad people can't see you so well for a while. There. Now – just as soon as I get our knight there to stand up and move over, you lift up that window seat. You'll find a staircase going down inside the wall. It'll take you to a secret underground passage that leads a good ways away from here before it surfaces. I'm sending Mr. Knight and Hawk with you. They'll take care of you.'

The booming sounds continued, growing louder, shaking the whole tower. Scared though she was, Lucy didn't look ready to abandon Torgrim.

'Don't worry, cupcake, I'll be all right,' the old man said. 'As soon as I get things sorted out here, I'll come after you. Now go! Oh, and take the lantern!' He waved a hand at the suit of armor, and it rose to its feet, joints squealing in protest.

'Take her to Summerland,' he told it, 'and wait for me there.'

Lucy cast a last, uncertain glance at Torgrim, his shape barely discernible under the debris from the roof. Then, reaching a decision, she unceremoniously dumped the cloak in the knight's arms, lifted the window seat, and climbed down the stairs after Hawk, who swooped in ahead of her like a bolt shot from the sky. Behind her, the knight squeaked and scraped his way down the narrow, spiraling staircase. The stairs went a long way down, the swaying lantern making shadows jump from under the stairs and flit along the walls, and Lucy went slowly, gingerly, using one hand to brace herself against the wall, careful not to lose her footing. Finally she reached even ground and waited for the armored figure to catch up. Hawk had already flown on, hooting softly somewhere up ahead.

Lucy motioned for the knight to go first, taking the cloak and handing him the lantern. She hesitated, eyeing the roots and cobwebs hanging from the passageway's ceiling. Visibly gathering her courage, she wrapped the woolen cloak around herself as best she could, ducked her head and set out after her creaking companion.

The damp, musty tunnel seemed to go on forever.

When it finally came to an end and she stepped out into the freezing night, the tower lay far behind them. Through the driving snow, lights could be seen flashing in the cracks and windows like far-off lightning, some a sickly green, some a dirty blue, some pure white, accompanied by a rumbling like distant thunder.

Suddenly fear, exhaustion, and loneliness caught up with the little

412

girl, and a great sob shook her small body. She reached out her arms to the armored figure. It bent down and ever so gently picked her up. Cradling her in its arms like a baby, it set out into the night while she cried herself to sleep to the soft, rhythmical creaking of the ancient, rusty armor.

❖　❖　❖

Not necessity, not desire, no, the love of power is the demon of men. Let them have everything, health, food, a place to live, entertainment, they are and remain unhappy and low-spirited: for the demon waits and waits and will be satisfied.

Friedrich Nietzsche

24 The Warren

eep in the labyrinthine halls and passages of the Warren, a summons was delivered to the demon Ykrit that set her two hearts pounding with fear. She had thought herself well hidden in her burrow on the outermost fringes of the demon demesne, but the messenger had somehow managed to find her nonetheless.

Ykrit was young, barely a hundred, a mere adolescent by demon reckoning and still firmly stuck on the bottom rung of the Warren's hierarchy, not least because she abhorred any form of violence – an entirely uncharacteristic spleen for one of her kind, and extremely dangerous to boot. Hence she existed in a state of constant terror, because at any time an older and more powerful member of her species could on no more than a whim decide to overpower and devour her, trapping and imprisoning her inside its greater self.

There, she would be forced to spend the rest of her life in the most horrendous form of slavery imaginable, aware but utterly helpless, denied a will and a voice of her own, a tiny, insignificant source of additional power with the status of, say, a minor involuntary muscle involved in bowel movements.

Now that she'd been found, she had no choice but to obey, sneaking through the warrens like a furtive shadow, fervently hoping that she wouldn't meet a major demon with a hollow tooth to fill.

Finally she reached her destination, though anything but sanctuary. Prostrating herself on the cold stone floor of the cavernous throne room before Xorth, Lord of the Warren, she trembled with apprehension and dread, prepared for the worst – though it was beyond her why His Awfulness would bother with a meager morsel like herself.

Xorth was the mightiest demon of all. He had incorporated scores, if not hundreds of lesser demons and at least a dozen major ones, the latter in contests that nearly always involved some form of trickery on his part, of sneaking up and striking from behind, something Xorth was reputedly very good at. And that wasn't even counting the human souls he'd devoured in his long and illustrious career, though forays into Upperworld had become increasingly dangerous and unprofitable since even the last halfwit up there had learned that it was well worth spending the coin to have his house warded by a halfway competent hedge-wizard. And that it was better to stay indoors after dark on the nights just before and after a new moon, with doors and windows firmly closed and shuttered.

Matters had become even worse since the founding of the Demon Hunters' Guild, a band of hard-nosed, seemingly fearless bastards who were as highly proficient with weapons as they were with spells, the kind of people who would shoot first and ask no questions later. She was not to know, but Xorth had had a hell of a time procuring the human body necessary for the mission she was about to be sent on.

'I see you foolishly persist in wearing that ridiculous human female form,' Xorth rumbled. Eyes like glowing coals burned down on Ykrit from the immense height of his shadowy bulk. Better not to look at him too closely. He was an expert at creating and displaying images of himself that faithfully reflected the beholder's worst nightmares.

'Though those knockers aren't half bad,' he added lewdly.

Suddenly the room was filled with an overpowering reek of rutting maleness, making Ykrit feel comprehensively violated. Knowing that Xorth was only yanking her chain didn't make it any better.

'You seem to believe that blue skin, purple eyes, and sharp teeth are enough to constitute a suitably demonic appearance.'

They're not purple, you big, pompous sack of jelly, Ykrit thought, surprising herself with a sudden flash of anger. *They're violet. Just like the flowers.*

'Well let me tell you something, honeybunch,' Xorth continued, his voice dripping derision. 'Though you might like to think of yourself as the pinnacle of demonhood, you're not. You're a disgrace, an embarrassment. In short, you're pathetic, and I'm of half a mind to consume you right here and now and have done with you.'

He paused, projecting an image composed of saliva dripping down multiple chins as well as a mammoth-sized phallus standing to attention and ready for action.

Ykrit nearly fainted with fear.

'But,' Xorth continued, 'luckily for you, I have a task to assign. One that calls for just such a miserable failure as you are. Look to your right and you'll see a human body, relieved of its soul but otherwise in good working order. You'll inhabit it on your mission topside, so crawl on over and hop in, there's a good girl.'

Anything to get out of here in one piece, Ykrit thought and slithered across the rough stone floor to where the body lay.

Then she stiffened in horror. The body was that of a male! A man! No! She couldn't do it, absolutely not! It was revolting. Unnatural. Perverse. The abominable bastard! The stinking, overgrown toad! Some day, she would make him pay for this.

'What's the matter, sweetheart?' Xorth gloated. 'Would you rather stay for lunch?'

That got her moving. With the mental equivalent of holding her nose she slipped into the waiting body, sat up in it, and vomited.

'Don't like it in there?' Xorth enquired. 'Well, it's going to be yours for a while, so get used to it.'

Ykrit threw him a defiant look from stunningly violet eyes.

'Oh, good grief,' Xorth said. 'Still up to your childish tricks. Keep them, if you must. Just pray you don't run into someone who knew the young fellow when he still had brown eyes. And remember: if you mess up, you'd best do yourself in quickly, before I get my hands on you. Get it right, though, and there'll be a nice reward waiting for you when you get back. So listen carefully. Here's what I want you to do.' The plan that Xorth outlined to Ykrit made her feel sick all over again.

❖   ❖   ❖

Ykrit had barely left when Xorth was suddenly seized by a series of violent convulsions, his mountainous form rippling and thinning into translucency. He was being summoned.

Shortly, he found himself in a dusty, seldom used tower room in a castle in Dunmark, trapped inside a design meticulously drawn with four different colors of chalk on the rough, wooden floor. Routinely, he checked the lines. As usual, the man had made no mistakes.

Xorth had long since given up trying to impress this one with colossal, gruesome appearances, which in any case were an impossible squeeze inside the bloody circle, so he chose something simple and materialized as a giant, upright slug wearing a human head.

The summoner studied him coldly. His thin, long-fingered hands were set in a thaumaturgic gesture that promised agonizing pain to Xorth should he try any tricks. Sometimes the little creep dealt out pain just for the fun of it.

'Hey, hey, no need for that,' Xorth said, making placating gestures with a pair of hurriedly extruded, arm-like appendages. 'Everything's going according to plan.'

'Very good,' the man said. There was something in his smooth, emotionless voice that gave even Xorth the shivers. 'I'm glad to hear it. You've sent the assassin?'

'On his way, your excellency. He's the very best. Trust me. Top notch. In fact, you can consider the thing as good as done.'

'Xorth, Xorth,' the man said, shaking his head sadly, as if he were dealing with an incorrigible child. 'Why is it that whenever you say "Trust me" I get this feeling that trusting you is the last thing I should be doing? I strongly suggest you don't make any mistakes in this, inadvertently or otherwise. The consequences for you would be quite unpleasant, to say the least. Quite possibly terminal. Trust *me* on that. On the other hand, if all goes well you will receive your bonus as agreed. It's entirely up to you. Are we understood?'

'No mistakes, your grace, I promise. Trust – er, rest assured. Can I go now?'

'You may go. But I expect regular reports from you, say, once every three days.'

'How about once every fortnight, your worship? These trips really wear me out.'

'It's every three days, Xorth. Do you need a little extra incentive, maybe?' The man began to rearrange his fingers in a gesture Xorth knew all too well.

'Every three days it is, sir. So, if there's nothing else? Much obliged, your honor.'

Back in the Warren, Xorth was quite pleased with how things had gone. The arrogant little turd thought he could summon the Lord of Demons as if it were just a matter of course. Big mistake.

It had been a long time since anything but lesser demons had been called across the barrier. It seemed that in the meantime the humans with their puny memories had forgotten some very important precepts and cautionary rules. Rules their forefathers had arrived at by way of several extremely harrowing experiences. While lesser demons could be summoned any number of times without affecting the barrier's stability, every human-induced crossing of a major demon such as Xorth left ripples in the boundary's intangible fabric. Like waves coming together from different directions to peak in an unforeseen, destructive surge, the ripple effects of several such transitions could accumulate and cause a dangerous weakening of the barrier – dangerous for the humans, that was.

The three-day timetable meant that Xorth would likely be summoned several more times before Ykrit's mission was over, hopefully often enough to make a sizeable rent in the boundary between the Warren and Vereld. A hole that would allow Xorth and his cohorts to travel not only on the three nights a month when the new moon's influence sometimes rendered the border permeable enough to squeeze through, but whenever and as often as they wished. Xorth was very much looking forward to glutting himself on human souls again.

And there was another matter he wished to look into, the unexplained disappearance of two of his major rivals. Three actually, though the first had gone missing years ago. Still, he smelled some kind of connection, and something told him he would find the answers topside. In any case, the inhabitants of Upperworld were in for a big, nasty surprise, thanks to that idiot practitioner who thought he was pulling Xorth's strings while in truth he was only getting himself hopelessly tangled in them.

❖   ❖   ❖

Never was anything great achieved without danger.

Niccolo Macchiavelli

25 Kingskeep

rrin returned to his place of birth incognito, a stranger. He'd stopped shaving since Caer Ceonad, and three weeks' growth had changed his appearance considerably. His hair, still worn in a page's cut when he left, now reached down to his shoulders. That, and the simple fact that seven years had passed and he was no longer a boy but a grown man, gave him fair confidence that he wouldn't be easily recognized even by those who had known him well.

He had remembered the Colors, would have even without Greybeard's message. Somewhat of an exception among Dunmark's nobles – as fractious, scheming and backstabbing a lot as you could hope to find anywhere – Tormod Tondern, Kerr Kildown and Barra Varna, sometimes collectively called the Colors after their respective duchies, Redfern, Blackwood and Whitelake, were considered men of honor, old school believers in things like valor, courtesy, loyalty and integrity. They had always been staunch supporters and dependable allies of House Avellin, a stance that more often than not put them at odds with the majority of their peers.

But the Colors, and Avellin, had survived countless plots and armed disputes, not least because their adversaries were habitually blind or indifferent to any but their own interests, with the result that there tended to be almost as many warring factions among them as there were Houses.

A week earlier, Orrin had paid a clandestine visit to Dearg Fearna, seat of House Tondern. Situated atop a steep hill, the large, formidable stronghold of the dukes of Redfern was widely held to be impregnable, a mainstay of their considerable power and influence making them a force to be factored by necessity into anybody's plans.

At the gate Orrin presented himself as Colm, Lord Kildown's man, bearing a message for Lord Tondern. He was shown to the inner bailey, where Iomar, Tormod's weapons-master, was putting a fresh batch of recruits through their paces.

Tormod, a bear of a man with black hair and a shaggy beard, neither of which seemed to have seen a comb or brush in weeks, was sitting on the rim of a horse-trough with a beaker of ale and leg of lamb for a second breakfast, watching with amusement as Iomar had a young recruit step up for a round of fencing with wooden swords.

The youngster, by the looks of him a minor noble's son, seemed to have come to Dearg Fearna with the idea that he'd already been born a great swordsman and was therefore the gods' gift to any force he deigned to serve in. He'd also made the mistake of taking a haughty and deprecating stance towards the farmers' sons he was to train with. Iomar, born on a farm himself and risen through the ranks in his duke's service, was swiftly and methodically helping the boy rid himself of his erroneous preconceptions along with a good portion of his youthful arrogance.

Orrin winced in sympathy as the weapons-master's lead-weighted sword unerringly sought out his opponent's every unguarded spot, leaving bruise after painful bruise. He knew exactly how it felt, having been at the receiving end of Iomar's merciless lessons often enough during his time as a page in Dearg Fearna, cut short by the sudden and untimely death of both his parents. Back then, Orrin had labored under his own illusions, namely that as future king of Dunmark he would be sending other men out to do the fighting, and consequently didn't really need to apply himself too intensively to the strenuous, sweaty business of becoming at least a competent swordsman. Iomar, with complete disregard for Orrin's royal standing, had quickly succeeded in disabusing him of the notion.

'Colm of Gormach, my lord,' the man-at-arms who had escorted Orrin from the gate told Tormod. 'With a message from Lord Kildown.'

Tormod, chuckling at the recruit's travails, dismissed the guard with a wave of his leg of lamb.

'Well, out with it, man,' he said to Orrin, his attention fixed unwaveringly on the fight. 'Or have you just come to stand there and block my sun?'

'The message is for your ears only, your grace,' Orrin said, casting a glance at the gaggle of recruits standing nearby. 'Those are my orders from Lord Kildown.'

Something in Orrin's voice caught Tormod's attention. He gave Orrin a sharp look, all the mirth draining from his lively blue eyes.

'Come then, "Colm" of Gormach,' he said, casting the halfgnawed bone to the waiting dogs. Standing, he had nearly a head on Orrin, and easily twice the width. 'Let's find ourselves a quiet place to talk, and maybe a bit of refreshment while we're at it. You look

425

like you could do with a drink and a bite to eat.'

'Thank you, my lord,' Orrin said. 'You're most kind. And yes, some small sustenance would be most welcome.'

'Some small sustenance!' Tormod snorted, leading the way to the kitchen. 'They've taken to talking Empire fancy now in Blackwood, have they?'

The kitchen was bustling with preparations for the midday meal, but the mere sight of Tormod sufficed to see them promptly presented with a basket of choice victuals and a pair of freshly drawn beakers. Armed with their spoils, they withdrew to a sunny bench outside the kitchen door.

For once though, Tormod forgot about sitting down to food and drink. Instead he just stood there, staring at Orrin.

'Lad,' he said, a host of emotions tugging at his features, 'am I going potty in my old age and beginning to see ghosts? Or is it really you?'

'It's me, Tormod,' Orrin said, fighting to control his own feelings. 'It's me, all right.'

'Well, I'll be damned,' Tormod said, enveloping Orrin in a bear hug that squeezed the air right out of him. 'I thought you were dead, dear boy. We all did.'

'I'm glad to see you, too,' Orrin said, his voice muffled against Tormod's massive shoulder. 'When you're finished breaking my ribs, do you mind if we have something to eat? I really am hungry.'

'Ach,' Tormod said, releasing Orrin and giving him a clap on the shoulder that nearly buckled his knees. 'Don't tell me they've turned you into a wimp who can't stand up to a proper greeting among

426

friends anymore. You do look skinny, though. Need some fattening up. Here's a roast chicken for starters. Cook does a really nice crust on those.

'So, tell me what happened to you. Last I knew, you'd been abducted by a bunch of Conaran brigands. Great tragedy, that, so soon after your parents died. All of Dunmark in mourning for weeks, and your uncle Logan sending Hightower and Longbridge with an army against Conara, putting it about that they were most likely responsible for the death of the king and queen as well and swearing he'd kill them all to the last man, woman and child if you didn't turn up forthwith, alive and unharmed.

'Thankfully, I have to say, the Conarans have always been better at scheming than at fighting. They surrendered before too many of them got killed, and our lads came out with nary a scratch. To keep the scoundrels in line, Logan stuck your cousin Eskil on Conara's throne. Even with the Conaran blood he's got from his mother's side, the poor boy's not sitting easy on the big chair, more like riding an unbroken horse. From what I've heard, they've tried to rid themselves of him near on a dozen times, gone through every trick in the book. Man must have the luck of the gods to have survived this long. But here I'm nattering away like a whole bunch of ladies-in-waiting comparing doilies when you're the one with the story to tell.'

'There isn't all that much to tell,' Orrin said, an unbidden image of the royal apartments where his parents had been slain appearing before his inner eye. No amount of cleaning and scrubbing had been able to erase the signs of the horrific carnage perpetrated in those rooms. After their deaths, Logan, first cousin to Orrin's father, had assumed the regency.

'After the rites for my parents were over, Logan said he wouldn't countenance another death in the family. He wanted me safely away from Kingskeep until the killers had been caught and their principal identified, though there was little chance of that ever happening. As you'll remember, the general opinion was that only a demon could have created such horrific mayhem. Though I don't recall anyone explaining how it could have gotten through some of the strongest wards in all of Dunmark, and on a full moon to boot.'

'There was an official finding some weeks later,' Tormod said. 'The conclusion was that the way had been opened for the demon by a mage. It didn't say who that mage was or for whom he'd been working, but after your disappearance, in which Conara was clearly implicated, your uncle didn't hesitate to point the finger and hold them responsible for your parents' deaths as well.'

'Mages aren't supposed to do things like that,' Orrin objected. 'And there hasn't been a mage strong enough to control a demon in hundreds of years. At least that's what I was taught.'

'Mage, sorcerer, whatever,' Tormod said. 'I've yet to see either, provided they exist at all. Though there was this one fellow came by here one day, oh, some twenty years back, asking if he could have a look at the library. Found more dust in there than reading material, I'd wager, but he seemed quite happy nonetheless.

'Any road, before he left he asked if there was anything he could do in return for the kindness I'd shown him. As it happened, there was. I asked him if he'd take a look at the vineyards, see why the grapes were always so damned sour, the wine hardly fit for anything but making vinegar. Now, he could have told me what I already knew, that it was simply the wrong climate for grapes. Too cold and rainy, and the soil was all wrong as well. But he didn't. Instead, he went and inspected the vineyards. Didn't say much, just that everything should be fine, and that if it wasn't too much trouble I should save him a small cask of next years vintage.

'As it turned out, that vintage was sensational, better than anything I'd ever dreamed of. And in all the years since, it's just been getting better. We've had record harvests for twenty years straight, three hayings every season, and never a sick or injured animal. Even the people seem to have been doing better. If all of that was his doing – and I can't see how else it could have come about – then I'd say that it was a sight more than you'd expect from your simple, run-of-the-mill hedge-wizard. Never came back for his wine, though. But you were saying.'

'Logan,' Orrin said.

'He said he was sending me back to Dearg Fearna, where he reckoned I'd be safest. Since you'd already left he asked Varna to take me with him as far as Caer Banlin.'

'And sent me a message asking me to pick you up there,' Tormod said. 'Very neat.'

'What do you mean?' Orrin asked.

'Well, now,' Tormod said, his brow furrowing. 'Mind you, I'm not saying your uncle Logan was behind all this. Haven't got a shred of evidence to support it. And I freely admit that I don't like the man, never did, so you could say I'm not exactly impartial as far as he's concerned. But if you ask yourself for a moment who stood to gain from having you and your parents out of the way, every road leads straight to his doorstep, and to none other.

'Unless you want to believe in some third party trying to desta-bilize Dunmark by killing off the royal family. Only question is, if somebody was after the kingdom, why didn't they follow through when the job was already three quarters done? If, on the other hand, it was Logan, then he did a very nice job of casting doubt on Varna and myself, two of the three people most likely to ask inconvenient questions. So you'll understand I'm quite curious to hear a first-hand account of your abduction.'

'Absolutely,' Orrin said, not overly surprised by Tormod's suspicions. 'As I was saying, I was supposed to travel with Varna's retine. But he was detained, and Logan pressed him to send me on ahead with a detachment of his men. Which Varna did, though he didn't seem happy about it. We were almost to Banlin when we were attacked by a force three times our number. They wore the Conaran colors all right, but if they were really Conaran soldiers, they were the most undisciplined bunch I've ever seen.

'They knew how to fight, though, and made short work of Var-na's men. I was the only one they took alive. They tied me up and forced some smelly, vile-tasting stuff down my throat that completely robbed me of my wits and will. Then they took me north to a place called Caer Ceonad and left me there with some rather unpleasant people who kept putting drugs in my food and drink until I'd forgot-ten everything, even who I was. That's where I've spent these past seven years, locked up and dumbed down to the state of a vegetable.'

'Caer Ceonad,' Tormod mused. 'Never heard of the place. So how did you manage to get away from there?'

'With the help of some unexpected friends,' Orrin said. 'Forest

430

folk, actually.'

'Fairies?' Tormod guffawed. 'Boy, that must have been pretty strong stuff they were giving you.' He chuckled. 'Forest folk!'

'Yes, forest folk,' Orrin said defensively. 'And they're not fairies. They're as real as you and I, just a bit smaller. You might even meet them eventually, and if I were you I'd be very careful about mentioning gnomes and goblins and the like in their presence. They don't like it when they're not taken seriously.'

'If you say so,' Tormod said, disbelief still written all over his face. 'So what's the plan, then?'

'I'm going to Kingskeep,' Orrin told him. 'I'm going to pay my uncle, the Regent, a visit and see what he says when I ask him – nicely, that is – to hand over the throne. I was hoping you'd come with me.'

'Lad,' Tormod sighed, 'if you're set on killing yourself, why not do it quickly and cleanly. Here, I'll even lend you my dagger. Sharp as a whore's tongue. Iomar himself took a whetstone to it just this morning.'

'Thanks,' Orrin said. 'But we're going to Kingskeep. Here's how we're going to do it.'

'You call that a plan?' Tormod said when Orrin had told him what he proposed to do. 'Sounds more like a sure recipe for disaster. Unless...' The big man scratched his beard, his gaze seemingly fixed on something in the distant sky beyond the castle walls.

'What the hell,' he finally said. 'With all the gods' luck, it might even work. And if not, we'll at least end up in the history books – probably as the bad guys, seeing who's going to be left to write them.

We should go soon though, before Logan gets a whiff of what's afoot. If we lose the advantage of surprise, we stand to lose everything.'

'If he's the one pulling the strings, he'll already know I'm coming,' Orrin said. 'But he'll expect me to hole up with you or one of the other Colors until spring. And then come at him with an army, provided I manage to raise one. If I just show up unannounced and in public, what can he do? Calling me an impostor isn't going to work. Too many people will recognize me. And having me assassinated is going to look really, really bad, and raise all the old doubts about who killed my parents.'

'There's that,' Tormod conceded. 'There's also the possibility that he'll decide he simply doesn't care about appearances any more, and chooses to present the iron fist instead. Sadly, there's quite a few of my peers would go along with it, if he whispers the right promises in the right ears.'

'There's also the fact that we're not even sure he's done anything wrong,' Orrin pointed out. 'He may be completely innocent.'

'Now that's the part that really has me worried,' Tormod said. 'Because if it's not him, then we haven't got the slightest notion who else it might be. Meaning, we won't know where to look for danger. Except everywhere at once, which is not a state of mind you can sustain for very long without putting your sanity at risk. We might well end up dead *and* looking very surprised and stupid.'

'You're right,' Orrin grinned. 'Things could get quite interesting.'

He didn't feel half as cocky as he was trying to appear. What confidence he felt was mostly due to the fact that Tormod was there and willing to help. He knew it couldn't always be like this, knew that eventually he'd have to find within himself the strength and self-assurance he needed to see through what he was about to begin. But he told himself that, for the moment at least, it was all right to borrow a little from the man who had always been a fatherly friend to him.

Orrin made the voyage to Kingskeep as just another member of Lord Tondern's retinue. It was a small party. Tormod, being a widower and childless, took only Iomar and a dozen men-at-arms with him, the minimum his station required. Not surprisingly, the forest folk preferred to travel independently, keeping to their hidden routes far from roads and villages.

Before departing for Kingskeep, Orrin visited their camp in the woods outside Dearg Fearna and agreed with Sedge on a place where they would meet again once they had all reached their destination.

On the way there, Tormod's party stopped over at Caer Gormach. Orrin had been dismayed to learn from Tormod that old Lord Kerr of Kildown had died the previous winter. Kerr's only son had been killed in tournament years earlier, and Kerr's grandson Cavan was now head of House Kildown. Tormod seemed sure that Cavan would hold with the family tradition and prove sympathetic to Orrin's cause, and it turned out he was right.

Cavan, a rather ungainly man about ten years older than Orrin, with a prematurely receding hairline and a voice that tended to squeak when he became excited, seemed awed to be part of such a momentous undertaking. He treated Orrin with something approaching reverence, calling him 'your highness' even though they were second cousins, and insisting on observing all the proper formalities. He promised that Kildown would support Orrin and his claim to the throne with an eagerness that to Orrin seemed almost excessive and led him to wonder whether it had been wise to include this excitable man in their plans. He was somewhat reassured when Tormod, in his usual blunt manner, cautioned Cavan to keep his mouth shut, even and especially with his pregnant young wife – women being what they were, prone to worry and easily overwhelmed by the task of keeping secrets, the more so the graver the information. He also strongly counseled Cavan to leave his lady and their two small children behind for the sake of their own safety. No one could guarantee that things wouldn't turn ugly, and nothing crippled a man's freedom of movement more effectively than his family being held hostage by the opposition.

Cavan agreed wholeheartedly, and said he'd follow them to Kingskeep in three day's time. Whether his complicity would prove boon or bane remained to be seen.

Flanked by Tormod and Iomar, Orrin set foot in the great hall of Kingskeep Castle for the first time in seven years.

It was the evening of the last day of All Gods festival. After a week of prayers and observances, piety and gravity had been aside, the celebration reaching its high point in a night of feasting, gaiety, and masquerade. Outside, Kingskeep Town was bursting with revelers dancing, drinking, and eating in the streets lit by food vendors' fires and hundreds of colored lampions. People were appareled in fantastic masks and costumes, most of them weeks if not months in the making, everyone trying to outdo their peers in magnificence and fancy and not a few holding great hopes of winning the purse of silver traditionally tendered by the King, and lately the Regent, as prize for the best costume.

In the hall, festivities were proceeding at a more sedate pace. Many of the older nobles in attendance hadn't bothered with more than a simple mask, while the younger folk wore elaborate costumes that lacked nothing in imagination and opulence in comparison with those on display in the streets.

It was a standing joke that the bear costume Tormod wore year after year was by now probably held together more by the moths infesting it than by the few remaining stitches, and Iomar's desert warrior wasn't exactly new or original either. Orrin, after some deliberation, had chosen for himself a fool's gaudy patchwork and bells, together with a white, long-nosed half mask that left his mouth and freshly shaven chin free.

Logan wasn't hard to find.

Dark-haired, of middling height and with a tendency towards pudginess, he wore his usual black silks and gold-embroidered doublet. His only concession to the occasion was a mask, a twin of the one Orrin was wearing. His immaculately trimmed beard didn't quite manage to hide the weak mouth and receding chin.

He was in the company of two men, standing either side of him. Neither was in costume, but both wore masks similar to Logan's. Orrin immediately noticed a wariness in their stances and in the way they avoided looking at each other that spoke of a deep mutual dislike more clearly than a shouting match or a fistfight would have done. Logan seemed oblivious to the barely contained hostility, addressing both his companions with what he probably considered witty comments that raised mirthless smiles thin as fresh knife cuts.

435

One of the two Orrin knew, had spoken to only a few hours ago. Seven years had carved more and deeper lines on his gaunt features and chased the last vestiges of color from the now completely grey fringe of long hair surrounding his bald dome, and he looked thinner than ever.

A stranger who saw Barra din Varna out of his court finery might have easily mistaken him for a scribe or a scholar. And in fact his appearance had misled many a young blade into questioning Barra's reputation as Dunmark's finest swordsman and challenging him to duel, always a regrettable decision for the contender. Barra had seldom been forced to kill or even seriously hurt one of them – he was that good. But, one and all, he'd sent them limping off with a piece of sound advice. 'Go back to the farm and practice on the sheep' had become a favorite turn of phrase all over Dunmark, not least among whores, pickpockets, and cardsharps.

The afternoon meeting with Barra hadn't gone well.

Tormod had invited him to his town house for a cup and a chat among peers. Barra had seemed not at all happy to find the lost prince returned.

'This is most awkward,' he said, glaring at Tormod and Orrin in turn, his long, thin fingers wrapping themselves ever more tightly around his silver cup until Orrin expected to see it crumple at any moment. 'You could not have come at a more inopportune time. I regret to say that House Varna cannot assist you in such a rash and hasty undertaking.'

'I'm very sorry,' Orrin said. 'It's not what I expected to hear from an old and trusted friend of my father's. But I suppose I'll have to accept it.'

'Well, I won't,' Tormod growled. 'Not without being given a good reason. Young Cavan didn't even blink when we told him what we're about, and gave his support willingly. Hardly needed asking.'

'You've told Cavan?' Barra exclaimed, looking aghast.

'Sure we did,' Tormod said. 'House Kildown – '

'Forget Kildown,' Barra snapped. 'That young blackguard has been in Logan's pocket from the start, and you can be sure the first thing he's done is get off a message to the regent. No better way to let him know you're coming than to tell Cavan. At least now you can be sure Logan's expecting you, if he wasn't already.'

'The craven, traitorous swine!' Tormod shouted, banging the table angrily and setting the cups rattling. 'Had us believing we could count on him. All the more reason for you to stand with us.'

'I can't,' Barra said, shaking his head as if he needed to remind himself to stand down.

'Barra, old friend,' Tormod said with quietly controlled anger. 'I'm not going to do you the injustice of asking whether you too are in Logan's pocket. But I do think I'm owed some kind of an explanation here. What the blazes has gotten into you that's got you throwing all your old loyalties overboard, not to mention friendships?'

'I can't say,' Barra said, rising to leave. 'I'm sorry to disappoint, but there it is. I wish you luck, nonetheless. You're going to need it. And beware Alba, Logan's adviser. The man's a snake. Don't bother yourselves, I'll find my own way out.'

'Devil's tits!' Tormod said when Barra had left. 'What's the sodding world come to if you can't even count on Whitelake anymore? Makes you wonder where he's really stood all these years. Makes you wonder about a lot of things, like who else besides Logan might have been behind your abduction. Still, I'm willing to carry on, now more than ever. Only way to get to the bottom of this is step on some toes and see who squeals first. What say?'

'We go ahead,' Orrin agreed, with more conviction than he felt.

Now, facing Logan and his two companions, he made an effort to silence his doubts. Up until an hour ago the alternative would have been to run far and fast with his tail tucked between his legs and spend the rest of a miserable life looking over his shoulder for the assassin he'd probably never see coming. That option, if it had ever truly existed, belonged in the past.

Barra noticed him, shot him a quick, unreadable glance before turning his attention back to the regent. The other man with Logan Orrin had never seen before. Shorter than Barra but just as thin, his shoulder-length hair was fine as spun silk and white to the point of having no color at all. Beneath the beaked mask resembling a bird of prey his mouth was a hard, almost lipless slash, and even from across the hall he exuded a presence that Orrin found more than a little disturbing. He squared his shoulders against a feeling of foreboding.

'Let's go,' he told Tormod resolutely, and together they marched across the hall, Tormod in the lead, Orrin and Iomar a step behind.

'Your highness, greetings,' Tormod addressed the regent, giving a sketchy bow that could be put down to his ample girth being in the way, or to a pointed lack of respect – however one wished to see it.

'Ah, Tormod. Greetings. I daresay I'd have recognized you even without the bear costume,' Logan said, snickering at his own witticism. 'And brave Iomar. In from the desert as every year, shoes full of sand and parched for a drink, no doubt. But pray tell, who's the young fool trailing your coat tails, or should I say, your bear's tail? Though bears don't have tails, do they?'

'A most welcome surprise, I should say, your highness' Tormod answered. 'Lost and found, and now returned to the fold, so to speak. My lord Regent, I present you prince Orrin, your beloved nephew, returned from captivity but most definitely not from an early grave that some would have prematurely consigned him to.'

Orrin removed his mask and watched Logan's jaw drop.
Either the man was a very fine actor, or he'd truly had no idea that Orrin was alive and coming to Kingskeep.

'What... Orrin?' Logan stammered, pulling off his own mask. His eyes seemed ready to pop out of his head. 'Orrin? Is it really you? Oh, my boy! My dear boy, come here and let your uncle embrace you. Praise all gods. What a joy to see you alive and well after all this time!'

Logan gave Orrin a weak little hug. Then he held him at arm's length, looking at him wonderingly and pulling a handkerchief from his sleeve to dab at the corners of his eyes, though Orrin wasn't sure there was anything there worth dabbing at, except maybe a few beads of sweat born of shock and confusion – or of a bad conscience.

'You must excuse me,' Logan said. 'I have to confess I'm some-what overwhelmed. This is all too much at once. As soon as is decent you must retreat with me to someplace quieter and tell me everything, dear boy, absolutely everything. Meanwhile, meet Barra din Varna, whom you'll remember, and Master Alba, whom you won't. He's all the way from Orr, and my most trusted and valuable adviser. Alba, this is my dear nephew Orrin, the loss of whom we mourned for years, and who now by divine grace has been returned to us.'

'Then I suppose we should all thank the deities for his safe return,' Alba said smoothly. 'Provided everyone's agreed it's actually him, that is, and the gods or his grace aren't playing along with a divine joke and slipping us a fool for a changeling.'

'What?' Logan blinked, a stricken look on his face. 'Why certainly it's... do you think?'

'Have a care, sir,' Tormod growled, and for the first time Orrin understood just how dangerous a man he could be. Without seeming to have moved at all, his face was suddenly an inch from Alba's. Hidden between their bodies, the point of Tormod's dagger was pricking the white-haired man's doublet precisely between the third and fourth ribs. 'You question the word of Redfern at your peril. I'll hear an apology, or I'll gut you on the spot.'

Seemingly unfazed, Alba gave Tormod a cold smile. 'You really don't want to upset his highness by creating a mess on his floor,' he said, adding, 'your grace' as an afterthought, making the title sound like an insult.

'Don't worry,' Tormod growled. 'I'll wipe it up with what's left of you. Now apologize.'

Logan cast nervous glances from one opponent to the other, making meaningless, soothing noises while his hands wrung the starch out of his handkerchief. Barra made no move, though he looked ready to kill someone. Iomar's hand was resting on the hilt of his sword. Orrin supposed it was up to him to do something about the situation.

'Tormod, stand down,' he said with all the firmness and authority he could muster. It seemed quite strange to be giving Tormod an order, when previously it had always been the other way round. But to Orrin's surprise it didn't feel altogether wrong.

The big man obeyed instantly, the dagger vanishing quicker than the eye could follow. Orrin could have sworn there was a glint of amusement in his eye.

'And you, sir,' Orrin addressed Alba, 'will do us the courtesy of removing your mask and showing us your face. And then you'll explain yourself to his grace's satisfaction, and to mine. Avellin will countenance a slur no more than Tondern will.'

With a small bow just this side of flippant Alba pulled off his beaked raptor's mask, revealing an unlined face that stood in stark contrast to his white hair. His close-set eyes were those of an albino, red as blood.

'I assure your highness that I spoke only in jest,' he said, the ironic undertone subtle but unmistakable. 'Though I'll admit the joke may have lent itself to a certain misunderstanding. My apologies to you and the bear.'

'I trust that in future you'll endeavor to show better taste in your choice of jests,' Orrin said calmly. 'And I'd counsel you to desist from further nettling the bear. It has claws, as you'll have noticed, and doesn't always heed the voice of reason.'

Iomar flicked an imaginary piece of lint from the pommel of his sword, as if that was all he'd ever intended. Barra's features were in the process of rearranging themselves – into what new expression was not yet clear. Logan was sweating freely now, and Orrin thought he detected something akin to apprehension, maybe even fear, in the look his uncle gave him. Until recently their little meeting had gone

441

largely unremarked, but now curiosity was impelling more and more onlookers to sidle closer to what looked to be shaping up into a tasty morsel of news, perhaps even scandal. Orrin recognized familiar faces among them and was tentatively recognized in turn, setting off a buzz that quickly spread through the hall.

'Uncle,' he said. 'You're upset, and rightly so. I apologize for taking you unawares with my surprise visit, which no doubt contributed to this deplorable misunderstanding. But I'm sure it's been cleared up now to everyone's satisfaction.'

'My dear nephew, you're too kind,' Logan said, darting a sideways glance at Alba. 'Alas, I fear we must postpone our private talk, as I shall retire early. Regrettably, I feel a fierce headache coming on.'

'By your leave,' Orrin said. 'I'll just greet a few old acquaintances. Then I'll be on my way. I'm staying with Tormod, biding other arrangements. As for our family reunion, I rest at your convenience. Tomorrow, perhaps?'

'Yes, yes, by all means,' Logan said, limply waving his damp handkerchief at anything and everything, his other hand searching for the support of the albino's arm. 'Alba, if you will?'

'Wouldn't it be wise to make at least a short announcement concerning your nephew's return before you retire, your highness?' Alba said, clearly fighting to retain at least some control over the situation.

'Tomorrow,' Logan said, passing a hand over his brow. 'Tomorrow will do. We'll make it official, then. Do let's leave now, my head is fit to kill me.'

He grasped the Alba's arm and let himself be led off like a stricken man to his sickbed.

Before they stepped through the side door leading to the regent's private quarters, Alba threw a glance over his shoulder. The look wasn't hard to read: a declaration of war, unspoken but clear as day nonetheless. Nor did it escape Orrin that it had been directed at him, not Tormod.

'Do you want I should say something to them, lad?' Tormod asked, surveying the crowd.

Though nearly everyone was playing hard at decorum, an air of excitement permeated the hall, measurable in the steadily rising buzz of voices as well as the sudden proliferation of calculatingly wrinkled brows and a multitude of ladies' fans fluttering double time like a host of startled butterflies.

'No,' Orrin said. 'Let's keep it unofficial for now, guests among guests. You can already see the cogs beginning to turn in their heads. Let them spin for a while before they decide which side they're going to come down on.'

With Tormod at his side Orrin worked the crowd, singling out those he deemed most friendly to his cause as well as those most inimical, and taking pains to demonstrate gracious attention towards both while divulging nothing past a sketchy and superficial account of his own adventures. Eventually, nearing the door, he came across Barra conversing with a young man dressed in fine but outdated and slightly threadbare clothes.

'Your highness,' Barra said, shooting him a look that seemed to betray a change in his attitude. 'My compliments. I'd venture to call your reentry a success, as far as it goes. I trust you'll consider your next steps with care. Allow me to introduce Desmond Fjolen, recently set out from Osona to see the world, with a thirst for adventure that has proved much larger than his purse. He's currently looking for gainful employ. Seeing as you'll be needing a squire, he might be just the man for you.'

'Your highness,' Desmond said with a bow. 'I'd be deeply honored.'

The eyes that met Orrin's were quite startling, a dark, vibrant violet that evoked the sweet scent of hidden things blooming behind high walls on warm summer evenings. Desmond's gaze sent a strange thrill through Orrin, a feeling of fate taking an unseen hand, of recognition almost. He shrugged it off as fancy but spontaneously decided he liked the man.

'Are you any good with a sword?' he inquired of Desmond.

'More than proficient, if I say so myself,' Desmond said, managing to convey self-assurance, sincerity, and modesty all at once, another point in his favor.

'Good,' Orrin said with a wry smile. 'Because I'm not, and I may be needing someone who'll have my back. I'm staying with Tondern. Why don't you come by his grace's house tomorrow morning, and we'll get things sorted.'

As he spoke Orrin realized that, with how things stood, he hadn't a copper to his name, and no idea where to find the money to pay a squire with. He'd have to borrow from Tormod, much as he disliked the idea of asking.

On the way out they ran into Cavan, red-faced and out of breath.

'So sorry I'm late,' he puffed. 'Did I miss anything important?'

'Now there's an inane question if ever I've heard one,' Tormod growled. 'The heir to Dunmark's throne shows up at court after he's gone missing for seven years, during which time everyone believed him dead, and you ask if that's important? What's kept you, anyway? A little parley with the regent, maybe? Or with his so-called adviser?'

'What?' Cavan squeaked indignantly. 'What are you implying? You know damn well I can't stand the red-eyed bastard, and Logan won't give me the time of day if he can help it. I'll have you know that I take serious umbrage at your insinuation, and will have to think whether it warrants satisf – '

'Oh, all right already,' Tormod interrupted. 'Enough with the fancy talk. I was just poking, making sure there's no meat on the bones of a nasty rumor I've heard. Never really thought there was, so you can keep your shirt on, laddie. Tell you what, why don't you drop by for a cup tomorrow and we'll get you up to speed?'

They left Cavan with his mouth hanging slightly open, not at all sure what had just happened – a state of mind they seemed of late to be spreading around generously wherever they went. No sooner were they out of sight of the castle and in the streets among the common folk than Orrin received another of Tormod's knee-buckling claps on the shoulder.

'Well done, lad!' The big man almost shouted with glee. 'Famously well done! By gods, you showed them all a true king tonight, gave them something to chew on. By the time they realize the bone is apt to break their teeth, we'll have done and you on the throne, if you carry on like this.'

'There was a moment there when I thought it was all going to go terribly wrong,' Orrin confessed. 'Would you really have stuck Alba if he hadn't apologized?'

'Nah,' Tormod chuckled. 'Just a bit of play-acting to give you the opening you needed. And damn if you didn't take it like we'd practiced it a hundred times. But mark my words: that fellow is a poisonous snake and may well need killing yet. So far he's stayed out of sight and slithered around in the shadows, which is why he's pretty much escaped my notice. But tonight his hand was forced a mite, and he's not going to thank us kindly for it.'

'I wonder what's going on between him and my uncle,' Orrin said. 'It's almost as if Logan's afraid of him.'

'Aye, nothing good, that's for sure,' Tormod said. 'Logan's never shown an overly stiff backbone, though he can be as cunning and clever as they come. But tonight was different. First time I've seen him in over a year, and I swear he's not the same man he was before. Mayhap he's ill and has kept it a secret for fear that the vultures will descend on him while he's still alive and kicking. And right he'd be.

'I'll bet anything he'd love nothing better than to have the crown for himself, but he's been prudent enough to see that he'd be stirring up a viper's nest if he tried. The duchies tolerate him as regent but only so long as it suits their interests. His position is far from secure. Let one of them feel strong enough to make a bid for the throne, and Logan will be gone in an instant, with the rest of them at each other's throats and Dunmark in a turmoil the likes of which we haven't seen since Connor Avellin forged the kingdom.

'In any case we'll need to tread very carefully around Logan and his pet snake until we know what's what with them. Just don't get it into your head that because you've put Alba in his place he's going to stay there. His kind will don a meek and pretty face just so long as it serves to let them sneak up from behind and stab you in the back. Actually, I'm beginning to have second thoughts on his account. Maybe I should have stuck him after all. Ah well, too late now. Another time.'

'Maybe when I'm king I should ban weapons from court,' Orrin mused. 'If only to keep rash fellows like you from doing something they might regret later on.'

Tormod laughed. 'Forget it, lad. It's been tried before. Last time was in your grandfather's day, if I remember correctly. Everybody was all for it at first, until someone realized that, for all that the nobles and even the king himself would be attending unarmed, the Kingsguard was not about to disarm as well. Suddenly everyone felt they'd be sitting ducks at court, and the motion was unanimously dismissed. Besides, it's far too easy to hide a dagger up your sleeve or down your boot, and you can't expect your enemies to play nice and stick by the rules. By the way, I have something for you.'

Tormod pulled a ring from his little finger and gave it to Orrin, who saw that it bore the royal seal, the Dunmarkan lion rampant.

'Your father gave it to me as a sign of our friendship. I want you to have it.'

'I don't know what to say. Thank you.' Orrin was deeply touched. 'I hope I can take it in the same spirit it was given to you.'

'That you can, lad,' Tormod said. 'That you can. And now to bed. It's been a long day.'

Orrin yawned. 'Gods, but I'm tired. An hour at court is as exhausting as a month on the road.'

'Well, you've earned your sleep today, laddie, three times over,' Tormod said as they turned into the courtyard of the Tondern town

447

house.

The massive building was unobtrusively set up as a defensible stronghold and well guarded by Tormod's men, a fact Orrin was coming to appreciate more and more as he traveled ever deeper into the labyrinth of deceit, treachery, and hidden machinations that in Dunmark as most everywhere else called itself politics.

And enough for me that when my hand touched your shoulder, you leaned on me; and when you felt me slip away, you called my name.

Orson Scott Card

26 The Three Quarters

nce, there had been a mighty kingdom north of Dunmark, reaching from the mountains to the sea and far to the north where the sun didn't set in the middle of summer and the dark months of winter were truly dark. In the Age of Battles, the old kingdom of Aldland had fallen before another kind of darkness, and though the forces of light had in the end prevailed, Aldland had never recovered, living on only in the part of its name bequeathed to the continent that had harbored it.

Well, not quite. If you asked the people of the Three Quarters, they'd tell you a different story. As they saw it, the Three Quarters were and always had been the very heart and backbone of the old kingdom. As long as they existed, so did Aldland, and some day it would surely rise again to its former might and glory. As for Dunmark's laying claim to their territory, it was the one issue that never failed to get them seriously riled. Mention the subject of an evening in a tavern, and the landlord would most likely find you a warm and cozy spot in his heart for launching his customers into a thirst-raising series of heated discussions, all centered on the insolent usurpers from the south.

Thankfully, Kingskeep was much too far away for any Dunmarkan reeve or tax collector to have set foot in the Three Quarters in living memory, and so an uprising against the oppressors seemed neither imminent nor pressing.

A good thing too, for the Three Quarters with its roughly three hundred farms and a dozen villages would likely have found conquering Dunmark a hard piece of work – or a long furrow to plow, as the natives would have put it.

One cold, blustery afternoon in early November, a stranger came to Nara, the Three Quarters' largest village and still too small to call itself a town.

He was a big man, bigger even than Eirik the smith, who stood a head taller than everyone else and whose arms were thicker than most people's thighs. The stranger came into Nara on foot, walked into the *Lost Traveler* and ordered a mug of ale. He immediately carried it outside, together with a chair he grabbed without asking, and sat down in the middle of the road, facing west, away from the mountains. There, bare-armed and seemingly impervious to the cold, he settled down, took out a whetstone, and applied it to the outlandishly curved blade of his huge sword that already looked sharp enough to split hairs with, occasionally taking a sip from the mug sitting on the ground beside him.

Not long, and the *Lost Traveler's* other patrons brought out their own mugs as well as various chairs and benches, settling on the inn's wooden porch the better to take the sun that intermittently peeked through the clouds, and quite incidentally to watch the events that were preparing to unfold in the street – for everyone felt certain that

450

something rare and highly entertaining was about to take place. The wait turned out to be longer than expected, giving them ample time to observe and speculate.

The man was clearly not from anywhere in these parts, as old Asgeir superfluously remarked. The stranger's skin was the tone of wild honey, and, apart from the dark, arched eyebrows that gave his face a slightly sinister touch, there wasn't a hair to be seen on his body. This last observation led to a lengthy but carefully muted discussion of whether it followed that his lower parts were hairless as well. Provided he had any at all, that was, seeing as hairlessness might well be a sign that he wasn't a real man at all, but one of those blokes who'd been relieved of their nuts – what were they called again? Whonucks? Younicks? Something like that.

Between the sword, the small, round shield the stranger had carried slung over his back and which now rested against a leg of the chair, and the boiled-leather cuirass he wore under his dun cloak, everyone agreed that they were looking at a fighting man, though which kind exactly was another question.

Was he a caravan guard? Hardly, so far off the beaten track. A mercenary? If so, he wasn't about to find any work in these parts. A soldier maybe, deserted from some foreign army. Or perhaps he'd been properly decommissioned – shouldn't start out immediately assuming the worst about a chap – and was simply looking for a quiet place to settle down. Opinions were divided on whether the stranger would fit into the Three Quarters, though Brocc, the innkeeper, just arrived with a fresh round of ale, rightly pointed out that it wouldn't be an altogether bad deal to have a man like the 'bloke over yonder'

451

around if it ever came to trouble.

Come to think of it, who knew but he was another dreamer come to join Gulfram's Ghosts, the fabled troop of rangers said to be secretly guarding against all manner of terrible nightmare creatures that supposedly haunted the mountains and high passes between here and Dunmark.

Children's tales, Ghosts and creatures both, and if that was the man's reason for coming here, he'd made a hell of a long journey for nothing.

Their line of reasoning was interrupted by a wagon arriving from the west, driven by Fingal, a retired soldier who'd bought Morten's farm some fifteen years ago. A good man, most reckoned, if not very forthcoming where personal matters were concerned. With him was his niece Seara, a scruffy slip of a girl, though the majority of the womenfolk insisted she'd clean up a rare beauty. At least half the young men in the Three Quarters seemed to agree with the assessment and were hopelessly smitten with her – with the emphasis on 'hopeless'. But, if she ever got a rein on that sharp tongue of hers and settled down to marriage and motherhood, her grandchildren might even some day become real, honest-to-gods Three Quarterers.

Evidently you'd first have to get her out of the boots and trousers she insisted on wearing, and into a nice dress. Only to do that, you'd first have to relieve her of the pair of short swords she never went anywhere without, something that had been tried twice in the past year by roaming brigands from down south. Intriguingly, none of them had survived the attempt, even though by all accounts the girl had been alone both times.

452

Speculations on Seara were cut short by the arrival of Fingal, finished stocking up on supplies and ready for a pint himself. He nodded a friendly greeting, signaled Brocc for a drink, and found himself a space on one of the benches. He'd just taken a deep draught from his mug and was leaning back with a look of contentment on his craggy features when the show everyone had been waiting for finally began. Seara walked up from the store and planted herself in front of the stranger.

'What the devil's she doing?' Asgeir asked of no one in particular.

'Probably something to do with the rashness of youth,' Fingal said, casually adjusting his weapons belt.

Seara addressed the stranger, and suddenly everyone was all ears, straining on the edges of their seats to hear what was being spoken.

'Waiting for someone?' Seara asked.

The man didn't react.

'Excuse me,' Seara said. 'I'm talking to you.'

'You're blocking my sun,' the man said. 'And I'm not talking to you.'

'Well you just did, so I suppose at least you're not deaf. Don't they teach people manners where you come from? Where *do* you come from, by the way?'

The man glanced at her, his eyes showing as much expression as a pair of dark pebbles, though there were little lines at the corners that looked more like the result of smiling or laughing than of squinting into the sun.

'Get lost, kid.'

'Suit yourself, good sir. I was only trying to make friendly conversation.' She sniffed dismissively and turned her back on him.

'You're still standing in my sun,' he said, beginning to sound irritated.

'Sorry,' Seara said, staying right where she was and making a show of cupping her ear as if she were hard of hearing. 'Did you say something?'

Grunting, the man got up, moved the chair three feet to the left and sat down again, only to find that Seara had moved with him and was again standing in his line of sight.

'Listen, kid,' he said with an exasperated edge. 'There's somebody coming. Not a nice person. Likely there's going to be a fight. You don't want to be hanging about and get caught in the middle of it.'

'Oh, but maybe I do.' Seara shielded her eyes against the low sun. 'Is that who you're waiting for?'

The man leaned to one side, craning his neck to see around her. On the porch, all heads swiveled to the right, taking in the newcomer, then back to the man, studying his reaction, as if the inn's patrons were spectators at a joust.

'Oh, damn!' the man groaned. 'I knew it. A woman. I don't fight women.'

He rose, gripping his sword. How he could tell that the four-square, chunky figure beneath all the chainmail belonged to a woman was a mystery to the onlookers, but as the newcomer drew nearer they saw he was right. Not yet thirty and just this side of plain, the woman had a stern, matronly air about her that was only slightly alle-

viated by her relative youth, the snub nose and the dirty-blond pig-
tails sticking out from beneath the rim of her helmet. A few paces
away she stopped and surveyed the situation. The hilt of an enormous
two-hander protruded over her shoulder.

'You, girl,' she said. 'You need to be somewhere else. Now.'

'He doesn't fight women,' Seara said pleasantly, unsheathing her
swords. 'So I'm standing in for him.'

'No, you're not,' the man growled. He reached for her with his
free hand, obviously intending to bodily lift her out of the way and
set her aside.

As if she had eyes in the back of her head, Seara whirled around
and gave him a hard smack on the wrist with the flat of her blade, ex-
acting a pained grunt. At the same time she did something in a blur of
motion and flashing steel that sent him stumbling backwards and his
sword flying into the dirt. Immediately she was facing forward again.

'Next time I'll cut it off,' she said over her shoulder.

'Next time, girlie, I'll have you over my knee,' he grumbled, rubbing his arm.

The woman's expression had turned thoughtful.

'Now, both of you,' Seara said sternly. 'I want to know what's going
on. I happen to live here, and I don't appreciate it when people come
trampling through town and leave behind a mess.'

'I have a commission to bring this man in,' the woman said stiff-
ly. 'All duly documented with the Orrian chapter of the Headhunter's
Guild. You have no call to stand in my way.'

'What did he do?' Seara asked curiously.

'He tried to kill a high-ranking member of the nobility. For that, he'll hang. Now step aside.'

'Just a moment.' Seara raised a hand. 'I want to hear what he's got to say for himself.'

'This is crazy,' the man said. 'I'm a Headhunter mysel – ' He stopped, frowning. 'Why am I telling you this?'

'Because you're such a nice, agreeable person?' Seara said. 'Or because I count three swords against your one? No, make that none.' She used a foot to flip his sword farther out of reach.

'Oh, all right, whatever. A while back I was commissioned to capture a man, dead or alive. Preferably dead. I was given a time and place and a description, but no name.'

'That's iffy right there,' the woman said disapprovingly.

'Yeah, fine. Easy for you to say. But the assignment came from Duke Rois personally, and you don't tell him no if you fancy staying alive and healthy. Besides, I was a bit strapped for coin at the time. It didn't hurt that I received a very generous letter of credit beforehand.'

'Now that's definitely against regulations,' the woman said.

'So sue me,' he said. 'Anyhow, I found the man, he put up a fight, I had to kill him. Next thing I knew, I was surrounded by the Duke's men, the dead guy turned out to be Rois's secretary and the signature on the letter of credit was Duke Adwin's, who happens to be Rois's worst enemy.'

'You didn't even bother to read it?' Seara asked disbelievingly.

'I'm not all that good with letters,' the man said defensively. 'I can read numbers fine, though. And I wish you'd stop interrupting. Now, where was I?'

'Over your head in the deep-and-smelly?' Seara prompted.

'Right. As it happened, I got a lucky break and managed to escape. I decided to find a quiet backwater, someplace I could lay low until things in Orr blew over. Only someone was on my trail. She' – he pointed an accusing finger at the woman – 'kept coming after me, and no way could I shake her. Stickier than pitch, that woman.'

'You swear you're telling the truth?' the woman asked, a deep frown wrinkling her brow.

'By whatever you like,' the man said.

'Then I believe we're done here,' she said, chewing out the words as if she loathed having to take them into her mouth at all. 'As it happens, the man who sent me after you is none other than Duke Rois. Told me you'd tried to kill him and mistakenly offed his poor secretary in the process. Seems I need to have a word with the man. I don't appreciate being jerked around, not by anybody, no matter how highborn. The sod was obviously using me to tie up his sodding loose ends.'

'Sodding right,' the man said with a humorless grin. 'And if you don't show up soon and deliver the goods, you'll move right up to the top of his to-do list. Welcome to the party.'

'Well,' Seara said. 'Looks like you two are out of a job. What would you say to a free meal and bed at my uncle's farm? After all the excitement you've caused here, old Brocc the innkeeper will probably charge you triple, just to see how far he can milk your providential arrival here for further revenues.'

The two strangers exchanged a look.

The man shrugged. 'I'm broke, anyway,' he said with a wry grin.

The woman shook her head resignedly. Then a small smile lit up her face, like a little sun rising over a barren landscape and throwing

457

it into a new and milder perspective. Suddenly she looked almost pretty. 'I'm Ailis,' she said, holding out a broad, calloused hand to Seara.

'Seara,' Seara said.

They both looked at the man inquiringly.

'Anak,' he offered, rubbing his bare scalp. 'You can call me Anak.'

Meanwhile, conversation on the porch was a jumble of sentences that all began with 'Did you see how...' and 'Damn if that wasn't...' and ended with brightly glowing exclamation marks. Only Fingal, sitting there sipping his ale and wearing a look akin to fatherly pride, remained silent.

'Who in hell taught that girl her fancy swordplay?' Asgeir wondered aloud.

'Ah, that would be me, I suppose,' Fingal conceded, smirking like the proverbial cat. He drained his mug, paid Brocc for everybody's drinks, nodded a friendly farewell and sauntered over to his wagon. As soon as Seara, Ailis and Anak had clambered aboard, he flipped the reins and they departed, leaving behind a small cloud of dust and enough food for talk to keep tongues wagging for days to come.

❖   ❖   ❖

'I've decided I'm going to have a company,' Seara announced on the way home.

Fingal, used to her sudden impulses – which more often than not weren't so much impulses as the fruit of unhurried and intelligent reasoning – simply raised a questioning eyebrow.

'I'm going to have a company,' she repeated. 'You're going to be my captain. You two' – she turned around to look at Ailis and Anak, sitting in the wagon's bed – 'are welcome to join.'

'And do what?' Ailis asked. 'Hire ourselves out to whoever pays the most and end up robbing shops and homes and killing unarmed civilians? No, thank you.'

'I'm paying,' Seara said. 'And we're going to hunt down and punish some very bad people. People who've had it coming for a long time.'

'I'm not sure revenge is a good basis for starting something like this,' Fingal cautioned. 'It tends to blur the lines between victims and culprits, and between a lot of other things as well.'

'This isn't about revenge,' Seara assured him. 'It's about justice, and protecting innocent people from harm. You brought me up. You should know.'

He had his doubts on that point but decided this wasn't the time or place to discuss this particular subject.

'All right then. But you realize this means giving up secrecy and subterfuge. Not that there's much to give up after your little act this afternoon. Gods, girl! What were you thinking? Anak here could have just as easily been lying in wait for you. But it's done, now. We'll be out in the open, and we might have them coming after us sooner than we like – before we're ready, even.'

'I know when I can trust somebody,' Seara said stubbornly. 'They're good people, both of them.'

Fingal rolled his eyes. 'Your words in the gods' ears, lass,' he muttered.

'And I'm ready,' she said grimly. 'Ready as I'll ever be.'

'Then we'd better start recruiting in a hurry,' Fingal said. 'What's with your two new friends? What have they got to say?'

'Sounds interesting,' Anak said. 'How's the pay?'

'Ask the captain,' Seara said. 'He'll be the one doing money stuff.'

'Oh,' Fingal said. 'Will I, now? And what will you be doing, young missy?'

'Everything.' Seara gave a humorless grin. 'Everything from grand strategy to slicing and dicing, if you get my drift.'

'I can't help much with the brainy stuff,' Ailis said. 'But I'm pretty good when it comes to handling sharp edges, so go ahead and count me in.'

'Good,' Seara said. 'Since you've both signed up, there's one more thing you should know, if you haven't guessed already. The captain and I, we're not quite who we seem. My real name is Anili, and his is Baran. The people we're going after, and who we must assume are still looking for us, destroyed a whole kingdom to find me. So being on our side isn't exactly going to be stroll in the meadows.'

'You're not talking about Larnakis, are you?' Ailis asked, eyes going wide.

'I am,' Anili said soberly. 'You having second thoughts?'

'Next time you chase me somewhere,' Anak complained to Ailis, 'could you find us somewhere that doesn't just *look* peaceful and quiet, but actually *is?*'

'You're the one who chose this place,' Ailis answered. 'I was only following you.'

'Now that's sorted,' Anili said, 'run those horses, captain. I'm starving.'

❖   ❖   ❖

Some time after midnight, all hell broke loose in Nara.

Old Asgeir, whose house stood last on the village's eastern end – or first, depending on where you were coming from – suffered from insomnia, and so was the first to notice that something was amiss. All his usual tricks for putting himself to sleep having failed, he'd just stoked the fire in the hearth to brew himself a cup of chamomile tea he intended to lace with a small dollop from his parsimoniously hoarded supply of poppy juice when he heard strange thumping and dragging sounds approaching from the east. Overcome by a nasty premonition, he hastily banked the fire, crept to the window and peered out through a crack in the shutters.

There was a half moon out, and what he saw in its uncertain light made his blood run cold. A multitude of dark, misshapen creatures were limping, stomping, shuffling and scrabbling along the road, some on two legs, others on more. Some were roughly man-sized, others a lot bigger, but as far as he could make out only a few bore a vague resemblance to human beings. And even those were so skewed and warped, so full of strange lumps and weird appendages sticking out from all the wrong places, he found it hard to say where they began and where they ended. The others were simply preposterous, so horribly perverted the eye shied away from them and the brain refused to reproduce any clear memory of them later on, after it was all over. It was the same for the other survivors of that terrible night, even those who, in the heat of a desperate battle and the light of their own houses burning, had gotten a much better look at the horde of nightmarish monstrosities.

461

Any reasonably sane person would have hidden under the bed, trembling with fear and praying to all the gods to let him remain unnoticed, but not old Asgeir. Living where he did, he was Nara's eastern lookout, and as such he had the duty and the means to warn the village of approaching danger, no matter he was a hair's breadth away from wetting his smallclothes.

Frantically, hands shaking, he scrabbled in the dark, searching on the mantlepiece and in the process knocking down just about everything he kept up there. Finally running out of patience, he raked up the coals and threw on a handful of shavings together with a fresh log. To hell with stealth.

He looked again, and there it was, his trusty old aurochs horn, passed down from father to son for more generations than he knew to count, and not for the first time Nara's savior in times of distress. It was sitting exactly where it was supposed to be; he'd just missed it in the dark.

Opening a shutter, he brought the horn to his lips and blew. All he got for his trouble was a cloud of dust and a coughing fit. He turned the horn around and looked into its mouth. The thing was full of cobwebs, insect carcasses and mouse droppings. Quickly, he cleaned out what he could reach with a finger, and on the second try he blew a sweet, clear note that rattled the shutters.

Twice more he sounded the horn. Then he set it down, lit a lantern, grabbed the pitchfork leaning against the wall just outside his door, and advanced to the attack.

By now the last stragglers had passed by his house.

But several other homes had not been so lucky, had flames dancing

462

on their thatch. He saw Brocc down the street in front of the *Lost Traveler,* defending the inn with a chair in one hand and a rusty sword in the other, chopping away with a vengeance at anything that came within his reach and bellowing curses and imprecations that would have made a wagoner blush. Eirik the smith was there, methodically swinging his two largest hammers, one in each hand, and Asgeir could hear their thudding impacts even over the screams and shouts and the crackling flames. A few men were reaping a grim harvest with pitchforks and scythes, but most had taken the time to string their bows, and the air was sizzling with arrows.

Hobbling along, Asgeir came upon one of the ghastly things lying on the ground, riddled with shafts but still twitching. It hissed at him, baring blood-smeared fangs. He dispatched it with his pitchfork, trying not to look too closely.

Of a sudden there was a lull in the fighting. Asgeir had a feeling that something more was coming, that they hadn't seen the worst yet.

Whatever it was, it was preceded by a wave of crippling terror. Friend and foe alike were struck with a palsy of fear so overwhelming it made grown men cower and wet themselves like snot-nosed toddlers.

And then a huge, shambling thing, a shapeless shadow taller than the tallest house, taller even than the trees, came moving through the village with a sound reminiscent of a snake slithering over dry leaves or the hide being ripped off a cold carcass. Asgeir, shaking so hard his legs threatened to give out under him, risked a quick glance. He thought he saw a human figure riding atop the darkness, clad in black, veiled. Moonlight struck a glint of sheer malice from the rider's eyes – or so Asgeir imagined, his own eyes tearing from the smoke – and then the apparition was past.

Only when the terrible thing was well and truly gone did the fighting resume, rapidly moving through the village and out the other end. Fumbling back to his senses, Asgeir found and killed two more injured monsters. He'd just sent off a fourth with a well-aimed stab of his pitchfork and a heartfelt curse when he heard the thunder of hooves approaching from the east and a score of men rode in on some of the finest horses he'd ever seen, all of them darkish grey in color, as were the cloaks of their riders. Asgeir reckoned that in the woods they'd have been hard to see even in daylight, and nigh on impossible to detect in the dark. As it was, only their black silhouettes against the burning houses and the firelight sparking the odd reflection off the riders' weapons and their mounts' sleek, shining coats betrayed their positions as they reined in when Asgeir gave a warning yell, sure he was about to be ridden down.

'Which way?' one of them shouted.

Asgeir was about to answer but thought better of it. This was no time to be careless. He wished he'd brought the horn. 'Who's asking?' he said. 'And which way what?'

'A Ghost is asking,' the man said impatiently. 'And we're hunting the Blight, old man. Now tell me, which way did they go?'

Asgeir merely pointed, his mouth hanging open and his eyes round as saucers. They were gone in an instant, thundering off like the Gods' Great Hunt, leaving a silence in their wake that was only interrupted by the hiss and spit of water hitting flames.

Asgeir collected his wits.

The first of the men were beginning to lay aside their weapons and join the womenfolk in putting out the fires. The monsters had been hard to kill, remaining a menace even when they were so badly wounded they should by rights have been good and dead – until somebody discovered that they caught fire easily and burned like torches, at least most of them. Those that didn't burn had to be chopped up into many, very small pieces before they stopped moving, though the ichory, hotly bubbling stuff that passed for their blood ruined blades and axe heads, eating away at the steel like acid.

All told, it looked as if the grisly host hadn't really been interested in Nara, had only been passing through on the way to some other, less fortunate place. Luck of the gods, they all agreed later. They'd not have stood a chance if the things had really applied themselves to the task. As it was, Nara had lost eight, three of them ripped to pieces by claws and fangs, two cut to ribbons by some kind of sharp-edged implements, and two crushed under a collapsing roof. Truls the storekeeper died lying on his back in the road, drumming his heels in the dirt while suffering bone-cracking convulsions and foaming red at the mouth, with not a mark on him other than a small and seemingly harmless bite on the back of his left hand.

When dawn broke and the last fire was extinguished, they prepared to drag the attackers' cadavers off the street and burn them outside the village, but all they found were ugly splotches and puddles of a stinking black substance like runny tar that caused painful burns where it encountered unprotected skin. They attacked the stuff with shovels and buckets, and when the street was its old, dusty self again they celebrated the Rites of Parting and buried their dead. The day after,

465

they began rebuilding the houses they hadn't been able to save from the fires, with everybody lending a hand, and after that the men again went out into the forest with axes and saws to fell trees for a stockade. The people of Nara weren't about to let themselves be taken by surprise a second time.

❖ ❖ ❖

Leaving Nara behind and moving through the darkness with inhuman speed, the grisly host turned towards Morten's farm, reaching it in less time than it would have taken a horse and rider to make the journey in plain daylight.

The shadow arrived with the vanguard, its rider intently surveying the terrain's layout. During the past weeks, he had sent most of his forces south along the mountains. With the watchers staring after them in puzzlement, he'd been able to slip by unnoticed with this smaller force.

The farm's current owner had turned the place into a small stronghold and cleared a wide space around it. The house itself had a roof of stone, and it formed the eastern side of a walled courtyard. The outward-facing windows of the two-story building had been bricked over on the ground floor, those above fortified with sturdy bars as well as armored, loop-holed shutters.

The shadow's rider studied the conditions for a time before deploying his forces. When he was satisfied that his orders were being followed precisely, he gave the signal to attack. Then he left, heading in a northerly direction. He had another, more pressing task to fulfill. Spies had reported that, after many years of absence, his master's oldest and most dangerous enemy had returned to the Grey Tower, a situation that needed to be addressed posthaste.

❖　❖　❖

Baran had never been one to ignore a premonition, and the feeling of foreboding stalking him that night was as strong and disturbing as he'd ever known it to be. He'd told everyone to sleep in their clothes and with weapons at the ready, and he'd put himself and the three farm hands, Haldor, Odd, and Stian, on guard duty.

So far, everything had remained quiet, the silence broken only by the occasional distant howl of a wolf while the moon slowly sank behind the western tree-line. Still, the feeling didn't go away but rather intensified as the night wore on. There were about three hours left until dawn when Odd, perched on the roof, gave a soft, trilling whistle.

Baran, standing above the gate on the wall's western walkway, knew with a sudden chill that his fears had been fully justified. Lighting a fire arrow from the brazier positioned within easy reach, he loosed it at one of the oil-drenched woodpiles that were evenly spaced around the compound a good sixty yards out, silently thanking the gods that it hadn't rained in almost a fortnight. Tall flames shot from the wood. What he saw in their light made his skin crawl.

If anything, he'd expected to find men out there, or at worst something like the uglies he'd encountered at Tinnan, but not… this. There weren't words to describe the horror he was looking at. Suddenly feeling nauseous, he swallowed a lump of fear and disgust that threatened to drag up the contents of his stomach. Sometimes the jitters before a battle were bad, and sometimes, like now, they were worse. He checked on his troops, a calming ritual.

Odd was wildly ringing the bell that hung in a small turret on the roof, normally used to call in the field hands at mealtimes. Haldor and Stian were following Baran's example, lighting up more of the woodpiles. Shooting from the roof, Odd ignited two piles at the back of the house, making it clear that they were surrounded on all sides.

Shortly, Anili, Anak, and Ailis clambered up the ladder and joined Baran on the west wall. Dagrun the cook opened an upper-floor window and stuck out her iron-grey head. She was past sixty but tough as old leather, and no mean shot with a bow.

'I've got the back,' she called out, an uncharacteristic tremor in her voice. 'But there's an awful lot of them. Tell Odd to hurry up and get in here.'

'Coming,' Odd shouted, already scrambling down from the roof.

Baran sent Anak to join Haldor on the north side, and Ailis to the south with Stian. All three of the lads were more than just simple farmhands, and Baran himself had seen to completing their training. He knew he could count on them, but the mass of creatures out there gave him pause. He reckoned there were close to two hundred of the things, and though there weren't many weapons in evidence and no arrows had come flying yet, he had a feeling they'd soon be seeing some nasty surprises. There wasn't a single black priest in sight, but the stink of sorcery lay in the air like a bilious fug.

A few of the things were ripping the doors off of an old wooden outbuilding he'd been meaning to tear down for ages, and he berated himself for not having done it sooner. Moments later, the shack was burning.

Using the doors as shields, a score of the creatures headed straight for the wall. Half of them made for the gate. The others chose a section to the left where, one by one, they left cover and began to climb up the wall with nightmarish nimbleness like fat, deformed spiders. Between them, Baran and Anili shot five of them down. Four made it to the top.

The doors were already going back for reinforcements. There was no time to do anything about them.

Three of the things went for Anili, the fourth turned towards Baran.

It walked upright on two legs, and he saw two arms swinging from a human-shaped torso with a human-shaped head sitting on top of it, but something about it looked completely wrong. Of a sudden it collapsed, fell apart into scores of smaller creatures that came swarming along the walkway, five-legged crawlers the likes of which he'd seen before, in what seemed like another lifetime. A fleeting image of Rupili crossed his mind, forcing him to acknowledge that his death would very likely be no prettier than hers. There was no way he could fight all of them off before one got its teeth in him. Chances were, that would be all it took to kill him. A quick glance at Anili told him that the opponents she faced were solid, as yet.

Almost without thinking, he kicked over the brazier, scattering the glowing coals right into the path of the oncoming swarm. Pushing, shoving, and crawling over each other in an unstoppable killing frenzy, the things ran straight into the red-hot embers. They immediately caught fire, crackling and bursting like kernels of corn on a hot griddle. Those few that got by he crushed under his boot.

The wooden walkway began to smolder.

Scraping off the worst of the coals with his boot, he prayed that the seasoned boards wouldn't go up in flames. No time for anything else. At least Anili had dispatched all three of her assailants. His relief was short-lived. Of a sudden she uttered a disgusted yell, swiping a sword along her lower leg, and he saw an ugly, clawed hand with part of an arm still attached to it clutching her ankle. The next moment, she'd regained her cool, slid her blade between the hand and her boot and sliced through the thumb. The thing came off, and she sent it flying off the walkway with a kick.

'Watch out for body parts,' she shouted. 'They go on moving even after you cut them off!'

It was a piece of news Baran could have done without. He looked around to see if it was true everywhere.

On the north and south walls, the defenders were busy shooting and hacking away at their share of the creatures, throwing the remains off the wall. Down below, several mutilated and supposedly dead bodies had begun to stir again. Some made it back onto their feet, others with legs missing limped, crawled, or dragged themselves back to the wall. Someone had cut both mismatched heads off one of the creatures, yet it was back on its feet almost as soon as it hit the ground, shuffling around in circles, thrashing the air with a pair of rusty swords.

During a short lull in the fighting, Baran heard a strange crackling and hissing somewhere below. Leaning over the parapet, he saw two of the larger creatures attached to the gate like huge, flattened leeches. Around their edges, smoke was rising from the blackening planks, as if the things were exuding some kind of corrosive substance that was eating away at the wood. It looked like they were already half-way through the outer ply.

Farther out, the doors were coming back with a fresh load of climbers. More were attacking without the benefit of cover, most of them making it to the walls unscathed. There were simply too many of them, and too few defenders on the wall. Baran was beginning to think they'd better their chances if they withdrew into the house, plugging every crack and hole after them.

He was about to order everybody in when he saw lights approaching down the track connecting the farm to the Nara road. He had no time to wonder what this might mean, for suddenly there was a sound like the crackle of lightning, followed by a thunderous BOOM! and part of the north wall collapsed, taking Anak and Haldor down with it.

❖   ❖   ❖

Anak was no great archer, but the bow he'd selected from the farm's armory was well made, with a smoother action than any he'd ever shot, and he missed only one out of three, a personal record. It probably helped that he was scared shitless.

He was no match for Haldor though, who was not only twice as fast, loosing two arrows to every one of his, but also made nearly every shot a sure kill. His long, blond hair gathered in a loose braid, his young, sparsely bearded face contorted in a grin of fierce concentration, the wiry muscles of his bare arms still deeply tanned from a long summer's work in the fields flexing with every pull, he looked the perfect picture of a northern warrior, sprung right out of the old songs and stories. The only thing missing was a pair of aurochs horns on his round, rimless helmet.

'This job,' Anak grunted, exchanging the bow for his sword and hacking at several creatures that had made it to the top of the wall, 'is already starting out a right bitch.' He sent considerably more pieces tumbling back down than had come up. 'I should have asked for double pay, seeing as they don't even give a man nights off.'

'Missing your beauty sleep?' Haldor said, scoring hit after hit in what seemed like one long, fluid motion of nocking, drawing, loosing and slipping the next arrow from the quiver even as the one before it still sped towards its mark.

'Exactly,' Anak said, breathing hard. 'At this rate, I'll be worn out and wrinkled in no time, and then who's going to turn all the pretty little wenches' heads and make them want to do naughty things?'

Looking down at the seething mass of twisted bodies, he frowned.

'Am I seeing stuff? Or are some of those ugly fuckers down there running around with arrows sticking out of places that mean they should be good and dead?'

Haldor replied with an absentminded grunt. He'd stopped shooting and was staring at something farther out. 'What the devil are the ugly bastards up to now?'

Anak strained to see what he meant. On the very edge of the area lit by the burning woodpiles, nearly two dozen of the things were massed into something resembling an untidy wedge pointed at the wall where Anak and Haldor stood. They were up to something, uttering a low, guttural chant that sent shivers up his spine. A dark, indefinable mass began to form in the air in front of the wedge. As Anak stood watching, it continued to grow in size until it reached the size of a cart wheel.

Then, with a sudden, earsplitting crack, it sped towards them as if shot from an unseen catapult, hitting the wall beneath their feet.

Briefly, Anak felt himself standing on nothing but air.

Then, without transition, he was lying in a jumble of timbers and stone, feeling more kinds of pain than he'd thought possible. Still numbed from the fall, he raised his head and saw a mass of twisted bodies and disjointed limbs scrambling and trampling towards the gap in the wall. The realization that he was lying directly in their path woke him up smartly, jolting him upright before he'd consciously thought to move.

For a wonder, he was still gripping his sword. Even more miraculously, the pile of rubble beside him stirred and Haldor stumbled to his feet, spitting dust and bleeding from a gash on his forehead. He too had somehow managed to hold on to his weapon, but the bow was useless now, the stave broken in two. Disgusted, he threw it away and drew his sword and dagger. Half a breath later, they were fighting for their lives.

Anak's panic was short-lived. Overcome by a battle rage the warriors of his people were well acquainted with, his world narrowed down to the reach of his blade, his ears filled with a buzzing like angry wasps. He hardly heard Haldor beside him, singing some northern dirge in no certain key but at the top of his lungs while malformed corpses piled up in front of him.

Then several of the really big buggers came lumbering up, truly hideous monstrosities towering over the two humans and swinging multiple blades with more arms than by rights there should have been. They were nearly impossible to kill. The only way to get them under control was by cutting them up into as many small pieces as possible, and even then one had to be careful of the still moving parts.

Things got mighty tight for a while. Two of the smaller uglies managed to get by Anak and Haldor. There was nothing they could do about it, and Anak expected them to attack from behind, ending it for him and Haldor. Instead, as soon as the beasts were clear of the fighting they collapsed into a multitude of small, crawly things that scuttled off towards the house.

Thereafter, things blurred together in a timeless stretch of bloody, inelegant chopping and slashing as Anak wielded his increasingly heavy blade with tired, burning arms. Only instinct and a stubborn refusal to die kept him going – until suddenly there was nothing left to hack and stab at.

For a time, he just stood there, braced on his sword, staring dumbly at the wriggling heap of undead flesh before him, his whole body trembling with fatigue, his aching lungs gradually finding enough air to breathe again.

Slowly, his normal sense of the world returned, and he became aware of Haldor beside him, in a state not much different from his own. Strangely, he thought he could still hear the echoes of a horn, as if one had sounded just moments ago.

Then the night lit up outside the walls as if the earth itself had caught fire.

❖   ❖   ❖

Anili was suspended between gratification and shock.

Gratification, because finally she'd begun to fulfill what she saw as her true destiny, all the countless hours of hard, rigorous training paying off and making actual, tangible sense.

Shock, because nothing Baran had taught her had even remotely prepared her for something like this, for an enemy so hideous, so monstrously deformed and perverted that eyes and mind alike shied away from the sight.

In her dreams, she'd always pictured herself leading her people, miraculously returned to life, from victory to glorious victory. She'd never imagined fighting in a battle that was this... horrible. Filthy. Revolting. It made you wish you didn't have to see to kill, or better yet, that you'd wake up and find it had all just been a nauseating, sweat-soaked nightmare.

But she stood fast and fought, though truth be told her first reaction had been a nearly overwhelming need to run into the house and pee and maybe never come out again.

Ailis was working the near corner like a grim, primordial goddess, dispensing death with a pair of long, wicked knives, the two-hander sheathed on her back all but useless in a fight at close quarters such as these, until it became clear that the creatures couldn't be killed by conventional means. She grabbed a torch from one of the brackets on the wall and took to setting the things alight before she toppled them off the walkway with well-placed kicks of her iron-shod boots.

'Fire!' she shouted. 'You've got to use fire! They burn really well!'

Anili replaced one of her swords with a torch.

More and more of the dreadful creatures were swarming up the walls and onto the walkways, and the greater part of them seemed to be heading Anili's way. Blade and torch whirling, she managed to keep them at bay, but more were coming up the wall, faster than she and Ailis could kill them. The pressure was rising, the balance slowly but surely tipping in the enemy's favor. She reckoned they'd soon be forced to retreat into the house, and was expecting Baran to give the signal at any moment.

Then the northern wall came crashing down, and it was too late.

But, for a wonder, Anak and Haldor both rose from the rubble and held the breach, a feat of guts and valor she envied them, though not the disgusting butchery that came with it. Distracted, she nearly missed one of the things, caught it on her sword at the very last moment, slavering jaws clacking together mere inches from her face.

Then she heard a horn blare, saw dark shapes coming out of the woods: horses, riders, at least a score of them, closing on the massed creatures with torches held high. Just before they reached the ugly horde, the riders reined in their mounts.

For a short while they seemed to be doing nothing at all. Then a dozen fireflies rose from their midst, arcing high and descending on the spot where the creatures were thickest, over to the north.

Where the flying sparks landed they burst into a raging inferno, setting everything around them alight in the blink of an eye. Flames shot thirty feet and more into the air. Burning creatures weaved and staggered and rolled on the ground, screeching and howling, unable to rid themselves of the clinging fire. The heat fanned an atrocious, sulphurous stench up the wall. A ragged cheer went up from the farm's defenders as the riders launched another flight of deadly sparks, sowing confusion and panic among the enemy horde and quickly breaking down any sort of coherent action. Methodically, the riders began to work their way around the perimeter.

An arm went around Anili's shoulders.

Baran was there, exhaustion and relief in every line of his face that was streaked with sweat, dust, and soot. Anili buried her own face against his broad, solid chest, unable to watch the grisly spectacle any longer. He gave her a strong, one-armed hug.

'Almorican fire,' he said. 'Did I ever tell you about it? Damned nasty stuff, that. A kind of jelly packed in clay jars. When they break, it splatters all over the place and ignites everything it touches. No way to get rid of it before it's burned itself out. Can't wipe it off, can't wash it off. Jump in the water, and it just goes on burning. Myself, I'd hate to use it even against creatures like these, but there's no denying it's saved our lives.'

Anili shuddered. 'I want to get the bastards responsible for all this,' she said through clenched teeth, fighting down the contents of her stomach that were trying to climb up her throat. 'I want to get them so bad it hurts.'

'We will,' Baran said. 'We will. Come, it's not over yet. There's still some mopping up to be done out there. But we'll handle it the traditional way, with clean, honest steel.'

Standing there on the wall with Anili, Baran experienced a flash of insight, one of those rare moments when the things a man has lived through suddenly fall together in a new pattern or in a different incidence of the light, thus revealing to him a deeper understanding of his own self.

With Anili, he knew, fate had bestowed upon him the greatest gift of all: a child, a daughter, something he'd most likely never have had on his own, given the flighty nature of his relations with women. Even if he'd ever considered binding himself to a single one, he'd have made a terrible husband, of that he was convinced. True, he'd loved them all, beginning with the mother he'd lost so early he retained only the faintest memory of her. But he'd always tended to love all women in a woman, rather than loving the woman for her own, individual sake – with the exception of Rupili, whom he had greatly admired and respected and yes, loved, if only from afar, for who she was.

That she of all people should have entrusted him with her child continued to fill him with amazement and awe, and with immense gratitude. Trusting someone with one's life was a momentous thing, but trusting a person with one's child was something so enormous, only a parent could understand what it really meant. And a parent he had become, thanks to a cruel twist of fate and Rupili's confidence in him. It was an experience he wouldn't have missed for anything in the world.

He'd given it his best shot, and thought he hadn't done too badly. Teaching Anili her weapons had been the least of it. She had proved extraordinarily gifted, and he strongly suspected that her natural fleetness and coordination were further augmented by a hefty dose of Talent. There was no other way to explain the speed with which she'd learned and surpassed him already a while ago. For him, all this was incidental, even the fact that having Anili around had likely saved him from himself – beset as he was by grief, doubts and self-recriminations in the aftermath of Tinnan and the fall of Larnakis.

It had never been his intention to assist in the creation of a super-warrior but to share with Anili the value of things like honesty, integrity, loyalty, modesty, compassion and kindness, to offer her the chance of growing into someone who could one day make a difference. A true queen of men, no matter in the world of material things she had no kingdom left to call her own, and in all likelihood never would. She had turned out more than he had ever hoped for.

Still, he couldn't help but worry for her. There was a part of her he couldn't reach, a part she kept hidden away from everyone, even from him. Even from Dagrun, who'd been as much of a mother to her as she'd ever known. He suspected there was a darkness there that went beyond the usual aches and pains of a young girl growing up – not that he knew a lot about those either.

She sometimes seemed so single-minded in her aim, so clenched around her one and only purpose in life. He feared what following it through to the end might do to her, and she to herself. He would have so wished for her to be able to allow herself something closer to a normal life – whatever that might be – but he knew well enough that fate or the gods had decided differently, had decided already long ago, likely before she was born.

It didn't help that all these years he'd harbored his own desire for retribution, a desire that hadn't grown weaker over time.

He gave her shoulder another squeeze. 'I'm proud of you, lass,' he said. 'I wouldn't miss a day we've had together.'

It was the closest he'd ever come to telling her how dear she was to him. Maybe he should have simply said, 'I love you'. If anyone he'd ever known deserved to hear it, it was Anili. But he wasn't good at that sort of thing, never had been. Hopefully one day, when she met the right young man, she'd do better with expressing what she felt.

Outside the walls, there was nothing left to kill.

Those creatures that had survived had fled into the forest, and the riders had gone after them, all but three. Their horses stood with empty saddles, their masters dead. One was burned almost beyond recognition, another had been hacked to pieces, and the last one they found among the carnage had fallen to one of the few enemy weapons in evidence, a rusty Larnaki spear with a broken and clumsily mended haft. Baran realized with a shudder where it must have come from.

Even in death there was something impressive about the third man, a gentility and majesty that still shone through the hard lines of his used and weathered face. With Anak and Haldor's help, they carried the three bodies out of the general carnage, laying them out as neatly and as far away from the dead creatures as possible.

Baran was about to send Stian and Ailis to see what had become of Odd and Dagrun when the riders returned, grim-faced.

'Well come, sirs,' Baran greeted them. 'We are deeply indebted to you, the more so as you have paid a high and bitter price for coming to our aid. Our heartfelt thanks, and our deepest regrets for your loss. I would offer you rest and food and drink, but we've yet to see what's happened inside the house.'

'Let us do that,' one of them said, removing his helmet and motioning two men towards the house. A young man, Baran saw, with raven-black hair already shot through with grey, and eyes rimmed red by exhaustion. 'We're better equipped to deal with the Blight.'

Baran had already noted that all of them wore light chainmail, not only hauberks but also leggings that tucked into the tops of thick, sturdy boots, and heavy leather gauntlets, the backs of the hands and fingers further protected by overlapping metal scales.

'I am Baran Kendarren,' he said, 'and these are my people. I take it you are Gulfram's Ghosts. May I ask which of you is the leader, Gulfram?'

'There is no Gulfram,' the young man answered. 'Never has been. The name was meant as a jest at the time it was chosen. And our leader lies dead before you: Torvald Halvassar, last direct descendant of Aldland's kings. I am Akon Halvassar. Torvald was my uncle.'

'A most grievous loss,' Baran said. 'I am very sorry. My condolences.'

'Thank you, my lord. He will be sorely missed.'

One of the Ghosts gone to examine the house returned.

'The place is crawling with biters,' he reported. 'There's people in one of the downstairs rooms, shouting and making a hell of a racket. Don't see how to get them out, though. If we use the fire in there, we'll burn the whole house down, and them with it.'

Baran thought for a moment. 'Which room are they in?' he asked.

The man told him.

'That's the kitchen. Here's what we'll do.'

A quarter of an hour later the house was ablaze, surrounded by Ghosts ready to finish off any creatures that managed to escape. At the northeastern corner Anak stood back, lowering the sledgehammer he'd used to smash through one of the bricked-up kitchen windows. Haldor stuck his head into the opening. Standing behind him, Baran saw Dagrun and Odd inside. They must have fled down here when

481

the biters began streaming in through the upstairs loopholes. They were each brandishing one of Dagrun's larger frying pans.

Dagrun brought hers down on the hearthstone with an ear-splitting clang, smashing one of the small creatures.

'There,' she said, shouldering her pan and peering into the darker corners. 'I think that was the last one.'

Smoke was seeping in through the cracks around the doorjamb.

'Hey, you two,' Haldor said. 'Playtime's over. Better come out, unless you want to get your arses roasted.'

'Language, boy!' Dagrun said sharply, and Haldor quickly withdrew his head from the opening before she decided to use her pan on it.

Moments later, they were all outside and retreating from the heat of the blazing house, but not before Dagrun had collected a large assortment of foodstuffs from the larder and passed them out through the hole in the wall, saying she knew her boys – the term including everyone except Anili, whom she liked to call her 'princess' – and was sure they'd all be good and hungry after a hard night's work.

That work wasn't over yet.

They still had to bury the fallen Ghosts. They piled stones from the destroyed wall over the graves they'd dug at the edge of the woods, and Akon wedged the dead men's swords upright between them, fitting markers for men who had lived and died in battle.

After the burial they found themselves a clear space away from the remains of the fight. Dagrun passed out bread, cheese, sausages, and a couple of wineskins, insisting that everybody have a bite, there being nothing better to steady the nerves than food and drink.

482

'Shame about the house,' Akon said, wiping his chin with the back of his hand after a deep draught from one of the skins.

'Not really,' Baran answered. 'It would have taken days if not weeks to clean out the beasts, and even then we'd have lived in constant the fear that we might have missed a couple. No, better like this. We're leaving anyway. What will you do now?'

'I don't know,' Akon said. 'Choose a new leader, I suppose. There don't seem to be any more of the Blight left in these parts. In all likelihood these here were the last. All the others have gone south. Though I'd not advise anyone to risk the passes. Most of the things left up there are more or less stationary, but, if anything, they're even more dangerous, so well hidden you'll never see them until it's too late. Especially Long Pass remains a death trap. Perhaps we'll go south for a spell, follow the Blight, though our charter is for the Three Quarters. I don't see us laying down our weapons just because the beasts have moved on. They've caused far too much grief for that.'

Baran saw Anili, who had been drowsing with eyes half closed, suddenly perk up.

'What would you say if you got a chance to go after the people who are responsible for all this?' she asked Akon.

'That would be for all the Ghosts to decide,' Akon said. 'Personally, I can't think of anything I'd like better.'

'All right,' Anili said. 'Here's the deal: we're forming a company to do just that. If any of you want to join, you're most welcome.' A stirring went through the Ghosts. 'Think about it,' she added. 'We'll be leaving soon.'

'We will, my lady,' Akon said, inclining his head, and Baran noticed a spark of interest in the young man's eyes that seemed to go beyond the business at hand. He and the other Ghosts rose and moved off to discuss their options among themselves.

'Damn!' Anili said suddenly. Being Dagrun's princess, she got away with a look of mild rebuke from the old woman. 'The jewels!'

'Not to worry,' Baran said, patting a bulge in his leather jerkin. 'I've got them right here.'

The jewels Rupili had given into Baran's care for Anili were worth a king's ransom, their only means of financing the company, and as yet untouched. Baran had bought the farm from his savings, deposited over his years of service with his brother in Dunmark, and saved the jewels for a rainy day. It looked as if that day had now arrived.

He turned to Dagrun, searching for the right words to tell her something she surely wouldn't want to hear. 'Dagrun. We're going to war, there's no other way to put it. I don't think – '

'Hold right there,' Dagrun interrupted him. 'I'm coming, and if you think otherwise you need to check whether with all the fighting your head's come unscrewed. War or no, you boys need to eat, and not a cook among the lot of you. It's my decision to make, and it's not up for discussion. So don't even start.'

'Well,' Baran said with a rueful smile. 'I suppose that's settled, then. Stian, Odd, why don't you go have a look over at the north meadow, see if we've got any horses left. You'll find saddles and tack in the barn down there. Seeing as we've got nothing left to pack, we should be ready to leave in an hour.'

Akon came back with the news that the Ghosts felt it was still too early for them to leave the Three Quarters unprotected. For the time being, they would stay and safeguard against trouble returning.

'Things might look different in spring,' he said. 'Perhaps we can join you then. For now, I'm sending young Hakan here with you.' He indicated a blond, rosy-cheeked young man who looked no older than Anili. Hakan gave Anili a shy smile.

'We Ghosts have our ways of staying in touch,' Akon said. 'He'll know to get a message passed along to us. Should the need arise, we'll find you. In the meantime, I wish you the best of luck.'

They said farewells, and in a rush of clattering hooves and snorting horses eager to be away from the fire and the stink of alien corpses the Ghosts rode off, leaving behind a silence and a sense of emptiness and exposure that spurred the rest of them on to a speedy departure.

Odd and Stian returned with the horses, all of them unharmed and eager to run. They had four spares, and would be able to travel that much faster, though there was no need for haste, seeing as they hadn't even begun to make concrete plans.

And so the first leg of their journey was a leisurely affair, taking them no farther than Nara, where much to Brocc's delight they stopped at the *Lost Traveler* for a bath, a meal, and a bed. Baran set up in the common room, where he haggled with several of the local farmers over a good price for the livestock left behind at the farm, making sure the buyer went out that same morning to milk and feed the cows. He also bought various supplies and three additional horses to carry them.

Two days later they set out in earnest, heading south towards a future that held no certainties but any amount of possibilities.

❖   ❖   ❖

From wonder to wonder existence opens.

Lao Tzu

27 Ravenstein

t was after tea-time. Lucy was playing downstairs, and Lisa had gone to buy some things in the village after reminding Jon to keep an eye on his little sister. He was lying on his bed reading a letter delivered to him by Franz. It was from uncle Richard. Over the past days the old man's health had increasingly failed, and he was bedridden. The doctor had been by several times, twice yesterday. He'd wanted to have Richard taken to the hospital but the old man refused, saying he'd managed so long to keep his distance from the world's idiots, he wasn't about to change that now. He preferred to die in peace and quiet in his own home, thank you very much. Apparently he'd had a minor stroke yesterday but remained resolute in his decision. The missive he'd sent Jon was a lengthy one, written in a slightly shaky but beautiful, old-fashioned hand, an art that had become nearly extinct with the advent of computers and cell phones.

❖　❖　❖

My dear Jonathan,

over the past week I have told you most of Ravenstein's history,
things that can never be written down but nonetheless must be passed

on from one guardian of the Gate to the next. There is one part I have left out, and now I must tell you it as well, if only to give you an example of how dangerous and ruthless an enemy we face, and to what ends he will go to achieve his goals. Even after so many years, I still find it very painful to speak about that period, the darkest in Germany's past, and in Ravenstein's, so for once I have broken with traditional rules and entrusted this account to paper – though I must ask you to read it forthwith and to destroy it as soon as you've done so.

I'm sure you'll have heard of Heinrich Himmler, Hitler's Reichsmarschall and chief of the SS – but perhaps not of the Ahnenerbe, an organization founded by Himmler in 1935. Its official mission was to explore ancient Germanic heritage and validate the theory of the Aryan master race, the 'Herrenmenschen'. To this end, archaeological expeditions were sent all over the globe, penetrating into places as remote as Tibet where, believe it or not, Himmler's 'scientists' discovered that Tibetans were really descendants of the Aryans, making them our distant cousins, so to speak. They also concluded that there was a distinct intellectual and spiritual affinity between Hitler's 'Mein Kampf' and the Buddha's teachings. What better example to illustrate the total insanity that ruled Germany in those days!

Ahnenerbe's real, clandestine mission was a very different one. In truth, its strings were pulled by a secret, esoteric brotherhood called 'Schwarze Sonne', or Black Sun, whose members wore an additional rune on the sleeves of their black SS uniforms: algiz, the rune of defense, of secrecy, or taboo. On behalf of Schwarze Sonne, Ahnenerbe was searching for ancient, occult artifacts that could be used as sources of theurgic power or, even better, as outright weapons in the struggle to force the world under Nazi rule. (In a sense, you could say that Nazism was one of the greatest esoteric movements of all times, with its 'Blood and Soil' cult and mass rituals. But then, spiritual madness has occurred throughout the ages, and to this day it plagues every religion and ideology, every esoteric or political offshoot ever invented by mankind.)

How he could be so blind and foolish I will never understand, but in November of 1941 my elder brother Maximilian joined the SS and was drawn into Himmler's inner circle. There can be no excuse for what he did, but I do believe it was mainly to spite our father, with whom he'd always had a difficult and oftentimes stormy relationship, culminating in a bitter fight in which father disinherited Max in my favor and Max went storming off to become a Nazi superhero. Had our mother still been alive to mediate, things might have gone differently. But she wasn't, and disaster was not long in the making.

Though father had never entrusted him with the secret of the Gate, Max had his suspicions, and late one evening in the fall of 1942 he returned to Ravenstein. I'll never forget the scene of his arrival. I couldn't sleep that night, plagued by a vague but insistent feeling of foreboding. It was drizzling outside, and banks of fog drifted by, sometimes so dense I could hardly see the light burning at the castle gate from my window. Around ten o'clock, I saw the long, ghostly fingers of headlights dancing through the trees as a car drove up the private road. It roared through the gate and stopped at the perron, spraying gravel. Three men in long military coats and SS uniforms got out. One of them was my brother Max, holding the door for a fourth passenger, obviously a person of higher rank. When he step-

ped from the car and I saw who it was, my heart fell into my shoes. Himmler himself! He looked around, the light reflecting on the round lenses of his glasses, then they all walked up the steps and hammered on the door.

I hesitated at first, unsure what I should do. By the time had I reached a decision and thrown on some clothes, I'd already missed the beginning of the confrontation that ensued in my father's study. When I got there, Himmler's two thugs were holding my father between them, and Himmler himself was yelling at him at the top of his voice. Even so, he noticed me storming in and interrupted his tirade to look me up and down with the eyes of a snake studying a mouse it intended to make its next meal. My brother drew his pistol and pointed it at me.

'You stay out of this,' he said, trying to sound authoritative but not quite bringing it off. I could see that he was nervous and insecure.

'No, no,' Himmler said with his insidious predator's smile. 'Quite the contrary. You're Richard, I assume? Very well. Since your brother has convinced me that it would be useless to try and tease your father's secret out of him using, let's say, the more direct means at our disposal, we'll try a different approach.'

He addressed my father, keeping his reptilian eyes on me.

'Graf Ravenstein, I find it very disappointing that you've offered only one of these strapping young men to serve in the Führer's great cause. So I've decided I'll take him with me and have him inducted into the Wehrmacht, and then sent directly on to the eastern front. The war effort needs young fellows like him, especially on the front lines. Naturally I could also find him a much less strenuous line of duty, but that is entirely up to you. All you need do is tell me what I

490

want to know. Until then, young Richard here will be having some very exciting experiences, I'm sure. It's in your hands. When you're ready to talk, a call will suffice. We're done here. Müller, Hansen, see that the young man comes along quietly.'

Himmler turned on his heel and strode out of the room with that ridiculously false military bearing all of the Nazi bigwigs affected. As the two thugs grabbed my arms and led me off I managed to exchange a last look with my father. All the agony of the moment, all the fear and regret were clearly written on his face, and though he didn't say a word I knew he was silently pleading my forgiveness.

And I understood.

For though, incredibly – no, absurdly even – neither Max nor Himmler had ever thought to ask whether I might know the secret they so avidly coveted, I did. (That's the Nazis for you: ruthless, crafty, and conniving, and at the same time dumb as cow pie.)

I ended up in Stalingrad just in time to be caught in the Russian encirclement. If there was a biblical hell, a real counterpart to Boschian visions of purgatory, I'd have gladly exchanged it for that city on the Volga, and counted it a marvelous vacation. As I found out later, of the three hundred thousand German soldiers caught in the 'Kessel' of Stalingrad, less than a hundred thousand survived to be taken prisoner, and of those a mere six thousand made it back home after up to fifteen years in the gulags. Between July '42 and February '43, somewhere around two million soldiers and civilians died on the banks of the Volga, and most of us who still lived had come to regard death as a promise of salvation. Mine came on the Christmas Eve of 1942.

I will spare us both a detailed account of the horrors of Stalingrad; a sketch will do. It was freezing, had been for months, an eternity of eternities. The cold had long since crept not only into the marrow of our bones, but into the very core of our souls, as had the hunger. There was not a dead horse left that hadn't been picked to the bones, and even the cannibals were starving, unable to find so much as a scrap of wood to light a fire and thaw a cut from a dead comrade's frozen body. I'd caught a piece of shrapnel in the leg some weeks earlier, but by then there were no more aeroplanes to take out the wounded, and the few doctors we had left were too busy with the more serious cases. Though superficially the wound was healing, the bomb fragment was still there, lodged against the bone and causing me considerable and constant pain.

That evening there was a cease-fire, and we could hear the Russians singing carols just a stone's throw away. It was then I decided I'd had enough. I crept away through frozen mud and dirty, bloody snow and rubble, all that remained of what had once been a thriving city. I left my gun behind. I was finished with the war. The only thing I took along was a book I'd found in a bombed-out house, a German copy of Stendhal's 'Le Rouge et le Noire'. It had played a central role in helping me hold on to my sanity, and even though I was going to my death, I was reluctant to part with it. Once I had left the ruins behind, I made my way south along the banks of the Volga. I knew that sooner or later I'd run into the Russian lines, but I wasn't planning to go that far in any case, only to find a secluded place where I could let the cold take me and give me a peaceful ending.

Somehow, I must have misjudged the distance I'd gone, for suddenly I found myself blundering straight into a Russian outpost. Ironically, the shock reawakened my atrophied survival instincts and I *ran, nearly fainting from the pain in my leg, fighting against the snowdrifts, thrashing my way deeper and deeper into a dense forest of young pine trees. They grew between the steeply rising sides of a ravine that led me inland, away from the river. Then the trees thinned and I skidded onto the frozen surface of a stream that flowed along the bottom of the ravine. Slipping and sliding, I followed it around several twists and turns until I reached a place where the sides of the gorge drew together in a jumble of boulders.*

Two of the largest stood upright on either side of the stream like a pair of natural menhirs, as if arranged that way by a freak of nature. Though I hadn't heard any sounds of pursuit, I went on, thinking that at least I'd found a good spot to leave this world. And when I passed between the standing stones, that was exactly what happened.

Next I knew, I was falling into the smell of wildflowers, into a world of sunlight and warmth I'd nearly forgotten existed. At first I thought I must have somehow managed to die without noticing it happen, and I felt only relieved that the next life's setting seemed so normal – which may serve to illustrate just how utterly confused I was during those moments. But as I lay there in the grass, listening to the buzz of insects and savoring the warm, gentle breeze on my face, slowly coming back to my senses, I began to grasp what had happened. Impossible as it seemed, I'd stumbled upon another Gate, and to this day my only explanation is that some higher power was guiding my steps that night.

I had no idea where I was – except not on Earth, that much was pretty well self-evident – or if I'd ever find a way to get back home, but of one thing was certain: I wasn't going back the way I'd come. I won't get into any details of what followed; suffice to say that by a tremendous stroke of luck – or the intervention of destiny, who can say? – I had arrived on Enemathea, Vereld's southern continent, and after eleven years and numerous adventures that would fill a book of their own, I was finally able to return to Ravenstein.

I found my father on his deathbed, felled by a series of strokes and unable to speak, so I sat with him, held his hand, and told him all about my adventures in Vereld. Three days later, he died, smiling. Though I was glad to be home again, it was by now 1953 and the world had moved on, picking up the pace with frightening speed. Between my experiences in Russia and those in Vereld, I had somehow lost the connection to this world, and I couldn't bring myself to be interested in the things that occupied the thoughts and hopes and wishes of my contemporaries. Still, I read philosophy and French literature in Munich and later in Paris, and I traveled extensively before settling down to the quiet life of a private scholar in Ravenstein.

I never saw Max again.

But I know he survived, choosing the right moment to slip into civilian clothes and a civilian persona and so escape the Allied purges, which in any case were half-hearted at best. He eventually married and had two daughters, your mother and your aunt Lisa. Their mother died from complications during Lisa's birth, and that seems to have been the last straw in Max's troubled existence. One evening in May of 1970, he left the two girls on Ravenstein's doorstep with a note saying he was sorry for everything he'd done. After that, he vanished, never to be seen or heard from again. Whether he killed himself or disappeared to some remote, godforsaken corner of the earth,

I have no idea. Presented with the task of caring for an infant and a five year-old, I did what I could, but I'm the first to admit that, as a surrogate father, I was lacking in all respects. I did grow to love them dearly and, notwithstanding my incompetence, they both grew up to become very fine women, and I –

❖   ❖   ❖

Here the missive ended abruptly.

Jon suspected that the stroke had intervened. In a hand so wobbly it was hardly legible, Richard had added a postscript:

Sorry – finished anyway. Please burn right away. Richard.

Jon realized with a start that it was dark outside. He hadn't heard Lisa come back, and he'd completely forgotten to check on Lucy.

He found some matches and set alight Richard's letter in the fireplace, stirring the ashes to make sure that no scrap of it remained unburned. Then he went downstairs to find Lucy. She wasn't there.

She wasn't in her room either, or anyplace else he looked, which in the end was pretty much everywhere in the castle, with Franz and Anton joining in the search. Dinnertime came and went, and for once nobody was interested in Maria's cooking. Lisa hadn't returned either. Hans was missing too, it seemed. The look on Franz's face grew increasingly worried. Anton drove down to the village to look for Lisa. Half an hour later he was back, his news not good. She'd been seen with Hans. The two of them had been standing on the sidewalk near the village pub when a large black SUV pulled up beside them. Lisa had gotten into the car, though it wasn't clear whether Hans had helped her in or given her a push before getting in himself and driving off with whoever was at the wheel. Franz was looking very grim by now.

Then the telephone rang, and Franz answered, speaking only in monosyllables. After less than a minute he rang off.

'They've got Lisa,' he said. 'They say they'll trade her for information.'

Nobody felt the need to ask what kind of information 'they' were after. Franz fetched two pistols from the weapons safe in the hunting room and gave one to Anton.

At this point Jon had a sudden inspiration, an image of Bear sitting alone and deserted in the downstairs corridor, right in front of the wall that hid the Gate. 'I need to talk to uncle Richard,' he said. 'I think I know where Lucy's gone.'

'We'll wait for you here,' Franz said. 'Don't say anything about Lisa. He's ill enough as it is.'

Jon hadn't seen Richard since before the stroke.

He was shocked by how shrunken and transparent his uncle had become, as if half of him had already crossed over to the other side. 'Uncle Richard,' he said, kneeling by the bed, 'I need your help.'

The old man opened his eyes and looked at him questioningly.

'Lucy's gone. I think she found out how to open the Gate, and I need to go and get her. But I still don't know how it works.'

Richard stretched out a pale, trembling hand, and Jon took it in his own. 'Walk the house,' he said, fighting for breath, each word an effort. 'Feel the lines… find the heart…'

He paused.

'Franz… help…' he went on, his words becoming more and more slurred, his eyelids drooping. 'You… master now…'

He fell asleep, exhausted. Jon gently laid Richard's frail hand on the bed-cover and left, wondering if he'd see his uncle again.

Downstairs Franz had sent Anton to close and bar the castle gate. 'They might not waste much time waiting for an answer,' he explained.

'Go,' he said when Jon told him where Lucy had likely gone and that he was going after her. 'Go. Anton and I will take care of things here. Don't worry. We know what we're about. Both of us used to work for GSG-9, and I still have good contacts there. We'll get Lisa back, I promise. Now go find your sister. But once you've found her, it might be a good idea to leave her where she is until we've got things sorted here. No use putting her in danger. Coming to think of it, you'd better stay away for a while yourself. They can't get any secrets out of you if you're not here.'

Jon walked the house, the old and the new – though calling the centuries-old castle 'new' seemed a bit extravagant, unless you compared it with its Roman predecessor.

He paced the rooms and corridors, trailing a hand along the walls and trying to get a feel for the 'lines' Richard had spoken of. For the longest time nothing happened. His anxiety for Lucy grew, beginning to interfere with his concentration. But then, eventually, almost unnoticeably at first, there was… something.

It was down in the old part that he had the first glimmering, a sensation akin to nearly but not quite seeing something out of the corner of his eye. Whatever it was, it vanished every time he tried to look at it directly. He gave up trying to catch it with his physical vision and kept moving. And then, all of a sudden, the lines lit up for him.

With senses he hadn't even known he possessed, he saw a simple set of glowing white strands, and knew they were the natural lines of the land. They were overlaid with a more complicated grid of blue, and he recognized how Corvinus' house had been placed just so, complementing and reinforcing the natural lines. There was a larger set of blue filaments delineating the castle, and they too were in harmony with everything else.

In a flash of heightened perception, Jon understood how the house had become almost a separate entity with something close to an awareness of its own, its foundations and walls standing on lines grown bright and strong over centuries, over millennia even, of supporting a structure that was right, laid out from the beginning with great care and consideration for what already existed in the land and further strengthened by countless generations of inhabitants whose repeated movements had drawn lines of their own, confirming those of the house.

He found the Gate only because he knew where to look, and even so it took him a moment. On its own, it would have stood out like a beacon. Bright filaments like the lines of a magnetic field arced out from its center where they sprang from a dazzlingly bright node of white light. But on this plane too, the Gate had been artfully hidden; the lines of the buildings surrounded it like a conductive fence, catching the observer's attention and sending it slipping and sliding along a defensive perimeter of false trails and counterfeit tangents. Reaching the Gate at its physical location, Jon felt his fingers tingle and sink into the wall, and without hesitating he stepped through.

It was the same tower room, and yet it wasn't.

He felt an immediate clutch of fear for Lucy when he saw the state it was in. There was a three-foot gap in the wall that seemed to run all the way up and down the tower. The crack had also spread across the floor, tearing a whole row of floorboards from the beams they'd rested on. Part of the roof had collapsed, and the far half of the room was a jumble of rafters and shingles, all of it covered with a dusting of snow.

Gingerly, Jon walked across the remaining floor and looked a-cross the gap. One of the window seats had been lifted up to reveal an opening. He saw a steep stone staircase winding down into impene-trable darkness, and wondered if this was a good or a bad sign, whether the stairs had given Lucy an opportunity to flee or served someone else as a means to intrude. He decided to risk making his presence known.

'Hello!' he called out. 'Is anyone there?'

'Outside!' a voice replied. 'Come on down. But do be careful on the stairs. No idea how long they'll hold up still.'

The only way to reach the rickety wooden staircase was to jump across the gap and land on an uncertain floor. Jon peered down through the gaping hole. The floor down there looked intact. He lowered himself over the edge until he was hanging from outstretched arms, and then let go.

It was still a five-foot drop, but he managed to land without spraining an ankle. The only furnishings in this room were a big four-poster bed and a wardrobe. The walls were lined with shelves cram-med to bursting with books, the overflow resting in dusty piles on the floor. Several rows had tumbled from the shelf where the crack ran through the wall, narrower than upstairs, but still wide enough to let in daylight and more snow.

The next lower staircase looked sturdy enough, and took him down to what was clearly the kitchen. Here, the crack in the wall narrowed down to a hand's breadth. Two rucksacks were sitting on the table, stuffed to bursting and ready to go. The door stood open. Outside, a long, steep flight of stone stairs led down to ground level.

An old man in a grey robe several shades darker than his unkempt hair and beard was poking around with a stick inside a large, blackened circle of bare earth where something had recently burned. Wisps of smoke still rose from what looked like charred sticks and the indefinable contents of a half-melted metal bowl. Splotches of some tar-like substance bubbled with residual heat, giving off a disgusting smell. At second glance, Jon realized that the sticks were bones, and the bowl was a helmet, or what remained of it. The old man turned, and Jon was met by a sharp, penetrating gaze from under bushy brows. Briefly, he had the weird feeling that the old man was looking right into him.

'Boy, oh boy,' the old man said appreciatively.
'She's sure keeping her promises. Glad you finally made it. We're running late, so we'd better get going as soon as I've found the danged... ah, there it is.'

He bent down, picked up a small, sky-blue bowl, and wiped it on his robe, leaving black smudges. Holding it up, he gazed at it admiringly. Instantly, Jon felt a strange, nearly irresistible pull from the thing. Entirely of its own volition, his arm began to rise and reach out towards it. With an effort, he stopped himself.

'Torgrim?' he said.

'That's me. And you're Jonathan. I've been expecting you.' Torgrim wrapped the small bowl in a crumpled handkerchief and stuffed it into a pouch hanging from his belt.

'I'm looking for Lucy, my little sister. Have you seen her? Is she all right?'

'She's fine,' Torgrim said, heading for the tower's stairs. 'As you may have noticed, there was a bit of unpleasantness here last night, but she's safe. Safer than the rest of us, no doubt.'

'Where is she?' Jon asked, moving to keep abreast of the old man. 'I need to see her.'

Torgrim stopped and gave him a searching look.

'She's with friends. Don't worry. No harm will come to her. She's in the best-protected place there is in the whole of Vereld, or anywhere else for that matter. As for seeing her, that will have to wait. Like I said, we're running late, and we've got things to do, things that will brook no further delay. Come on, we've got to find some proper clothes for you. You'll stick out like a sore thumb running around here like that.'

'Do what kind of things?' Jon asked, feeling increasingly out of his depth with this strange old man.

'Things like keeping a couple of worlds from going down the drain, for instance,' Torgrim said. 'Didn't she tell you anything?'

'Didn't who tell me anything?'

'Oh dear, feckless, bumbling gods!'

Torgrim rubbed his brow with a soot-blackened hand, leaving a dark streak to complement a smudge already decorating his nose.

'I'd hoped she'd have spoken to you. You haven't had any extra-ordinary dreams lately? No visitors in white?'

Jon told him about the people wrapped in bandages.

'Ah, no,' Torgrim shook his head. 'That's definitely not her. She must have been unable to get through to you for some reason. Which means you'll know nothing about your Talent, either.'

'Talent? What talent?'

'What I feared,' Torgrim sighed. 'All right. Here's the extremely short version. It's all we have time for right now. Some thoroughly bad people with truly disgusting characters are running loose on Vereld. And I'm not talking about your usual, run-of-the-mill mass murderers, the kind you've got back home, though those can be a major pain, too. To put it more succinctly, we're staring extreme evil in the face, or will be soon, and somebody's got to do something about it in a hurry. That's where you and I come in.'

'But I – '

'Right. I was getting to that. You know about magic. I'm sure Richard's told you that much at least. Well, not to beat around the bush, you've got a talent for it – the Talent, with a capital T – and you've got it in spades. Trust me, I can see it. Now all we've got to do is find out exactly what it is, and teach you how to use it, and we'll be all set to tackle the bad guys. Only problem is, it usually takes between five and ten years for a mage to fully develop his Talent. But then, you've got me to teach you, so by the time we reach Kingskeep in a couple of weeks you should be getting the hang of it. Now. Clothes, packs, and off we go. There are people we need to catch up with before they get themselves into serious trouble.'

'But Lucy – '

'I told you, she's fine. We'll go see her as soon as there's time. Which, right now, there isn't.'

Back inside the tower, Torgrim went upstairs and rummaged in the wardrobe. He dropped several items of clothing down the stairs and came back down.

'Here's a robe for you,' he said, holding out a fairly clean garment of faded green wool. To Jon's surprise, when he pulled it over his head it wasn't musty at all, but smelled pleasantly of lavender and cedar. There was also a warm, hooded cloak of a similar color to go over it. Torgrim donned a slightly moth-eaten, weathered blue cloak and a wide-brimmed, flat-crowned hat, reached for a wooden staff, and with packs shouldered they set off – out the door, down the stairs, and down the hill, with Jon dazedly wondering what he was doing, and whether it was at all the right thing. But he didn't seem to have much of a choice at the moment, except to go along and see what would happen.

Torgrim wasted no time, and lessons began immediately.

They crossed a brook gurgling along between ice-rimmed banks at the foot of the hill on which the tower stood, and were entering a dale with an old, widely spaced growth of thick-trunked, gnarled larches, their branches not yet shed of their orange-gold needles and bowed under their load of snow, when Torgrim stopped and pointed.

'That tree there,' he said. 'See if you can get the snow to fall off. And I don't mean by going over and shaking it.'

'How in the… How am I supposed to do that?'

'Just go ahead and do whatever comes to mind. You'll likely try all the wrong stuff first, but that's perfectly all right. It's called learning by elimination. Go on, the tree's not going to bite you.'

Jon thought it best to humor the old man by at least going through the moves, so he concentrated on the tree, imagining all the snow avalanching off its branches in a swirling cloud of white. Nothing happened.

'Again,' Torgrim said.

This time Jon focused on the trunk, willing it with all his might to tremble and shake off the snow covering the tree's branches. Again, nothing happened.

'And again.'

Grasping at straws, Jon tried to conjure up a gust of wind to sweep through the limbs, with no result other than that fifty yards away, a crow sitting on the very tip of a tree rose with a squawk and flew off, heading for another perch several trees farther down.

'That's better,' Torgrim said.

'What?' Jon said. 'I didn't do anything.'

'It doesn't matter whether you did anything or not. You wanted something to happen, and something happened. That's all that counts. The crow. It almost dislodged enough snow to set off the rest and clear the whole tree. That wasn't bad, only it was the wrong tree. You need to focus, lad. Now, since we can't stand here all day I want you to go on picking trees that are far enough ahead and go to work on them. Once we're past one, choose another. Got it?'

They resumed walking.

Jon was beginning to feel frustrated, and just a little bit angry. This was totally ridiculous. He didn't feel any hint of this so-called Talent within himself, not even enough to hit the tree with a damned snow-

ball. But he went ahead anyway. Useless as it seemed, at least it helped pass the time. An hour and several failed attempts later, they were
walking along a stretch where the trees were more densely crowded
and stood closer to the trail when something caused Jon to stop. No
idea what.

'Wait,' he said, holding out an arm.

The old man halted and looked around bemusedly. Jon had a sudden, crazy notion that, any moment now, he'd pull out a camera and
begin clicking away like a busy Japanese tourist. Suddenly, with a
mighty whoosh and thump, a tree standing just a few paces further on
dumped its entire load of snow onto the trail.

Torgrim looked at Jon curiously.

'That was interesting,' he said.

'I didn't – ' Jon started to say.

' – do anything, I know,' Torgrim said. 'But you knew it was
going to happen. Very interesting, indeed. It would seem you have
more than one Talent. Well. Don't just stand there. Choose your next
tree, and let's get going.'

Jon was beginning to get a feeling that the old man was pulling his
leg, assigning meaning to completely random occurrences and making believe Jon had anything to do with them just for kicks. He was
just waiting for Torgrim to say, 'Got you!' and then laugh out loud
and tell him what a gullible, entertaining fool he was.

His mood continued to plummet. Even the sun coming out to
warm them as they held a short lunch break didn't do anything to
assuage his rising resentment. Being studiously ignored by Torgrim
didn't help either. The old man was silently munching away on hard-

tack and cheese with the hint of an amused smile playing around his lips.

Staring at a distant tree in a huff, Jon felt his anger turn to fury, both at himself and at Torgrim. Without thinking he directed it at the tree, with an intensity that blotted out everything else around him. He felt a bittersweet darkness rise inside him, like the one and only time he'd thrown a tantrum as a child when something he wished most dearly to possess was denied him.

Suddenly the tree exploded – literally – as if it had been struck by lightning or hit by a mortar shell, snow and branches flying every which way, its trunk splintering and cracking with a sound like gunfire. Afterwards, Jon just sat there, dazed and trembling with shock and confusion.

'Let me tell you a few things about how magery works,' Torgrim said in a conversational tone, though Jon could see that he wasn't quite as unruffled as he pretended. 'There are some mistakes you only want to make once. What you just did was one of them. Never, ever, do anything like that again, unless it's a matter of life and death and you've exhausted every other possibility. Now get up.'

'What?'

'Go on, get up.'

Jon tried to rise but found that his legs were too weak to support him. His heart was hammering away in his chest at a frightening rate, and he felt nauseous, close to blacking out.

'Right,' Torgrim said. 'I'll bet you're feeling pretty lousy right now. That's because you used up part of your own substance, physical and mental, to blow up that tree. Now you know one reason why a mage tries to avoid that kind of thing at all costs, even if he's been hoarding and has power to burn, which you haven't.'

'The second reason is, it's too close to how the Dark Side does things, particularly if it comes from a place of anger, or worse, hatred.

'And the third reason is that, again like in sorcery, it goes completely against the natural flow – against the grain of creation, you could say. It's unnecessarily brutal and destructive, and too much of it eventually brings on uncontrollable repercussions. Do it too often, and it can and will cause considerably more damage than originally intended, to yourself as well as to your surroundings.

'Jonathan, lad.' Torgrim suddenly looked very serious. 'I'm giving you some homework. You need to figure out where that' – he gestured at the ruined tree – 'just came from. And then you need to face it, get a handle on it. A mage has to put his own house in order before he can take on the rest of the world.'

Jon nodded. 'I'm sorry,' he said. And he was. Somewhere deep inside, he'd known very well what he was doing, he realized. He'd known it was wrong, and for a moment hadn't cared. 'I wasn't thinking. It was wrong.'

'Not entirely,' Torgrim said, smiling. 'Don't forget: this is a crash course, and you need to make mistakes in order to learn from them. Actually, that was a very valuable lesson just now. But I want you to forget the practical stuff for the moment, and absorb some theory instead.'

'Now,' Torgrim said, taking up the thread as soon as they were back on the trail again. 'A sorcerer is someone who sees only obstacles, things to be met with aggression, using brutal force to blast them out of the way, just like you did with that poor tree. The cost in energy expended is enormous, which is why sorcerers prefer to use other peoples' power rather than their own. And make no mistake: they do kill people in the process.

'A mage on the other hand sees opportunities, looks for things that are ripe and ready to do what he needs them to. All he does is give them a gentle nudge in the direction they're already leaning anyway. It takes a little more imagination, and sometimes a bit of patience. But it costs very little, seldom more than you can afford without exhausting yourself. Take this tree here, for example. There's a small, weak branch very close to the top that's almost ready to give under the weight of the snow. See if you can find it.'

Jon looked up into the tree, seeing only snow. Then he remembered what he'd learned during his search for the key to opening the Gate, and closed his eyes. He relaxed and concentrated, looking for a different perspective, and suddenly the world opened up to him on a new and completely unexpected level.

It was magnificent, staggering, exhilarating.

He saw lines everywhere, and found that the tree, too, existed within a network of lines, had lines of its own. As did absolutely everything, from living, breathing beings to objects he had learned to think of as 'dead' matter, though now he saw they weren't inanimate at all, but very much alive in their own slow and measured way.

He turned his attention back to the tree, and found the branch in question easily. 'Got it,' he told Torgrim without opening his eyes.

'Good. Now give it a nudge. Just a caress will do.'

Jon did, and the small branch sagged, releasing its burden of snow onto the next-larger branch beneath it, which in turn shook off its load, and so it went until everything came whooshing down, liberated boughs springing back and swaying in rapidly fading arcs while the main body of snow thumped to the ground. An ephemeral shroud of crystalline powder went lazily drifting off on the barest of breezes, glittering like fairy dust in the golden light of late afternoon.

'There you go,' Torgrim said, looking quite pleased. 'Easy as pie. Now. Time to find a shelter for the night. There's an old barn not far down the trail. Half a roof to spend the night under, if it hasn't fallen down, with a bed of hay and plenty of firewood thrown in, and all of it for free. By tomorrow night we should be in Nara, where old Brocc had better have the horse and buggy he promised me waiting if he doesn't want all the ale in his cellar turned into rat piss. And then it's straight to Kingskeep, hopefully in time to stop some errant fool from causing more trouble than there already is.'

'Torgim?' Jon said when they had resumed their journey.
'Is there a rational way to explain what just happened, or do I simply take it on faith that this stuff exists, and works?'

'Both,' Torgrim answered. 'If you were a simple soul, I'd tell you to just believe and be happy, and you would. Anything else would only complicate matters for you. But since you're clearly the intellectual type' – here the old man pulled a face, making it clear that this was not necessarily an advantage – 'you'll need an explanation. If only to give your busy mind something to chew on, something to keep all those annoying questions and doubts from tripping you up.

'Well. Where to begin? First of all, what we're dealing with here is paradox. Take the famous question you earthlings are so fond of torturing yourself with: if the Creator created the universe, then who or what created the Creator? The answer is, the Creator and the universe created each other, at the same time, and they're still doing it, or neither of them would be there for us to wonder about.

'Time, by the way, is another paradox. Does time flow in one direction, or do the past, the present and the future all exist simultaneously and we've just invented the flow of time to keep ourselves from going instantly and totally insane? And again the answer is, both versions are correct.

'To put it all in a more individual perspective: God created, creates, and will create you. And you did, do, and will do the same for Him, provided you think He's worth the trouble. If not, don't worry. There's always somebody else who'll take care of Him. Or Her. It?'

'But what's all this got to do with magic?' Jon asked.

'Patience, lad. I'm getting there.' The old man had picked up the pace. The topic seemed to have an inspiring and invigorating effect on him. 'Let's talk about subatomic space-time turbulence. Quantum foam. That's where the paradox is resolved, or resolves itself, in a sense. If there's anyone on Earth who's close to understanding magic, then it's your modern physicists, especially since Planck and Heisenberg, and I'll be forever grateful to Richard for acquainting me with their work. Any road, where was I?

'Right. Quantum foam. The foundations of the fabric of the universe. That's where – and when – everything is, was, and will be, including magic. And, as follows logically, it's where everything is, was, and will be possible. It's also the stuff mages work with, at least in theory. Once you've learned to access it, you can do almost anything. Every possibility you can imagine and every one you can't is

510

there, just waiting to happen. Choose one that suits your purpose, find its analogy in the foam, define the place and the level of presence and density on which you want it to materialize, and give it a nudge. That's it. Sounds simple, doesn't it? Well it is, and it's not.'

'But how do I do it?'

'You don't. That's the trick. There is no "how". It just happens. All you need is a good reason and the honest wish to help it occur, and it will. Did you weaken that branch in physical space? Or did you manipulate it by speeding things up in the time frame? The answer is' – Torgrim mad a dramatic pause – 'who the hell cares?'

The old mage chuckled.

'This all sounds pretty theoretical to me,' Jon said. 'What if I run into a sorcerer and have to fight him? What do I do then? Argue theory with him?'

'Why not?' Torgrim replied. 'As long as you're better at it than he is. Though it helps if you also know how to put it into practice. But seriously. It's the same as with that little branch, basically. You're dealing with a person who wants to destroy something, or kill someone – in this case, you.

'Opportunely, he'll do most of the work for you, and you probably won't even have to nudge him along. You just let him get on with what he's doing, and then you turn whatever he throws at you around and send it right back at him, reflecting it like a mirror. But we'll get to that later. It's actually not quite as simple or as easy as it may have just sounded.'

'I didn't think it was,' Jon sighed, realizing the sheer impossibility of the task that lay ahead of him. He thought for a moment. 'So what you're saying is, the creator and the created are identical. God is me.

I am God.'

'Yes!' Torgrim beamed a happy, silly grin at Jon. Then his mien changed to exaggerated sobriety. 'And no,' he added, tapping the side of his nose with a finger. 'Don't forget: paradox. Ah, here we are. Not quite the *Lost Traveler* yet, but it'll do.'

They had reached the end of their day's journey. The barn was where Torgrim had said it would be, with half the roof still standing. The hay was old but mostly dry, the firewood plentiful, and though the night was clear and bitter cold, Jon slept soundly, better than he had in a very long time.

❖ ❖ ❖

When you are dining with a demon, you've got to have a long spoon.
Navjot Singh Sidhu

28 Dunmark

he summoner of demons was thoroughly out of patience with the creatures he'd been calling up from the Warren, especially Xorth. Nearly a month had passed since he'd given the demon lord a simple task, and so far absolutely nothing had happened. The target was still very much alive and kicking. Luckily, while studying a rare compendium he'd stolen from a most secret collection in Orr, the summoner had found a new and much more promising method of achieving his aims and removing his enemies. Now, this very night, he was about to put his discovery into practice.

Over the past week he'd procured every item but one on the list of things necessary for his undertaking, surreptitiously stashing them in the remote, unused cellar he used for the more dangerous of his hidden activities.

He had just finished drawing a chalk design on the floor, but not the usual one. This time, instead of a pentangle he'd drawn two tangent circles, one large, one small, like a very lopsided figure eight. He'd left a narrow gap where the circles met, no wider than the wetted finger with which he'd erased the line at that point. The most difficult part of the preparations had been finding a way to close that gap later on without disturbing the circles.

Nothing at all, neither objects nor spells, could cross those lines when a demon was present inside them, or else the containment would be broken and the demon set free. As sure as night followed day, the first thing it would do was devour the summoner, body and soul. At that point, there would be absolutely nothing he could do to defend himself and prevent the demon from gobbling him up. He'd be helpless as a choice morsel of food invitingly laid out on a silver platter. The only reason he could influence a demon caught in the lines at all was that, with the mudras he used, cause and effect were not really connected, at least not in a direct, line-crossing sense. In reality, the gestures were no more than a sort of reverse placebo, suggestions that played on the demon's innate fears and preconceptions. The summoner didn't actually *cause* pain, only suggested that now might be the proper moment to *feel* pain. The rest, the demon did all by itself. Very convenient, and very neat.

He'd solved the problem of the gap, though not as elegantly as he would have liked. No matter. On the line beside it, he'd drilled a hole into the floor-boards and stuck an upright, wooden rod into it. One end of a string was tied to the top of the rod, the other to a piece of chalk that was leaning at an angle over the gap, the string the only thing keeping it from falling over. Under the string, he'd placed a candle stub. Each piece, rod, candle and chalk, was perfectly centered on the line, and he'd experimented with different lengths of candle and various types of string until he knew to within a few seconds how long it would take for the candle to burn through the string and release the chalk, which would then fall over the gap and close it.

The last thing he did was place a small sphere in one circle. No larger than a cherry, it was made from a very special alloy of rare metals that had been hard to find and harder still to coax into bonding with one another, especially as a small amount of fresh human blood as well as hair belonging to a certain person had to be incorporated into the mix. But he'd taken that hurdle as well.

He lit the candle and performed the summoning.

Xorth materialized in the larger circle, wearing the same form as always when he was summoned.

'Blast me,' the demon groaned. 'Not again! You called me only a few days ago.' He looked around. 'You've moved.'

'So I have,' the summoner said.

'This had better be good,' Xorth grumbled. 'I'm already having a bad day.'

'Better save the whining for later, old chap,' the summoner said, his lips twitching with cruel amusement. 'Your day's about to get a lot worse.'

'What?' Xorth complained, beginning to look seriously worried. 'Haven't I done everything you asked? I've found you the perfect assassin, and he's right where he's supposed to be, the prince's best buddy. What more can you ask?'

'Too much best buddy, too little dead prince,' the summoner said. 'Let's face it, it's not going to happen. Your assassin is a dud. You've let me down, Xorth. You've let me down, and now I want my pound of flesh. Or rather, I want my pound of demon.'

Xorth's human head, balanced precariously atop the giant slug he'd again chosen as a body, blanched.

'Y-you can't do this,' he stammered. 'I'll find another one, a better one, right away, I promise – '

'Too late,' the summoner said, shaking his head in false regret. 'And I can. I will. But I'm not without mercy. You get to decide whether you're going to give me what I want voluntarily, or whether I have to cut it out of you. The first option will cause you only some slight discomfort, and a minor lessening of your status that I'm sure you'll be able to make up for in no time at all. The second entails an amount of pain you can't even begin to imagine. It's up to you.'

'W-what exactly do you want?'

'Not all that much, really. Just a piece of you, one of the major demons you've incorporated. Ashotl, for example, or Qazarr, or Cratch... no, I think I want Ashotl. Mean bastard, that. Just what I need. Hand him over quietly, and we can part as friends.'

Xorth squirmed and wriggled, trying in vain to find a weak spot in the circles. He sent a questing feeler through the gap, hurriedly retracting it when he encountered the sphere. The eyes of his human head widened in panic.

'You can't do this,' he whined. 'It's indecent. You're breaking the compact. You're way out of bounds, and you know it.'

'I know no such thing. And your time's running out.' The summoner interleaved his slender fingers, forming a promise of pain.

'All right, all right,' Xorth said hurriedly. 'Since I don't seem to have a choice, I'll give you Cratch – '

'Ashotl.'

'Ashotl, yes. But I'll have you know that I deeply resent this and will lodge a formal complaint with the arbitrators of the Incantaria. This is absolutely no way to treat an old and faithful associate. There *are* rules, you know.'

'Be my guest. And now, spit him out. I want him in the other circle, and I mean immediately.'

Xorth extruded a finger-like appendage and stuck it down his throat, his face turning a greenish hue as he choked and heaved. He swayed, quickly extending three pseudo-pods to steady himself.

His mouth opened wider than should have been possible, jaws stretching until they dislocated with an audible crack. The head of a fat, black snake appeared in his maw, testing the air with a forked, darting tongue.

Xorth gave one last, tremendous heave, and the rest of the snake slithered out of his mouth and thumped to the floor in the smaller of the two circles, coiling in a puddle of slime.

Instantly, it reared up and began to grow, morphing into the shape of what was probably the most hair-raisingly ugly demon that had ever sprung from the Warren's murky bowels. It was black as a subterranean cave at midnight, its humpbacked, twisted body covered with random patches of ugly warts and needle-sharp spikes.

Xorth and Ashotl stared at each other hungrily, facing off across the narrow gap between their respective prisons. Even in their current, precarious positions, their primal demonic feeding instincts were drawing them towards uncontrolled mayhem.

Just in time, the string parted, burnt through by the candle's flame. The piece of chalk fell over the gap, sealing it.

The cherry-sized ball of blood and rare metals began to glow red, and did what it was supposed to do. Before the demon Ashotl had time to react or even grasp what was happening, the artifact sucked him up, helpless like a leaf before the maw of a cyclone. Xorth looked on in horror, bug-eyed and trembling.

'Atrocity,' he whispered. 'Abomination. Anathema. This will have terrible consequences. Terrible.'

'Oh, get out of here, you old washerwoman,' the summoner said, releasing Xorth without further ceremony. As Xorth faded, the demon's gaze remained fixed on him, and the summoner saw hatred congeal in the demon's eyes, a hatred so overwhelmingly intense it caused even him, the hardened manipulator of demons, a frisson of unease.

He shook himself. Irrelevant. He had what he needed.

Scuffing the chalk lines with his shoe to open the circle, he bent down and picked up the sphere. It was hot to the touch, as it should be. Compressing a demon into such a miniscule space necessarily led to a certain amount of internal friction. He dropped the sphere into his coat pocket. Then he blew out the candle, shrugged on his cloak, grabbed a shovel leaning against the wall, and left. One last element missing. One more task to perform before the night was over.

Making less noise than the wings of a moth, he climbed up two sets of stairs to ground level and left the building through the servants' entrance, casting a simple spell that blinded the guard at the door to his passing.

Outside, he directed his steps towards the burial ground adjacent the temple of Sulcen the Smith. Contrary to the other denominations, all of whom preferred cremation, the Greys buried their dead. He happened to know that there had been an interment this very day. Perfect.

As he walked through the dark, deserted streets and alleys, he mulled over another recent development. Two days ago, he'd heard disturbing news from the priests of Amut. Though he was only very loosely affiliated with the Kingskeep chapter of the Temple – or with any of them, for that matter – he kept himself informed on what went on there, thinking the Blacks might eventually come in handy at some later stage in his plans.

It seemed they'd had a visitor from the east, an emissary from someone who called himself Ummuz, purporting to be the reincarnation of the god Amut himself. The emissary had apparently gotten the whole lot of them to swear fealty to this Ummuz, extracting their solemn oaths to faithfully and unquestioningly follow and obey his master. And Kingskeep hadn't been this envoy's first stop, either. Reportedly, he'd crossed the mountains sometime this past spring and had been touring the kingdoms ever since.

Religion aside, the summoner found all this rather disturbing. The Blacks were not your usual meek, trusting, and malleable flock of sheep. Many of them, he knew, paid only lip service to their so-called faith, saw it as a convenient front behind which to carry on all the more undisturbed with their true vocation, the dark arts. For them to swear away their autonomy was a highly uncharacteristic thing to do, and he could think of only two explanations for their unexpected behavior.

The first was that they'd sent the emissary off with an oath in his baggage they never meant to keep, which implied that they'd seen some way to turn the whole thing to their own advantage. In that case, he'd have to watch them a lot more closely than he'd been doing so far. It was one thing to keep them as a reserve force in case he ever needed such a thing. If they got ideas of making their own bid for power in Dunmark, he'd have to do something about them.

The second scenario was far more worrisome. It entailed the Blacks giving their oaths neither entirely of their own free will nor with their judgment unclouded, exposed to an influence stronger than their own ingrained penchant for tampering, rigging, lying, and cheating. The manipulators manipulated. The fathers of all hypocrisy conned into another's fold.

He himself didn't believe in gods, nor did he usually care how others chose to relieve themselves of their devotional urges unless he saw some way to exploit those needs for his own purposes. Just what he'd had half a mind to do with the Blacks. And now it seemed someone else had usurped them, preempting him on what he regarded as his own, private patch.

By itself, that wasn't much of a problem; he could do without the Blacks, work around them. And as far as the intrusion onto his territory went, he did possess the pragmatism to put expediency before pride. No, what bothered him was the speed of this 'conversion', and the extent to which the Blacks had given themselves over. It implied foul play at a level he couldn't but secretly admire. It reeked of masterful manipulation, of a skillfully employed fanaticism that bordered on the rabid, and, worst of all, of a self-assured grab for power that seemed almost surely predestined to collide with his own interests sooner or later.

He had an uneasy feeling that, before too long, he'd be hearing from this Ummuz character in a more direct fashion. He sincerely hoped the man was nothing more than an – albeit highly intelligent – religious fanatic, however powerful, ruthless, insane or corrupt, and not something much, much worse. There had been rumors. So far, he'd taken note but refused to give them any credence.

He resolved that, should he ever have reason to believe otherwise, he'd not see his carefully laid plans and the patient work of years overthrown by what had to be, if those rumors were even half true, a raging madman on a path of belated revenge.

He'd find a way to work around that, too. And if not, he'd kill the man. Thankfully, with his newly discovered method of employing demons, he'd have a clear shot at the usurper. A sure kill. Once the man was eliminated, his followers would likely scatter or, better yet, the summoner might make use of them himself.

He reached the graveyard and pushed open the creaking gate, only a few short steps away now from the completion of his task, and one step closer to the fruition of his plans.

Duty is not collective; it is personal.

Calvin Coolidge

29 Digger's Row

s Hunsicker had foreseen, the FBI's presence was short-lived. CIA and Homeland Security put in guest appearances, but the military – DIA, he reckoned – ousted them practically before the rotors of the choppers they flew in on came to a standstill. Lying in the brush thirty yards from the clearing, he studied the as yet small and provisional military installation going up on the eastern edge of the clearing.

Under the cover of night, several camo-colored prefabs had been airlifted in by heavy-duty choppers: a couple of labs, an HQ and comms unit, antennae and satellite dishes, a mess hut and tents for barracks. Everything, including the artifact itself, was hidden under camouflage netting. Army engineers were putting up an inner perimeter, clearing brush and trees and erecting a twelve foot-high chain-link fence in a neat, regulation rectangle, no matter the space it was to enclose was almost perfectly round.

Another work detail was almost done clearing a way of access from the nearest road, a two-lane blacktop cutting through the forest twelve miles to the east. For most of those twelve miles, all they'd had to do was follow an old logging road and a series of firebreaks, with nothing bigger than brush and saplings barring their way. Only the last couple hundred yards or so were old-growth forest. They'd started clearing that less than two days ago, working day and night, and he could hear the chainsaws and bulldozers in the distance, cutting up felled trees and removing stumps. Where the access road forked off from the blacktop they'd put up a gate and a guardhouse, and from there they were already busy surveying and preparing the ground for the construction of a second fence, an outer perimeter that would likely enclose an area of close to sixty square miles, if not more, once it was finished.

Hunsicker hated to think what it would do to the wildlife in the area, cutting off game trails and migratory routes used by countless generations of animals.

A gaggle of military and civilian scientists had set up all sorts of instruments at a minimum safe distance from the artifact, poking, prodding and measuring to their hearts' delight, though very, very cautiously. In other words, the thing had them fascinated beyond their wildest scientific dreams – and it scared them shitless.

Hunsicker crawled a couple of yards closer. Thankfully, they hadn't cut the brush in the clearing itself yet, leaving him some cover. So long as one of them didn't actually step on him, he was good. But time was getting short. Once the chain link was up all the way a-round, things would get a lot more complicated. He had a feeling that when it was done it would be more than just a simple fence. They'd probably electrify it, install motion sensors, maybe, and whatever other gizmos they had nowadays. Animals would get electrocuted, and likely play havoc with the sensors.

If Marge could see me now, he thought wryly, *she'd probably tell me I was acting like a silly old fool, sticking my nose where it was apt to get bitten off, crawling around the wintry woods like an over-aged boy scout, getting myself in trouble way over my head.*

But he knew she'd also be secretly proud of him, for not giving up on a missing boy whom nobody else was interested in anymore.

And he did know something about what he was doing.

Though he'd never served in the armed forces, as a boy he'd been lucky enough to receive a different kind of education from his Salish grandfather, his mother's father. He'd spent whole summers out in the woods camping, fishing, and learning the old ways, and he'd kept up the skills his grandfather had taught him ever since. He could say without conceit or boastfulness that there probably weren't that many people who could out-stealth or out-stalk him in a natural surrounding, and even less who could best him at tracking. Hunting was in his genes, and he was good at it.

He'd never fired a gun in his life, not even in his job in law enforcement. But give him a bow, and he'd hit anything he aimed for – nine times out of ten dead center. His way of hunting was a bit unconventional, though. When his grandfather had judged him ready, he'd let him kill a single animal, a lame old deer that wouldn't have survived the winter. Then he'd told the boy that, next time he killed something, it would be out of true necessity or not at all. Hunting was no game, nor should it be seen as a sport.

Since then, Hunsicker hunted, but not to kill. He could spend hours stalking an animal until he had the perfect shot, until he and his prey were in the best possible positions in respect to each other, him with arrow nocked and bow drawn, knowing with absolute certainty

525

that if he released – now – it would be a quick, clean kill.

Only he never made the shot. Instead, he slowly released the tension from the string, unnocked the arrow and put it back in the quiver. It gave him all the satisfaction he needed. Especially if he managed to slip away afterwards without the animal ever realizing he'd been there in the first place.

Second to his deep, unconditional love for Marge, the wilderness was his one true passion, and he continued to spend as much time in it as he could. Marge deeply disapproved of killing living things, but because he didn't kill, and because Marge was a generous person, she'd allowed him all the time and solitude he needed. And she'd had her own passion: horses. She'd inherited a dilapidated farmhouse and fifty acres just four miles outside of town from an eccentric bachelor uncle and always kept between three and five horses there. After their only son Rick had died of leukemia fifteen years ago, they'd fixed up the house and moved out there for good.

When Marge knew she didn't have much longer to live, she'd begun selling the horses, the ones that were more particular and difficult to handle first, because she wanted to make sure they ended up in good hands. But she'd died with two still in the stables, Doug and Sheila, a bay gelding and a dun mare. Hunsicker had kept them for reasons that had more to do with Marge than with the horses themselves. Being around them always made him feel nearer to her, as if at those times her loving spirit somehow drew closer to the world of the living. As if she were there, just beyond the great divide, invisible but watching, intangible but participating nonetheless. It made caring for them no trouble at all. Now, he was doubly glad he'd kept them.

Listening to the people gathered at the artifact, he'd reached several conclusions. One: if the eggheads had their way and nobody interfered, they'd go on measuring and recording until doomsday, theorizing about singularities, wormholes, folded space-time, and multiple parallel universes without ever actually touching the thing. Two: there was some level of disagreement between them and the army guys, who were, three: definitely the more enterprising lot.

An hour ago, to vehement protest from the nerd faction, they'd begun doing some more practical experimentation, tossing all sorts of objects tied to strings through the faintly shimmering curtain between the columns, and then pulling them back out to see what had happened to them. The results were quite interesting.

A stick, for example, came back unchanged, was still a stick. A knife remained a knife. A screwdriver returned still recognizable as a screwdriver, though its synthetic grip had turned to wood. Then they tried tossing through a handgun with the magazine and chambered round prudently removed beforehand. When they pulled it back out by the string to the horrified screams of the lone female scientist present – obviously a serious sufferer of murophobia – it wasn't a gun anymore, not even close. There was now a dead rat attached to the string. A large dead rat, as Hunsicker gleaned from various excitedly shouted comments. There seemed to be general agreement on the fact that this was no normal rat, either. Not with such long, wicked teeth and claws, and definitely not with scales instead of fur.

Unsettled and slightly abashed by the lady scientist's reaction more than by the results of the experiment, the army guys momentarily ceded ground in the struggle over procedure, and the eggheads resumed their explorations by remote control. Half an hour later, the

527

clearing operation broke for lunch, and blessed silence descended on the forest once more as everyone convened on the mess hut.

The people at the singularity interrupted their work as well, heading for the source of food in two distinct groups, the techs leading with single-minded purpose. The scientists distractedly ambled along behind them, debating and gesticulating, the whole group stopping every few feet when one of them had what he or she thought was a particularly relevant point to make.

Only a guard remained behind, a young soldier who looked like he still belonged in highschool, tightly gripping his submachine gun and surveilling the perimeter with restless, darting eyes as if he expected hordes of Russian spies or bomb-girdled jihadists to come pouring out of the woods at any moment.

Hunsicker had seen and heard enough.

He was about to back out and make for the tree line when he noticed movement out of the corner of his eye, something that didn't fit the overall pattern. He went still and waited, letting his vision unfocus and open up to a wide-angle view.

Something stirred again, and this time he got a fix on it. It was a soldier, wearing some kind of sci-fi battle dress, the camo so perfect he was practically impossible to see unless you caught him moving. Even then, he wasn't more than a slight disturbance in the landscape. Something you might easily mistake for, say, a branch swaying in the wind or a bird flitting by.

As Hunsicker watched, the man removed an access panel from the mess hut's heating unit. He pulled an object that looked like a soft drink can from one of his cargo pockets, twisted something on the top, shoved it inside the unit and replaced the panel. Then he went still again. Within seconds, Hunsicker's eyes had drifted ever so slightly and he'd lost sight of the man. It was eerie.

He stayed put and waited. After a few minutes, there was motion again. The man crept up to a window in the side of the hut and looked in. Apparently satisfied with what he saw, he raised an arm and signaled all clear. Moments later, Hunsicker heard several engines approaching. He watched as four quads and a humvee with a heavy machine gun mounted on the cab's roof came curving and bouncing through the cutting at a speed just short of reckless.

The guard at the artifact, who had noticed nothing of what had been going on, suddenly went tense and alert. The mess hut door stayed closed, nobody coming to see what the commotion was about. Hunsicker reckoned they were all fast asleep in there.

The newcomers drove up to within twenty feet of the column and stopped in a neat row, the lead vehicle's bumper nearly touching the array of instruments that blocked further progress. The quads were civilian models, black with leaping panthers stenciled on the tanks in gleaming gold. The four soldiers riding double on the quads dismounted, and another two scrambled from the back of the humvee, forming a defensive perimeter as if they were in the process of invading an enemy camp. All of them wore the same, futuristic-looking battle dress, though theirs was set to a neutral olive. Their visored helmets looked like something out of a science fiction movie, and were probably stuffed with all the latest gimmicks dreamed up by the arms industry's overpaid nerds at the expense of the unsuspecting taxpayers. Hunsicker hoped they didn't start looking around in heat-seeking

529

mode. If they had it and were using it, they'd spot him immediately.

The drivers and the soldier manning the machine gun stayed put, leaving the engines running. An officer stepped from the humvee's cab, approaching the guard with the kind of steroid swagger that shouted two-hundred-percent alpha dog.

Hunsicker didn't get more than a fleeting glimpse of his face, but it was enough to tell him that here was a man firmly and unquestioningly grounded in the material side of things, a man to whom pumping iron and killing people was likely a religion of the self, and the military his cathedral. This was the type who took it for granted that God was always on his side, no matter what he did. Which was even true – if you had Him confused with your own, over-inflated ego.

Hunsicker had had dealings with such men, and he knew that it was mostly a question of chance which side of the law they came down on. Wherever that was, they were dangerous. A uniform didn't make them better men, only bad men in uniform. The guard saluted.

'At ease, soldier,' the officer said.

'Sir,' the guard said.

'We'll be moving through here shortly,' the officer said. 'And we need to get this stuff out of the way.' He gestured dismissively at the array of highly sophisticated and probably exorbitantly expensive machinery.

'Sir,' the soldier said, squinting at the officer's nametag. 'Major Brown, sir. With all due respect, sir, I can't let you go through. Orders from general Grady, sir.'

'Yes, well,' the major said. 'I have orders that outrank the general's, and they say I'm going through here, no matter what. Now step aside smartly, and let my men get on with it.'

'Sir,' the guard replied, visibly uncomfortable. 'I think it would be a good idea if you talked to general Grady.'

'You think, huh? Well, should you ever make it to a pay grade where you're required to do any thinking, let me know, and we can talk about it. Meanwhile, get out of my way.'

'Sir. All due respect, sir, it could be dangerous,' the guard blurted out.

'Dangerous? Hell, soldier, what exactly do you think you signed up for? This is the military, not a goddamned belly-dancing fag parade. Now move over, or I'll have you moved.'

Stung, the guard found his backbone. He straightened, bringing the muzzle of his gun up to point, if not exactly, then almost, at the officer.

'Sorry, sir. I can't do that.'

The major gave an almost imperceptible hand signal, and one of his men fired a silenced shot from a slim, long-barreled pistol. The guard stood swaying for a moment, a surprised and rapidly dulling look in his eyes, the business end of a stun dart buried in his neck. Ever so slowly, he began to topple. Another man stepped forward to catch him and ease him to the ground.

Brown barked an order, and his men began to move the scientists' instruments out of the way, not very gently.

'Excuse me!' a voice suddenly called. It was one of the eggheads. The chief egghead, actually. He'd just come out of one of the port-a-johns and was stumbling towards the soldiers, still fumbling with his fly. 'You there! What the dickens do you think you're doing?'

Huffing and puffing, he reached the scene where his precious

531

work was being vandalized.

'Please don't touch those,' he told the soldiers sternly. 'They'll take hours to reposition and recalibrate.'

'And you are?' the major asked.

'Alfred Herkenheimer. Professor Alfred Herkenheimer,' the scientist said, drawing himself up. 'I'm the head of the scientific team here. Please tell your men to immediately desist from further disturbing my instruments.'

'Sorry,' the major said. 'Our mission is top priority, and your stuff's in the way.'

'In the way of what? And who are you, anyway?' Herkenheimer asked, studying the officer's nametag. 'Brown?' Then it began to dawn on him. 'You're some kind of commando, aren't you? What are they called, black somethings?'

'You got that right,' Brown said, grinning humorlessly. 'Blacker than the devil's asshole. Needless to say, you've never seen us. Right?'

'R-right,' the professor stuttered as another, even more disturbing revelation hit him. 'Y-you're not intending to enter the singularity, are you? Because you can't. Most assuredly not with those weapons and vehicles, and quite probably not without them, either. To even try would be not just extremely foolish, but quite possibly lethal. And besides – '

Brown sighed. 'Mancuso. Shut this guy up, will you?'

Mancuso, the man with the stun gun, was already in position. He shot the professor neatly in the buttock, catching him as he blacked out and easing him down beside the unconscious guard.

The major studied the monitor connected to one of the scientists' machines for a moment. Then he touched a control unit on his chest, and his suit changed colors, morphing into something that looked like it would render him nearly impossible to see in an environment consisting mainly of grey, jumbled rock. His men followed suit.

He raised his hand and made a circling motion. The soldiers on foot took up flanking positions on both sides of the small convoy. Five of them carried assault rifles that looked to Hunsicker as if they were several generations ahead of mainstream military technology; the sixth held a rocket launcher balanced on his shoulder.

Brown vaulted onto the humvee's bed and stood behind the machine gun, feet planted wide. An überwarrior hungering for battle, Hunsicker thought, a titan unleashed, eager to face whatever hell might choose to throw at him. The man was a walking cliché, but that made him neither safe nor predictable. He slapped the cab's roof twice with the flat of his hand. Engines were gunned, and the convoy moved off, vehicles and soldiers disappearing one by one into the artifact's shimmering curtain.

Not having to bother with stealth anymore, Hunsicker got up and hurried back to a dense stand of cedars half a mile away where he'd left Doug and Sheila. This was the best chance he'd get, a godsend if ever he'd seen one.

The horses were saddled, packed, and ready to go. Though he hadn't known about the artifact's being so peculiar concerning certain objects, nothing he'd brought along should be a problem. He had his two favorite bows, a sixty-pound recurve and an eighty-pound yew longbow, two quivers with twenty-five arrows each, broadheads and round-points, extra strings. He'd made all of it himself, using only natural materials. He had a razor-sharp skinning knife and a twenty-four inch Bowie that was heavy enough to serve as a hatchet. Hooks and line for fishing, a couple of tarps made from waxed canvas. Two woolen blankets, a small pot and pan, eating utensils, flint and tinder, provisions for a month. He was wearing a padded woolen jacket over buckskins and long, woolen underwear, moccasins, and a leather hat. He was somewhat dubious about the treaded rubber soles on the moccasins, but any other footwear he possessed would have presented the same problem. He'd just have to see, and hope for the best. He could have taken only a knife and a blanket and used his woodsman's skills to make what he needed to survive, but that would have been a time-consuming undertaking. Besides, he wasn't a young man anymore, so providing for a minimum of comfort seemed only sane and sensible. Which was why he also carried twenty Silver Eagles in a neck pouch under his shirt. He disliked the idea of money as a matter of principle, and the damn coins had cost him close to seven hundred dollars, but you never knew.

As of yesterday, he was on a long overdue, three-week vacation. He'd left the department in Clyde's capable hands, and knew there wouldn't be a problem even if he was forced to stay away longer than planned. He'd already hinted at the possibility to avoid undue worry in case he wasn't back on time.

As he headed back to the clearing with the artifact, Sheila took a not so playful nip at Doug's withers, clearly offended that she'd been relegated to lowly packhorse duty. Hunsicker turned around in the saddle and looked her straight in the rebellious eye, raising a warning finger. She got the message, though she continued to sulk, letting him feel her sentiments through the lead by hanging back and allowing it to tighten every so often, just a little, but enough to jog Hunsicker's arm and thus make her point. He let her.

Twenty minutes after he'd left the site of the singularity, he was back. Nothing had changed in the meantime. Herkenheimer and the guard were still out cold, and there was no sign of activity in the huts. He stopped twenty yards from the Gate to collect himself, taking a couple of deep breaths. Then he heeled Doug to a canter, and the three of them plunged into the shimmering curtain.

Feeling as if he were tumbling head over heels, Hunsicker fell through a crack in reality. With a gut-churning wrench of deceleration, time stopped. It simply ceased to flow, became eternity, a non-place where any attempt at measurement was as impossible as it would have been pointless. There was nothing left to measure, and nothing to measure it by. He was caught up in darkness, in a river of shadows and shades, but he had no perception of movement or direction. He could have been sweeping along in a rushing torrent, or immersed in an endlessly drawn-out, stagnant pool.

He also seemed to have lost his physical self – at least it was somewhere far, far away, attached to his awareness by the flimsiest of strands, good only for sending vague and muffled signals of distress, frantic warnings from a panic-drenched organism he was powerless to heed.

Plus the connection went only one way. He couldn't communicate back, couldn't command his body to move even a finger, much less do anything about the distant, wildly pounding heart and the desperately laboring lungs. He was unable to tell whether he was still sitting

535

in the saddle, or falling, or sprawled senseless with a split skull and broken bones.

But what happened to his body seemed minor compared to the smothering darkness his spirit-self was suspended in, a terrifying, shadowy nothingness that wrapped itself around him like a poisonous cloak, compressing and reducing his very soul to a pinprick in a single, lightless dimension.

For this was not merely a darkness, not in any sense.

It was a metaphorical ooze of blood, shit, vomit, and tears, a creeping flux of moans and sobs, wails and screams. It was a dreadful current filled with the sum of all horrors, comprised of every imaginable variant of human suffering, of humiliation and degradation, confusion and pain, misery and grief. Fed by every cruel and heartless act, by every expression of baseness and inhumanity mankind had ever concieved of and executed, it was violation, rape, torture, mutilation, murder – physical and psychological. It was a perpetually renewed fluency driven by arrogance and intolerance, by hypocrisy and manipulation, by greed and selfishness, by all manner of abuse and oppression, by hatred and bitterness – and above and beyond all else, by fear.

Helpless, he was carried along, surrounded by the fragments and shreds of souls ripped and sundered from the millions of victims and perpetrators of an infinity of crimes. He was touched by every single one of them, was pierced, penetrated to his very core by the sad and terrible fate of each one of these debased and damaged beings. He was immersed in their agonies, felt what all of them had suffered. It was like being held under and slowly drowned in an emotional cesspool.

The whole of it was a vast, dark force, a terrible energy, and in a fleeting, half-glimpsed instant he understood the most terrifying thing of all: there was an intent behind it, a will, malevolent beyond all comprehension. There was a purpose and a direction to this insanity.

He nearly broke then. Less than a hair's breadth separated him at that moment from losing himself in every sense, not just the physical, and only a desperate act of will saved him from a violent free fall into utter madness.

With a sudden rush, velocity returned, wrenching him from zero back to the normal speed of existence. The dispersed elements of his self came together again as he broke through, out of the Gate and onto the other side.

He half slipped, half fell from the saddle and sat on the stony ground for long minutes, gasping for breath, shivering uncontrollably, tears streaming down his face. He felt abused, sullied, debased. He felt terribly, painfully ashamed to be part of a species that was capable of such unspeakable behavior.

Very slowly, he began the painful work of putting himself back together again. Only when he was convinced that all of him had come through and he hadn't lost a part somewhere along the way did he begin to take in his surroundings. Miraculously, he was still holding Doug and Sheila's reins, and a good thing too. They were as frightened and shaken as he was, snorting and sidling, blowing and sweating as if they'd run for miles. Unchecked, they would have likely bolted and run until they broke a leg or simply dropped dead from exhaustion.

With a pang of apprehension, he remembered the black ops team that had come through before him. He heaved himself up and stood on weak, trembling legs, looking around. There was no sign of them, only a jumble of rocks and boulders that seemed to stretch on forever in every direction.

There was a huge standing stone right in front of him, matte black and humming like a high-voltage transformer. Behind him stood two dark, slender columns exactly like the ones back in the clearing, and beyond them a tower of the same black stuff rose into the grey sky like an alien skyscraper, all smooth, seamless surface and sharp, bladed angles.

The place had an abandoned, empty feel to it, but he had a distinct impression of being watched, as if the building itself possessed some kind of awareness and was scrutinizing him.

And something else emanated from the tower, something that raised goose bumps on his skin and made him shudder involuntarily. If he'd wanted to go there and put a name to it, he would have said it was pure Evil.

He took time to calm the horses, stroking their necks and speaking soft, soothing words, benefiting from the moment of communion as much as they did. Then he led them around the upright stone, careful that neither he nor they came in touch with it. There was a cleared track leading up to the tall, closed double doors of the tower, and another, wider one crossing it at right angles and leading off to either side. Hunsicker squatted and studied the dusty surface, remaining that way for several minutes.

When he rose, he knew at least something of what had happened in this place. Most important of all, Billy had been here. He'd come stumbling through the Gate, probably even more disoriented than Hunsicker himself, only to be yanked off his feet by something that walked upright on three-toed, clawed feet. The size of those tracks did not bode well for Billy. On the other hand, there was no blood, so it was likely he'd still been alive at this point. It looked like the thing, whatever it was, had carried him inside the tower.

Hunsicker slowly moved over to the great doors and saw that at some stage the boy had come out again, walking on his own. Some-one else had left the tower with him, and both sets of tracks stopped where they intersected with parallel lines made by the wheels of a wagon or coach. The coach, drawn by a team of four, had arrived from the left, turned around, and then driven off again after having taken on the passengers. The three-toed creature and another one like it had also left, probably at the same time as the coach, loping along behind it.

The main thing was that Billy was alive.

Hunsicker would go after him, and sooner or later he'd find him. What troubled him more were the other tracks he found. The imprints of the soldier's combat boots were unmistakable, and all of them were accounted for, but, starting this side of Gate, there wasn't even the ghost of a tire tread to be found.

What was there instead, deeply impressed in the dirt and flanked by the tracks of what looked to be four big cats, was something Hunsicker had never seen before. He could have made an educated guess at what had left those impressions, but the notion was just way, way too crazy. And the idea of having to go after and get around something like that to reach Billy scared him more than he cared to admit.

But it didn't stop him from going anyway. Grim-faced, he heaved himself into the saddle and set out, heading due west, the way everyone else had gone.

❖　❖　❖

In this our age of infamy / man's choice is but to be / a tyrant, traitor, prisoner: / no other choice has he.

Alexander Pushkin

30 Kingskeep

krit was wildly, madly, hopelessly in love. One look into the prince's eyes was all it had taken. One short instant. Standing there in that draughty antechamber with Varna, pretending she was the person who belonged in this handsome, masculine body that wasn't hers and – gods forefend – never would be, nauseated by the blur of pompous, vapid, inconsequential faces passing by, tarted-up strangers strutting with self-importance but to her eyes only parading their utter insignificance, she'd almost been ready to discard the whole idea of looking for a subtle approach and to just settle for getting the job done any which way as soon as the first viable opportunity presented itself. Until.

Until, suddenly, *he* had appeared, and her world had been turned upside down in one violent, extra-systolic leap of the heart. Everything she knew and believed, everything she was had been completely dismantled in the time it took to exchange one glance with him, and now she was left with the impossible task of putting back together a myriad of disparate pieces, fragments of her former self that simply wouldn't fit anymore, no matter how she tried to make them. Disconcerted was a much too mild description for the state she was in. In a complete shambles, was more like it.

One moment, she'd fall into the blackest of depressions, the sheer impracticality of it all swatting her down into utter hopelessness, smearing her all over the dank bottom of the deep, dark pit of self-loathing, and she'd see herself as what she was: an impostor, a lie, and worse, a traitor. A demon, for gods' sake, who fancied herself a female, imprisoned in a body that was not only stolen but male, the complete antithesis to the self-image she'd cultivated and cherished already in the Warren, a persona she'd come to wholly believe in because it just felt so absolutely, inescapably right.

Then again, she'd find herself woolgathering in some inopportune corner of the house or the keep, waking from a dream, a blissful fantasy in which she had a body that perfectly suited her disposition – meaning beautiful, gorgeous, human, and above all, female. Her beloved prince was hers, the boundless wealth of feeling she held for him was wholly reciprocated, he was going to make her his princess bride, or maybe his mistress, that would do too, would do wonder-fully, she wouldn't ask for more; she'd be quite content with that, as long as he loved her...

Gods! Here she was, at it again, and in the middle of the keep's lower main passage. Two young chambermaids, their arms laden with lin-ens, had interrupted their errand and stopped to watch her daydream-ing, whispering in each other's shapely ears, a look of amused curi-osity on their faces.

To distract from her embarrassment, and just for the hell of it, Ykrit flashed them a dazzling smile that predictably elicited blushes and giggles and, just like that, conjured up a sexually charged atmosphere that practically set the air crackling.

Immediately, she blushed too, hating herself, and hastened off without a backwards glance, in all probability leaving behind two very baffled maids and another tidbit for the rumor mill that had likely already begun to grind over the odd behavior of the very attractive but slightly deranged squire from Osona.

She needed to hurry. This morning she was supposed to accompany Orrin on an outing, a ride in the countryside to meet some friends of his. She was already running late, having been sent to deliver a message at the keep and then tarried on the way out. Yet another note to the Regent, to remind him of the meeting he'd been putting off for three solid weeks now, citing his bad health as the reason. It was true he hadn't shown himself in public since All Gods. But, sick or no, he was still the Regent and ought to make an effort, was what *she* thought.

A blind person could see that the nobles were up to no good, plots and intrigues brewing right and left, and the town's usually bustling, cheerful atmosphere seemed to be flagging lately, as if even the ordinary folk sensed that all was not as it should be. Mayhap their deeply ingrained sense for approaching hardship was sounding a first, faint warning, and they were instinctively preparing to duck away and hide from whatever difficult times were coming; after all, it was always the little people whom adversity hit first and hardest.

Orrin had so far refused to force the issue, not wanting to cause bad blood and strife, and rightly so. But in Ykrit's opinion the time was fast approaching when he'd have to change his thinking, or else see the kingdom plunged into chaos and torn apart by the vultures already circling in strength.

Love, intrigue, rebellion; it was all too much for her.

Not even counting the totally overwhelming experience of having been unceremoniously dumped into this alien and frighteningly fascinating world of humans, it was all enough to drive a person to the brink of insanity, she thought with a mixture of anger and despondency, hastening her steps.

As Desmond, she could have probably had all the wenches she wanted, whenever she wanted, but she felt no desire at all in that direction. And the one person she wanted as herself, as Ykrit, she couldn't have. One thing was for certain though, and that was that Orrin hadn't the slightest inclination towards young men, no matter how attractive, and in any case the mere thought of that kind of liaison turned Ykrit's stomach. Thoroughly. She was a woman, gods damn it! And there she went, invoking the gods again, so help her, entreating with the arch-enemies of demonkind like a good, mindless little human – and how she wished that she was!

But, human or demon, she was a woman, and not about to betray her love with a double, no, a threefold deception. It would make her not only a demon pretending to be a human, and a woman pretending to be a man, but also a woman pretending to be a man pretending to be interested in other men, and specifically, in Orrin. Shameful! Disgusting! Out of the question.

Actually, there was a fourth element of deception in play, something she'd been putting off for much too long and had yet to deal with decisively: she was pretending to be Orrin's faithful squire, his friend and protector – when in truth she'd been sent here for the express purpose of murdering him. Three weeks, and she hadn't lifted a finger. If Xorth ever got his hands on her... no, better not think about it.

She made it back to the Tondern townhouse just in time.

In the courtyard, the grooms had four horses saddled, stamping and snorting and eager to run, their breath pluming white in the cold air. Orrin was just that moment clattering down the perron stairs, Tormod and Iomar following at a more sedate pace, all of them as happy as the animals to be getting out and about on a day that promised to be perfectly gorgeous.

They wore fur-lined cloaks, hats, and gloves, for it was the beginning of December and winter had arrived in earnest a week earlier, bringing a foot and a half of snow and freezing temperatures.

Iomar was carrying saddlebags with oats for the horses and provisions for a midday meal, as they probably wouldn't be back before late afternoon, and Tormod had brought with him a basket of leftover bones from last night's dinner, which he threw to the dogs as consolation for not being allowed along this day. Orrin had been firm on that point, saying that the friends they were going to visit would be less than thrilled to see them show up with a pack of huge, slobbering hounds. Ykrit didn't find them all that big or fearsome – but then, what did she know?

'Stay!' Tormod told the nervous, yipping dogs, torn between their treats and the vain hope that a hunt was in the making.

Last to mount, he handed the freezing groom the empty basket in exchange for the reins. He heaved his considerable mass into the saddle with surprising ease, and then they were off, riding down the street, a white band of hard-packed snow churned, pitted, and tamped down again by countless feet and hooves, unsullied as yet except for the occasional pile of frozen horse droppings.

Their mounts daintily avoided the icy ruts left by carts and wagons bringing produce to town and keep. Despite every storeroom, larder and cellar having been filled to the top during the autumn months and the merchant traffic having dwindled down to a seasonal trickle, there were always things to be transported into and about the town: flour from the mills for the bakers, meat from the farms for the tables of the lords and the wealthy, hides for the tanners, stones and timber for the masons and carpenters renovating and adding a new wing onto the venerable but time-worn temple of Elil, their work going on uninterrupted even in this bitter cold.

They reached the gate, and suddenly they were out of the shadows, out in the sunshine and a pristine, glittering landscape straight out of a winter's tale, the cloudless sky a vault of deep, vivid blue spanning a sheer boundless expanse of dazzling white.

Orrin, riding in the lead, gave a whoop of pure joy and spurred his horse to a canter, and they all followed suit, letting the animals run for a stretch. Ykrit would have fallen after scant yards, but Desmond was – or had been – an expert rider as well as an accomplished fighter, and the body she was wearing retained the memory of every skill its original owner had mastered during his twenty-five or so years of tenancy.

As it was, she enjoyed the ride, appreciated the feeling of the large, warm beast beneath her, the great strength and firmness of it, muscles bunching and stretching as it ran, seemingly tireless, its every movement more deliberate, more exaggerated and at the same time more fluid in the deep snow. All around her was pureness and silence, accentuated rather than disturbed by the soft, muffled thumping of hooves, the jingle of tack and creaking of leather, and the snorts and whickers of the beasts, content to be out in the open and running after days of being confined to the stables.

The first rush of energy burned off, they slowed to a walk, and she dug out her Desmond persona, guiding her mount up alongside Orrin's.

'Desmond. What a day,' Orrin said, glancing over at her but avoiding her eyes, as they had both been doing for some time now, shying away from the jolts and the charged atmosphere that were the unfailing result of any direct eye contact between them, something neither of them knew how to handle and that only led to fumbled silences. It was infinitely awkward for her, to want nothing more than to be able to communicate her feelings by any means possible, and at the same time having to constantly rein herself in and watch her every step, terrified that Orrin might get the impression Desmond was interested in him in an unnatural way and put and end to an embarrassing and intolerable situation by sending her away. So she did her best to play the hearty fellow and faithful squire, and hoped that Orrin would continue to go along and not see through her falseness, though she couldn't help but feel that it must be glaringly obvious to everyone around them.

'Splendid, my lord,' she said. 'I feel lucky.'

'Lucky, indeed,' Orrin said. 'And not just to be gifted with such beauty, but also to be on your way to meet some very special people. Folks right out of a fairy tale, though they hate it when you say so. I suspect they think of us as big, bumbling, and slightly daft fellows, precariously balanced on two large left feet, not altogether safe to be around, and best avoided whenever possible. But they're great company, and very funny sometimes. I'm sure you'll like them.'

'I already do,' Ykrit said, 'just hearing you describe them. Not at all like the pinched and serious faces hanging about court.'

Orrin laughed. 'Definitely not,' he said. 'In fact, they're the exact opposite, and very refreshing. Let me tell you about them.'

After little more than an hour, they turned off the road and onto a narrow lane between white-capped hedgerows that led by a couple of farms, cozy-looking places with snow-laden roofs and smoking chimneys, their inhabitants settled in for the season, the only visible tracks running from houses to barns or woodpiles and back.

They reached the edge of a woods and found a trail that wound in among the trees. There was less snow on the ground here under the old-growth pines, and the trail was wide enough to give the horses another run, though there were branches to watch for and duck under and once, a fallen tree to jump.

Orrin, once again in the lead, managed in passing to tug at a snow-laden bough, dumping its load squarely onto the others behind him, following too closely to dodge the cold deluge. Faces stinging from the melting snow, they reined in to brush themselves off, Tormod and Iomar cursing Orrin good-naturedly. Ykrit, to her great surprise, found herself laughing happily, for the first time ever, which made her immediately want to burst into tears. She was distracted from her conflicted feelings by two small figures stepping out from under the trees.

'You kids lost?' one of them said. 'Or just horsing around in the woods on a dare?'

'Gods,' the other one said. 'Even the children are huge. You think they feed them some kind of special diet to make them grow faster?'

Ykrit goggled, as did Tormod and Iomar. Then Tormod let out a great, bellowing laugh.

'I like these fellows,' he told Orrin, still chuckling. 'Right after my own heart, they are. Well, are you going to introduce us, or what?'

They dismounted, and Orrin made introductions. Sedge and Burr, the two little men were called, and though most of them were strangers to each other, all were greeted as friends. Sedge and Burr led them in among the trees. In short order they reached the camp of the forest folk, as inviting as a temporary shelter could be made. There they were greeted by three more of the little men, Alder, Holly and Hock.

Using deadwood and pine boughs, the little people had built five small sleeping huts, stuffed and insulated with dry leaves and grass, all grouped around a central space and a cook fire, roofed over with boughs as well, and protected by a windbreak against the cold winds from the north. There was a warming fire going, old hardwood that burned nearly smokeless, and sections of fallen trunks to sit on, enough space for all of them.

Ykrit marveled at how cozy it all seemed, out here in the forest in the middle of winter. During the ride out, Orrin had told her of his travels with the forest folk, and so she knew they were capable of breaking camp on the shortest of notices, leaving hardly a trace to show that they'd ever been there.

Though it was cold, they'd still taken care that the horses didn't break a sweat, and there was no need to rub them down. They covered them with blankets that were strapped to the saddles and gave them each a nosebag with oats to munch on. Then they all settled around the fire, and Iomar broke out the provisions: bread baked freshly that morning, cheese, smoked fish, cold chicken legs, apples, dates, cider, wine.

It was a welcome change of fare for the forest folk, she saw, and there were overly generous amounts of everything, enough so that the leftovers would last the little men for a few days. On their part, they contributed tough but tasty strips of dried venison, and Sedge made a huge pot of delicious herb tea, a wonderful mix of many-layered aromas recalling meadows gay with summer flowers, hedgerows ripe with berries, and shady places where woodruff and peppermint grew along burbling brooks.

Everybody seemed to have a hearty appetite except Ykrit, who was too filled with new and wondrous impressions to fit in anything more. But she loved the tea, was content to drink cup after cup of it as she listened to the easy banter between Orrin, Tormod and the forest folk.

Suddenly Sedge held up the chicken leg he'd been gnawing on, signaling for silence. 'Somebody coming,' he said.

Ykrit immediately feared the worst. Someone had followed them. Assassins sent after Orrin. Logan's doing, or Alba's. She rose, as did Iomar and Tormod, drawing their swords and surrounding the prince in a defensive perimeter, so close that Orrin had trouble freeing his own blade from its scabbard without cutting one of them.

'You're supposed to guard my back,' he hissed at them, 'not coddle me like an infant.'

'Better coddled than dead,' Ykrit hissed right back, feeling violently protective of him, surprising herself yet again.

'No need for that,' another voice said, and a very old man wearing a tatty, grey cloak and a wide-brimmed hat stepped out of the trees, followed by second man, this one young, hardly more than a boy. 'You can stow the sharp stuff. We're friends.'

'Greybeard,' Sedge said. 'Nice of you to still show up before everyone's frozen their pizzles off.'

'Well,' the old man said with the hint of a smile. 'Since that smart mouth of yours obviously hasn't frozen shut yet, the cold can't be all that bad, can it?'

❖   ❖   ❖

They were only about an hour from Kingskeep, or so Torgrim said, when Jon had another of his strange intuitions. He'd just climbed back onto the cart after having walked behind it for a few miles to warm up, something Torgrim said he should have learned by now to do without having to resort to physical exercise. But, try as he might, so far he hadn't even begun to get the knack of simply telling himself to be warm, and then being warm. Every hour or so, he had to get off and trudge through the snow that had been getting steadily deeper the closer they got to Kingskeep, and had already slowed them down pretty much since they'd left Nara.

The trip had taken them longer than expected. But, hurry or no, they could ask only so much of Einstein, as Torgrim had christened their horse, a good, strong animal that valiantly ploughed its way through the snow without so much as a snuffle of complaint.

'We have to go left here,' Jon suddenly said, surprising himself

551

more than the old man, who simply nodded and turned Einstein onto a narrow lane that led past some farms and then into the forest beyond.

Torgrim didn't touch the reins, preferring to 'nudge' the horse into doing what he wanted of it, saying it cost him less effort than handling the reins. He'd had Jon practice it too, who'd gotten the knack of that much easier than with the staying-warm bit, though it was still hard labor for him and worked only half the time at best. He'd caused poor Einstein some confusion along the way, turning him in the wrong direction more times than he cared to count, and the resulting round-abouts had added a mile or two to the trip, which was long enough as it was.

Passing the farms, Torgrim shot him an inquiring look, but each time Jon shook his head. 'Keep going,' he said. 'It's in the forest somewhere.'

They were following someone else's tracks. Several horses had come this way not too long ago. He saw a pile of dung in the middle of the lane, some last wisps of steam rising off it. Jon wondered who the riders were, and if they were the reason he'd made Torgrim turn off the main road when they were almost in sight of Kingskeep and a warm, cozy inn with soft beds and lots of food.

The lane turned to a forest track, still navigable until they came to a large, fallen tree that completely blocked their progress. The riders had jumped over it, but even if Einstein had been Pegasus, he couldn't have made the cart fly along behind him. With a certain smugness, Jon thought that here was a feat that was likely even beyond Torgrim's capabilities. There was simply no way around the obstacle, trees crowding in close on either side, and it would take considerably more than a nudge to move the mighty trunk out of their way.

'I guess we'll have to walk from here,' he said, unhappily working his freezing toes in boots that were already uncomfortably wet.

'Nah,' Torgrim said, waving a hand. 'Let's try going around that way. There seems to be enough room for us to get through between those two trees.'

Jon could have sworn that 'those two trees' had been standing much closer together just a moment ago, but he said nothing as the old mage directed Einstein through the gap, wide enough for the cart to pass with room to spare. A hundred yards on, the tracks led into the trees, and they stopped.

'Now we walk,' Torgrim said. 'There's a damn sight too many trees here, and only so much nudging a man can do in a day without tiring himself out.'

Jon spread a blanket over Einstein, and then they trudged off into the woods, following the tracks of horses and men, until they caught up with them. The sight that greeted them left Jon staring openmouthed.

Three men with swords drawn stood around a fourth, protecting him as if Jon and Torgrim were a horde of bandits come to slit his throat.

But what really astounded him were the five little guys, their faces brown as ripe hazelnuts and, he thought, somehow full of humor and mischief, as if they'd go the extra mile and cause all sorts of friendly mayhem for a good laugh. They were obviously adults, all five of them, but none was taller than a ten year-old child.

The oldest of them said something to Torgrim about freezing pizzles, and Torgrim told the big guys that it was okay, they could put their weapons away. Then everybody got to know each other, and Jon was pulled out of himself and into the fray of introductions.

He couldn't have said why, but he thought that this was a momentous meeting, an important step on a road whose further course still lay concealed in the shadows of the unknowable, at least for him, and he was glad, and not a little proud, to have played a part in their coming together.

❖ ❖ ❖

Ykrit was frozen in terror.

Mages! The newcomers were mages, both of them. And not just any old mages, either. Their auras were so strong they made her legs wobble.

And she a demon!

Everybody knew what mages did to demons they caught in Upperworld. It was clear to her that she had only moments left to live. She didn't know what to do – so she did nothing, just stood there, shaking like a leaf and waiting to be exposed, for the hammer to fall. After that, it would be a swift and merciless end for her, total extinction, final death from which there would be no return.

Maybe it was better this way, she thought. Better than suffering through a few more days or weeks, which was the most she'd get before she either was recalled and subsumed by Xorth or went through with her mission, killed Orrin, probably to be gobbled up by the Demon Lord anyway. Her eyes met those of the young mage.

Now! She thought, cringing. *This is it!*

He gave a small start, but then he smiled at her and nodded a friendly greeting, as if he had no idea what she was. Could it be?

554

Could it really be that he was blind to the creature that stood before him, masquerading as a human being? And the other one, Torgrim? Surely not. Just with his being so close, her eyes were beginning to water and her bladder was threatening to release its contents, considerable after all the tea she'd drunk. Inexorably, he was drawing closer, greeting those in front of her one by one, the gap between herself and oblivion narrowing with every hand he clasped.

'My lord Tondern,' Torgrim was saying. 'It's been a while. How's the wine coming? You still owe me a cask, as you may remember.'

'I do, I do,' Tormod said. 'And the wine is sensational, I have to tell you, and getting better every year. As is everything else in Redfern, thanks to whatever miracle you performed back then. I suppose it would be forward to ask what it was you actually did? Secret of the trade, and so on?'

'Oh, no secret at all.' Torgrim smiled. 'Good, hard-working folks in Redfern, good soil for them to work, and a good lord looking after them. What more do you need? Just the tiniest of nudges, maybe, no more than that.'

'Well, I'll take your "tiniest of nudges" any time,' Tormod chuckled.

'Iomar,' the old mage said. 'Sharp as ever, I see. Tormod can be glad to have you. And this young man – Orrin, it must be – can be glad to have the both of you. You've set yourself on a straightforward course, lad, and I expected no less of you. But these are dangerous times, and you'll need all the friends you can find.'

'I do,' Orrin said. 'And I owe you my deepest thanks for helping me escape from Ceonad. You've saved my life, or at least given me back a life worth having. I very much hope that I may count you among the friends you just spoke of.'

'You can, my boy, you can. That's why we're here, in fact – and by the way, this is Jonathan, my apprentice. If things go well over the next ten or so years, he might yet learn to treat, say, a mild case of flatulence without killing the patient.'

Ykrit had time to note the look of disbelief on the young man's face, as if he'd expected something altogether different from the old man. Then it was her turn.

Torgrim looked at her, his sharp gaze penetrating beyond her eyes, she felt, and all the way into her soul – if she had a soul at all. He frowned, and she braced herself for the inevitable, stealing a glance at Orrin, wanting to see his face one last time. Still the old man didn't speak. Was he toying with her?

'Well, well, well,' he finally said, following her gaze and looking at Orrin for a moment before turning the full force of his attention back on her. 'I've been around for quite some time, but this is a first even for me. I don't know if it's wise, but I'm going to trust you. I sincerely hope you'll not give me reason to regret it later on.'

None of the others seemed to be listening, as if Torgrim had somehow willed them not to pay attention to their exchange. At his words, Ykrit felt herself sagging, her insides going soft as warm wax with a mixture of relief, a feeling of having been redeemed in some mysterious fashion, and with a sudden, irrational affection for this strange and powerful old man that threatened to overwhelm her and brought tears to her eyes.

'I won't,' she said. 'I swear it, I won't. I love…'

'I know,' Torgrim said, patting her arm. 'That's why I'm taking a chance with you. I've never seen anything quite like it. It would be a shame not to see how this particular story continues.'

❖   ❖   ❖

Jon felt humiliated, and not a little angry.

He knew his limitations well enough, knew how far he still had to go to become at least competent at this weird business of magery. But there was no call for Torgrim to present him as a slow-witted, bumbling fool and embarrass him in front of these people. It was ungenerous, and totally unfair. In lessons, they hadn't even touched on anything to do with healing, for God's sake! He had gotten the hang of nudging, more or less, and he'd become pretty good at self-defense – at least against pinecones, sticks and snowballs. That's how Torgrim had taught him to deflect sorcerous attacks, by throwing stuff at him – not spells, but *things*.

They'd still been in Nara, waiting for Einstein's owner who was two days late, no fault of Brocc's. The man had gotten his days mixed up, it turned out when he finally showed up.

They'd just settled into their room at the *Lost Traveler*, and Jon thought he'd take a nap and catch up on some sleep, but Torgrim had other plans.

'Let's go for a walk,' he said, in a tone that Jon had come to recognize. It meant lessons, and it meant his participation wasn't optional.

They walked east, in the general direction of the mountains. When they were well past the end of the village and into the forest, Torgrim stopped.

'Remember what I told you about dealing with sorcerers?' he

said, stooping to pick up a dozen or more pinecones and gather them in his hat. 'About turning the stuff they throw at you around and sending it right back at them? Well, it's time you learned how. Stay right there.'

He paced off a dozen steps. Then, without warning, he turned around and threw a pinecone at Jon. The man had a mean pitch. The cone came literally whistling through the air and hit him square in the chest.

'Ow!' Jon complained. 'That hurt.'

'Good,' Torgrim said. 'Means I have your attention now. Do you think a sorcerer about to attack is going to announce himself nicely, give you fair warning? All's fair in love, war, and magery, they say, and it applies all the more when you're dealing with the bad guys.'

Jon barely managed to fend off the next of Torgrim's missiles with his hand, though it stung mightily. Torgrim wasn't bothering with old, dried-out husks but had picked only the fresher and heavier ones. Another one grazed the top of his head. The next one he ducked, but the fifth hit him on the cheek, drawing blood.

'Wait,' Jon said. 'I'm – '

'Sorry,' Torgrim said, launching another cone. 'I'm a sorcerer, remember?'

Suddenly Jon was fed up with this stupid game, and the next missile exploded in midair.

'Well, hello, how are we, good morning,' Torgrim said, lowering the cone he'd been about to throw. 'Had a nice snooze? What you just did there was pretty crude, but effective – against a pinecone, that is. Try that with a bad guy who's even halfways worth his salt, and you'll regret it.

'It would be too nice if you could just blow up a spell like that, but you can't. At least not without blowing yourself to smithereens as well. The law of conservation of energy, and all that. Ever heard of it? No? I'm beginning to suspect you dozed your way through physics classes, too. Now. Try and concentrate, and don't let me hit you again.'

The next pinecone came whizzing, stopped about an inch from Jon's face, and fell to the ground. Jon was puzzled.

'Who did that?' he asked Torgrim.

'Not me,' the old man said, grinning, and launched another one.

Again, it halted in mid-air, as if it had smacked into an invisible wall, and dropped straight down.

'But how – '

'Doesn't matter how, doesn't matter who,' Torgrim said, 'as long as it works. Hold on a moment, I'm out of ammunition.'

'Now,' he said when his hat was full again. 'Think, spell. You can stop a spell with what you just did, but that's not going to make it go away. And, unlike a pinecone, it's not going to meekly drop down and die, either. There's a sorcerer's will and power behind it. You block it, and he's just going to push harder. And then you have to push back harder still, and so on and so forth. Suddenly you're locked in a struggle, man against man, magic against magic, and before you know it you're entangled with evil up to your ears. Which is exactly what you wanted to avoid in the first place. So. Let's try an intermediate step. Deflecting, instead of reflecting. Ready?'

They stayed at it until it got to dark to see, but Jon didn't progress beyond the stopping-dead phase, not that day and not the next, nor the one after that. Which didn't keep Torgrim from throwing stuff at him. Whenever they halted for a meal or for the night, whenever Jon got off the cart to walk for a spell, he would unfailingly be bombarded with whatever the old mage had to hand. Torgrim seemed to find a childish pleasure in the game, and even stuffed his pockets with small pebbles he flicked at Jon when they were sitting side by side on the cart. It got to a point where Jon could have happily strangled him.

Then one day – Jon was sitting by their midday fire and Torgrim was going through their stores – a rotten apple suddenly came flying. Jon didn't even see it, just knew with the clairvoyance of the sorely tested that it was coming. Before he could even think what to do, the apple changed course and went off on a tangent. It smacked into a tree, bursting in a spray of rotting pulp.

'See?' Torgrim beamed. 'Told you you could do it.'

He seemed so happy over Jon's success that Jon simply couldn't be angry with him anymore. So the hunk of overripe, runny cheese he threw at the old man was launched with nothing but love and affection. A second later, it hit Jon square in the face, an oozing, stinking mess that clung to his skin like rubbery glue.

But he'd seen how Torgrim had done it, had seen it with that strange, capricious extra sense of his that on rare occasions lit up the world for him, gifting him with sudden insights and unexpected cross-connections, though most often it left him fumbling in the dark, especially when he needed it most. No matter. He'd seen Torgrim reverse the cheese in mid-flight, and he knew how to do it himself now, notwithstanding the fact that 'how' and 'do' didn't really come into it at all.

He threw another piece of cheese at the old man, and turned it around when it came streaking back. Torgrim laughed, and sent it back. The cheese went flying to and fro several more times before the old mage had had enough and sent it straight up into the sky, where it vanished into the lowering clouds.

'You peeked,' he told Jon with mock reproach.

'Yup,' Jon grinned. 'I sure did. You said so yourself: all's fair in magery.'

'That's right,' Torgrim said, looking smug. 'And besides, I *let* you to peek.'

The old devil always had to have the last word.

For once, Jon hadn't minded.

But he did mind now. As far as he was concerned, Torgrim could go find himself a new apprentice. He'd had it with the old man's stupid games and autocratic whims. He'd go find Lucy, get them both back to Ravenstein, and to hell with saving a world that wasn't even his.

Ykrit got to see the forest folk break camp for real.

Torgrim said they had a situation, a term that by itself didn't tell her much, but he had several such outlandish turns of speech in his repertoire. Where he'd picked them up she couldn't begin to imagine. He had a few quiet words with Sedge, and right after that the camp began to disintegrate around them.

The huts and windbreak came down, their components spread around on the snow-free ground under the trees in a manner that made it seem as if they'd always lain there, had never been moved to begin with, and all of it in less time than it took the old mage to give a quick and very sketchy explanation of what he meant by a 'situation'.

He suggested they repair to Near Greening, the last village he and Jonathan had passed through, only a few miles back down the road and graced with an excellent inn, stating that he expected their conversation to be a rather lengthy one and that at his age, sitting around in the snow any longer than absolutely necessary was plain stupid.

Ykrit noticed Jonathan pull a face at these words, as if the old man was having them on, which she doubted; he looked like he was close to eighty, if a day, though he seemed spry enough for his age. As it was, the mention of an inn was met by enthusiasm all around, especially by Tormod. Despite the fact that he'd just eaten heartily, he managed to convey the impression that he was already half starved again.

They barely had time to stand before the logs they'd been sitting on were rolled out from under them, the fire was extinguished with armloads of snow, and the stones that had surrounded it were repositioned in a more random and natural order, blackened sides down. Holly and Hock brushed over everything with pine branches. When they were done, Sedge made a last tour of inspection, nudging a stone here and a piece of deadwood there, until he was completely satisfied with the overall result. He noticed Ykrit watching him.

'Everything's got to be in the right place,' he explained. 'You can't just put stuff down any old way and expect it to be happy. And happy is important. You come back to a place you left in a mess the last time you were there, things are not going to go well for you. You'll be uncomfortable, wet, cold, won't find what you need, your knife won't cut, the fire won't start, that kind of stuff. That's just the way it is.'

Ykrit nodded thoughtfully. 'Sounds like the big folks could learn a few things from you people. Sometimes, it seems to me that the world out there is nothing but unhappy clutter.'

Sedge, who was sweeping away their tracks as they walked back to the forest track, made a rude noise. 'Anybody feels like teaching them is welcome to try. Me, I'd rather teach bears to shit in chamber pots. Well, here we are. Time to say goodbye.'

'You're not coming with us?' Ykrit asked.

'Nah,' Sedge said. 'Big-people houses ain't no place for us. Besides, we gotta go find out some stuff for Greybeard.'

'Be safe, then,' Ykrit said. 'I'm glad we met.'

'Yeah,' Sedge said, looking her straight in the eyes. 'Me too. Not even the high meadows in June can compare.'

'Huh?'

'June is when the gentian blooms,' Sedge said. 'It's a riot of blue you can't imagine. Your eyes. They're even better. Person with eyes like that has gotta be all right.'

'Well, thank you,' Ykrit said, blushing. 'A person who knows how to tell a wom – ah, how to turn a nice phrase like that has got to be all right, too.'

Sedge grinned. 'Just because a person lives in the forest don't mean he ain't got no culture,' he said, giving her a wink. 'Which goes to show that hardly anybody's what they seem, once you take a closer look.'

Ykrit suddenly felt very transparent. She wondered whether to ask Sedge what exactly he'd meant by those last words, but before she'd made up her mind he'd vanished among the trees with the other forest folk, leaving so little trace of their passing that it already seemed doubtful whether they'd ever really been there in the first place.

❖   ❖   ❖

'You can untwist those knickers now, lad,' Torgrim told Jon as soon as they were back on the cart and had Einstein pointed in the direction of the inn. 'You've made good progress, even given the amount of Talent you have, but there's no need to shout it from the rooftops just yet. These are all good people, but what they don't know, they can't tell, and I want to keep you out of the firing line for as long as possible. The enemy will have you in their sights soon enough as it is. Besides, it never hurts to have an ace up your sleeve.'

Jon was relieved and mollified by Torgrim's words. They actually amounted to lavish praise, given how sparingly the old man usually parsed out his approval where Jon's achievements were concerned. He realized he'd been acting childish, and felt foolish all over again for not having trusted that Torgrim as usual would have a good reason for what he did. Still, it smarted to think that the others probably now saw him as stupid or lazy, or both.

'All right,' he conceded. 'But why mention healing, of all things? We've never even talked about it so far.'

'Because you haven't got a lot of Talent for healing,' Torgrim replied. 'Just as you seem to have very little inclination for using your head. If everyone's made to believe that your Talent lies in healing, and that you're obviously no good at it, then it'll take a very nosy and determined enemy to figure out the real danger you represent. As long as you don't go showing off, that is.'

Jon sighed, admitting to himself that he was pretty dense sometimes. One thing still nagged at him, though. 'So you're asking me to
lie about my Talent to everyone I meet,' he said.

'Exactly,' Torgrim said. 'And not just about your Talent. I didn't
know whom we'd find back there, and I didn't really have the time to
think things through properly, but you're going to need a story that
explains where you're from and how you got here. There can't be a
word of Earth or Gates in it, as I'm sure you'll understand. And we
need to have it ready by the time we reach the inn.'

'Why not say I fell off a horse and hit my head,' Jon said, half
joking. 'And now I've got amnesia and can't remember anything except my name.'

'Splendid!' Torgrim beamed. 'That way, we don't have to invent
anything at all, and we don't risk getting our stories mixed up and
running afoul with different versions later on. And it goes a long way
towards explaining why you're so slow at learning. It's perfect. Simple, but effective. You're beginning to think like a true mage.'

'You found me in the Three Quarters,' Jon said, getting into the
game. 'Nobody there seemed to know me, so you figured I was from
somewhere else. You decided to take me with you, hoping that eventually my memory would return, or that you'd find some other means
of discovering who I am.'

'Good lad. I knew there was more than just solid bone between
those ears of yours.'

'Well, thanks a lot. To hear you talk, I'd have never thought so.'

Torgrim chuckled. 'All in your best interest, lad. All in your best
interest.'

Once they were ensconced in front of a blazing fire in the *Headless Chicken's* side-room, away from the curious ears of the patrons in the common room filled to bursting in the late afternoon, Torgrim began by telling them the story of Larnakis. He seemed to know a lot of details, almost as if he'd heard them from someone who had been there when it happened.

Not for the first time, Jon marveled at the old man's network of informants. It had apparently survived his absence of twenty years as if he'd been gone only a few months. He'd spoken to all sorts of people on the way from Nara, farmers, clerks, priests, merchants, store owners, innkeepers, and from each and every one he'd gleaned something valuable but unsettling as well, to judge by the worry lines that settled ever deeper onto his features.

There had also been a couple of more clandestine encounters with rough-looking men who appeared when Jon and Torgrim were camped on the lonelier stretches of road, shadowed wraiths stepping out of the night-dark woods to share a meal and what information they had, and afterwards disappearing as silently and stealthily as they'd come. 'Ghosts', was all Torgrim would say about them when Jon asked who they were.

Somehow, the old man seemed to garner a lot more information from these meetings than Jon did, maybe because Torgrim suddenly found all sorts of tasks and errands for him when these men were around, stuff like collecting more firewood and hauling more water than was really needed, or seeing to Einstein who was already munching his hay and oats and was perfectly fine.

Much of what Torgrim recounted was news to his listeners.

Shocking news. And Larnakis wasn't the worst of it. It seemed the danger was much more present than any of them had thought.

'You all know of the black priests of Amut,' he said, 'and of the rumors and suspicions surrounding them, implicating them in anything from unhealthy sexual practices to stealing little children. Allegations made on the quiet, and only half believed, if at all. No secular authority has ever followed up on them. Which is probably a good thing. Because no secular authority exists that could take them on and hope to succeed in shutting them down, or even make a noticeable dent in their plans and machinations. They're more than simple priests, however perverted. For centuries, they followed their dark god, dabbled in black magic, and fancied themselves sorcerers.

'Unfortunately, they're not dabbling anymore. Nearly fifty years ago, following a tenuous trail of scraps and legend, a handful of them found their way to Tothmar, a land that lies far to the south and east, between the Middle Sea and the Fire Mountains. There, they found Fellmere castle. Once, a very long time ago, it was the seat of some of the most powerful sorcerers the world has ever seen, and even though it had stood empty for nigh on two thousand years, they found the castle and everything in it well preserved, protected from the ravages of time by potent wards and spells put in place by true adepts of the Dark Side.

'A wealth of knowledge awaited the first Blacks who returned to Fellmere. In all likelihood, they had to learn from scratch, but with what they found in the castle's secret vaults they were able to make rapid progress. Too rapid. Though they never came close to attaining the powers wielded by their precursors, the sorcerers of old, they learned much, enough to become a real danger to the rest of the

567

world, as the fate of Larnakis shows all too clearly. Would that I hadn't been away at the time. Perhaps I could have shoved a spoke in their wheel.

'In any case, it was from Tothmar that the disastrous campaign against Larnakis was launched. It cost the Blacks dearly, but they've had sixteen years to recuperate, and I fear that during that time they've become stronger than ever.'

Outside, the sun had set, and darkness gathered in the corners of the room as the old mage spoke. Not for the first time since coming to Vereld, Jon felt a strange sense of the unreal, as if he were merely dreaming all of this and might turn into a diaphanous ghost at any moment, to be sucked away back into the waking reality of his own world.

'But what made them go after Larnakis in the first place?' Tormod asked. He'd ordered a trencher and a mug of ale, both standing untouched. 'What could they have hoped to gain from raiding the smallest and probably poorest kingdom in all of Aldara? I can't see the sense of it.'

'To understand that,' Torgrim said, 'you have to know that they got hold of a prophecy, or at least a snippet of one, that foretold their ruination at the hands of certain – agents. Redeemers, you could call them. One of which is described as a lizard. So the Blacks looked around and discovered that Larnakis' arms showed a dragon. On this most tenuous of connections, they decided to strike first and ask questions later, a decision that cost the lives of thousands, including their own.

'As campaigns go, it was an unmitigated disaster. You could say

568

they got a taste of the prophecy's accuracy, if it wasn't for the fact that their leader, the man who instigated the whole sorry business, survived. Since then, he's rebuilt. And after how things went in Larnakis, he's got something to prove. The chip on his shoulder is probably the size of a wooly mammoth.'

'How ever did you manage to find out about this prophecy?' Orrin asked. 'And do you think there's anything to it?'

'A little bird told me,' Torgrim said. 'A little bird bearing a message from a very courageous person inside the sorcerer stronghold. That the message reached me at all, over the distance of a thousand miles and seventeen years, is a wonder in itself. And yes, I believe the prophecy should be taken seriously. I think it's neither the fabrication of a self-aggrandizing fool nor the outpourings of a delusional madman, but knowledge dragged by the cruelest and most brutal of means from an utterly sane and very reluctant subject. And prophecies like that don't just pop up out of nowhere. It takes times like these, critical, dangerous, pivotal times, to give rise to true prophecy.'

'These sorcerers,' Iomar said. 'You seem to think them a renewed threat. A threat to us here in Dunmark. What would they be after now?'

'Though I can't be sure,' Torgrim said, 'I suspect they might not have found whom they were searching for in Larnakis. And there is more than one of these Redeemers. I think the black priests are now ready to come looking again in earnest. If they proceed as they've done in the past, they'll come knocking with battering rams and siege towers and ask their questions with fire and sword. Not to mention sorcery. But I believe that Larnakis might have taught them a lesson, and they'll try something different this time before they reach for the big hammer. Something more subtle but no less dangerous.'

'And what are we supposed to do about it?' Tormod asked. 'You say there's no – how did you put it? – no "secular authority" that can stand up to them. Sounds to me like this is a business for mages.'

Jon noted how everyone had slipped quite easily into accepting Torgrim's authority. He wasn't surprised. The old man had that about him. And he wasn't a mage for nothing. As Jon had already seen on the road, things just seemed to somehow fall into place around him and go his way more often than not.

'It is,' Torgrim said. 'Or it would be, if there were any other mages left to speak of. I'll do what I can, but I can't do it alone. I need your help.'

'What would you have us do then?' Orrin asked. 'Pay them a visit in Tothmar?'

'No,' Torgrim said grimly. 'It's too late for that now. Even when Fellmere stood empty, it would have taken a powerful mage, an army of workers and several years to take it apart. Gods know I tried often enough to convince the western kings to do just that, but to no avail.

'Why should they embark upon such a far-fetched, costly enterprise to tear down an abandoned heap of stones a thousand miles away, they asked. Most of them hardly knew where Tothmar was, and had much more pressing projects at home, like waging another of their endless petty wars or building more impregnable keeps and grander palaces for themselves. Alas, they said, as I could see, their armies and builders were all tied up, and their funds stretched as it was. The one or two who actually saw sense in my proposal never got beyond intents and promises, stalling and delaying until they were

570

either dead or deposed.

'Now, with a full complement of sorcerers ensconced in Fellmere, you'd need all the armies of the West united under a brilliant general, and a score of first-rate mages to even dream of breaching those walls and ousting the black rats. But the West is divided, and as things stand now, none of the kingdoms will agree too merge their forces, much less entrust them to someone they fear they won't be able to control.

'As for the mages – they just don't make them anymore the way they used to. You'd be lucky to find even two of them competent enough to dismantle the *Headless Chicken's* outhouse without injuring themselves, not to mention taking down a fastness like Fellmere, held together by a tangle of wards so potent, fooling with the least of them could probably blow you and half your army into oblivion.

'No, we have to begin here, put our own house in order if we're to stand a chance at all. For now, our tools must be diplomacy and espionage. We have to convince the kingdoms that the threat is real, and that their only chance to survive is to set aside their differences and cooperate with one another. At the same time, we have to find out all we can regarding the Blacks and what they're up to, and thwart them wherever possible. By now, the Great Temple of Amut in Orr has branches in every major city in Aldara, some overt, some secret, depending on the level of acceptance the Brotherhood encounters with the authorities and populaces.

'I suspect they have agents in towns and villages as well. They'll have surely tried to infiltrate the guilds, the various branches of officialdom, even the nobility. They'll have been very circumspect and underhanded about it, and their agents may be all but impossible to dig out. But we have to assume they're there. Anything else would be irresponsible folly.'

Jon, who had actually decided that his 'amnesia' called for him to keep his mouth shut for the time being, had a hundred questions of his own. Before he knew it, he found himself asking one of those he found most pressing.

'These redeemers,' he said. 'Who are they? Shouldn't we be looking for them? Get them together, see that they're protected? Make sure they stay alive, so they can do whatever it is they're supposed to do?'

Torgrim studied him for a moment, seeming to weigh what to say, or maybe whether to say anything at all. Then he sighed.

'All right,' he said. 'I suppose you need to know. But this is dangerous knowledge. Gods forbid it should happen, but if any of you should fall into the hands of the Blacks, it would be better you were ignorant in this. On the other hand, they're smart enough to figure it out for themselves.

'This is what the prophecy said, word for word: "Come summer solstice, the last of three eggs will hatch. One is the egg of a cat, one is the egg of a carrion-bird, and one is the egg of a lizard. Three will hatch, and these three will be the doom and downfall of you and all your ilk and spell your master's end as well, and mankind shall know again the pleasure of being alive."

'The prophet called them the Warrior, the Wizard, and the King, and there was also a mention of a Wild Card. The lizard is the dragon of Larnakis. I think they got that one right. There was a royal child born in Larnakis not long before the Blacks' invasion. But, as I said,

572

they might not have been able to fulfill their objective, which was to capture or kill this child. It might still be alive.'

'The cat,' Orrin said, pulling a ring from his left hand and laying it on the table. It was set with a lapis lazuli, it's face engraved with a lion rampant. Looking pale and shaken, Orrin stared at the ring. Then he looked questioningly at Torgrim.

The mage nodded. 'Yes. I think we can safely assume that this is the cat in question. Though there are other arms bearing the lion, and there may well be young men of the right age attached to those Houses, none of them is here.'

'So that's why you had Sedge and the others spring me from Ceonad,' Orrin said. 'You knew.'

'Not for sure,' Torgrim said. 'Not then. But I do know now, seeing how certain things – and certain people – are beginning to come together. There is no such thing as coincidence where prophecy is involved. All of you here are caught up in it to some degree, and from this moment on, you should work under the premise that nothing of what happens to any of you is accidental. And secrecy is vital. I trust you all understand that this must go no farther than the ears of those present here today.'

Everyone nodded.

'What about the carrion bird?' Jon asked, forgetting himself for the second time.

'Ah,' Torgrim said. 'The raven. Nothing more should be said about it for now.' He threw Jon a glance that seemed casual but was filled with meaning, and contained a warning. Jon swallowed, trying not to betray his shock.

'Some secrets,' Torgrim continued, 'must be kept even from

friends – when the implications and consequences of revealing them pose too great a danger to all involved. So much for the Redeemers. Each of the three will hopefully find his appropriate place and the role he is to play in the events to come. I for my part will do everything in my power to make it possible.

'And then there is still the Wild Card. Before you ask: I haven't the slightest idea who that might be. And neither do the Blacks, that much I can promise you. It's in the nature of the Wild Card to remain unknown and unknowable until it chooses to reveal itself. Which will probably happen when you least expect it, and even then you may well miss it and have only the repercussions to tell you it's been played at all.'

Torgrim was about to continue when suddenly Jon sat up as if pulled by invisible strings, struck by a foreknowing.

'Somebody's coming,' he said with utter conviction. 'Somebody important.'

All eyes came to rest on him, and he felt the others' regard like a palpable weight. Or maybe it was just his own, pressing expectation, his need to prove to them that he wasn't as useless or stupid as they might think.

The noise from the common room seemed suddenly louder, as if for the last hour they'd been sitting in a bubble of quiet, and he thought fleetingly that Torgrim might well have had something to do with that.

Tormod raised his mug and took a deep draught. Iomar and Orrin followed suit, though they drank more sparingly. Torgrim was leaning back in his chair, studying the ceiling above their heads as if he

might find denial or confirmation of Jon's claim lurking up there between the age-blackened beams. A minute passed, two, three, and Jon
was beginning to think that, for once, just when it would have been
most convenient to be able to rely on his gift, it had misled him into
making a laughing stock of himself.

Then they all heard the jingle of harness and the thudding of
hooves outside as the newcomers rode around the side of the inn and
to the back where the stables lay. Iomar rose to peer out through one
of the room's tiny bulls-eye windows.

'Nine,' he said, his hand automatically coming to rest on the hilt
of his sword. 'They're armed, and they look like they know how to
handle themselves. Sellswords, maybe. Not the kind you'd want to
mess with, and they've got us outnumbered.'

'It's all right,' Jon said, deciding that his intuition had been trustworthy after all. 'We need to meet these people.'

'Yes,' Torgrim said. 'I think the lad has got it right. Let's wait and
see what happens.'

Iomar remained standing by the window.
Orrin and Desmond sat in tense silence. Only Torgrim and Tormod
appeared relaxed, the former staring into the flames in the fireplace
with half-closed lids as if he were about to fall asleep, the latter finishing off his ale and giving a resounding belch before attacking his
trencher filled with cold meat and gravy.

Not long, and they heard heavy footsteps enter the common room.
The door to the side-room opened, and the landlord stuck his head in.

'Pardon the disturbance, my lords,' he said. 'But there's a lord
and young lady just arrived with their retinue, and seeing as the com-

mon room's full up, I'd ask if you'd be willing to share this room with them. There's enough space for all of you, without you getting in each other's way. I'd be much obliged.'

'By all means,' Torgrim said, coming out of his reverie. He sat forward and pulled down his hat, the wide brim throwing his face into shadow. 'Show them in. We'd be most happy to share.'

'Thank you, my lord.' The landlord bobbed, opening the door wide and stepping back. 'You're very kind.'

The first to step through was a tough-looking man whom Jon guessed to be in his early fifties. There was a soldierly air about him, in his weather-lined face, the straightness of his bearing, and the economy of his movements. He gave a formal nod of greeting and turned towards the large, empty table at the far side of the room. Behind him came a young girl, slight but self-assured, the hilts of two short-swords poking up over her shoulders in a very business-like way and standing in sharp contrast to her almond eyes and full, sensuous mouth.

Jon thought her quite pretty but far too boyish and arrogant for his taste. She didn't spare him or anyone else in the room more than a passing glance and a curt nod, until Torgrim, still hidden under his hat, suddenly spoke.

'Behold the dragon,' he said, so softly Jon wasn't sure he'd heard properly.

Of a sudden it was very quiet in the room, and somehow markedly colder than a moment ago. The soldier and the girl seemed to possess a keen hearing; Torgrim's words had escaped neither of them. The man immediately turned and, seeing that the girl was about to go for her swords, laid a restraining hand on her arm.

'I'm sure it's only a misunderstanding,' he said, speaking both to the girl and to Torgrim, though his right hand was gripping the hilt of the dagger sheathed on his belt. 'A case of mistaken identity, most likely.'

As the rest of the party filed in, the old man's face lit up in a beatific smile.

'Not at all,' he said, removing his hat and giving the dagger a pointed look. 'Baran Kendarren. Are you going to stick that thing in your late father's best and oldest friend, or give an old man who dandled you on his knee when you were still prone to piddle on it the greeting he deserves?'

The man's face was a sight to see. Astonished didn't quite cut it, in Jon's opinion. Words like gobsmacked or discombobulated came to mind. Then the soldier grinned.

'Torgrim of Eldinga!' he said. 'Do you have any idea how often in the past sixteen years I've been out to that crumbly old tower of yours? Where the blazes have you been all this time? I was beginning to think you'd finally retired for good.'

'Retirement!' Torgrim snorted. 'I should be so lucky. No, I was merely on vacation for a while, though maybe a wee bit longer than I'd originally intended. And my tower is not crumbly – or at least it wasn't until very recently. Had a spot of bother the other day, and the old pile took a nasty hit. But do have your friends come in and close that door. And all of you sit down. There's a draft, and you're looming.'

The old man rose to clasp hands with Baran. Then he turned to the girl and gave a perfect courtier's bow, flourish and all.

'My lady,' he said, taking her hand. 'There are hardly words to say how glad I am to see you alive and well, and to meet you under such auspicious circumstances.'

He looked around to make sure the door was closed, and continued in a lower voice.

'May I present to you his highness, prince Orrin of Dunmark. His grace, Tormod Tondern, duke of Redfern. Iomar Caereven, weaponsmaster. Desmond Fjolen from Osona. And Jonathan, my apprentice.

'Sirs,' he addressed his own companions, 'meet her highness Anili Tavore, the Dragon Princess. And now sit, everyone. I've got a lot of explaining to do, for the second time today.'

He guided Anili to a seat between himself and Jon, who stood, heart suddenly thumping, and essayed a bow that didn't come out nearly as elegant as Torgrim's. In fact, he just barely got through it without losing his balance and falling on his face. All he received in return for his trouble was a cool glance and a slight and very regal inclination of her pretty head.

Fine with me, he thought. I think I don't really like her much anyway.

While Torgrim brought the newcomers up to speed, Jon drifted off into his own thoughts, mulling over his current situation.

His previous life seemed to be drawing farther and farther away, receding from the realm of the tangible into that of memory, slipping from his grasp as he battled with the here and now, immersed in this strange other world that day by day became more demanding of his exclusive attention.

Notwithstanding his resolve to keep a separate perspective, to not become so used to these new surroundings that he risked forgetting where he really came from and belonged, he found himself being drawn ever deeper into this world and its ongoing story. Habit, he realized, was as powerful as any natural force, time and gravity combined to slowly but surely erode a person's will to resist. And it wasn't the big events that worked the changes in him so much as the small things, the seemingly unimportant, endlessly repeated rituals of everyday existence that took bite after miniscule bite out of him, like drops of water striking a stone until finally, one day, it was hollow enough to be filled with something else entirely.

With a pang of guilt, he thought of Lucy, and wondered how she was doing, cast without warning into an alien world just like himself, but only five years old. He yearned to see her, make sure she was all right, but all he could do for the time being was fervently hope that she was as safe and well cared for as Torgrim had said.

And Lisa – was she safe by now? Had Franz and Anton managed to fulfill their promise and rescue her from whoever had taken her? If so, she must be worried sick over Lucy and himself. Would that he could send her a message to allay her fears, though he wasn't all that sure that such fears were unfounded.

Uncle Richard – was he still hanging on to life? Franz would have a hard time keeping what had happened from him, and in his state, it wouldn't take much at all to push him over the brink. Jon hoped not, hoped the old man he'd come to love and respect in such a short time was alive and as well as could be. He still missed his parents, and uncle Jude, missed them with a fierce sorrow whenever he thought of them, though he hadn't dreamed about them in a while.

But he'd had another recurring dream of late, of the kind that

579

seemed more real than waking life. He'd dreamed of riding down a succession of dips and rises on a grassy mountainside in the last, fading light of a clear, cold autumn day, the brighter stars already visible like diamond pinpricks in the darkening sky touched with the last afterglow of sunset. Topping a rise, he saw the lights of a small village nestled among the hills, warm, welcoming lights from hearth-fires and tallow lamps. He heard sheep bleating and cows mooing in the stables, heard dogs barking and children laughing and shouting. He caught the scent of hay and animals on the fresh, clean air, laced with whiffs of the evening's cooking, and above all, the smell of wood-smoke.

To his great chagrin, he always awoke before he reached the first houses. The children would stop their play to look and point at him and his companions – for he had the feeling he wasn't alone, that there were other people with him, though he never actually saw who it was that rode behind him. Then, when he was nearly there, preparing to rein in his horse and dismount, the children swarming towards him with open faces and welcoming smiles, he and his party seemed to dissolve and blow away on the evening breeze like the smoke rising from the chimneys.

Each time, he awoke with such an intense and painful longing for that place, it took his breath away and left him on the verge of tears. It felt like the ultimate essence of home to him, this small dream-village, like the one and only place in the entire universe to which he absolutely belonged, and it to him. He felt he would have gladly given this world and his own for the chance to reach that place among the hills, to settle into it like a hand into a well-worn glove and never leave again.

But there was also something disturbing about this dream scene, something infinitely sad and tragic, the reason for which he could never quite grasp, though he suspected it might have to do with who came behind him.

Gradually, the fact that a different voice than Torgrim's was speaking penetrated his awareness, and he roused himself from his reverie.

' …over two hundred of them,' Baran was saying, 'and if it hadn't been for the timely arrival of young Hakan here and his friends the Ghosts, I doubt we'd have survived the night. The things were nearly impossible to kill, at least until we discovered how well they burn. But by then they'd started using some kind of sorcery and brought down the wall.'

Torgrim had Baran describe the part about the sorcery in every detail. Jon had never seen the old man look so troubled. The lines on his face had deepened into shadowed crevasses, and he seemed to have aged a decade in a few, short moments.

'Ah,' he said. 'This is bad. Very bad. There's only one explanation as to the origins of those undead. Who could have known that the tragedy of Larnakis would give rise to something even worse than the end of a whole people? For all their terrible suffering, not even true death was granted them. Instead, in the aftermath of Tinnan their remains must have mixed and fused with those of their enemies, and they became undead monstrosities, driven by nothing but mindless hunger and an inhuman hatred that was never theirs. We can only hope that, before this is over, we will be able to release them all from a fate too horrifying to contemplate.'

'Gods!' Baran exclaimed in a strangled voice, pressing the bridge of his nose with white-knuckled fingers and clearly fighting for composure. A furtive glance told Jon that Torgrim's words had hit Anili just as hard. Her cheeks were wet with tears, though she didn't make a sound, and looked more angry than heartbroken.

They all waited until the two of them had regained some semblance of equilibrium. Finally, Baran heaved a great sigh and looked up.

'Well,' he said, and there was an audible tremor to his voice. 'We've come to hunt the black scum down, and what you've just told us – hard as it is to grasp – makes for another seal on their fates, another shovelful dug out of their graves. It seems we've come to the right place, and our meeting may turn out to be more than just fortuitous.'

'Yes,' Torgrim said. 'As I said earlier, we've arrived at a time where coincidences cease to happen. We haven't any clear idea of what awaits us, only that much of it will be bad and likely get worse before there's a chance of things taking a turn for the better. But we have the prophecy to at least point us in the general direction we should be headed. Still, it's time we started making some plans.'

❖ ❖ ❖

A babe in the house is a well-spring of pleasure, a messenger of peace and love, a resting place for innocence on earth, a link between angels and men.

Martin Farquhar Tupper

31 Summerland

ll through the night the silent, armored figure walked, animated by whatever strange force inhabited it, rusted hinges creaking softly with the rhythm of its untiring progress. Wrapped in Torgrim's thick, woolen cloak and gently rocked in the suit of armor's arms, Lucy slept peacefully while it consumed mile after mile with long, regular strides, crossing snow-covered mountain meadows gleaming in the otherworldly light of a full moon, and then shadowed stretches of forest where nothing stirred save Hawk flying ahead, wending his way among the still branches of the sleeping trees, occasionally hooting softly and swerving back along the trail to make sure his companions were still following.

They'd left the snow behind and were traveling alongside a stream that tumbled down its bed of clean-swept pebbles in a gurgling rush when the first rays of the rising sun found their way through the winter-bare branches and tickled Lucy awake.

For a while, she remained still, only turning her head slightly to better present her face to the warming sunlight. Curiously, she seemed quite content. Perhaps it was because, like all human beings and especially children, she possessed the ability to adapt to almost any situation, and her young mind was still blessedly free of the ruts that habit engraves on older brains, those magnetically attractive grooves in which worry and fear tend to lodge and trap a person's thoughts in endlessly repeated, deleterious cycles.

Gifted with a child's natural curiosity and facing a fresh, new day brimming with promise, she seemed – for the moment at least – to have completely forgotten all about fear and loneliness.

She squirmed around, looked up at the closed visor gently nodding above her with each powerful step.

The helmeted head tilted down enquiringly.

She squirmed some more, making it clear that she wanted down. The knight came to a halt and carefully set her on her feet. Gathering up the folds of Torgrim's much-too-long cloak as best she could, she headed for some nearby bushes and emptied her bladder, happily managing to do so without getting anything on her pajama bottoms. When she was done, the knight offered to carry her again, but she declined.

The path continued to run more or less parallel to the creek, always descending. Gradually, the water's rushing diminished, and the burbling brook became a measured, tranquil stream, flowing sedately between moss-covered banks. They'd arrived at the end of the foothills, and the forest had changed as well. Here, the trees were truly ancient, venerable grandmothers and grandfathers with trunks so wide it would have taken several people holding hands with outstretched arms to reach all the way around.

Their progress was slower now with Lucy walking on her own,

584

finding a hundred interesting things to look at and declaring numerous rest stops. Later, she made it clear that she was tired and wanted to be carried again, and soon fell asleep in the knight's arms.

She awoke to find him standing stock still at the river's edge. He seemed to be gazing intently at the other side, as if he were waiting for something or someone. When she looked a question at him, he put her down, raised a cautioning finger to where his lips would have been behind the visor, and then pointed across the river.

The forest on the opposite bank was very different from the grey, winter-bare woods on the near side. The trees were clad in the vibrant greens of early summer, and the sun-drenched air was so crystal clear one could see every individual leaf, needle and twig. A warm breeze carried over, filled with the sweet scents of forest loam, sap, young grass, and blooming wildflowers.

Birdsong trilled across the water.

For a time, nothing happened. Lucy began to fidget. She tugged at the knight's hand, wanting to leave. He shook his head and pointed again. Where a moment ago there had been only a dark, sluggish expanse of water, there was now a slender bridge of light grey stone, spanning the river in a single, elegant arch. On the other side, a gap had opened up in the vegetation and a figure in white was just stepping out from among the trees. A woman, it became apparent when she came down to stand at the far end of the bridge, holding out a welcoming hand to the little girl.

Lucy seemed hesitant at first, perhaps not sure whether this new person could be trusted.

Then Hawk flew past her and alighted on the woman's outstretched arm. The knight gave Lucy an encouraging nod, offered her his steel hand. She took it, and, crossing the bridge together, they walked out of time.

❖   ❖   ❖

Is there not some chosen curse, some hidden thunder in the stores of heaven, red with uncommon wrath, to blast the man who owes his greatness to his country's ruin?

Joseph Addison

32 Kingskeep

ot at all sure whether this was really such a brilliant idea, Orrin stood beside Torgrim as the mage knocked on the door to the Logan's private rooms. There'd simply been no stopping the old man. Ever since he'd shown up unexpectedly in the forest and gathered them all together at the *Headless Chicken,* everyone seemed to take his leadership for granted, though quite how this had come about remained a mystery to Orrin.

Not that he minded. By himself, he'd gotten pretty much bogged down just trying to get in and see Logan, so he was glad that now things finally seemed to be picking up momentum. If only Logan had responded to any of their notes, his and Torgrim's – though Torgrim had sent only one, and made it clear he had no intention of wasting his time on a second – they wouldn't have had to barge in on the regent like this, unwelcome intruders at best.

But, as they had all agreed back at the inn, it was the only sensible course of action that might break the impasse resulting from Logan's newfound reclusiveness. The regent was an important part of their plans. They needed him, it was as simple as that.

They'd already had a run-in with the soldiers guarding Logan's door. Orrin had successfully pulled princely rank on them, though he doubted he could have brought it off if Torgrim hadn't been there, working his sneaky magic without anyone really noticing what he was doing. It was obvious that the guards weren't happy with what was filtering down the chain of command from inside the regent's apartments, but from there to openly disobeying explicit orders was still a giant step – one that Torgrim helped them make. This much Orrin understood, though he'd be damned if he knew how the old man did it.

A servant cracked the door, eyeing them warily.

The man's expression was pinched, and he looked unhealthily pale, as if he hadn't seen the sun in a long while. 'His highness is not receiving visitors,' he informed them dismissively, making to shut he door on them.

It wouldn't close because the heel of Torgrim's staff was in the way, an unsightly length of wood he'd picked off the forest floor at the little people's camp. It looked rather rotten and tended to shed pieces of crumbling bark and shreds of dry moss. There were even a few small, white agarics clinging to the upper half of the worm-eaten branch.

'I've been told his highness is indisposed,' Torgrim said amiably.

'Yes,' the servant said, trying in vain to dislodge Torgrim's staff with the toe of his shoe. Torgrim just leaned on it a little harder. 'Exactly. And he's not receiving – '

'Then his highness will be delighted to see us,' Torgrim overrode him with a big, confidential smile, reminding Orrin of a horse trader preparing to pass off a nag for a racehorse. 'I'm a physician.'

'His grace, Duke Alba is the Regent's physician,' the servant said, looking more and more uncomfortable.

'His *what?*' Orrin said, immediately incensed. 'Last time I look-ed, the bloody fraud was still a commoner.'

'Yes, well. His highness… promoted him. Just this morning, in fact.' The man was looking decidedly uneasy.

'You're worried,' Torgrim stated matter-of-factly.

'I'm – '

'Worried for his highness.'

'What… '

'You know that things are badly amiss.'

'I…' Beads of sweat stood on the servant's brow. His earlier haughtiness had all but vanished. Suddenly he looked drained, des-perate. He *was* worried, Orrin realized. Very worried.

'That's why we're here,' Torgrim said in a kind, grandfatherly voice that would have broken down even the most stubborn repro-bate's resistance. 'To set things right again. You *want* us to set them right, don't you?'

Orrin was grazed by what felt like the fringes of a warm, comfort-ing aura of compassion and benevolence. Tears suddenly appeared in the servant's eyes, tears of relief and gratitude. Wordlessly, he open-ed the door, stepping aside to let them in.

The old rogue had done it again.

Inside the apartment the air was close, heavy with the odors of old food, stale incense – and something stronger, at once musky and sharp, unpleasant.

Alba stepped from a door leading off the anteroom, closing it firmly behind him, his colorless cheeks flushing red with anger when he saw who the unwelcome intruders were.

'Your highness,' he said with a minimum of civility. 'This is most inopportune. The Regent is – '

'Is going to see us, whether you like it or not,' Torgrim said. 'Nobody's asking your permission, Whitey.'

Furious, Alba looked around for the servant, but the man seemed to have put prudence before valor and retreated to some remote part of the apartment, or perhaps left it altogether.

'You leave me no choice but to ask you straight out to leave,' Alba grated, his red eyes burning with ill-concealed hatred. 'I can't have you further endangering his highness's delicate health by bursting in on him like this. Now please go, or I'll call the guards.'

'Cut the crap, buddy,' Torgrim said sharply, surprising Orrin yet again with one of his outlandish phrases. 'Already I'm of half a mind to turn you into something that better fits your slimy little character. If only I could think of something that's base enough to suit you.'

Alba drew himself up, cocksure and arrogant. 'With all due respect, your highness,' he addressed Orrin frostily. 'May I ask what this... this overblown hedge-wizard is doing here? I find it most unfitting – '

'Hedge-wizard?' Torgrim rumbled. 'I'll show you hedge-wizard, you vermin-infested little gutter rat... Ha! That's it. Rat.'

The old man suddenly loomed – there was no other way to describe it. Alba responded immediately, quickly intertwining his spidery fingers in a weird, arcane gesture pointed at Torgrim. The light in the room grew dim, shadows seeming to creep from the corners and gather around the albino.

The mage didn't react in any visible manner, just stood there leaning on his staff and staring at Alba curiously.

Suddenly the albino's expression turned panicky. He began to tug at his fingers, trying in vain to pull his hands apart, but they seemed to be stuck together more thoroughly than if they'd been joined together with a tightly knotted rope or a generous dollop of strong glue.

'Gotcha,' Torgrim exclaimed with an evil grin. 'Amateur,' he told Orrin breezily. He walked around the anteroom, opening and closing doors until he found one that led to some sort of closet. 'Ah. This'll do for now,' he said. 'Orrin, lad, why don't you escort his nibs into this fine waiting room here, and then we'll go see your dear uncle.'

'You have no idea what you're getting yourself into,' Alba hissed as Orrin stuffed him into the closet. He threw a hate-filled look at Torgrim. 'He'll pay for this. And so will you, sooner than you think.'

Orrin shut the door on him.

It was dark and close in Logan's bedchamber.

The heavy curtains were drawn and the air was hardly breathable, rank with sweetly cloying fumes and the unpleasant odor of an unwashed body.

Logan lay sprawled on the unmade bed, half clothed and unkempt. He had food stains on his shirt, dirt under his nails, and dried snot on his cheek, a far cry from his usually so dapper appearance. He was lying with his face close to a brass censer resting on a low nightstand and giving off a sickly-sweet smoke that permeated the air and made Orrin's head swim.

Torgrim leaned his staff against the nearest wall. Moving quickly, he drew back the curtains and opened both windows. Next, he fetched the censer and unceremoniously threw it out the window, brass bowl, coals and all. Orrin heard it crash onto the courtyard cobbles three stories below.

Logan didn't stir. Torgrim sat on the edge of the bed. He felt for Logan's pulse, pulled up his lids and smelled his breath. 'What I thought,' he told Orrin. 'Drugged to the gills but otherwise healthy enough.

'Ah, here we have it.' He picked up an empty glass bottle that had been half hidden under the bedclothes and sniffed at the opening. 'Poppy juice, blackroot, dreamwort, my, my. And he's been inhaling the smoke of ooja leaves. No wonder he's not been prompt about answering his correspondence. Friend Alba's been keeping himself a tame regent, it would seem. Makes you wonder about other things as well, doesn't it? Your stay in Ceonad, for instance.'

'Oh yes,' Orrin said grimly, fighting down an urge to drag the albino out of the closet and do something painful to him. 'It certainly does. Logan looks worse off than I was. I expect he'll have a bad time coming off it, which means he'll be as good as useless for a week or so.'

'Not necessarily,' Torgrim said. 'We can put him on a maintenance dose, too little to addle his thinking but enough to allow him to function normally. We'll have to get Alba to cough up an adequate supply of the stuff. But first, we need to sober up Logan. Why don't you go ask one of the guards to run down to the kitchens and fetch a big pot of strong, hot kaf.'

Orrin went to do as Torgrim had asked but was back in under a minute.

'Alba's gone,' he said. 'The closet door's open and he's nowhere in sight. Somebody must have let him out.'

'Darn!' Torgrim groused. 'My fault. Seems I underestimated the rat. Stupid, but it can't be helped now. Means I'll have to waste time finding an apothecary who carries the ingredients we'll need to make up a new batch of Logan's happy juice. Oh, well! Let's bring him round first, and worry about the rest later.'

It took hours to rouse Logan to a point where it became possible to have an intelligent conversation with him. While the regent was still coming round, Torgrim sent for Tormod and asked him to see if he could find out where Alba had gotten to. The big man returned sooner than expected.

'Found the bugger,' he announced, cheerful as if he'd just flushed a prize boar. 'He's taken himself to Fagin Stonebridge's house. Tied himself to Fagin's apron strings and thinks himself well hidden. Took two silvers to get the guards to talk. Corruptible beggars, just like their master.'

Fagin Stonebridge, Duke of Dalborn, headed the faction of nobles who professedly supported Logan – bargained with Logan, would have probably been a more accurate description. Tolerated his regency in exchange for favors. They were the worst lot of calculating, insidious manipulators that Dunmark had to offer, and they did nothing that didn't further their own interests or turn them some sort of profit.

'Thank you, Tormod,' the old mage said. 'It's always good to know where your enemies are. It might not be a bad idea to have someone keep an eye on the place, just in case he decides to run farther afield.'

'Already done,' Tormod said, rubbing his stomach. 'All this running around has made me hungry. In case you need me, I'll be down the kitchens.'

'Oh, Tormod,' Torgrim said. 'One more thing, if you please. Have someone go round the apothecaries' and see if they can get the things on this list.' He handed Tormod a scrap of parchment. 'If they can have it made up to the specifications I've written down, even better. By this evening will do.'

Towards evening Logan was finally clear-headed enough to absorb what Torgrim had to tell him. He was sitting up in bed, his back braced by several pillows, looking wasted and scared, uncertain eyes darting back and forth between Torgrim and Orrin.

'Where's Alba?' he asked.

'Alba, yes,' Torgrim said. 'Seems he's left.'

'What do you mean, he's left?'

'Scarpered, skedaddled, done a runner. I think he wasn't exactly thrilled by our meeting.'

'What? Where is he?' Logan said, becoming agitated. 'You have to bring him back immediately. I... need my medicine.'

'Your medicine,' Torgrim said. 'I was meaning to talk to you about that. How long have you been taking it?'

Of a sudden Logan looked furtive. 'I... I can't remember. And who are you, anyway? What are you doing here?' He threw Orrin a plaintive look. 'Orrin, what's he doing here?'

'Sorry, uncle,' Orrin said. 'This is Torgrim of Eldinga.'

'You?' Logan goggled. 'But I thought...'

'Lots of people have *thought,*' Torgrim said. 'Yet here I am, still

594

alive and kicking. I'm glad you've heard of me. That way, I don't have to explain to you that it's not a good idea to mess with me, no matter how high up you are in the food chain. Now, try to remember. When did you first start taking Alba's "medicine"?'

'I was terribly sick,' Logan recalled, shivering. 'Fever, bad cold, dreadful cough. That must have been…' He pondered for a moment, looked surprised.

'Two years ago? Alba gave me medicine, cured me. Said I should take it until I felt completely restored. Somehow there always seemed to be more of it. I… I got used to it, I suppose. I've taken it ever since.'

'Used to it,' Torgrim mused. 'That's a cute way of putting it. I imagine at some stage you tried to do without, and discovered what happened when you stopped taking it?'

Logan nodded mutely, looking guilty as a child caught stealing from the cookie jar.

'Right, then,' Torgrim said. 'Here's what we'll do. You'll receive your medicine from me from now on. But only as much as you need to function normally. No more excesses. And only until there's a breathing spell in all this madness and we can get you properly weaned. Agreed?'

Again Logan nodded. Orrin thought he looked relieved, as if a burden had, if not lifted altogether, at least lightened considerably.

'What madness?' Logan inquired abruptly.

'Ah,' Torgrim said. 'We've arrived at the main point of our visit. Listen well, highness, because the fate of Dunmark hangs on what I'm about to tell you.'

Logan did listen, somewhat distractedly at first, and then ever more raptly, as Torgrim reiterated for him exactly what he'd told Orrin and the others back in Near Greening, leaving out nothing save for the identities of the three Redeemers.

Logan may have been many things, not all of them favorable, but stupid wasn't one of them. He studied the ring he wore on his left hand. It bore the same seal as Orrin's. He looked up, stared at Orrin, realization dawning in his eyes. Torgrim raised a finger to his lips.

'Don't speak of it,' he said, softly but urgently. 'Not now, not here, not anywhere. It's more than possible you'd as good as kill him if you did.'

'Understood,' Logan said, looking shaken.

'Now,' Torgrim continued. 'As I said, we need to get the kingdoms to present a united front when the time comes. Which means we have to begin working towards that end now. Preferably yesterday. What I need from you are letters of accreditation for Orrin, myself, and Baran Kendarren, officially naming us ambassadors of Dunmark.'

'Baran?' Logan wondered. 'I thought he'd gotten himself killed in that awful business in Larnakis. Where has he been all this time? His brother was devastated at the time. Well. I'm glad to hear he's alive. And you shall have your commissions. But what about me? What am I to do? Do you want me to step down?'

'No,' Orrin said. 'That is something we can discuss some other time. For now, I would ask you to stay exactly where you are. As you've heard, Torgrim has other things for me to do. Someone has to stay here and hold Dunmark together, and you're the only one I can trust to do the job properly.'

Logan pulled himself up, his weakness giving way to a shaky resolve, but resolve nonetheless. There were tears in his eyes.

'My dear boy,' he said, and for the first time it felt to Orrin as if he really meant it. 'I won't disappoint you. I'm sorry for not being there for you earlier, and I hope you'll forgive me.'

'It's all right,' Orrin said, feeling awkward. 'Alba's gone, and the only thing that counts now is where we all go from here.'

'Alba,' Logan said, looking unsure again. 'What will he do? What if he comes back?'

'Don't worry about him,' Torgrim said. 'I'm leaving Tormod in Kingskeep to look out for you. He won't let Alba come anywhere near you. Ah, Tormod. Speak of the devil.'

'Highness,' Tormod boomed heartily. 'Good to have you back among the living. You already look much better than when I last passed through here. I've taken the liberty of ordering you a good meal sent up, should be here any moment.'

'Thank you, Tormod,' Logan said. 'That's kind of you. I do feel like I could do with some food. And a bath.' He wrinkled his nose at his own smell.

'Here's the stuff you asked for,' Tormod said, handing Torgrim a good-sized glass bottle that was filled to the stopper with a thick, dark liquid.

Orrin noticed Logan staring at it hungrily as it passed from hand to hand, and realized his uncle was far from out of danger. His weakness was a liability, a threat to all of them. But it couldn't be helped. There was no one else to fill his post.

Sending him out in Orrin's stead was clearly not an option. And, with all his drawbacks, he was still infinitely more experienced in dealing with the intricacies and pitfalls of governing a kingdom and keeping a fractious and unpredictable nobility in check. Orrin still didn't see how they would ever let themselves be persuaded into combining their forces.

'Somebody's got to start getting our army here in Dunmark sorted,' he said.

'Quite right,' Torgrim said. 'Thanks for reminding me. I was going to have a talk with Varna about that. And about some other things. I suppose now's as good a time as ever. Orrin, lad, would you care to accompany me?'

Tormod raised a hand, opening his mouth to speak, but Torgrim cut him off. 'Sorry, old chap, but someone's got to stay with his highness, and you're it.'

'You could have told me earlier,' Tormod grumbled, 'then I'd have ordered dinner for two.'

Orrin smiled, sure that the big man would be quick to correct the oversight and reward himself for having to stay behind with the best the kitchens had to offer.

❖   ❖   ❖

Varna received Torgrim and Orrin in the study of his town house. They'd obviously interrupted his evening meal, which didn't help to improve his mood.

'Highness,' he addressed Orrin bluntly, casting a doubtful glance at Torgrim. 'If you've come to enlist my support against your uncle, you're wasting your time. My answer remains the same. I can't help you.'

'Quite the contrary,' Orrin said. 'It's your support for Logan I'm asking for. He needs someone who can gather our forces and forge them into an army. Yours was the first name that came to mind.'

If Barra was surprised by the fact that Orrin was openly supporting the Regent, he didn't show it. In any case, he was far too well acquainted with the plots and intrigues that plagued the kingdom to take Orrin's declaration at face value. For all he knew, the prince might just as well be implementing a clever, convoluted plan to depose his uncle and hasten his own ascendancy to the throne.

'What does he suddenly need an army for?' Barra asked. 'Last I heard, we weren't at war with anyone. If he's had news of the pot boiling over in Conara, it must be very recent indeed.'

'Your grace,' Orrin said. 'This is Torgrim of Eldinga. I'd like you to listen to what he has to say. I'm believe you'll find it very interesting.'

'Torgrim of Eldinga?' Barra said coldly. 'Impossible. The man's a legend. I remember hearing stories about him from my great-grandfather's time. I don't for a moment believe that this fellow – '

'Believe what you like,' Torgrim interrupted him. He sounded like his patience was running thin. 'It doesn't change the facts. And just so you know: your great-grandfather Conlan wasn't your great-grandfather at all. The lecherous old bender was far too enamored of young boys to beget any himself.

'If not for a little meddling on my part, House Varna would have ended with him, and you wouldn't even be here today. As it was, I took it upon myself to introduce your charming and sadly neglected great-grandmother to the royal heir, prince Seorus, and that was how your grandfather came into existence. Which means that you and Orrin are actually cousins, or something of the sort.'

'How could you possibly know… ' Barra looked flabbergasted.

'Because I was there,' Torgrim said crossly. 'Take my word for it. But don't worry, your little family secret is safe with me. And now, if you don't mind, I'd like to get to the point of our visit. There are things you need to know.'

While the old mage talked, Orrin watched Barra.

It was interesting to see the duke's expression slowly change as he listened to Torgrim's story unfold. By the time Torgrim had finished, Barra's initial disbelief had given way to thoughtfulness. The old man's charisma seemed to be at work again as well, for when Barra finally spoke, it was with new respect for the old mage.

'So you say these priests are really sorcerers,' he said. 'That is indeed worrisome. I've never trusted the black bastards myself. And if it's true what you say about the things that have emerged from that sorry business in Tinnan, I find that even more disquieting, not to say frightening.'

'Oh, it's true all right,' Torgrim said grimly. 'We've just recently met some people who had a run-in with a relatively small mob of the things, and it wasn't pleasant. But that may still not be the worst of it. I've had some troubling reports from beyond the Ard Dromlach, and it's beginning to look increasingly as if something even more dangerous were running loose in the east. If it's what I fear – and I truly hope it isn't – then we won't just need to have every man, boy, cripple and dotard in the kingdoms under arms. We'll need the gods' own luck if we're to stand even the ghost of a chance of surviving, once it decides to head our way.'

'From what you've told me,' Barra said, 'it does look like one should prepare for some sort of unpleasantness, wherever it may lastly decide to come from. Very well. Provided I'm charged by the Regent directly, I'll do it. I'll see that what forces we have are shaped up and ready, put the Kingsguard and the city watch through some extra drills, get them used to working together.

'And then there are my own forces – and Blackwood's and Redfern's, I suppose. Bringing them anywhere near Kingskeep right now would only cause one hell of a commotion and have the factions yelling bloody murder. I'd think it best to put them on alert and leave them where they are for the time being. But ready to march at a moment's notice. You'll understand that, as far as the southern duchies are concerned, there are no guarantees. One can only hope they'll see the light of necessity and decide to heed the Regent's call.'

All the while, Torgrim had been studying Barra curiously.

'What have they got against you?' he asked abruptly.

'Well, it's not news that the Colors – '

'No,' Torgrim interrupted. 'I mean, what have they got *on* you. What are they holding over your head that's kept you from declaring for Orrin here?'

Barra seemed ready to give a sharp retort. Then his anger abruptly deserted him. His features collapsed, leaving him suddenly looking old and desperate.

'He's got my youngest son and his family,' he said. 'He's promised to kill them very slowly and painfully if I don't cooperate.'

'Who has?' Torgrim asked.

'Who do you think? Logan. Or Alba.'

'Logan?' Torgrim said. 'I rather doubt that. Tell me everything,

601

from the beginning.'

'He sent someone,' Barra said, his features twisted with resentment and worry. 'Someone with a message saying he had my son and his family in his power. If I did anything to support Orrin's claim to the throne, their lives would be forfeit. I immediately dispatched a fast rider to Whitelake, to see if it was true. It was. They'd been quietly abducted during a harmless outing, a picnic by the river Ormel. It's only a half hour's ride from the keep, and they took no guards, only a squire to see to the horses. They found the man, and the children's nurse, slaughtered like animals. There was no trace of my family.'

'This messenger,' Torgrim said. 'What can you say about him?'

'Not much,' Barra answered. 'I was on my way here from the keep when he accosted me. It was after dark, and he wore a deep hood. Nothing about him caught the eye, and I'd never heard his voice before. He delivered his message and said that if I harmed or followed him, one of my relatives would suffer for it.

'I followed him anyway, very carefully. Too carefully, as it turned out. In the alleyways down near the west gate, I lost him for a spell. When I found him again, it was because I nearly stumbled over his corpse. Someone very handy with a crossbow had put a bolt through his eye. I fetched some guards from the gate to pick him up, but when we got back to the spot where he'd lain, he was gone.'

'His principal, tying up loose ends,' Torgrim surmised, 'obliterating the back trail.'

'My thought exactly,' Barra said bitterly. 'Clearly, the bastard leaves nothing to chance.'

'What makes you so sure it's Logan?' Orrin asked.

'Stands to reason, doesn't it? He's the only one who gains from it.'

'On the face of it, yes,' Torgrim said. 'But that may very well be exactly what the real culprit wants you to believe. You've been a-round long enough to know that, in politics and power games, nothing is ever what it seems. There are always layers and layers of deception and misdirection involved. In this case, I'd wager almost anything that Logan has no idea what's been going on.' He told Varna what they'd found at the Regent's apartment.

'Then it must be Alba,' Barra grated. 'The poxy swine! I've a mind to pay him a visit this very hour and wring it out of him.'

'Bad idea,' Torgrim said.

'I know,' Barra sighed resignedly. 'I know. He's in bed with Stonebridge, that conniving rat. I'd need a small army to drag the filthy, red-eyed scum out of there.'

'And besides,' Torgrim said, 'I'm not so sure it's Alba who's behind this either. At least not as principal, and likely not even as errand boy. He may have the character for it, but I doubt he's got the balls. I have some... contacts I can ask about this. Let me see what I can find out.'

'All right,' Barra said. 'But I'm not going to sit on my hands forever. I want my family back. Safe and sound, if possible.'

'Understood,' the old mage said, heaving himself up from his seat with the help of his staff. 'You'll be hearing from me.'

Orrin hoped it would be soon. The Duke of Whitelake didn't look as if he had any great reserves of patience left.

❖   ❖   ❖

It seemed that Torgrim had barely gone to sleep when he was roused by someone gripping his shoulder and shaking it. It was Baran, his cloak dripping icy water, obviously just come from Near Greening through some very bad weather.

'What is it?' Torgrim asked, immediately wide awake.

'It's Anili,' Baran said, his tone urgent. 'She seems to be caught up in some kind of horrible dream, and we can't get her to wake up.'

'Crap!' Torgrim said. 'I'm coming. Find me a horse while I get some things together. I'll meet you at the stables.'

Half an hour later, they passed through the west gate and headed out into the night. The weather had suddenly worsened, and they had to fight their way against a squalling westerly that drove flurries of small, icy flakes almost horizontally into their faces, seemingly intent on slowing them down or stopping them altogether.

❖ ❖ ❖

All that we see or seem is but a dream within a dream.

Edgar Allan Poe

33 Near Greening

hroughout the day, Anili had been restless. She'd never been good at waiting, and sitting around the *Headless Chicken* with nothing to do was driving her up the walls. Ailis and Anak were rolling dice with the boys, Dagrun had befriended the landlord's wife and was helping her dice vegetables in the kitchen, and Baran and Iomar were sitting in the side room sketching maps and conferring in low voices. Anili spent an hour in the room she shared with Dagrun, sharpening her already sharp swords. After that, she paced the empty common room until the first patrons began to show up and sneak surreptitious glances at her, looks that were everything from wary to lecherous.

Finally, she couldn't stand it anymore. Feeling an urgent need for solitude, she grabbed a cloak and stepped outside. The sky was overcast, dark clouds ripe with snow leaking first, stray flakes. The streets were nearly deserted, a steady, freezing wind keeping everyone inside who didn't have an unavoidable errand to run, and even those few who did weren't tempted to tarry even for a moment.

Anili didn't care. Shrugging deeper into the fur-lined cloak, she set off down the village's main thoroughfare. She walked for nearly an hour, leaving the village a good ways behind, following the road past wind-scoured fields where frozen earth and stubble alternated with drifts that sometimes reached up to her knees, and then through a woods, the trees crackling and groaning under the frost. Her thoughts were stilled to a lazy murmur by the simple tasks of walking and dealing with the cold – until her feet began to grow worryingly numb and her face felt like a frozen mask and she was finally forced to turn around.

It was growing dark when she reached the outskirts of Near Greening. As she passed the first house, a dark bundle of feathers launched itself from the eaves. A crow. She didn't pay it much attention until she realized it was headed directly towards her. Instinctively, she raised an arm, just in time to bat the crazy bird aside as it flew straight at her face, beak and talons outstretched and a mad glint in its beady eyes. With a startled squawk, the bird caught itself in mid-tumble and flapped off into the quickly descending darkness.

Surprised and a bit shaken, Anili didn't notice the black-clad figure cautiously parting the curtains behind one of the windows and watching her intently for a few moments.

Feeling vaguely troubled, she hurried on towards the *Headless Chicken,* where blessed warmth awaited and the prospect of human company didn't seem all that undesirable anymore. Neither the severe scolding she got from Baran for wandering off on her own nor the acute pain of her toes slowly thawing could diminish her relief at being out of the cold.

Under the circumstances, she didn't think it advisable to further upset Baran by mentioning her brush with the crow, so she kept the incident to herself, and soon forgot it.

That night, she dreamed.

In the dream, she stood on a high boulder overlooking a dark, barren wasteland, a vast expanse of shattered stone that seemed to reach beyond the horizon in all directions. There was a sound of many voices, muted at first, sobbing, wailing, groaning, screaming. Then the voices seemed to notice her presence, and swiftly rose up towards her, engulfing her in a mad cacophony of pain, terror, and despair.

With a heart-stopping wrench, she realized where she was. She was looking at Tinnan valley – or what was left of it. The voices belonged to her people. The ghosts of her people. In a blinding, crippling flash of insight, she understood that all of this was her fault. Hers alone.

If not for her, none of this would have happened. Larnakis would still exist, whole and undamaged, and there would be no ghosts but living people. Had she never been born, the Larnaki would not have been irredeemably forsaken, damned to an undead afterlife too horrible to contemplate. She felt dirty, guilty, evil. She should not exist.

Abruptly, the scene changed. She was on another battlefield. Here, the dead were still a minority. A battle raged, and she was in the midst of it, at the head of an army, leading her shining company against an enemy she couldn't lay hands on. An enemy hidden in a roiling mass of shadows that rained bolts and arrows and sprouted disembodied claws and fangs, scything through her army and consuming it piecemeal, while far behind her the exultant cheers rising from a vast crowd of onlookers gradually faltered and were replaced by screams of fear and terror. Inexorably, the shadow tide engulfed everyone around her, soldiers and civilians alike, until only she was left, spared for some obscure reason.

Her fault, she thought. All of it her fault. A part of her knew this was nonsense, since what she'd just seen hadn't even happened yet, and maybe never would. But another part insisted she should simply kill herself before this horror too came to pass. She tried to wake up, struggled with all her might, seized by mounting panic and clawing for the surface like a drowning person. In vain.

Just when she felt desperation begin to veer off into madness, an open doorway appeared before her out of the impenetrable brume. She saw clear, unblemished daylight beckoning from beyond, escape, freedom.

Had she been less agitated, had she possessed the calm to wait and take a closer look, she might have noticed that the light was somehow wrong, not quite consistent, shimmering with a false promise. As it was, she missed the telltale darkling around the edges, the faint flickers of illusion. Seeing only the promise of relief from this horror of a nightmare, she stepped through – and right into the waiting trap.

At the very last moment, already crossing the threshold, she had a fleeting impression of someone reaching for her, trying to hold her back. But whoever it was must have missed her, for she felt nothing more.

In the blink of an eye, she lost all awareness of her own self and the world.

❖   ❖   ❖

Jon had long since transcended the limits of his strength and endurance, and still he held on. He was deep in a dream but aware that he was dreaming, and he was acting with what felt like lucid purpose, though it might also have been blind madness.

The dream had started out normally enough, until at some stage he'd found himself wandering aimlessly through a featureless grey fog. Though he was sure something momentous was happening just beyond his ability to perceive, it stubbornly eluded him.

Suddenly a gap appeared in the mist, and he saw what looked like a brightly lit doorway standing isolated in the uncertain landscape, completely incongruous without the supporting reference of a building or at least a piece of wall. A slight figure, shoulders bowed as if under a great weight, was about to step into the shining quadrangle. Fear gripped him.

With a dizzying wrench as if he'd been turned inside out, he awoke, not into the world of here and now but into a state of heightened awareness, bright as a clear day and keen as a razor. With it came the absolute knowledge that he had to keep what he was seeing from happening, had to stop whoever it was from crossing that distant threshold, no matter the cost.

Otherwise, there would be nothing left worth fighting for.

He knew without knowing how that, as in the waking world, there were lines in this dream realm as well, and in less than a heartbeat he'd found one and crossed the distance to the doorway, hurtling himself down it like a high-speed train on a magnetic rail, already reaching out to grab the person by the collar and haul them back.

He missed.

In a flash, he realized his mistake. Instead of trying to catch the other's body in a physical sense, he should have gone for the essence, the soul, or spirit, or whatever you wanted to call it. Didn't matter. It was too late.

Desperate, he sent out a line of his own anyway, hurled it through the door and after the person, and to his surprise he managed to get a grip, though not a good one. He pulled. Hard. Hauled on the fragile line with all his might, to no avail. Something was straining in the other direction. A malevolent intent, a virulent power stronger than his. It was all he could do to hold on and not let himself be dragged over the threshold as well.

And so he dug in and held, though as time stretched ever longer he felt his own self begin to attenuate as well, and knew that his strength and capacity to resist were finite, slowly but inexorably coming to an end. At some stage he'd have to let go, or be swallowed himself. He decided that, with what hung in the balance, he'd put that moment off for as long as possible – and then put it off some more, if he could.

After what seemed like several eternities, he suddenly felt a strong, steadying presence nearby. Torgrim was there, standing beside him, taking his hand in a firm grip.

I've got you, lad, he heard the old mage say. *Go ahead and see if you can pull her out now.*

Her?

Sorry. Thought you knew who it was. It's Anili. Got herself caught up in something truly nasty. Go on, let's give it a try.

Jon heaved on the line, afraid that it would break or that his precarious grip on Anili might slip and he'd lose her. With that thought, he found something more in himself, something that went beyond the impending doom that hung over two worlds and threatened to come crashing down for a certainty if he failed.

With Torgrim anchoring him, he was free to use every ounce of his power against whatever was resisting him on the other end, and slowly, slowly, inch by painful inch, he forced it to cede ground. Then, so suddenly it nearly sent Torgrim and himself tumbling over backwards, it let go, and Jon woke up.

He was lying on his bed in the room he shared with Hakan at the *Headless Chicken.* On the other bed, the old mage was just sitting up, groaning and holding his head in both hands, and Jon suddenly realized that he too had a splitting headache.

'What – '

'Not now,' Torgrim said in a hoarse whisper, fishing around in the pockets of his cloak with his eyes closed. Finally, he found what he was looking for, a small vial containing a colorless liquid. 'Here,' he said, holding it out to Jon. 'One tiny sip. For the headache.'

Jon fumbled with the stopper and took a sip, though somehow it ended up being a lot more than he'd intended. He handed the vial back to Torgrim and gingerly lay back on the bed. His head felt like an overripe melon, ready to burst or just fall off.

'Greedy little bugger,' he heard the old mage say. 'That's going to put you to sleep for a good, long while.'

Jon didn't care. He was in the grip of a wonderful lassitude. Torgrim's last words already had a strange, echoing quality to them, as if they were reaching him from far away. The headache was receding, and that was all that mattered. He drifted off.

❖ ❖ ❖

Orrin urged his mount to a slow canter.

The horse was one of Tormod's, and Orrin had taken a liking to it. Its name was Duty, and in addition to the fact that he favored a good, dependable beast over a flashy charger, he found the name quite fitting. He was a royal prince, had been brought up to see duty as the defining factor of his existence, and still did.

He certainly wasn't seeking the throne for himself out of ambition or a craving for power. Under different circumstances he'd have been quite happy to tread a simple and ordinary path through life – happier even, he thought. It was his deeply ingrained sense of obligation and responsibility towards the kingdom, and more importantly towards the people of Dunmark, that determined his course and kept him on it. He knew well enough that he wasn't blessed either with irresistible charm or with a brilliant mind, but he thought of himself as dependable and persevering. Much like the horse Duty.

When he'd risen early in the morning, he'd found Torgrim's note, shoved under his door some time during the night. In it, Torgrim said he had to see to some kind of emergency in Near Greening, though he didn't elaborate, asking Orrin to come as soon as he could and urging him not to travel without an escort. Orrin was pretty sure the old mage had envisioned something more substantial than just Desmond, but he felt it was too much bother and a waste of time to go looking for Tormod and ask him for more men.

As it turned out, Tormod had already been up and busy since the early hours, with reports pouring in of some strange and frightening new phenomenon. It seemed that quite a few people who had gone to sleep as usual the night before weren't waking up as they should. They lay in their beds like wax statues, hardly breathing and with only the faintest of pulses, impossible to rouse. At last count, their number stood at over forty.

Orrin could practically see Tormod chomping at the bit when the big man heard where the prince was going. He would have come himself, would have liked nothing better actually, but as Logan's designated minder and with the brewing crisis he was firmly stuck in Kingskeep. He did insist that Orrin take at least Iomar and two of his best men-at-arms.

The weather had changed again.

The snow on the fields, sculpted into a relief of runnels and ridges by last night's storm, was tinged with a reddish dust, carried on an unseasonably warm wind blowing steadily from the south. Sand from the faraway Jemmarraa, Orrin guessed. There was even a pinkish hue to the overcast sky, and he hoped it wouldn't rain any time soon, else the peasants would soon be going on about bloody portents and omens, terrified that something awful was about to overtake them. For once, they'd likely even be right.

The warm air had turned the ice on the road rotten and brittle, giving the horses a passable footing and allowing them to travel at a reasonable pace. It took them less than an hour to reach Near Greening and the *Headless Chicken.*

They found Halvor lounging outside the inn's front door, and Odd and Stian around the back, sitting on a bale of straw and rolling dice. Casual as they seemed about it, the three were undoubtedly standing guard.

Leaving Tormod's men-at-arms, Hurn and Malley, to see to the horses, Orrin made for the common room with Desmond and Iomar.

The landlord nodded them towards the side room, where they found Baran and Torgrim, heads stuck together and poring over a map.

'What's going on?' Orrin asked. 'Where is everyone?'

'Ah, there you are,' Torgrim said. He looked tired, but alert. 'There's been an attack on Anili, is what's going on.'

Orrin's hand automatically went for his sword.

'No, not that kind,' Torgrim said. 'The black rats have learned a new trick, it seems. Dreamsnatching. Very worrying. One of them laid a nasty trap for Anili, and she traipsed right into it. Poor lass never saw it coming. Interesting though, that they chose her, one of the three.

'Any road, by a huge stroke of luck, Jonathan was dreaming as well at the time, and he managed to catch her, if just barely. We got her out, but it was a close thing. Afterward, we went through the whole village looking for the bastard, but it seems he got out in time. Anak and Ailis are still out there patrolling the streets, just in case. Anili is sleeping it off, and Dagrun is with her. So is Jonathan. He's sleeping on the floor beside Anili's bed, protecting her dreams, otherwise she wouldn't have let herself go to sleep at all. Hakan is standing guard outside her door. I suppose you saw the farmboys on your way in. That's it, everyone accounted for. What's up in Kingskeep? How's Tormod holding up?'

'He's got his hands full,' Orrin answered. 'At least forty people didn't wake up this morning in Kingskeep. Just like Anili.'

'Oh, bloody hell!' Torgrim exclaimed. 'Bloody catastrophe! Just what we needed. And, unlike Anili, there was no one around to save those poor souls.'

'Isn't there anything we can do to get them back?' Orrin asked.

'It's too late,' the old man said grimly. 'They're gone, the lot of them. If Jonathan hadn't happened to be dreaming at just the right moment, we'd have lost Anili as well. Once the soul is severed from the body, there's nothing anyone can do. The flesh will live on for a time, but that's it. Nobody home anymore, and nobody coming back, ever. And what worries me even more is that, short of finding and killing every damned Black in, oh, all of Aldara probably, there's nothing we can do to stop it from happening again.'

'There's one thing we can do,' Baran interjected. 'We can go on as planned. It's the only way I can see to get the bastards in the end. Bitter as it is, we always knew that people were going to die along the way.'

'You're right,' Torgrim sighed. 'So let's get on with it. Here's what we'll do, and how. Orrin, you'll take Desmond, Anak and Ailis and go west, to Harad, Ardath and Tirlangan. I want you nowhere near Conara. Meaning, you, Baran, will take the southern kingdoms, Conara, Osona and Deasor, with Hakan and the farmboys. Anili needs to be around someone who can keep her dreams safe, so she'll be coming with me. Dagrun's not going to let her precious princess go off unchaperoned, so I guess she'll be tagging along with our party as well. I know you hate letting the girl out of your sight, but, believe me, she'll be a lot safer with us.'

'All right,' Baran agreed. Orrin could see how hard it was for him. 'But what about you? You seem to have divided up all the kingdoms between Orrin and myself. So where are you planning on going?'

'To Orr,' Torgrim said. 'And a bit beyond. To see if I can find a mage or two who are still worthy of the name. We should get going as soon as we can. If nothing else, the Dreamsnatcher attacks have proved that the opposition isn't dawdling. And neither should we be. Oh, and one of you should go by way of Kingskeep, let Tormod and Logan know what's going on. It certainly wouldn't do for all of us to just take off and leave them wondering.'

❖   ❖   ❖

Orrin took it upon himself to inform Tormod and Logan of the latest developments. Returning to Kingskeep, he wasn't overly surprised to find the city in an uproar. Putting the commotion down to the Dreamsnatcher attacks, he made his way through the anxious, angry crowds to the keep.

He found Tormod in Logan's study, conferring with the Regent in urgent tones. The expressions on both their faces when they looked up spelled trouble, bad trouble, and filled Orrin with a fresh sense of foreboding.

'Uncle. Tormod,' he said. 'What is it now?'

'Orrin, boy,' Logan said, his face tight with apprehension and worry. 'Thank the gods you're here. Varna has gone and killed Alba and Stonebridge. The bailiffs have him locked up, and Stonebridge's cronies are screaming for his head.'

'Weird thing is,' Tormod said, 'he swears by all the gods he didn't do it. And they found a days-old corpse just around the corner from the Stonebridge house, with a ball made of some mighty strange metal in its mouth.'

Suddenly Orrin felt the whole world closing in around him with the single purpose of boxing him in and squashing him to a pulp. He sat down heavily, staring into the middle distance like a man bereft of his wits, at a complete loss what to do next.

Everywhere they turned, the enemy was already there. For every move they made, the opposition seemed to be two steps ahead of them. They were so few against so many. How in all the gods' name were they ever going to catch up?

And we haven't yet seen the half of it, he thought wearily. *Not half of the half of it.*

He stepped down, trying not to look at her, as if she were the sun, yet he saw her, like the sun, without even looking.

Leo Tolstoi

34 The Jemmarraa (AD 1998 / 1194, 4th Empire)

hree years earlier, long before the Redeemers met in far-away Dunmark, Rather and the other inhabitants of Massarit experienced a sudden and unexpected upheaval of all their lives, a pulling up of stakes and certainties, forcing them to take a huge leap of faith that plunged them into the complete unknown – all of it caused by things Rather had mistakenly believed were done and lost in the past.

One night in Massarit, he'd awoken with a start.

He'd had a dream, something disquietingly violent, though he couldn't remember what it had been about. Thankfully. He sometimes still had nightmares of Fellmere, tortured dreams in which he was back in his cell trying to reach the open door through which he could see blue sky and freedom, only to find that he had no hands with which to free himself from the clinging tentacles that held him in his prison, and no feet to carry him out of it.

He lay listening for Nissa's steady breathing, and heard nothing. Then he remembered they'd had a spat the evening before. She'd gone storming off to spend the night somewhere else, most likely the next room. It wasn't the first time, and it wasn't serious, just vexing, and it continued to baffle him even though he thought he knew all the reasons.

It was about patience, and fire. He had too much of the former and too little of the latter, Nissa maintained. He thought that with her it was the other way round: hardly any patience to speak of, and her knickers always filled with fire ants. She tended to want things done yesterday. Sometimes she wanted things done just so she knew that something was happening, even if what she'd decided to set her sights on wasn't strictly necessary.

But she did keep many things moving, sometimes over the groans and protestations of Chinua and himself, things that otherwise would have risked being neglected – he gave her that, no question there. And as much as he preferred to think things through before he acted, he was well aware that he sometimes took too long, getting bogged down in details.

In any case, he knew that by tomorrow morning all would be forgiven and forgotten. Her temper subsided almost as quickly as it flared. Most of the time, their differing natures complimented each other nicely, but once in a while their respective speeds diverged so far, it took a small eruption to get them into synch again. This time, things went faster than expected. It was still dark when Nissa slipped under the covers and snuggled up beside him.

'I'm sorry,' she whispered.

'So am I,' Rather said, and everything was okay again.

They made love, and then fell asleep in each other's arms.

It seemed like only minutes had passed when Rather awoke for the second time that night. Although this time he couldn't remember dreaming at all, he was out of breath, and his heart was pounding furiously. Nissa stirred awake beside him, and he felt the soothing touch of her small, warm hand on his chest. He lay there searching for calm when without forewarning the prophecy took hold of him again, appropriated him like a tool with no will of its own.

Suddenly he was back in Orr, in that strange boy Jareth's room, staring at a passage of text written on the wall, scratched into its surface as indelibly as it was etched into his memory. The words he was meant to see were illuminated by some indefinable source, the rest remained shrouded in darkness. He found that he had no will to resist the prophecy, and so he let it compel him to do its bidding, to recall and speak the words of a certain passage from the text that had been faithfully preserved in his eidetic memory all these years. When it was over, he knew exactly what had to be done, though the prospect frightened him no end.

Nissa had heard, and would be happy: finally there would be activity. Lots of it, more than enough to satisfy even her extravagant needs.

In the morning, he convened a meeting of the elders – meaning the Unborn, Chinua, Tolui, Nissa and himself. They sat by the lake where none of the children could overhear. Especially the younger kids were not above satisfying their curiosity by sneaking up on their elders and listening in on what wasn't meant for their ears.

If only they'd listen as avidly to the things they're supposed to hear, teaching them the stuff they need to know would be a whole lot easier, Rather thought as they settled on the sandy shore.

'My friends,' he said. 'You all know the story of the boy Jareth

621

and his prophecy, and the part I played in it, leading to my abduction by the sorcerers of Fellmere, and finally to our coming to Massarit. You're also aware of the fact that, though I didn't have much choice in the matter, my revealing a part of the prophecy led to the destruction of a whole people. We've all heard the news of the fall of Larnakis, which I'm pretty sure is where the sorcerers' army was headed back then. It's the only thing that makes sense.

'Since then, the prophecy reawakened only once, speaking of dark creatures soon to emerge from the Ard Dromlach and haunt the lands along the mountains' western edge. That was three years ago, and since then we've had the truth of it confirmed by the caravans. Last night, after three years of blessed silence, the prophecy chose to hand me another one of its two-edged gifts. If the message I'm about to pass on to you doesn't make you feel like jumping for joy, let me say that I wholly share the sentiment.

'Here's what it said, word for word: "In the fourteenth year after the ravaging of the Hollow Rock, the hosts of Darkness will spill over the Worldspine and into the West, a plague of monstrous locusts that will scythe through the fields of life until hardly a stalk is left standing. Then is the time when the Children of the Lion must collect their weapons, their tools and livestock, everything necessary to seed a new beginning, and go forth from their abode. They shall travel through the desert until they reach the Golden Mountains, where lies Sahida the Hidden, lost and forgotten since the Age of Battles. Here, they must prepare for the Last Days, and be ready to receive those who will come before. Sahida is the fulcrum, it is Vereld's nemesis and its salvation, and only if the Children reach it in time will the End of All Things not be a forgone conclusion. And this I also say to the

622

Children: beware the Living Dead, who ever wait and seek to thwart the Light."'

There was a heavy silence, broken only by the distant shouts and laughter of the children working in the gardens, hoeing and watering and likely having a little mud-fight on the side.

Tolui stirred. She didn't look happy. 'The children are the last of the Assenai. Have we saved and nurtured them, only to lead them into danger and ruin on the word of a dead prophet? They are safe here. I say, let others who are more suited to the task deal with this evil.'

Rather wasn't surprised. He fully sympathized with her. She had two children of her own, hers and Chinua's. When the period of mourning for the victims of the plague had ended, Chinua had somehow made it clear that he was interested in her, though much to Nissa's amusement Rather hadn't had an inkling of what was going on until it was a done deal. Tolui had consented, more out of necessity and compliance with the logic of the situation than anything else. But her attitude had soon undergone a remarkable transformation, and she and Chinua had become a true couple, as close as two people could be.

'News of what's been crawling out of the Ard Dromlach has reached even us,' Rather said. 'If the prophecy's right, there's much worse to come. There will be no safety here, or anywhere else. As I see it, we can either hide and wait for them to find us – and they will, sooner or later – or we can do something, even if it seems like something crazy. It might even be exactly what's called for, precisely *because* it's crazy. You know, like foiling the enemy by doing the unexpected. But I know as much as you do, and I'm only guessing

623

here. Maybe I'm wrong.'

'No,' Chinua said. 'Rather is right. Massarit is no secret. Not many caravans come through here, but enough for the world to know that we are here. If I had a thousand men, or better two thousand, I would have a hope of holding Massarit even against a much stronger enemy. But we are few, and there are too many ways by which a determined invader can get in.

'As for the children, most of them are hardly children anymore. Temur is turning twenty-seven this winter. He and Nasan are expecting a child of their own, the first of the next generation. The "children" can take care of themselves. They are warriors, all of them, down to the youngest. They need not fear comparison with the bravest of their forefathers, and they know the desert as well as anybody can.'

Chinua, war-leader of the Assenai before the plague, had been adamant about teaching the kids everything he knew about staying alive in a fight and surviving in the desert. Rather, who was no fighter himself, had seen the wisdom in this, and even taken lessons with Chinua. Useless with a sword, middling with a bow, he'd finally discovered a partiality to the quarterstaff and become passing good with it. At some point, Chinua had added spearheads to both ends of Rather's staff. Now it made Rather feel really dangerous, though whether he posed more of a threat to a hypothetical enemy or to himself he still wasn't quite sure.

'There's another thing,' Nissa said. 'The children have grown up together like a large band of siblings. They're very close, and they're used to looking out for each other, more than any tribe living together under normal circumstances. I think that this, together with what

624

they've learned from Chinua, makes them a force to be reckoned with, strong and dangerous far beyond their years and numbers. What bothers me a lot more is, how are we going to find this place, this Sadi-something?'

'Sahida,' Rather said. 'That's a good question. Has anyone ever heard of it? Chinua?'

'No,' Chinua shook his head. 'Nothing.'

'Are there any maps we could look at?' Rather asked.

'No,' Chinua said. 'We desert people keep our maps in our heads and our hearts, in our eyes and our feet. We learn the ways by traveling them, and the places by seeing them. Which means that if I've never heard of this Sahida, it must be far away, farther than any Assenai has ever traveled.'

'Or very well hidden,' Nissa said.

'Either way,' Rather said, 'it looks like we're stumped. Gormin, Striving. You saw the maps in Fellmere. Any ideas?'

'None,' Gormin said. 'I'm sorry.'

Striving Four shrugged.

They sat there, mulling over their predicament.

'Since it seems we've somehow reached the decision to take this prophecy by its word,' Tolui said into the silence, 'there is something. An old song.'

Rather saw what it cost her to speak.

'There's an old song,' she repeated. 'Not a very nice one. It's about a king and queen dancing on a carpet made from the bones of their people. Erdene used to sing it when she was in one of the strange moods that sometimes overcame her, back when I was still a

625

child. Did you know she was my great-aunt? Anyway, Sahida's not in it, but golden mountains are. This is how it went.'

Tolui sang, a haunting tune with a jarring note of false merriness that made it all the sadder.

'Come dance with me in Neverwhere
beyond the sands of glass.
Of gold are made the mountains there,
of emerald the grass.
Merry must the people make,
in mirth their sorrows drown.
They dance until the mountains shake,
and then they all fall down.
The king and queen dance on their bones,
a carpet white as snow.
They dance until they turn to stone:
a royal perch for crows.

'There was more to it, but that's all I remember. It might not be any help at all.'

'The sands of glass,' Chinua murmured. 'I've heard of them. Batukhan told me about them once. Didn't sound like a place anyone in his right mind would want to go.'

'Tell us,' Rather said.

'Hottest, driest spot in the whole desert,' Chinua said. 'Bad for your health in other ways too, it would seem. As Batukhan told it, there was some heavy fighting there in the Age of Battles. He said today's mages can only dream of what the Old Ones were capable of, and even so, the things they did in that battle were so extreme, they ended up wiping themselves out along with their enemies. They set the desert itself on fire, melting the sand and turning it into glass for fifty miles in every direction.'

'Sounds bad,' Rather said. 'Can you find it?'

Chinua nodded.

'South and east, on the edge of the desert,' he said. 'Maybe twenty, twenty-five days. Water might be a problem.'

'All right,' Rather said. 'I think this needs to be done. After what the prophecy brought down on Larnakis, I can't really ask anybody to come. I'll go alone if I have to, but somehow I don't think that's going to be enough.'

'Silly man,' Nissa growled. 'You're going nowhere alone.'

Chinua and Tolui exchanged a long look. Tolui sighed. 'We will come,' she said.

Chinua nodded, as if to say he'd expected no less – or perhaps in acknowledgement of the fact that the course of their fates had just taken an inevitable turn. A few words had completely distorted the familiar face of the future, turned it into something completely alien. It was, Rather thought, as if they had all been gazing at a well-known, reliable landscape. Then, without warning, a heavy fog had rolled in, and now anything could be out there, or nothing at all. He bestirred himself. This was no time for abstract musings.

'And you, my friends,' he said, addressing the Unborn. 'What do you say to all this?'

They exchanged glances among themselves; then Rain Seven answered for all of them. 'For us, the decision is simple,' he said. 'We go where you go.'

'So be it,' Rather said. 'But the children must have their say in this as well. Let's get them all together this evening and see what they think.'

What the children thought of this mad idea of Rather's was that it held an irresistible promise of adventure. Here was a chance to finally leave the walls of Massarit and get to see something of the bigger, wider world. Rather suspected that most if not the whole lot of them were already imagining themselves the heroes and heroines in the songs and stories of future generations.

He tried his best to impress upon them the dangers and hardships awaiting them but succeeded only in further stimulating their imagination. The more he and Chinua cautioned and warned, the more eager the children became to have done with all the talking and get on with it.

Not all of them, though. Temur and Nasan decided to stay in Massarit, and with them fifteen others.

'This has been the home of the Assenai for countless generations,' Temur said. 'If all of us leave, it will be forever lost to us. The law of the tribes says that, once a place is abandoned, whoever comes first can claim it as their own. No one can say what you'll find out there, and those of you who go might need a place to come back to.'

Rather half expected Tolui to have second thoughts, but if she did, she didn't say so. And though he worried for them, he was also strangely relieved by Temur's and the others' decision to stay. Chinua seemed to feel the same.

'Pay attention,' he told the other children. 'Witness. It's a brave thing to go out and prove your worth in the tests the world will no doubt put before us. But greater still is he who thinks first of the tribe and second of himself, who puts the welfare of his people before his own advancement. I honor Temur and the others who choose to stay behind, and I count them warriors no less brave than those who go to fight elsewhere.'

The following weeks went by in a blur of activity, every hour of every day filled to bursting with the thousand and one tasks necessary in preparation for their exodus.

Rather and Chinua discussed the possibility of taking out a scouting party first, to reconnoiter the route, to look for Sahida, and to figure out what they were getting themselves into. But they reckoned that, all told, it would cost them at least two, possibly three months – time Rather wasn't sure they had.

They left with fifty of the tribe's eighty camels, two thirds of the goats and sheep, together about two hundred head, and all the hay, provisions and water-skins the beasts could carry. Their most precious cargo were seeds from every variety of plant that grew in Massarit, from grain, fruits and vegetables to medicinal herbs to plain grasses and even flowers. Carefully packed in hundreds of bags and satchels made of leather that had been smoked for weeks until it turned almost black and became as impermeable as waxed canvas, their hope for long-term survival rode in the camels' panniers and in the packs on their own backs alongside spears and bows and well-filled quivers.

It wasn't an easy or cheerful farewell, since neither those who went nor those who stayed behind knew what awaited them, and whether or not they would ever see each other again.

❖   ❖   ❖

They struck out eastwards, towards the mountains and the narrow strip of savannah that ran along the foothills, retracing the route along which Rather, Nissa and the Unborn had come to Massarit all those years ago.

For Nissa, the journey was a first, since back then she'd been nothing but baggage, fevered, unconscious, and barely alive. Rather on the other hand couldn't stop reminiscing, as if it had all been a grand adventure. She supposed it had been for him, and even though she'd heard the story countless times and in every detail, seeing the actual places, especially the water holes, suddenly made the whole thing real for her. She found herself listening almost avidly as Rather and the Unborn recounted those past events yet again, spellbound as if she were hearing it all for the first time.

Only when their memories took them back towards the beginning of that distant journey did they begin to tread more carefully. Fellmere remained a painful topic for all of them who had come over the mountains, and they still tended to shy away from it.

But, sitting here under the desert stars beside one of the night's many campfires, surveying what she thought of as her brood, her family, Nissa thought that, for all the evil that had driven them here, an immeasurable amount of good had lastly come of it, and what at first had seemed like an overwhelming burden, a prison of responsibility and honor, had borne unexpected fruit and proved itself a great reward instead, a most precious gift.

As much as she would have loved for Rather and herself to have had children of their own, she was more than content to be the mother of a hundred and fourteen adopted ones, a job she happily shared with Tolui and the Unborn, the latter having proved surprisingly adept at surrogate mothering.

There were even times when she thought the children were closer to them than to their human foster parents. And sometimes it seemed to her that the Unborn, alien as they seemed, were becoming better humans than the rest of them. Their unfailing kindness and seemingly infinite patience paired with an unassuming humbleness never failed to touch her heart, and made it impossible not to love them dearly. She thought that what the children learned from the big, misshapen creatures by example was as precious a lesson as anything she, Rather, Tolui or Chinua could teach them, maybe even more so.

It had not been easy to deal with the knowledge that she was barren – likely due to the weeks she had spent in an overheated coma – but she was not the kind of person who let her life and the lives of those around her be destroyed by useless grief and pining over something that couldn't be changed. Not that Rather hadn't tried. But even his magically enhanced capabilities, grown to a surprising extent during the harrowing experience of the plague, had reached their limits here. He'd finally given in and admitted his inability to help her, and then gone so far as to suggest it might be his fault, seeing as his relevant parts weren't the originals anymore, but replacements for those taken by the Blacks. If nothing else, he'd succeeded in making her laugh and shake herself out of the anger and bitterness that had kept her from moving on.

It was as it was, and she had nothing to complain about, except sore feet and aching calves. Caring for so many children, she'd long since grown used to spending the greater part of her day on her feet, but ten hours of walking through the desert were something else again.

No doubt she'd get used to that as well.

Once they'd reached the standing stones and turned south, Chinua had them travel at a more leisurely pace, allowing the beasts to graze on the savannah and fatten up before the hard part of their journey began. Water was still plentiful, at least by desert standards, and there were days when they found two or three water holes along their route, springs fed by subterranean veins descending from the mountains.

It was a rare abundance but nothing compared to home – not Massarit but the place where she'd been born: the island of Almorica, some two hundred miles off the southern tip of Aldara, a tropical paradise in the middle of a warm, nurturing sea, a green gem set in a vastness of blue. Thinking of it still made her violently homesick, and she'd promised herself she'd at least pay it a visit some day. Rather had promised to come with her, but their commitment to the children had forced them to put the trip off until their wards were independent enough to do without them for a while.

That point had come and gone a while ago, and Nissa had lately been nurturing hopes that she and Rather would now finally be able to make the voyage. Rather's prophecy had put and end to that for the foreseeable future, maybe for good and all. Which made it even less probable that she'd ever get to see Rather's home, something she was quite curious about, though from the little he'd said it must be very, very far away, and it seemed he didn't even have a clear idea of how to get there.

Sooner than any of them wished, the good times were over.

Twelve days after departing from Massarit, they reached the end of the savannah, and with it the end of the map in Chinua's head. From here on, they were in the hands of fate and the Assenai's ingrained ability to cope with the harshest desert conditions, placing their whole trust in nothing more than a secondhand prophecy and an ancient song. They had all been well educated in the ways of the desert by Chinua, but even he admitted that, where they were going now, all their knowledge and skills might not suffice to see them through safely.

With that in mind, Nissa spent a large part of their last evening on known ground alone, absenting herself from the camp to perform a prayer ritual for Moricanna, the goddess of fire. She thought the choice fitting not only because Moricanna was her patroness, but also because, by all accounts, the place they were headed for was overwhelmingly dominated by the fire element.

In other words: hot as hell.

❖   ❖   ❖

There was no blue left in the sky, only blinding light and heat.

Six days out from the end of the savannah, Rain Seven wished fervently that his name had bestowed him with the magical power to wring even a few drops from that implacable sky, an inverted cauldron where the air itself seemed to be consumed by the sun's fire before it reached their lungs, scorching hot and unfit for breathing.

It was too hot and dry even for sweat, every drop of excess water long since evaporated. Their bodies, Unborn and human, were desiccated to a point where they were beginning to look like mummies, their skin turned dark and leathery by the unrelenting glare.

As Chinua had foreseen, water was becoming a problem. They

were subsisting on minimal rations, a mere fraction of what their parched throats cried out for. A few of the younger children were beginning to show signs of exhaustion. Rain and his brethren would have happily carried them, had offered in an offhand, general way that cost nobody face, but the kids were too proud or stubborn, or both – Assenai to the bone.

Rain was proud of them, and feared for them. But there was nothing he could do, except be there when he was needed.

Food at least was adequate, if not plentiful. Nearly a fifth of the sheep had succumbed to the impossibly harsh conditions, and their meat went to feed the people, a necessary loss that Chinua had factored into his plans from the outset. The goats were faring better, and the camels hadn't reached the limits of their reserves yet, but they needed to find water soon, or they'd all end up a scatter of bleached, wind-scoured bones.

They'd passed the point of no return yesterday, the crucial moment when their waterskins still held enough to get them back to the last, faraway water hole, though it would have meant abandoning the herds.

Towards evening they got lucky.

With the sixth sense of the desert dweller, Chinua suddenly turned sharply east and led them into the barren, rocky foothills. Far away, too far from their chosen course, hints of green clung to the distant mountainsides. Somewhere up there, there must be water. But nothing suggested that even a drop of it had somehow made its way down to where they stood now, on a red sandy bottom between untidy piles of black, igneous rock that looked more like slag heaps than natural outcroppings.

Chinua had stopped. Using the butt of his spear, he drew a wavy line in the sand, walking towards the upper end of the small depression. In no time at all, the kids had shovels out and sand was flying in every direction. Soon Rain heard excited shouts. They'd found a qashqash, a melon-like fruit that sometimes grew under the sand in places where there was sufficient humidity in the ground. Qashqashs could store large amounts of water, and they tasted quite good, like something between a watermelon and a sweet potato.

Following the line Chinua had drawn, the children unearthed more and more of the fruits. Chinua himself had passed out of sight, but he soon gave a high-pitched, warbling cry from somewhere farther up. He'd found water.

Rain rounded up two dozen kids to carry the waterskins, and they went to join Chinua. It was important they fill the skins first. If the beasts got wind of the water, there would be no holding them back, and so many of them would foul the source and leave it unfit for human consumption for days. If everything went well, they'd lead the animals to the hole later on in small groups, thus keeping it clean and fit for future use.

The water hole was actually a small lake, sheltered between overhanging cliffs that joined farther back to form a deep cavern, dark, cool and iresistibly inviting after the day's inferno. And there was a wide, sandy bank with room enough for all of them to camp on.

That evening, things were looking up. They had water, they had shelter, and even though the kids had assiduously followed desert wisdom and taken only every other qashqash, they had nearly three dozen of the sweet, succulent fruits, easily enough to go around and give everyone a welcome change from their usual diet of tough, stringy mutton.

But Rain Seven knew intuitively that this was only a brief respite, and that the worst still lay ahead. Though he had no gods to pray to, only an unproven notion that a Creator might exist, he asked Him and the universe in general to be merciful with the children and let them reach their goal alive and well.

He didn't know if his plea had been heard, but he did sleep exceptionally well that night, surrounded by what he too had come to regard as family.

❖   ❖   ❖

On the day they left the last water hole, everyone was in good spirits. Everyone except Chinua. An hour out, Rather joined him at the head of the column.

'What do you think that big lump on the horizon is?' Rather asked. 'Could it be Sahida?'

Chinua, blessed with exceptionally good eyesight, had already noticed the dark smudge the day before. It hadn't filled him with confidence then, and it didn't now.

'No,' he said. 'It's too big. I reckon we're still at least three days away from it. Which means it's likely close to a mile high.'

'What could it be, then?' Rather wondered.

Chinua shrugged. 'We'll find out soon enough,' he said. 'Whatever it is, it's right on our path.'

His estimate proved correct – and the thing on the horizon turned out to be something very strange indeed. Over the three days it took

them to reach its outskirts, the heat ratcheted up several more notches.

Chinua had never encountered anything like it.

Nor had he seen anything like the sheer endless expanse of scorched,
molten sand that stretched out before them, a plain of dark glass, for-
sooth. Though it was black, it was nearly impossible to look at,
reflecting the sun's relentless glare like an enormous mirror. And it
reflected heat as well. From a mile away, it was hot enough to redden
and blister unprotected skin. What it must be like over the glassy
surface, Chinua didn't dare imagine. The superheated air rising from
it created a funnel, sucking in more air all around its periphery. A
dark, whirling dust cloud stood over the plain, reaching a mile and
more into the sky. A stationary sandstorm of gigantic proportions.

Even where Chinua and Rather stood, a strong wind was pressing
against their backs, tugging at their clothes, fluttering and snapping
the loose ends of their veils and driving loose sand along the desert
floor in streaming sheets and rivulets, making it seem as if the ground
they stood on was rushing forward under their feet.

'There's no way we can go through that,' Rather shouted above
the wind and the humming, thundering rush of the storm.

Chinua pointed to the left. Since noon, they'd been traveling
along an escarpment of golden-ochre stone, a straight and vertical
slash in the landscape, as if the foothills had been cut off from the
desert plains with a knife. Its height varying from three to five hundred feet, it stretched on ahead of them into the far, hazy distance.
Between the rock face and the plain of glass, there was a stretch of
hard-packed sand.

'That's the way we need to go,' he shouted. 'Sahida must lie that way. No use going out and around through the open desert, even if we could. We'd only find the same conditions on the other side, and have to come back in from there.'

Rather nodded agreement. 'All right, let's do it!'

Chinua didn't point out that they were looking at a rough circle preposed in front of a straight line, which meant that the farther they traveled, the narrower the gap between the two would become. If the strip of virgin sand narrowed down to less than a mile, they were in trouble. Between the black-glass furnace and the rock face contributing is own share of reflected heat, they'd be roasted alive.

But there was no turning back now. They'd have to take their chances and hope for the best, though the best might well turn out to be a quick death. He gave the signal to move on, leading with Rather at his side.

It was pure hell.

They lost another ten sheep in less than the half-day it took them to reach the deadly circle's apex, too weary to do anything but leave the poor animals to die where they'd collapsed. Several of the children wouldn't have made it through the afternoon either, if Chinua hadn't ordered some of the camels stripped of their loads, the last of the hay, and the stragglers placed on the beasts' backs instead. The Unborn would have carried the children, but Chinua could see that they too were near the end of their endurance. As were they all.

Without Nissa, they wouldn't have survived at all. Using her Talent, she walked up and down the column of people and beasts, somehow managing to absorb a part of the immense, murderous heat

638

radiating from the glass.

Every fifty steps or so, she shed the collected heat, stretching out her arms and releasing great, arcing gouts of fire back into the cauldron, flaming discharges a hundred and more feet long. But she too was pushing her limits, and looked like she wouldn't hold out much longer.

As Chinua had feared, the gap eventually narrowed down to a mile, and then less. What they suffered in those hours was far beyond anything he could fit into the term 'unbearable', even his desert dweller's vocabulary exhausted in the face of such murderously hostile conditions.

Just when he was sure they were all about to go up in flames, the escarpment to their left fell back in a large half-round, forming a natural amphitheater nearly a mile across. With all haste, they made for the point farthest away from the plain's inferno. They were still fighting towards the rock face against the raging wind when the sun dipped behind the western horizon that was hidden somewhere behind the sandstorm's whirling cloud.

Darkness fell quickly, and with it the wind lessened, dying down to a harmless breeze in the time it took them to cross the last hundred yards. Soon after, the temperature began to drop as well. An hour later, huddled around the campfires, they were grateful for the warmth still radiating from the rock wall behind them. The sandstorm's thunderous noise had receded to a low rumble, and against the stars Chinua saw that its height had shrunken by half.

They'd survive the night, at least.

❖ ❖ ❖

Rather slept fitfully.

All around him, the Assenai were dead to the world. Only the animals seemed restless. He could hear them clattering back and forth along the low scree slope at the foot of the escarpment, but at some stage they too must have given in to exhaustion. When next he awoke, all was quiet, with only the storm's muted roar rumbling away in the distant background. He finally fell into a deep, dreamless sleep.

No one had thought to keep a watch, either because nobody thought there was anything to guard against in this remote and isolated spot, or because they were all simply too tired. And so it was that no one noticed when the sand began to churn and boil around and beneath the sleepers – not until it was too late. In less time then it took for any of them to fully awaken, everything was calm again, still and quiet.

A short time later, the moon rose over the escarpment's rim, its mild light revealing a campsite that looked largely untouched except for the fact that not a single living being was left there, or anywhere else in the great, silent semi-circle of stone and sand.

When the sun rose in the morning, nothing had changed. As it climbed into the sky, the heat increased and the wind started up again, quickly rising to gale force. Slowly, gradually, sand began to accumulate on the possessions left behind.

Over time, everything would be buried beneath it, leaving no trace that there had once been life here, if only for a short while, nothing to bear witness that either man or beast had ever come this way.

No, that wasn't quite true. In an early morning frenzy, as if it had to make up for the hours of activity lost during the night, the wind rushed and whistled down a deep, dihedral groove in the escarpment's face. Where it first met the ground, it swept away the sand so violently that a short stretch of flat, worked stone was laid bare – stone that hadn't seen the light of day in a very long time. The huge, golden-ochre slabs were part of an ancient road that in another time had led to the fabled city of Sahida, now lost forever.

❖   ❖   ❖

It is not in the stars to hold our destiny but in ourselves.

William Skakespeare

35 Aldara (AD 2001 / 1197, 4th Empire)

ll across the continent of Aldara, fear began impercep-
tibly to creep into people's hearts – a slow, insidious poison that stole the joy, the levity and laughter from their
lives while seeming to somehow accelerate and shorten their days,
leaving ever fewer hours in which to accomplish all the many chores
that needed doing. It was as if a great fist were inexorably squeezing
the land, as if the very atmosphere were subtly changing, growing
ever more clenched and nervous.

Though only a very few had even an inkling of how great and real
the threat actually was, there were signs enough for the rest to see,
time-tested portents that told them all they needed to know.

There was the blood rain that dyed the snow in four of the Seven
Kingdoms a haemal, heart-stopping red.

Cows and sheep bore calves with two heads.

In Ardath, a woman gave birth to a child with three eyes, the third
being right in the middle of its forehead and enabling it to see
everything that was hidden from the sight of ordinary mortals – or so
people swore.

In Deasor, the king himself was seized and possessed by a demon and had to be locked up in his own dungeon, wracked by spasms, foaming at the mouth, alternately howling like a wolf and screaming unspeakably vile invective.

And, like spots of deadly rash appearing here and there, the Dreamsnatchers' traps continued to reap souls throughout the kingdoms, sometimes in ones and twos, sometimes by the dozen.

Self-appointed seers and prophets suddenly abounded, offering their fearful audiences a plethora of forecasts as to what horrors awaited them and how and when the world would end, though on the latter point they all seemed more or less agreed: the Last Days were imminent.

The small handful of people who knew at least a part of what was really going on found themselves expending increasing amounts of precious energy as they struggled against the hopelessness and despair threatening to defeat them in the face of an enemy who seemed as overwhelmingly powerful as he was impossible to grasp and nail down to some more tangible perspective.

But the latter aspect was about to change. Encounters of a more direct and violent nature lay ahead, and though the few who fought against the evil tide may have already felt sorely tested, there was worse to come. Much worse.

Had someone been in a position to watch them all as they strove onward on their difficult and dangerous paths, that person might well have felt compelled to fervently wish that the gods existed after all, and that they were furthermore inclined to lend a helping hand, else there seemed to be no hope at all.

❖   ❖   ❖

Appendix

The Cast

(by place and in order of appearance)

Orr

Rather, doctor of medecine
Joceyn Frair, night watchman
Felda, his wife
Jareth, their son
Par Severt, Black Priest

Larnakis

Lansing Durpa, bone gatherer
Ügmen, his brother-in-law
Jalme and Pasong, Ügmen's sons
Dorting, Durpa's son
Ramen Lobsang, mayor of Sirida
Anskar Tanore, Radj of Larnakis
Rupili, his wife
Narayan, monk
Jeje Rinpong, master of martial arts
Tönden, abbot of Anpok monastery
Asha and Soonil, Rupili's maids
Baran Kendarren, Captain of the Watch
Mepe, monk
Tamsin, sergeant of the Watch
Anili, Anskar and Rupili's daughter

Fellmere

Kuruma, Supreme Brother

i

Tano, senior brother

Gracklin, senior brother

Poder, novice

The Oracle

Rain Seven, Unborn

Gormin, Unborn

Noburo, senior brother

Durstin, minor brother

Marden, senior brother

Striving Four, Unborn

Changing Grey, Unborn

Three Flower, Unborn

Counting Clouds, Unborn

Stone Blue, Unborn

Once Green, Unborn

Rinner, novice

Bodra, senior brother

Nissa, fire witch

Ilario Zamaròn, mercenary captain

The Madal Skog

Morlic Silt, member of the Mud Clan

Jekkim Flint, chief of the Stone Clan

Asukan, High Priestess of Uilmaz

Halima and Tomay, priestesses

Fasik, clan elder

Hurim, shepherd

Samad, clan elder

Sosha, murder victim

Nesud, her brother

Munnir, chief of the Mud Clan

Tomman, chief of the Snake Clan

Kassem, chief of the Sky Clan

Hamad, clansman

Rasid, clansman
Femaz, clansman
Rezak, clansman
Jessop, peddler

The Jemmarraa

Batukhan, Assenai elder
Chinua, Assenai war chief
Erdene, Assenai elder
Mongke, Assenai
Tolui, his wife
Sube and Checheg, Assenai
Temur, Assenai
Nasan, his wife

Earth

Billy Perkins
Eric Sandersen
Jon, a young man
Grand and Nana, his grandparents
Lisa, his aunt
Lucy, his sister
Jude, Lisa's husband
Dwight D. Hunsicker, sheriff
Clyde, his deputy
Martha Poors, town resident
Bob Cummins, plumber
Joe Hanks, town resident
Franz, bodyguard and majordomo
Anton, bodyguard and groundskeeper
Maria, cook
Hans, Franz's nephew
Richard von Ravenstein, Jon's great-uncle

Flavius Corvinus, an ancestor

Major Brown, special forces

Alfred Herkenheimer, scientist

Sergeant Mancuso, special forces

Dunmark

Orrin Avellin, Prince of Dunmark

Searc, castellan

Eithne, housekeeper

Sedge, Burr, Alder, Holly, Hock, Forest Folk

Torgrim of Eldinga, mage

The Summoner of Demons (?)

Iomar, weapons-master

Tormod Tondern, Duke of Redfern

Cavan Kildown, Duke of Blackwood

Logan Avellin, Orrin's uncle

Barra din Varna, Duke of Whitelake

Alba, Logan's advisor

Desmond Fjolen, squire (Ykrit)

Hurn and Malley, men-at-arms

The Three Quarters

Anak, headhunter

Asgeir, resident of Nara

Brocc, innkeeper

Fingal, farmer (Baran)

Seara, his neice (Anili)

Ailis, headhunter

Eirik, smith

Haldor, farmhand

Odd, farmhand

Stian, farmhand

Dargun, cook

Akon Halvassar, leader of Gulfram's Ghosts

Hakan, a Ghost

The Warren

Ykrit, demon

Xorth, Lord of the Warren

Ashotl, demon

www.vereldan.com

greg@vereldan.com